P9-DUX-569

An excerpt from *An Off-Limits Merger* by Naima Simone

She closed her eyes and a niggling sense of familiarity flickered in the back of Bran's skull.

Had they met? No way in hell he would've forgotten her.

"Hey, baby girl," he said, voice low, shifting closer to her.

"Don't call me that."

She probably meant to snap at him. But the words emerged as a low rasp.

"Okay," he said, deliberately softening his voice. "What should I call you then? What's your name?"

Her lips parted.

"Tatum Haas."

That nagging sense of familiarity finally clicked into place.

Tatum Haas.

The daughter of the man Bran was in Boston to see.

Well, damn.

He shook his head and straightened, stepping away from the woman who'd gone from pure temptation to off-limits in the blink of an eye.

Yeah, who was he kidding? She was still pure temptation.

NEW YORK TIMES BESTSELLING AUTHOR

BRENDA JACKSON

&

USA TODAY BESTSELLING AUTHOR

NAIMA SIMONE

ONE STEAMY NIGHT
&
AN OFF-LIMITS MERGER

HARLEQUIN

DESIRE

HARLEQUIN®

DESIRE™

Recycling programs
for this product may
not exist in your area.

ISBN-13: 978-1-335-45784-4

One Steamy Night & An Off-Limits Merger

Copyright © 2023 by Harlequin Enterprises ULC

One Steamy Night
Copyright © 2023 by Brenda Streater Jackson

An Off-Limits Merger
Copyright © 2023 by Naima Simone

For questions and comments about the quality of this book,
please contact us at CustomerService@Harlequin.com.

Harlequin Enterprises ULC
22 Adelaide St. West, 41st Floor
Toronto, Ontario M5H 4E3, Canada
www.Harlequin.com

Printed in U.S.A.

CONTENTS

Brenda Jackson is a *New York Times* bestselling author of more than one hundred romance titles. Brenda lives in Jacksonville, Florida, and divides her time between family, writing and traveling. Email Brenda at authorbrendajackson@gmail.com or visit her on her website at brendajackson.net.

Books by Brenda Jackson

Harlequin Desire

The Westmoreland Legacy

The Rancher Returns
His Secret Son
An Honorable Seduction
His to Claim
Duty or Desire
One Steamy Night

Westmoreland Legacy: The Outlaws

The Wife He Needs
The Marriage He Demands
What He Wants for Christmas
What Happens on Vacation...
The Outlaw's Claim
Second Time's the Charm

Visit the Author Profile page
at Harlequin.com for more titles.

You can also find Brenda Jackson on Facebook, along with other Harlequin Desire authors, at Facebook.com/HarlequinDesireAuthors!

ONE STEAMY NIGHT

Brenda Jackson

To the man who will always and forever be the wind beneath my wings and the love of my life. My everything: Gerald Jackson, Sr.

A man that hath friends must shew himself friendly: and there is a friend that sticketh closer than a brother.

—*Proverbs* 18:24

ACKNOWLEDGMENTS

In loving memory of my childhood friend and Delta Sigma Theta Soror, Lynda Ravnell. Losing you was hard, and I will forever appreciate the memories. Rest in peace.

Prologue

Jaxon Ravnel threw out a card before glancing around the crowded room. Including himself, there were over fifty men in attendance at the first ever Westmoreland Poker Tournament. Some were men who were born a Westmoreland or who, like the Outlaws, were cousins of the Westmorelands. Then there were those who'd married into the family. All were accounted for and all but four players had been eliminated from the game. Those were the ones who were either sitting around observing or hanging out at the bar. An assortment of whiskeys were in decanters and everyone was helping themselves. There was also beer in a huge refrigerator.

The room was quiet for now. Storm Westmoreland was no longer cursing, which meant he was either holding a good hand or he wanted the three others seated at the table with him to assume he was. The room where the game was being played was the spacious poker room, located on the third floor of Westmoreland House.

Westmoreland House was the three-story building Dillon Westmoreland had built on his property, located in what the locals in Denver referred to as Westmoreland Country. Because the Westmorelands were big on family and enjoyed get-togethers, the building contained a humongous kitchen on the ground floor and a huge banquet room with the capacity to seat anywhere from two to five hundred people.

There was also a theater room for the ladies to watch movies, as well as a huge playroom for the younger children that resembled an indoor playground. Not to be overlooked, the teens had their own game room equipped with arcade consoles, mounted televisions, pinball machines, pool tables, board games and a refrigerator stocked with energy drinks.

The entire third floor belonged to the men. That's where the bar, pool tables, man cave and sleeping quarters for overnight poker games were located. Jaxon thought this was a nice setup. The beginning of the tournament required several games going on at once and this room was spacious enough to accommodate everyone. There was a men-only rule and food had been catered by a restaurant in town.

It was close to midnight now, and this was night two of the tournament. Over the past year he'd gotten to know all the Westmorelands, those based out of Atlanta, Montana, Texas, California and Denver. And he was building a bond with his newfound cousins, the Outlaws.

Since the Outlaws and their Westmoreland cousins were such a close-knit group, Jaxon had been included as an honorary member of the Westmoreland family. As an only child, he wasn't used to a huge family, but he was finding out just how such a family operated, thanks to the Westmorelands and the Outlaws. Getting to know all of them, which included the wives and husbands who'd married into the family, had been overwhelming at first. Now he felt comfortable and at ease around them.

More than anything, he appreciated their acceptance of him as one of them. That was the main reason he figured here at the tournament was just as good a place as any for the announcement he needed to make. He wasn't sure how the men would take what he had to say, but he wanted to be up front and honest with them, and then let the chips fall where they may.

Another hour passed before the intensity of the game lessened as King Jamal Yasir of Tehran, who was married to Delaney Westmoreland, told everyone about the new school that had been built in his country. When he'd finished talking, Jaxon decided to make his announcement in a voice loud enough to be heard by everyone.

"Just so all of you know, I plan to marry Nadia."

Like he figured it would, the room became quiet. More than fifty pairs of eyes stared at him. At first no one said anything, and then his cousin, Senator Jess Outlaw, the only one who'd been privy to Jaxon's plan, made sure everyone's mind was free of confusion by asking, "Nadia Novak?"

Jaxon fought back a grin. That was the only Nadia he

knew and would guess that was the only one the others knew as well. "Yes, Nadia Novak."

"I didn't know you and Nadia were seeing each other," Zane Westmoreland said after taking a sip of his brandy.

"We aren't."

"Then how are you going to marry her? What's your plan of action?" Derringer Westmoreland asked.

A slow smile broke across Jaxon's lips. "A very serious courtship."

"Good luck with that," his cousin Maverick Outlaw said. "I think all of us have heard Nadia say more than once that she plans to stay single for a long time. Possibly forever."

"Hey, that's what Gemma claimed," Callum Austell said in his strong Australian accent. "It took me three years, but I eventually won her heart."

Jaxon had heard the story of how Ramsey Westmoreland's best friend from Australia had come to Denver to help Ramsey start his sheep farm. One day he had seen Ramsey's sister Gemma and what had been intended as a one-year trip to America for Callum had become three. It had taken the man that long to win Gemma over.

"I don't have three years," Jaxon said. "I want to marry Nadia before New Year's." He knew that was a big initiative given this was August.

"I hate to be the bearer of bad news, but Nadia doesn't like overconfident men," Canyon Westmoreland said, grinning.

Jaxon noticed several others nodding their heads in

agreement. "I don't consider myself an overconfident man. Just a self-assured one."

"You're also a very disciplined one, but with Nadia it won't matter," Stern Westmoreland piped in to say. "I suggest you think things through, Jaxon. Trying to win Nadia over might be taking on a little too much. I love her to death but she's a renegade. She's headstrong, opinionated and sassy."

"Sounds like she hung around Bailey too long." Walker Rafferty grinned, commenting on his wife. "At least I've never heard Nadia use any curse words."

Jaxon raised a brow. "Bailey curses?" He couldn't imagine such a thing of the woman he'd gotten to know.

Laughter broke out around the room. Hilarious laughter. "Worse than a sailor," Ramsey Westmoreland said, taking a sip of his drink. Jaxon figured Ramsey should know since he was Bailey's oldest brother. "Bailey would use curse words not even in the English language," Ramsey kept on. "You wouldn't believe how many times Dillon and I had to wash her mouth out with soap. Now we let Walker deal with it."

Jaxon had heard how the parents, the aunts and uncles of the Denver Westmorelands had died in a plane crash over twenty years ago, leaving Dillon, the oldest cousin and Ramsey, who was next to the oldest, with a family of fifteen. Several of the siblings and cousins had been under sixteen at the time. When the state of Colorado tried forcing Dillon to put the youngest in foster homes, he had refused.

Walker chuckled. "Now that we have kids of our own,

Bailey's gotten a whole lot better and rarely says a curse word. Thank God."

"So, in other words," Sloan Outlaw said, "Nadia will be a challenge you might not want to take on, cuz. We've seen her give more than one guy the boot. We'd hate for you to be the next."

Jaxon didn't say anything for a minute as he glanced around the room and met each man's gaze. "I am very much aware that Nadia has a strong personality. However, I don't have any choice about taking Nadia on. I've fallen in love with her."

Words like "damn," "crap" and "shit" escaped several of the men's lips.

"Have you taken the time to get to know her?" Riley Westmoreland asked.

"No, but it doesn't matter. I fell in love with her the moment we were introduced. But then that's how things work in the Ravnel family."

"They work that way in the Austell family, too, so I know where you're coming from," Callum said, grinning. "Falling in love for some men might be a slow and reluctant process, but for me it was automatic. I fell in love with Gemma the moment Ramsey introduced us."

"It was that way for me, as well," Dylan Emanuel said. He'd become the most recent addition to the Westmoreland family when he'd married Charm Outlaw ten months ago. "I'm a firm believer in love at first sight."

"That's all well and good, but I'm not sure five months will give you enough time to grow on Nadia. She can be stubborn," Reggie Westmoreland, the other senator in the family, said.

Jaxon leaned back in his chair. "I believe it can be done…without any interference from any of you."

"As long as you don't plan to do anything illegal or break her heart."

It was the first time Dillon had spoken. Any input from Dillon meant a lot since Nadia was his wife Pam's youngest sister. Jaxon knew Nadia was not just Dillon's sister-in-law, but that he also considered her the baby sister he never had since his parents had had six boys.

"I won't do anything illegal, and I won't break her heart. I just need all of you to know my intentions. And like I said, I prefer no interference."

"That means we can't tell our wives," Thorn Westmoreland said. "That shouldn't be a problem. We abide by the rule that whatever we say in this room stays in this room."

All the men agreed. However, Dillon said, "I'm telling Pam. Nadia is her youngest sister and I feel she has a right to know. Don't worry about her interfering because she won't. She knew about Aidan and Jill and didn't interfere with them."

Jill was another of Pam's younger sisters. Jaxon had been told of Aidan and Jill's secret love affair during medical school. Little had they known that Pam and Dillon had been fully aware of what was going on between them.

"You and Pam were too perceptive," Aidan said, grinning over at Dillon.

"Some things just can't be hidden," Dillon responded. He glanced back at Jaxon. "I'm trusting you to do the right thing by Nadia."

"And I will, I promise you. Like I said, I want her to be my wife and will do my best to win her over."

"Well, just be prepared that with Nadia, your best might not be good enough," Durango Westmoreland said, shaking his head. "To be honest, Nadia isn't the one I'm worried about."

"Same with me," Stone Westmoreland said, laughing. "In other words, Jaxon, we'll be here to help tend to your bruises when Nadia gives you the boot."

Jaxon actually saw a look of pity in a number of the men's eyes. Even Dillon's.

"You guys aren't scaring me any," Jaxon said, laughing and tossing out another card.

"Don't say we didn't warn you," Jared Westmoreland said, smiling.

At that time, King Jamal Yasir, who'd acted as dealer, went around the table to ask each player if they wanted to bet or call. No one raised the bet, and they began showing their hands.

Everybody groaned loudly when Jamal proclaimed Storm Westmoreland the winner of the tournament.

One

"**D**id you hear us, Nadia?"

Nadia Novak rubbed her temples and wished she hadn't heard what her sisters Jillian and Paige had said. Jaxon Ravnel was in Gamble scouting out land to expand his business. Why? Hadn't he bought enough land last year in Forbes, Texas, for the same reason? Besides, it wasn't like Gamble was a major city in Wyoming, even if it had grown in population over the past few years.

When her oldest sister, Pam, had married Dillon Westmoreland fifteen years ago and packed up a thirteen-year-old Nadia, a fifteen-year-old Paige and a seventeen-year-old Jillian to live with them on his huge spread in Denver called Westmoreland Country,

Gamble had been a town with a population of barely five thousand. There had been only one hotel, few fast food places and a theater that showed movies months after they were released.

Now thanks to a progressive mayor, Gamble's population had quadrupled. There were several hotels and theaters and a slew of fast food places. Sprawling housing developments had sprouted up as well as a megamall. With rumors circulating about a possible ski resort coming in about five years, Nadia figured one day Gamble would be as popular as Jackson Hole.

Years ago, her great-grandfather Jay Novak Sr. had purchased the two-hundred-acre spread that he named the Novak Homestead. More than anything, she appreciated her sister Pam for not selling it when they'd moved to Denver. She'd retained it as part of their family legacy.

Nadia didn't regret moving back to Gamble. She would admit it got lonely here at times, living in this huge house by herself. There had never been a boring moment in Westmoreland Country with so many Westmorelands living close by each other. It helped, too, that since Denver was only an hour's flight away, she often returned to Westmoreland Country for visits.

Her sister Jillian, who was fondly called Jill, was a neurosurgeon and was happily living in Florida with her cardiologist husband, Aidan Westmoreland. Nadia thought it was awesome that her sisters—Pam and Jill—had married Westmoreland men who were cousins.

Her sister Paige had followed in Pam's footsteps to become an actress in Hollywood. She'd made a name for herself and had starred in several movies. Paige hadn't hesitated to give up the glitz and glamor to marry Senator Jess Outlaw. Jess was a cousin to the Westmorelands, and he and Paige made their home in the nation's capital.

Nadia had attended the University of Wyoming for four years, before graduating from Harvard with an MBA. She had returned to Gamble three years ago. The timing had been perfect since the acting school her sister Pam owned, the Dream Makers Acting Academy, had been in need of someone to manage it. Nadia loved her job and found it rewarding as well as challenging.

Over the past year the student count at the academy had increased substantially, mainly because of Pam's contacts back in Hollywood. Oftentimes an actor friend would teach a class for a semester or two, or would do a once-in-a-lifetime symposium or workshop. Last year they'd added classes for aspiring stuntmen taught by folks from Hollywood. The academy was now in demand and already there was a waiting list for the next school year.

Although Nadia and her sisters now lived thousands of miles apart, they would carve out time to share a conversation or two at least once a week. Because of Pam's hectic schedule, she would jump on the call whenever she could. Although Pam was twelve years older than Jill, fourteen years older than Paige and sixteen years older than Nadia, the four of them were extremely close.

"Nadia, are you listening to us?"

"No," she said honestly. They'd lost her after mentioning Jaxon's name and that he was in Gamble to scope out land. The idea of them being in the same town was troubling. There was no way she would tell her sisters the impact the man had had on her from their initial meeting. For some reason, she couldn't shake off her intense attraction to him. What was pathetic was that whenever their paths crossed, he barely seemed to notice she existed.

Except for that one time at Charm's wedding last year. They'd held a pretty long conversation. Nadia figured the reason had been he'd been too kind to walk away when the others in the group had dispersed, leaving them alone.

"Well, get your mind off the acting school for a minute," Jill said.

Nadia had news for them. Her mind had not been on the acting school, although maybe it should have been since she was in a dilemma. The new school year had begun two weeks ago and yesterday the sponsor for this year's holiday play, the Dunnings Financial Group, had filed for bankruptcy. That meant she needed to find another sponsor and fast. The students had returned energized and ready to start work on the play. Auditions were already being held.

"Okay, what did I miss?" Nadia asked, turning her attention to the conversation with her sisters.

"You didn't make a comment when we told you how to treat Jaxon."

She frowned. "And just how am I supposed to treat him?"

"We want you to be hospitable to him, Nadia," Paige said.

Hospitable? "Why wouldn't I be? I don't recall being any other way around him."

"When you're not trying to avoid him. And what's up with that?" Jill asked.

Nadia rolled her eyes. Leave it to Jill to notice. "I just don't see the need to fawn over him like the rest of you do."

If only they knew that, in private, she did more than fawn over him. She had naughty thoughts that actually made her panties wet. Not to mention those dreams she had of him, the contents of which would probably give her sisters a stroke.

"We don't fawn over him, Nadia," Paige defended. "We just think highly of him for what he did. Can you imagine what would have happened if he had not come forward with that information on Phire's father?"

Phire was married to Maverick Outlaw, the youngest brother of Paige's husband. Nadia had never met Phire's father, but she'd heard about all the money he'd swindled from the Outlaws for close to twenty-five years. "And?" Nadia braced herself knowing her sisters were about to sing Jaxon Ravnel's praises.

"And," Paige continued, "Jaxon is the Outlaws' newfound cousin, and the Westmoreland family has embraced him as one of theirs, so you know what that means."

Yes, she knew. The Westmorelands and Outlaws were now one big happy family. Heck, her three sisters were married to Westmorelands and an Outlaw, which made them official members of the clan. "Like I said, I'm always pleasant to Jaxon, but I refuse to fawn over him." But she had no problem drooling in private.

"Well, please don't cause problems, Nadia. You can be rather hard on men and for no reason," Jill said.

A deep frown settled on Nadia's face as she leaned back in her chair. "I have plenty of reasons whenever I'm hard on a man. Should I remind you about Kemp, Paige?"

Kemp had been Paige's actor boyfriend who'd made news when he'd betrayed her with another actress while filming a movie. The news had caused a scandal that had taken social media by storm.

"And the three of us can't ever forget Fletcher Mallard and what he tried to do," she added.

Fletcher had been engaged to marry Pam with devious intentions. Luckily Dillon had arrived on the scene and put an end to that foolishness. He'd stopped Pam and Fletcher's wedding ceremony just in the nick of time.

"Those are just two men, Nadia. You can't judge the entire male population by them," Jill said.

In all honesty, there were three. One she'd never told her sisters about. Namely Benson Cummings. He was a guy she'd met during her first year at the University of Wyoming. He'd been a senior and she'd thought she was in love until she'd discovered her name was on a Freshmen Girls to Do list. A list circulated by senior guys, and Benson had been assigned to do her. She was grateful she'd found out about the list before sleeping with him.

"Just think of all the Westmoreland and Outlaw men and how wonderful they are," Paige tacked on for good measure.

"Okay, I will admit they're one of a kind," Nadia

said. "But then I'm partial where they are concerned. I don't know Jaxon Ravnel that well."

In truth, she didn't know him at all. She only knew how he made her feel whenever he was around her. Just being in the same room with him reminded her that she was a woman. A woman whose body sizzled every time she saw him. That was a reaction she'd rather do without and that was the primary reason she avoided him.

"Well, now is your chance to get to know him since he'll be in Gamble for a while."

Nadia's frown deepened. "How long is 'a while'?"

"He told Jess he planned to be there for at least three months," Paige said. "Possibly four."

"Why don't you invite him to dinner?" Jill suggested. "You love to cook and always complain about wanting to prepare all those dishes but having no one there to eat them."

They had to be kidding. There was no way she would invite Jaxon to dinner. What if he picked up on just how attracted she was to him? That's the last thing she wanted to happen. However, if she didn't invite him, her astute sisters would figure out why. "Fine, I'll call him in a few days to see if he's available. Give me his number." Paige wasted no time in rattling it off.

"And Nadia?"

"Yes, Jill?"

"Please remember Jaxon is a nice guy. Don't do or say anything that will make us regret suggesting you invite him to dinner."

"Well, if he's as nice as the two of you claim, then you won't have anything to worry about. Now, can we change the subject and talk about something else?" she asked.

The conversation about Jaxon stirred up sensations inside of her that she didn't need to be stirred. She was convinced it was merely a phase she was going through. It had to be. At twenty-eight her body was trying to convince her it was past time to end her virginal state. But she refused to do so merely to quench a case of lust. For her sex had to be more meaningful than that. But what if nothing meaningful ever came along? Should she continue to deny herself the experience of making love to man? Especially if it was anything like Jill and Paige claimed it was? Nadia couldn't help but be curious as to whether the real thing was anything compared to her dreams.

"I got a call from Taylor today," Paige said, intruding into Nadia's thoughts.

Taylor Steele Saxon was the sister to Cheyenne, who was married to Quade Westmoreland. "How is she doing?"

"She's doing fine. Quade is giving Cheyenne a surprise birthday party next month and Taylor is helping him with the invitations."

Nadia smiled, thinking about Quade and Cheyenne's triplets. While in high school she had kept the three for a week while their parents had celebrated their fifth wedding anniversary in India. Now the triplets were in their early teens.

"Give me the date so I can mark it on my calendar. Now if you guys don't mind, I need to finish this report before I can go home."

After ending the call with her sisters, Nadia glanced at her watch and then looked at the stack of papers on her desk. Standing, she moved to the window. The Dream Makers Acting Academy had once been a spacious house on two hundred acres of land that had been owned by Pam's high school acting instructor, Louise Shelton. Ms. Shelton, a former actress herself, had been instrumental in getting Pam a scholarship to attend college in California.

When Ms. Shelton died, she willed the house and all the land it sat on to Pam with stipulations. Pam could never sell it and it had to be used as an acting/drama academy. Pam had managed the school until she'd married Dillon, but then had left her friend Cindy in charge. When Cindy's husband, Todd, who'd been mayor of Gamble for several years, decided to run for state senator, and had won, Todd moved his family to Cheyenne, the state's capital. That's when Pam had offered the job to Nadia.

Pam had since opened a second school in Denver. Like this one, it operated at full capacity. A couple of years ago, Pam purchased land for a third drama academy in the DC area. Currently Paige was managing that one.

Returning to her chair, Nadia sat back down. The school had closed an hour ago, but she was still here. Some of the students were rehearsing downstairs, all excited about this year's holiday production. She refused to think it wouldn't be happening unless she found a replacement sponsor and fast. The Dunnings Financial Group pulling out was a hiccup of the worst kind.

Starting tomorrow she would begin making calls to several businesses in town. She wasn't sure how that would work out since most of them had already donated to the school and were contributing to other local charities.

Leaning back in her chair, she wondered where on earth would she get the extra money needed for the school's holiday play.

Jaxon Ravnel stood at the window in his hotel room and gazed out at downtown Gamble, Wyoming. If anyone had told him two years ago that the decision to expand his family's technology business would bring him here, he would not have believed them.

The home office for Ravnel Technologies was in Virginia, and so far he'd purchased land to expand into Forbes, Texas. Now he was considering, of all places, Gamble. He would admit it was mainly because of a particular woman. At least that had been the case a few days ago when he'd first arrived in town. However, it didn't take him long to discover Gamble was Wyoming's best-kept secret.

Although the town's growth began a few years ago, there were a number of national corporations unaware of the city's potential and attractiveness. That lack of awareness was in his favor. He could purchase all the land he needed at a fair market price before there was a business boom. He was also satisfied knowing there would be adequate housing for his employees who relocated here. There was no doubt in his mind that Gamble would be an ideal place to live, work and raise a family.

As for him personally…it was the perfect place to pursue a certain woman he wanted. Nadia Novak.

Jaxon was a man who could appreciate a beautiful woman whenever he saw one, and Nadia had taken hold of his senses the first time he'd laid eyes on her. That had been a little over a year ago at his cousin Maverick Outlaw's wedding reception. The minute she'd entered the banquet room of the Blazing Frontier Dude Ranch there had been something about her that demanded a second look and then a third. Never in his life had he been so captivated by a woman. He'd asked his cousin Jess about her and when Jess had said Nadia Novak had a rather feisty personality, that had made Jaxon even more interested.

Unlike some men, he preferred a woman with a strong personality mainly because over the years most of those he'd dated had had anything but. They'd assumed in order to capture the interest of the Ravnel heir, they had to be mild, meek, the epitome of social decorum, grace and sophistication. That's where they'd been wrong since he found that type of woman boring as hell.

Jaxon wanted a woman who was tough, independent and spirited—like his mother. His father, Arnett Ravnel, said the first thing that had attracted him to Ingrid Parkinson was her energy, sassiness and spunk. Those were traits Jaxon's mother still possessed and his father still admired.

His father had also said that a Ravnel man would know the woman he was destined to share his life with the moment he saw her. Jaxon had always assumed it would be someone from his home state of Virginia.

He hadn't been prepared to be taken with the likes of a Wyoming-born beauty named Nadia Novak.

Getting Nadia to be as taken with him as much as he was with her would be a challenge, but like he'd told the males in her family, it was one he was up to. Whenever he'd seen her she'd been friendly and pleasant, but she never had much to say. At least not to him. And there were times when he thought she was avoiding him. Jaxon figured the main reason for that was because she hadn't gotten to know him. That assumption was what had led him here.

Never in his thirty-three years had he ever pursued a woman. Because of the Ravnel name and wealth, it had always been the other way around. He'd been warned by the Westmorelands and Outlaws that he had his work cut out for him. There were some who even jokingly referred to her as the "Renegade Novak."

He had to be patient and not overplay his hand. For her to get to know him, they needed to spend time together. He'd been in Gamble a little more than a week and as part of his plan, he had deliberately not looked her up. Tomorrow he would drop by the drama academy and invite her to lunch or suggest dinner. It would come across as nothing more than a friendly gesture on his part since they were connected to the same families. He smiled, liking that approach.

He turned away from the window at the sound of his phone. Moving across the room he picked it up off the nightstand, not recognizing the caller's ID. "Yes?"

"Jaxon, this is Nadia Novak."

He pulled in a surprised breath. What were the odds

that the very woman he'd been thinking about would call him? "Nadia, how are you? This is a surprise."

He felt sensations in his lower extremities just from hearing the sound of her voice. "What can I do for you?" He asked the question while his mind was filled with several scenarios of all the things they could do for each other.

"I was talking to my sisters earlier this week and they mentioned you were in Gamble."

"Yes, I'm here on business."

"That's what they said, and I'd like to invite you to dinner."

"Dinner?"

"Yes. Tomorrow. In my home at the Novak Homestead. It's the least I can do since we have close ties to the same families."

A smile spread across his lips. That had been the same angle he'd planned to use. "I wouldn't want you to go to any trouble."

"I won't. I enjoy cooking and look forward to doing so for someone other than myself for a change."

"All right, if you're sure?"

"I'm positive."

"In that case, I accept. What's your address?" he asked, reaching for the pen and notepad off the nightstand.

She rattled it off to him and he jotted it down. "Thanks for the invitation. What time do you want me to come?"

"How about five o'clock? Will that work for you?"

Little did she know he would make any time work when it came to her. "Yes, five o'clock is fine."

"Good. I'll see you tomorrow. Goodbye, Jaxon."

"Goodbye, Nadia."

Jaxon's smile widened as he disconnected the call. Of all the luck. Getting that call from Nadia had certainly made his day. He couldn't wait to see her tomorrow.

Two

What a man, what a mighty good-looking man...

Nadia stood at the kitchen window and watched Jaxon get out of his car. She definitely appreciated what she saw and from where she was standing, she was seeing a lot. This particular window was designed in a way that gave anyone looking through it a good view of approaching visitors without being seen. In other words, you could watch them without them knowing they were being observed. It was a clever idea and she appreciated her great-grandfather Jay Novak for having thought of it.

Jaxon was carrying a huge bouquet of flowers and she figured they were for her. How thoughtful. The women in the Westmoreland and Outlaw families who'd gotten to know him thought he was considerate and kind, a true Southern gentlemen who had a strong sense of doing what was right. He'd certainly proved the latter when he'd exposed the wrongdoings of Simon Bordella to the Outlaws.

Nadia placed a hand over her heart when it began beating fast. The closer he got, the more he worked on all of her female senses. There was something about Jaxon Ravnel that did things to her each and every time she saw him. What was there about him that made her feel vulnerable? Make her want to toss caution to the wind and...

And do what? Risk giving her heart to another man? Have another man place her on his *agenda*? Trample both her heart and her pride? Refusing to think about what Benson had done to her, she concentrated on studying Jaxon instead. Why did he have to look so good?

He had coffee-colored skin, dark brown eyes and a solid, bearded jaw. She also knew he had black hair under that Stetson he was wearing. He had handsome features on a definitely sensual face, features any woman would drool over. He was also tall with muscular shoulders, a tight abdomen and a broad and powerful-looking chest. Definitely a body that was well-built.

The business jacket he wore over a white, collared shirt fit him perfectly, and she figured his taut thighs were why those slacks looked so darn good on him. Altogether—his looks, clothes and walk—made up a very alluring package. Now for the umpteenth time she was wondering if she should have her head examined for following Jill's and Paige's advice and inviting him to dinner.

She nearly jumped at the sound of the knock at the door. Drawing in a deep breath, she moved away from the window and left the kitchen. She glanced around the living room and wondered what he would think of her home. Although the Novak Homestead encompassed a lot of acres of land, the two-story, five-bedroom, four-bath house wasn't all that big. At least not in comparison to the monstrosity of a ranch house she'd heard Jaxon owned in Virginia. Paige had visited there a few times with Jess. Dumfries, Virginia, was less than thirty miles from the nation's capital. Paige had told her all about Jaxon's horse ranch and the beautiful thoroughbreds he owned.

Not wanting Jaxon to know she'd been spying on him from the moment his car had pulled into her yard, she asked, "Who is it?"

"Jaxon."

She opened the door. Although she'd seen his approach, every single step of it, she still blinked. Up close he was even more handsome, and when he smiled, making dimples appear, she was a goner. She forced her attention from his face to the two top buttons on his shirt that were undone, exposing a dark, hairy chest. Her heart rate increased. She couldn't help but appreciate his total maleness although she resented her reaction to it.

"Hello, Nadia."

His greeting made her look back into his face. "Jaxon. Welcome to my home," she said, easing back for him to enter while pulling herself together. He smelled good. She thought that same thing each and every time she was around him.

"These are for you," he said, handing her the flowers and then removing his Stetson and placing it on the hat rack by the door.

"Thank you. They are beautiful. You didn't have to," she said, lowering her head to draw in the scent of the flowers. They were a beautiful mixture of pink daisies, white peonies, orchids, bluebells and roses. But what had really gotten her was the feel of his hand when he'd given her the flowers. She had felt the touch all the way to her toes.

She glanced back up at him, smiled. "But I'm glad you did. I love flowers and these are some of my favorites."

"I'm glad."

"Excuse me while I put them in a vase of water. Make yourself at home. The table is set and dinner is ready."

"It smells good."

"Thanks." She'd asked his Outlaw cousins about his favorite foods. Not surprisingly most were Southern dishes. One year while in high school she'd spent the entire summer with the Atlanta-based Westmorelands. That summer she had worked in Chase Westmoreland's restaurant and learned how to cook most of the foods Jaxon liked.

It didn't take her long to find a vase while recalling her reaction when their hands had touched. Just remembering it made her feel light-headed. Why now? She'd been around him before, although for short periods of time. That one time the two of them had engaged in a longer conversation was at Charm's wedding. She had felt somewhat light-headed then, and had to fight back from drooling.

Now that they were completely alone in her home, more than anything, she needed all the self-discipline she could muster to handle her attraction. The last thing she wanted or needed was for her body to look for some excuse to be drawn closer to him, to desire him any more than she already did. That had been her mistake with Benson. She had been taken with him from the first.

After putting the flowers in water, she headed back to the living room.

Jaxon turned from studying the huge portrait when he heard the sound of Nadia returning. He watched, appreciating her shapely backside as she crossed the room to place the vase of flowers on a table in front of a window. She then turned to him with a huge smile on her face.

"I think they look perfect here, don't you?" she asked.

He honestly thought she looked pretty damn perfect in her blue maxi-dress. It had a drawstring that emphasized her small waistline, and she'd complemented it with a short suede vest and a pair of black leather boots.

He'd seen her a few times in a shorter dress and knew she had a gorgeous pair of legs. He especially liked the outfit she was wearing because it showcased all her shapely curves. "Yes, they look nice there," he said. He then turned back to the huge portrait he'd been looking at earlier. Last thing Nadia needed to see was how aroused he'd gotten from looking at her.

"This is a nice family picture," he said, trying to concentrate on the huge, framed portrait that hung over her fireplace. It was a picture of an older couple surrounded by four beautiful younger girls. "You look so young."

He knew the moment she'd come to stand beside him and glanced over at her. For a second, maybe two, their gazes held. That's when he felt it. A sexual connection she was trying to fight the same way he was. Had he misread her all these times? Had this been the reason she'd avoided him?

She quickly broke eye contact with him to glance up at the picture. "I was six. This picture was taken a few months before Pam left for college in California. Although we were all smiling, my, Jill and Paige's hearts were breaking. We didn't want Pam to leave us and go so far away."

He nodded. "The four of you are close?" Although he asked the question, he already knew the answer. Anyone observing the four whenever they were together could see that.

"Yes. Pam is the best oldest sister anyone could have. We have different mothers. Her mother died when Pam was three and Dad married my mother, Alma, on Pam's tenth birthday. Pam says my mom was the best birthday present she'd ever gotten. Mom filled the void she'd had in her life after losing her mother."

He glanced back at the picture. Alma Novak had been a beautiful woman and he could see her catching the eye of the widowed rancher Jay Winston Novak Jr. It was probably the same way her youngest daughter had caught his. "Your mother was a beautiful woman and your father, quite a handsome man. They had a beautiful family," he said, glancing over at her.

"Thank you. If you want to take off your jacket, there's a closet near the door next to the hat rack, Jaxon."

"All right." He removed his jacket and then walked over to the closet to put it in before returning to the living room. He saw that she was staring at him. "Is anything wrong?" he asked.

"No. Nothing is wrong. In fact, dinner is ready," she answered. "I left work early to come home to prepare it."

"You didn't have to go to all that trouble." He said the words, although he was glad she had since this gave him the opportunity to not only see her again but to spend time with her.

She waved off his words. "No trouble since I love to cook. Unfortunately, there isn't anyone here to cook for."

It was on the tip of his tongue to say that she could cook for him anytime but he decided to keep that to himself. "Is there a place where I can wash my hands?"

"Yes, just follow me."

She led the way and he couldn't help how his heart missed a couple of beats while admiring the sexiness of her walk. "Here's the powder room. The kitchen and dining room are through that door."

"Okay."

Moments later when he walked through the door that led to the kitchen and dining area, he paused. She was leaning down to take a tray of bread out the oven. He couldn't help appreciating the shape of her backside while she did so.

He cleared his throat to let her know he was there. She glanced over at him while placing the tray on a cooling rack on the counter. "Please have a seat at the dining room table. What would you like to drink?"

"What do you have?"

"A little bit of everything. Thanks to Spencer, I never run out of wine and I make sure I have beer, wine coolers and coffee on hand for whenever those Westmorelands or Outlaws decide to visit." Spencer Westmoreland and his wife, Chardonnay, owned Russell Vineyards which was located in Napa Valley.

Jaxon tilted his head to look at her. "They do that a lot? Come visiting?"

She grinned as she placed several rolls of bread on a tray. "They do it enough, just to check up on me. Not as much now as they did when I first moved back here. I guess they're now convinced that I can take care of myself."

He was glad to hear that. When he had arrived on her property and had seen how massive it was and how far away the location was from town, he became concerned with her living here alone. The good thing was all the security cameras installed around her land. "Wine will be fine," he said.

It was only when she finally sat down at the table that he did so as well. After she'd said grace, she glanced over at him. "I hope you like everything." She then took the lids off the platters.

He couldn't stop the smile that spread across his lips. All the things she'd uncovered were foods he loved to eat. There was no way this was a coincidence. He was not a person who believed you had to wait for Thanksgiving to feast on turkey and dressing. Then there was a medley of garlic roasted mixed vegetables, potato salad and hot yeast rolls.

"Dig in and make sure you leave room for dessert. I baked a chocolate cake."

His eyes lifted. "You did?" Chocolate cake was his favorite.

"Yes."

He looked at the platters again before gazing back at her. "You did all this for me?"

He watched her shrug a pair of feminine shoulders. "Like I said, I enjoy cooking and finding out about the foods you liked was easy." She chuckled and said, "Chase told me whenever you're in Atlanta and patronize his restaurant you always get the turkey and dressing off the menu. Jason told me that you do the same thing whenever you're in Denver and go to McKays restaurant."

"True. I'd eat turkey and dressing every day of the week if I could."

"Well, just so you know, I learned how to make the turkey and dressing from Chase, so it ought to be good."

"I'm sure it will be." After taking his first bite, he saw that it was. "Nadia, this is delicious."

He watched her lips ease into a smile. "Thanks."

Now they were getting somewhere. He could still feel sexual chemistry flowing between them, and he had a feeling she was trying hard to suppress it. He didn't want it quelled one iota. In fact, knowing she wasn't immune to him as he'd thought, gave him hope.

However, he wanted her to feel relaxed around him, at ease and to lower that guard he felt she'd put up for whatever reason.

They began eating. When he glanced up to look at her, he saw her looking at him. Like they'd done earlier in front of the fireplace, their gazes held for an intense few seconds before she looked back down at her food. Whatever he'd been about to say had been wiped from his mind, so he resumed eating while thinking just how strikingly beautiful she was. So much so that she'd nearly taken his breath away just now.

But then that's the same reaction he'd gotten the first time he'd seen her at Maverick and Phire's wedding reception. Even from a distance, the first thing he'd noticed were her eyes. They were chocolate brown and almond shaped. Then there had been her hair, a thick mass of dark brown sister locks that flowed around her shoulders and complemented her honey-brown skin tone.

Jaxon figured the silence between them would continue unless he said something, so he did. "I understand you moved from Gamble when Dillon married Pam."

She looked over at him. "Yes, that's right."

"What made you move back?"

She smiled again and he felt a deep fluttering in the pit of his stomach from that smile. "For the longest I had no intention of returning here. There was even a time when Paige, Jill and I tried convincing Pam to sell, but she wouldn't. She wanted to hold on to it for our legacy. I'm glad she did. I hadn't known how much I'd missed the place until we came back one weekend to attend a play at Pam's acting school. That's when I realized something."

"What?"

"That saying 'there's no place like home' was true."

She took a sip of her wine then added, "Don't get me wrong, I love Westmoreland Country, too. But I was born here. In this very house, and coming back that time made me realize it means a lot to me." She paused for a moment. "What about your home in Virginia, Jaxon? I heard it's beautiful."

There was no need to ask where she'd heard that from since her sister Paige and his cousin Jess were frequent visitors whenever Jaxon was home. He liked that DC was less than an hour away from his ranch. "Thanks. Like you, I was born on the Circle R Ranch. My parents signed it over to me when they retired and decided to move closer to the city."

"They were involved with your family's company, right?"

After taking a sip of his wine, he said, "Yes. My father was CEO of Ravnel Technologies, and Mom was CEO of the Ravnel Institute of Technology. Now I'm CEO of both. Luckily, I have good people working for me."

He paused a moment and said, "The Circle R Ranch will always be home for me, although because of all my travels I'm not there as often as I'd like."

She nodded. "I understand you raise horses, Jaxon. And that you own several prized thoroughbreds. Some of which have competed in the derbies."

It seemed that she was trying to keep the conversation on him and not her. He intended to remedy that.

"Yes, the Circle R started out as a horse ranch with my great-grandfather. It still is and I have a devoted staff whose job is to handle the horses."

He leaned back in his chair. "Now, enough about me. Tell me about you, Nadia."

Three

Nadia glanced over at Jaxon again, wishing he hadn't said her name like that and wishing even more that her body didn't react whenever he did. He pronounced it with a Southern drawl that seemed to roll off his lips. Those same lips she enjoyed watching every time his mouth moved. Was there anything about him that she didn't find a total turn-on?

"There's not much to tell," she finally said after forcing herself to stay focused on their conversation. "You already know that I'm Pam, Jillian and Paige's youngest sister. And I'm sure you've heard the story of how we tried to ruin Pam's engagement to this guy name Fletcher."

He chuckled. "Yes, I heard about that."

"Pam thought going through with a loveless marriage was something she had to do to save us from losing this house. It was a blessing that Dillon stopped by when he did. I don't want to think where we'd be if he hadn't."

Jaxon nodded and then took a sip of his wine. She couldn't help looking at his lips again. "There's a lot about this house that reminds me of Dillon's home," he said, after placing his wineglass down. "They are similar in design."

She smiled. "Yes, and there's a reason for it. My great-grandfather Jay Winston Novak Sr. and Dillon's great-grandfather Raphel Westmoreland were once business partners. I'm told that Raphel liked the design of this house so much that years later when he settled in Denver and built his own home, he used this same architectural design."

"Dillon mentioned that the two great-grandfathers had been business partners here in Gamble. What sort of business was it?"

Nadia thought he was doing a good job of keeping the conversation flowing between them. She was glad since it eliminated any awkward moments, and she was beginning to feel comfortable around him. However, that comfort level didn't decrease her attraction to him.

"It was a dairy business. However, from the journals Pam and Dillon discovered in a trunk in the attic, Raphel took care of the horses. I understand he was very good with them. Those Westmoreland cousins in the horse-training business probably inherited their love of horses from him."

"Your great-grandfather raised horses?"

"Yes, and he passed his love of them to his son and my father. I'm sure Dad wanted at least one son instead of four daughters but that didn't stop him from making sure we loved horses, too. He also made sure we knew how to take care of them, and he taught us how to ride."

She took a sip of her own wine and then added, "I've been riding since I was two. Dad was a wonderful trainer and over the years all his girls had received awards for their riding skills."

"All four of you?"

"Yes. Pam was a pro since she'd been riding longer. Jill wanted to be as good as Pam, and since Dad thought she had potential he sent her to horse-riding school. She competed nationally until Dad got sick. That's when money was needed to pay for his medicine and care."

"Did you enjoy living in Denver?"

Evidently, he saw the sadness in her eyes from remembering that time when her father was sick and he had quickly changed the subject. She appreciated him doing so. That hadn't been easy time for the Novak sisters. Pam, who'd had a bubbling career in Hollywood as an actress, had come home to help take care of their father as well as her three younger sisters.

In a way Nadia knew that's what made Dillon and Pam the perfect couple. Just like Pam had put her sisters' needs before her own, Dillon had done the same by raising his siblings and cousins after his parents, uncle and aunt had died in a plane crash.

"Yes, I enjoyed living in Denver. When Dillon married Pam the entire Westmoreland family claimed us as theirs. Pretty much like they're doing to you now. That's the Westmoreland way. They are big into family."

She watched the smile that spread across his lips and

fought hard for her body not to respond. "I can see that," he said. "I had a younger sister who died before her first birthday of a heart defect. I grew up without any cousins and admit the Westmorelands and Outlaws were a bit overwhelming at first. There are so many of them."

"I'm sorry to hear about your sister." She touched his arm. "But you seemed to have fit right in with our families."

"They didn't give me much of a choice," he replied, grinning.

She couldn't help but grin back, knowing exactly what he meant. It had been that way for her and her sisters as well. In no time it was as if they'd known the Westmorelands all their lives. She'd observed Jaxon with them over the past year and like she'd told him, he seemed to fit right in. They included him in just about everything. She'd heard he'd flown to Denver, Montana and Atlanta a number of times to take part in those infamous Westmoreland poker games.

"I understand you attended Harvard," he said in a voice that felt like warm honey being poured over her skin.

"Yes, I did. However, first I attended the University of Wyoming for my bachelor's degree. Then I went to Harvard for my MBA."

He nodded. "An MBA is impressive, especially one from Harvard. I was in a long line of Ravnel men who'd attended MIT and decided not to break tradition. I did, however, go to Harvard Law School."

"Did you practice law?"

"I did for a couple of years as one of the firm's attorneys. However, when my father let it be known he would be retiring in a few years I figured that was my cue to get ready to take over the reins as CEO."

Nadia had googled him and knew all about his family and how they'd acquired their wealth. She'd read how Jaxon's paternal grandfather founded the Ravnel Institute of Technology and how it was revered the likes of MIT in providing technological advances in higher learning. There was a waiting list to get master's degrees in technology management from the institute and the majority of the students were all but guaranteed six-figure jobs upon graduating. A good number went to work for Ravnel Technologies Incorporated, which was reputed to be one of the most successful technology firms in the nation. At some point, the firm had decided to expand in several parts of the country.

"I understand you're VP of the acting school here," Jaxon said, intruding into her thoughts.

"Yes. My original plan was to move back to Denver after college and go to work at Blue Ridge Land Management," she said, mentioning the billion-dollar corporation owned by the Westmorelands. "However, Pam knew I was interested in moving back to Gamble and when this position came up, she thought I'd be good for it and she offered it to me."

After taking another sip of her wine, she added, "The school depends on donations to award scholarships to deserving students as well as to put on special programs and projects each year. One of my jobs is to make sure we continue to receive funds for all those things."

"Sounds like you're kept pretty busy."

"Not too busy. Once in a while it requires some travel,

but I like what I do." That was true. Even now when she needed more funds for the upcoming play and had no idea where they would come from.

They continued conversing through dinner and it was easy to tell that Jaxon was confident with himself but not overly so and definitely not cocky. He had the type of voice that whenever he spoke, she couldn't help but listen. It was just that captivating. She was glad she was taking this time to get to know him and a part of her wished she would have done so sooner.

The reason she hadn't done so was her fear of him realizing just how attracted she was to him. Even now she hoped he hadn't figured it out. The thought that he might have sent panic skidding up her spine. More than once he'd caught her staring at him. Each time, he'd just given her a friendly smile before striking up another conversation.

"I understand you're looking for land to expand here in Gamble," she said when they had finished their meal and had pushed their plates aside.

"Yes, that's right."

"Why Gamble? What made you turn your sights here, Jaxon?"

Jaxon fought back telling her that *she* was the reason he had set his sights on Gamble. However, if truth be told, once he had visited the town, he'd discovered it was truly a hidden treasure.

Something similar had happened last year. His actual reason for arriving in Forbes, Texas, was to expose Simon Bordella and his betrayal of the Outlaws. His claim about wanting land to expand had been a ruse. But, in the end, just like in Gamble, he'd seen the potential of actually expanding his business in the area.

"The suggestion to expand here actually came from Dillon," he said. That much was the truth. It had happened the night of the poker tournament, when he'd announced his intentions toward Nadia. "He mentioned he'd thought about expanding Blue Ridge Land Management to Gamble because land was plentiful here and at a reasonable price."

She nodded. "I recall Dillon changed his mind after deciding Wyoming was too close to Colorado and if he was going to expand it would be best to do so in another part of the country."

"Yes, and he suggested that I come and check out Gamble. I've only been here a little more than a week and so far I'm impressed with what I see. Wyoming is the least populated state in this country. There's a lot of untouched land here and a lot of ranches. I can see why Wyoming is considered the Cowboy State."

"Yes, we are known to have our cowboys, which equates to plenty of rodeos," she said.

That made him wonder. Nadia was a beautiful woman and with so many cowboys around, he could see her catching their attention. Had none caught her eye? A lot of women went for the rugged, bronco, chaps-wearing type. Jess and Maverick claimed they'd never known her to be involved in a serious relationship. The Westmorelands had claimed the same. He couldn't help wondering why. Had some man broken her heart at some point in time?

Then there was that sexual attraction flowing between them. Sensations seeped through his veins every time he looked at her and every time she looked at him. She had to be feeling it. He now knew for certain that she wasn't as immune to him as he'd originally assumed. It had taken them being alone for him to hone on to it.

"Are you ready for dessert, Jaxon?"

He recalled she'd made a chocolate cake. Dessert was the end of the meal and the thought of that dampened his spirits. He had enjoyed the time he'd spent here with her talking and getting to know her. Listening to the sound of her voice stirred all sorts of longing within him.

It had taken all his willpower to contain himself as he watched her eat. Damn, he actually envied her fork each time she'd stuck it in her mouth. He could just imagine her tongue twirling around it. Another thing he thought was that he had yet to see the renegade side of Nadia. Was she putting on her best behavior for his benefit? Why? More than anything he wanted her to be herself.

Knowing she was waiting for a response, he said, "I'm ready for dessert. Everything was delicious, Nadia. You're a wonderful cook. I find it hard to believe there aren't any hungry cowboys around these parts who would appreciate a home-cooked meal."

He hoped his comment would open the discussion as to why, at twenty-eight, she wasn't seriously involved with anyone. He saw the expression on her face change from a smile to a frown and wondered why. Had what he'd said hit a nerve? She stood and tossed him a haughty look. He had a feeling he was finally about to see the very sassy, outspoken Nadia.

"You're right, there are quite a few hungry cowboys around here, but trust me when I say that I have no interest in feeding them."

Whoa… Well, she'd certainly told him. However, he felt there was a deeper meaning in her answer, and he had no problem digging. He leaned back in his chair. "Care to share the reason why?"

Her frown turned to a glare that sharpened on him. "Let's just say I'm picky when it comes to men."

"Picky in what way?"

"That's none of your business."

He couldn't help but smile because everything about her was his business. This was the Nadia Novak he'd heard about and the one he'd been waiting to see. "Remind me to never ask you a question."

"Oh, you can ask all you want, just as long you know that I reserve the right not to answer."

"Touché. And just for the record, I understand your position because I'm picky as well when it comes to the opposite sex."

She lifted a brow denoting her curiosity. "Are you?"

"Yes. So, I guess you can say we have something in common."

He could tell by the stiffening of her shoulders that she didn't agree with that assessment. "If you'll excuse me, I'll go get those slices of cake." She then walked out of the dining room toward the kitchen and said over her shoulder, "I'm not sure if we have anything in common or not, Jaxon Ravnel."

He couldn't help the way his lips twitched into a smile and was glad she hadn't turned around to see it.

Four

Nadia leaned against the kitchen cabinet, determined to get her anger in check and her desires under control. Dining with Jaxon had been nice, especially with them getting to know each other. But then his question about inviting cowboys to dinner had rubbed her the wrong way because it had reminded her of that incident with Hoyle Adams.

When she'd moved back to Gamble there had been men—namely cowboys—practically coming out of the woodwork, asking her out. It was a full year before she'd decided to go out with Hoyle. She'd played it safe and accepted his invitation to the movies a few times before inviting him to dinner. That had been a mistake. He had assumed she would be the after-dinner delight. After the meal she'd prepared, while she'd been in the kitchen to get the banana pudding she'd baked, he'd slipped out to his truck for his duffel bag. He'd actually assumed he would be staying the night and couldn't believe it when she'd asked him to leave.

That's when he'd acted like a total ass. He even had the nerve to tell her that all the single women in Gamble, and a few married ones as well, wanted him, and that she should be grateful she was the object of his attention. She'd told him just what he could do with all that attention.

He'd left with a bruised ego, but not before accusing her of being frigid just because she'd refused to sleep with him. Newsflash! She didn't do anything just for the hell of it, especially when it concerned her body. As far as Nadia was concerned it was no big deal that at twenty-eight she hadn't yet met a guy she felt was worthy of sleeping with. In fact, she'd never thought of making out with any man…

Until she'd met Jaxon.

Her sisters didn't know that since meeting him, she dreamed about him most nights. In secret he'd become her fantasy man. There was just something about him that pushed all her buttons in ways she hadn't thought was possible. During dinner when he'd licked a dab of gravy from around his mouth with his tongue, she could imagine him using that tongue to lick all over her the same way. She'd never had such thoughts before, but she had imagined them with Jaxon.

Nadia let out a frustrated sigh. She had to pull herself together. Sitting there talking with him, eating and sipping wine while getting to know him, had made her lower her guard and get too comfortable. But then why did she think she had to be uncomfortable around him? He'd been a perfect gentleman since he'd arrived. It wasn't his fault that bringing up the issue of her feeding a cowboy had pressed the wrong button and set her off. She could just imagine what he thought of her now. Probably Dr. Jekyll and Ms. Hyde.

Knowing she had hung out in the kitchen long enough, she drew in another deep breath and grabbed both plates of cake to walk back to the dining room. He looked up when she entered and stood. "Need help with those?" he asked.

"No, I got this," she said, setting plates with slices of cake on the table and then sliding one across to him.

He didn't sit back down until she did and she couldn't help but admire his manners. The Westmorelands and Outlaws behaved the same way. They might get rowdy at times but they respected women. She knew that some men didn't bother with all that chivalry stuff anymore because they assumed most women preferred they didn't. She wasn't one of them. Her father had raised his daughters to expect men to treat them like ladies.

"You think I can eat this huge slice?" he asked, picking up his fork while eyeing the cake she'd placed in front of him.

It didn't seem like her earlier flippant remarks had bothered him and she was glad they hadn't. "Yes, I think you can handle it," she said, wishing her gaze wasn't drawn to the hand that had picked up his fork. Why on earth would she think he had sexy fingers?

When he smiled over at her, flutters invaded her

stomach. "Maybe, but I'll be hitting the hotel's fitness room in the morning," he teased.

She watched as he sliced into the cake with his fork and then slid a bite into his mouth. Seeing the way his lips parted sent an intense throbbing between her legs. Nothing like that had ever happened to her before. Not with Benson or Hoyle and she'd seen both men eat. In fact, the way Hoyle had chomped on his food had been annoying.

"This is delicious, Nadia." He took another bite before glancing over at her with bunched brows. "Aren't you going to eat any?" He was probably wondering why she was sitting there staring at him. Specifically, his mouth. Instead of answering, she nodded and reached out to pick up her fork.

"Don't bother. I got this," he said, leaning across the table to bring his fork with a bite of cake on it to her mouth.

She met his gaze. Did he not know how intimate such a thing was? It was his fork, the same one he'd used. He continued to hold the cake close to her mouth while she studied the look in his eyes, thinking there was something in the dark depths staring back at her. She didn't want to consider the possibility of that being true. Her attraction to him was one thing. The thought the attraction might be reciprocated was something she wasn't sure she could handle.

She could tell him thanks but no thanks, that she could very well slice into her cake and use her own fork. But there was something about the way he was staring at her and the patient way that cake was being held close to her lips. Sensations rushed through her at the thought of them sharing the same fork.

Without saying a word, she parted her lips and he fed her the cake.

The moment Nadia parted her lips Jaxon knew he'd made a mistake.

Or, maybe not if her soft moan was anything to go by. He had a feeling the sound wasn't because her taste buds were exploding from the sensational flavor of the cake. Instead, he chose to believe it had everything to do with another type of sensation entirely. One he could feel himself. All the way down to his gut. And when her tongue darted out to grab a crumb left on the fork, he nearly lost it.

"You like it?" he asked her in a voice that sounded way too throaty for his own ears.

Still holding his gaze, she nodded and said, "Of course I like it. I baked it, didn't I?"

He couldn't help but smile at the bit of defiance in her voice. "Yes, you baked it."

She then asked him in a somewhat mellow tone, "You liked it?"

He was trying like hell to concentrate on what she was saying and not how turned on he was getting each and every time her lips moved. "Yes. I told you it was delicious. Didn't I?"

Then, as if she accepted his comeback as her due, she nodded and said, "Yes, you did. Thanks for letting me sample yours, but I can eat my own. I can also feed myself."

"I know you can, but I enjoyed feeding you."

"Why?"

She would have to ask. "I like the thought of us sharing the same fork."

The surprised look on her face was priceless. It started at her eyes and then spread to her cheeks. Although his response had been honest, maybe he should not have been so bold. His only excuse was that at that moment… or any moment he was around her… Nadia had an impact not only on his male senses, but on his mind.

"Why?"

She was certainly asking a lot of questions. As far as he was concerned, he had no problem telling her whatever she wanted to know. He didn't like playing games anyway. "For me, doing so was a form of intimacy. I wanted to know how you tasted and I wanted you to know the same about me."

Before her mouth could form the word *why*, he quickly added, "I'm sure by now you've figured out that I'm interested in you." He wouldn't go so far as to admit to falling in love with her. She wouldn't believe him. However, he had no problem to at least admitting to being attracted to her. He had a strong feeling the attraction was mutual.

He saw a defiant look appear in the depths of her eyes before she placed her fork down. The gaze staring at him was sharp, like it might rip him to shreds at any moment. "You're interested in me for what reason, Jaxon?"

He figured any other man would clam up under her piercing gaze. Instead, he was trying like hell to ignore a multitude of sensations escalating through him. Did she not feel the heat flowing between them? It was heat he welcomed, but he had a feeling she was fighting hard to control her reaction.

"For the reason any man would be interested in a woman, Nadia," he said, then took a sip of wine.

Something flashed in her eyes. Was he mistaken or was it disappointment? If so, why? Granted, a number of people were never prepared for his outright honesty. He would have thought, however, that she would be. She didn't come across as a woman who preferred a man spouting bullshit.

She sat up straight in her chair and her gaze sharpened even more. "If that's your way of letting me know your interest in me is nothing more than sex, then let me set you straight. That's not how I roll, and I'm disappointed you think that I do." And then as if that ended the conversation, she picked up her fork and began eating her cake.

"Sex?" he asked, surprised. "What makes you think that's my only interest in you?"

"What other interest would there be? You did mention the word *intimate* earlier. And what's more intimate than sex?" she asked. "Just so you know, the last man I invited to dinner who assumed it was all about sex was asked to leave. Should I show you to the door as well?"

She had it all wrong. Damn did she have it all wrong. He wouldn't say he didn't think about making love to her, because he did. A lot. Every night. But to him making love to her was synonymous with the love he felt for her. "You misunderstood me, Nadia. And you definitely misunderstood my intentions."

"Did I?"

"Yes," he said, placing down his wineglass.

"Then what did I misunderstand? What are your intentions?"

Jaxon hadn't wanted to tell her so soon. At least not before spending more time with her, before courting her properly. However, she left him no choice. It was either tell her what she needed to know or let her group him in the same class as the other assholes who hadn't left a positive impression on her.

To make sure she fully understood what he was about to say, he leaned slightly toward her. Holding tight to her gaze, he said, "My intention, Nadia Novak, is to marry you."

Five

Nadia tilted her head and stared at Jaxon. He didn't look as if he was teasing. That could only mean... Sliding back her chair, she walked around the table and placed the back of her hand to his forehead.

"What are you doing?" he asked.

"I figure you must have a high temperature for you to be so delusional."

"I'm in my right mind, Nadia."

Removing her hand, she returned to her chair. "There's no way you can be to say something as asinine as that, Jaxon. Think about it. There's no way you can want to marry me. You don't even know me."

"I would like to get to know you."

She didn't say anything for a moment. "Who put you up to this? Sloan or Maverick?"

She watched as a dumbfounded look appeared on his face. "What makes you think they put me up to anything?"

"Mainly because the three of us are known to play tricks on each other. I figured they owed me for that time I set them up with blind dates from hell a couple of years back."

"Trust me, Sloan nor Maverick have nothing to do with my decision to marry you."

His decision to marry her? Honestly, she didn't believe for one minute he was serious. And even if he was delusional to think such a thing, what man told a woman they barely knew of his plans to marry her? As if it was a done deal and she didn't have anything to say about it?

She wasn't born yesterday and knew she wasn't his type. It wasn't just the fact he was wealthy, since the Westmorelands and Outlaws had plenty of money as well. She would think a man like Jaxon preferred a sophisticated type, a cultured and graceful woman. A woman totally opposite from her. That one time she'd looked him up on the Internet she'd seen images of him from the society pages of several newspapers. In all of them, his date looked the part of a high-class, refined goddess.

"First of all, Jaxon, you won't be marrying me so stop saying such nonsense. And if Sloan nor Maverick put you up to this foolishness then who did?"

"No one put me up to anything. I'm speaking the truth."

She rolled her eyes. "Get serious."

"I am serious, trust me."

She leaned back in her chair and crossed her arms over her chest. "No, you aren't if you think for one minute that one day you'll be my husband."

"Don't you plan to marry?"

She shrugged her shoulders. "Possibly."

"Then what's the problem?"

She couldn't help but glare across the table at him. "The problem is you. How dare you say something like that, like you have the ability to speak such a thing into existence regardless of how I might feel about it happening. Marriage isn't and never will be at the top of my to-do list. Unlike some women, I don't worry about a biological clock ticking."

There was no way he didn't hear the irritation and strong conviction in her voice because she meant every word. "So, just in case you fell and hit your head on the way over here and are serious about thinking of marrying me, let me go on record to say that it won't be happening." She frowned when he had the audacity to smile.

"We shall see, Nadia."

We shall see? Had he actually said that? In that case, now was the time to show him the door. Easing from her chair, Nadia said, "I think you should leave now, Jaxon."

He glanced down at his cake. "I haven't finished eating."

"Then I suggest you take it with you."

He stared at her for a minute and then said, "I'm sorry if what I said upset you. However, it's my belief that honesty is the best policy."

Nadia stared at him and then she eased back down in her chair, totally confused. Although she hadn't gotten to know Jaxon as well as the others in her family had, at no time had she assumed he wasn't operating with a full deck. Until now. Therefore, she decided to use another approach.

"When did you decide you wanted to marry me?"

"The moment we were introduced."

Now she'd heard everything. "You honestly want me to believe that?" she asked, chuckling, finding what he'd said totally absurd.

"I don't see why not when it's the truth, Nadia."

Nadia would admit to feeling something when they'd first been introduced as well. However, she would call it what it was. Lust of the worst kind. She then thought about what he'd said. If he'd been taken with her from the first, why hadn't he approached her before now? The only reason he was here was because she had called and invited him to dinner. He'd even admitted he'd been in town a while, yet he hadn't looked her up. So how was she supposed to believe he was interested in her to the point of intending to marry her? That made this entire thing even more outrageous.

"That was truly delicious."

She blinked and glanced down at his plate. It was clean. He had eaten all of his cake. "I'm glad you enjoyed it."

"I've enjoyed everything about this evening with you, Nadia."

She drew in a deep breath, refusing to get baited. Standing, she said, "I had a rather interesting and enjoyable evening with you. Now it's time to call it a night."

"When can I see you again?"

She shrugged. "Not sure that's a good idea."

"Why? Because I told you of my future plans for us?"

He was frustrating her to the point where she wanted to stomp her feet. "There are no future plans for us, Jaxon. I am absolutely sure of that."

"If you're so certain of it then there should be no reason for me not to see you again, right? Dinner will be on me the next time. You pick the place." He then he stood as well. "I know it's a workday tomorrow for the both of us. I'll be seeing more land."

"So you are in town for that purpose?"

He smiled over at her. "That's one of them, yes."

"Meaning?"

"Meaning, while I'm here I hope to get to know you better." Then he changed the subject by saying, "I'll help you clear off the table."

"That's not necessary."

"It is for me. I'll even roll up my sleeves and wash the dishes if you need help."

"I don't. And you don't have to help clear off the table."

"You sure?"

"I'm positive." What she needed was for him to leave. Now. She couldn't think straight with him around. And she desperately needed to think. Do an instant replay and a total reevaluation of everything he'd said, especially the part about his future plans for them.

"Okay, if you're certain, Nadia."

"I am."

"Then please come walk me to the door."

She should have declined his request. After all, he knew the way there without her assistance. But then she decided to extend the same courtesy to him she would have expected of him had she been his guest for dinner. Besides, she didn't want him to think he'd rattled her with his nonsense, even if he had.

"You didn't say if you'll have dinner with me," he said.

They had walked side by side from the dining room and had reached the front door. He opened the closet to get his jacket. She was so focused on him sliding the jacket over his broad shoulders that she almost missed what he'd said. "I'll think about it." Although she'd said she would, she honestly knew she wouldn't. Right now, she needed him gone.

"All right. And like I said, I want you to pick the place."

Although she hadn't agreed to anything, she asked, "When?"

"Doesn't matter. I'm free whenever you are." He was standing there in front of her. She was about to take a step back when he reached out and placed both hands at her waist. The moment he touched her, heat spread to all parts of her body.

He was going to kiss her. She didn't say anything as she absorbed that fact into her brain. Regardless of the craziness he'd said about marrying her, what he'd said earlier was something she couldn't deny. She *had* wanted to know how he'd tasted and licking that fork hadn't been enough. Even with the sweetness of the chocolate cake, a part of her wanted to believe she had also gotten a taste of him. And it was a taste she wanted to experience again.

"Nadia?"

"Yes?"

"I hope you don't lose much sleep over what I said tonight."

She lifted her chin. "I don't plan on losing any sleep when I know it won't be happening."

"We'll see."

"No, you'll see," she said in an annoyed tone.

They stood there, staring at each other, squaring off. She wished all those sensations she'd felt all through dinner weren't still there. Jaxon was taking her breath away without even trying. If that wasn't bad enough, the nipples pressed against the material of her dress suddenly seemed achy. That was a first for her as well.

"It's getting late," she said, trying to dismiss the desire for him that was hitting her full force. It couldn't be helped, with the way his dark eyes were latched on to hers as if daring her to look away. For some reason, she couldn't. She felt herself falling victim to everything about him. Never had she been so mesmerized with any man, and she couldn't understand why she was this way with him. And then there was his mouth. The shape of it from corner to corner and that little dip in the middle fascinated her. She didn't have to be a rocket scientist to know that she was out of her element with Jaxon. The man was definitely out of her league. Yet…

"Then I guess I need to say good night."

His words cut into her trance. Before she could offer a response of *Yes, you do*, he leaned forward, drew her closer and captured her mouth in his.

* * *

Her lips immediately parted under his. The moment
their mouths touched, thoughts fled from her mind.
She'd needed this to happen. Was glad it was happening. For the past year, she'd wondered about his mouth.
Fantasized about it. Dreamed about it. Not only how it
would taste but also how well he could use it for kissing.

Now she was finding out and had no complaints.
He'd stuck his tongue inside her mouth at the exact moment she released a sigh of pleasure. There was something about the way he was kissing her that sent jolts of
heat through her. Never had she been kissed this way,
with such mastery and finesse. So vibrantly and with so
much passion. It was both mind-blowing and torturous.

He was devouring her mouth with one stoke of his
tongue while slowly mating with it with another stroke.
It was as if he was methodically and intentionally creating an avalanche of need and pleasure within her. Unable to help herself, she wrapped her arms around his
neck to hold, certain if he stopped kissing her, she would
melt in a puddle at his feet. Needs she didn't know she
had, and a degree of pleasure she hadn't known could
be derived from a kiss, were taking over her senses.

Without warning, he deepened the kiss and drew
her even closer. That's when she felt him. His aroused
body hard against the junction of her thighs. Knowing
he wanted her as much as she wanted him had temptation running rampant through her. Temptation to try
some of those things with him that she'd dreamed about.
Fantasized about doing.

Suddenly he broke off the kiss, but she soon discovered that he wasn't through with her yet when he traced the tip of his tongue across her lips, corner to corner. Then he stopped and slowly eased back, although he hadn't removed his hands from around her waist.

"I have to fly out tomorrow to Forbes to check on a few things but will return in a day or so. I will be thinking of you, Nadia and I hope you'll be thinking about me."

Before she could respond, mainly to tell him that she wouldn't be thinking about him, he grabbed his Stetson off the hat rack, opened the door and left.

Jaxon had driven a mile from the Novak Homestead when he pulled his car to the shoulder of the road to inhale and exhale. Never had kissing a woman left him so weak. He'd only stopped kissing her when breathing had become a necessity. Then it had taken all his strength to finally release her and walk out the door.

He rubbed his hand down his face. It had not been his intent to tell her he planned to marry her, and, as expected, he'd put her on the defensive. She would probably avoid going out with him for that reason. He could see her putting roadblocks in his paths.

But Jaxon could never forget the look on her face when he'd broken off the kiss. She hadn't been happy about how she was feeling, if the look on her face was anything to go by. And yet, she had enjoyed it as much as he had. He was certain of it. He'd also felt the way the hardened nipples of her breasts poked into his chest. That was a sure sign of arousal.

His plan was to tear down any wall she tried erecting between them, one brick at a time. Although more than anything he would love to be married to her by New Year's, he knew that some things just couldn't be rushed. He loved her and he had to be patient for her to fall in love with him. He had to believe that eventually she would.

He would give her a few days to think about tonight, just like he would. Then he would call and follow up on his invitation to dinner. No matter what she might be thinking now, there would definitely be a next time for them.

He would see to it.

Six

"You can close your mouth now, Rissa," Nadia said the next morning to the woman sitting across from her desk. Marissa Phelps had been Nadia's best friend since second grade. When Pam had moved her sisters with her to Denver, Nadia and Rissa had stayed in touch by engaging in summer visits, occasional sleepovers and then attending the same university after high school. It was at the University of Wyoming where Rissa had met Shayne, the man she married. The couple had three beautiful children under the age of ten.

Rissa closed her mouth but leaned forward in her chair with her eyes still widened. "Jaxon Ravnel actually told you that he intends to marry you?"

"Yes, that's what he said. Can you imagine anything so downright ridiculous?"

"I guess you can," Rissa said, eyeing her speculatively.

"Of course I can. What man tells a woman something like that?"

Rissa shrugged her shoulders as she sat back in her chair. "A man who knows the woman he wants and intends to get her. A man who wants more than a bed partner. He wants a future with the woman he loves. A man who—"

"Love has nothing to do with it," Nadia interrupted, frowning. "Jaxon doesn't even know me." Rissa's words had put her on the defensive. "You can't love someone you don't know."

Rissa scoffed at that. "I heard it happens that way at times. Otherwise, there would not be any of those love-at-first-sight situations."

Nadia shook her head. She didn't believe in that kind of phenomenon either. "Get real, Rissa. Jaxon Ravnel doesn't love me. Besides, I'm definitely not his type. He's a man who'd prefer a woman with a high degree of sophistication. One who possesses style, grace and pedigree. Not someone who for years was a tomboy. Even now I only act prim and proper when there's a need. I have no problem being outspoken and opinionated. Being known as a rebel and renegade doesn't bother me one bit."

"Maybe he likes you the way you are."

"Let me say this again, Rissa. Jaxon doesn't know the way I am because he doesn't know me. Besides, I'm not sure I even like him."

Rissa smiled. "If you recall, I didn't like Shayne at first either. However, he eventually grew on me. But then, maybe not liking Jaxon right off the bat is a good thing. You were smitten with Benson the minute he got in your face at that football game, and you see what happened with that."

She wished Rissa didn't make her remember that day or the guy. Yes, she might have been smitten with Benson the first time he'd turned those dreamy hazel eyes on her, but it was only after he'd taken her on a couple of movie dates that she had convinced herself he was a supernice guy. That's when she had fallen in love with him. Supernice her ass. He had proven just what a scum he was.

"Well, I don't want Jaxon, or any man for that matter, to grow on me nor do I want to grow on him. I'm not in the mood."

"Obviously you were in the mood for that whopper of a kiss he laid on you last night," Rissa said, grinning.

There were days Nadia regretted that Rissa kept her in check. Unlike her sisters, who hadn't a clue about her attraction to Jaxon, Rissa knew everything. She'd even told Rissa about the kiss that still had her swooning. When Paige and Jill had called that morning to see how dinner with Jaxon had gone, Nadia had told them everything had gone well. What she hadn't told them was what he'd said about marrying her. Nor had she told her sisters about their heated kiss.

"That kiss took me by surprise. I hadn't been kissed in a long time, so my mouth was more than ready for some action."

Rissa chuckled. "I guess it helped that the action was delivered by the same man you've been dreaming about for over a year. Don't you want to compare the dream with the real thing? You can't even say it's been a long time since you've slept with a man because you've never slept with one. I've told you more than once what you're missing."

Yes, Rissa had. Too many times. To the point where Nadia had gotten curious, too curious for her own good. It didn't help when Jill and Paige would go on and on about how much they enjoyed their husbands in the bedroom. That was one of the reasons Hoyle had been such a disappointment. She had figured although she hadn't been looking for anything long-term with him, that maybe after they'd gotten to know each other better, a little roll between the sheets wouldn't be so bad. It would have rid her of her virginity and appeased her curiosity. Like with Benson, she was glad she'd discovered just what an ass he was before sharing her body with him.

"Are you going to tell your family what Jaxon said about his plans to marry you?" Rissa asked, interrupting her thoughts.

"Heck no. They like Jaxon. If anything, they would pity him for even contemplating such a thing and warn him off." She paused and then said, "Benson taught me a hard lesson. When I do marry…if that day ever comes…I will marry for love. I will know beyond a shadow of a doubt that the man I marry loves me. Truly loves me. I won't take a chance with my heart again."

"Does that mean you won't sleep with a guy until you marry him?"

"No, I didn't say I had to love whatever guy who will

become my first. To be quite honest, he doesn't even
have to love me. However, I need to feel that I truly do
know him and there won't be any surprises later on that
I couldn't handle."

"So, what are you planning to do, Nadia? You might
want to come up with a plan because I have a feeling
Jaxon Ravnel has one of his own. Sounds like he intends to wear down your resistance like Shayne did to
me. And if that kiss is anything to go by, he's already
begun his attack."

The last thing Nadia wanted to think about was that
the kiss had been part of a planned attack by Jaxon. In
fact, she didn't want to talk about him at all anymore.
That meant it was time to send Rissa on her way; otherwise he would remain the topic of their conversation.

Looking at her watch, she said, "Shouldn't you be
leaving for work?"

Rissa was the assistant manager of a bank that was
a half a mile up the road. Since the bank didn't open
until ten, it was Rissa's normal routine after dropping
her kids off at school to stop by Dream Makers Acting
Academy every weekday morning to share a cup of coffee and girl-talk with Nadia.

Rissa gave Nadia a knowing eye, fully aware of why
she'd asked. "Not yet." After taking another sip of her
coffee, Rissa inquired, "Has anyone signed on as a sponsor of this year's Christmas play yet?"

Nadia released a frustrated breath. She honestly
didn't want to talk about that either. "No. Although I
can go to the Westmoreland Foundation as a last resort,
I prefer not doing so since they bailed this place out a

couple of times before I began working here. The reason Pam hired me is because she believed I could keep sponsorships intact. I can't disappoint her."

"It's not your fault that the Dunnings Financial Group went bankrupt."

"I know, but I should have had a Plan B in place."

"I disagree. Dunnings has always been one of the most prominent employers in the city. A company that could be depended on to fund community projects. It's unfortunate they had to close their doors when they did. Just think of the number of people who lost their jobs. People who were making good salaries." Rissa took a sip of her coffee then added, "At least I can admire them for giving everyone a nice severance package with enough funds to last them for the next six months. Everyone is hoping that by then another huge employer will come to town."

Nadia hoped so, too. Rissa was right. Dunnings was one of the few corporations in Gamble to pay top salaries and who readily funded community projects. They had been sponsoring the Christmas play for years. No one had asked who the new sponsor would be. She figured most people thought she had one.

"Just so you know, Nadia, the mayor and Gamble's Better Business Bureau had a meeting yesterday. Jaxon Ravnel's name came up. They know he's in town looking for land to expand his business. They're hoping he likes the area. Ravnel Technologies is three times the size of what Dunnings was."

"Although Jaxon is looking for land here, there's no guarantee he'll buy any," Nadia interjected.

"I know, but we can all hope," Rissa said standing. "It will certainly solve the unemployment crisis Gamble will be facing within a few months." She glanced at her watch. "It's time for me to skedaddle. I'll see you again this time tomorrow."

After Rissa left, Nadia leaned back in her chair and for the umpteenth time replayed in her mind everything that had transpired last night between her and Jaxon. He'd been the perfect gentleman the entire time. She'd been so busy fighting her attraction to him that she hadn't noticed he'd been attracted to her.

Until he'd fed her that cake.

She had noticed him staring at her a number of times but assumed he'd done so because he had caught her staring at him. It now appeared they had been staring at each other. She figured the reason she hadn't picked up on an attraction on his end was because he hadn't been giving her any predatory, I-want-to-take-you-to-bed looks.

What had rocked her world more than anything had been that kiss. What she'd told Rissa was true. She hadn't been prepared for it. She doubted any woman would have been. What man kissed like that? The way he had taken her mouth, locked his tongue around hers while he greedily mated with it had sent sparks escalating through every part of her body.

And talking about a body… While he'd held her tight in his arms, with her body pressed hard against his, she had felt him. Namely his arousal. Just knowing the intensity of his desire had matched hers sent a wave passion rushing through her. She was convinced if he hadn't stopped kissing her when he had, she would have gotten her first orgasm ever, right there in his arms. His kiss had been hotter than any she'd ever shared with a man before. Just thinking about it sent sensuous chills through her. That was the last thing she wanted or needed.

A couple of hours later Nadia was working through the stack of papers her administrative assistant, China Evans, had placed on her desk earlier. She glanced up at the knock on her door. "Come in."

China walked in carrying a huge vase of flowers. Nadia grimaced and sat up in her chair, having an idea who'd sent them. But that didn't make sense when Jaxon had brought her flowers yesterday when he'd arrived for dinner. Why would he be giving her more flowers today? But if they weren't from him, then who else would have sent them?

"These are for you, Ms. Novak." The younger woman of nineteen, who was attending the local community college, smiled from ear to ear as she placed the a dozen red roses on the desk.

"Thank you, China," Nadia said, not bothering to pull off the card that was attached.

"You're not eager to see who they're from?" China asked. "I've never known you to get flowers when it wasn't your birthday or Valentine's Day."

That was true. She always got flowers from various people on her birthday, and Dillon had always sent his Denver Westmoreland female cousins—Megan, Gemma and Bailey—flowers on Valentine's Day. After marrying Pam he'd added Nadia, Paige and Jill to his list. He was such a thoughtful brother-in-law. The best.

"I'll read the card later," Nadia said, turning her attention back to the stack of papers on her desk.

"I guess that means you know who sent them."

"Maybe," Nadia said and that was all she would say on the matter. China was at that impressionable age where she believed in love. The forever kind. Nadia remembered when she had been that way as well. Her parents, as well as Dillon and Pam, had been great role models. Then Benson had broken her heart and from that day forward she'd shied away from falling in love.

Seeing she was not getting any information out of Nadia, China said, "Well, I guess I'll get back to my desk."

As soon as China closed the door behind her, Nadia pulled the card off the arrangement and read it.

Thinking about you,
Jaxon

Nadia placed the card back in the envelope and slid it into her desk drawer. If Rissa was right and Jaxon was trying to wear down her resistance, first by feeding her cake, then the kiss and now with more beautiful flowers, she had her work cut out for her. She had to make sure he knew a marriage between them wouldn't be happening.

She sighed deeply as she stared at the beautiful red roses. Of course she would thank him for the flowers. However, she would text him instead of calling him, not sure she could handle hearing his voice. And as far as his dinner invitation, she might as well decline that, too, while she was at it. Hopefully, in due time he would discover she would not participate in whatever games he wanted to play.

Jaxon drove to the airport, glad to finally be leaving Forbes. The trip had taken a day longer than planned due to a glitch in the data system of one of the firm's top clients. He was glad the malfunction had been corrected and now he was on his way back to Gamble.

He wished he could say he'd been too busy to think about Nadia, but that had not been the case. He had thought about her a lot. Each time her face entered his thoughts, he felt emotions so profound that more than once he had to pause to pull himself together and re-focus.

If there had been any doubt in his mind that Nadia was the One, it had been dispelled on the night they'd shared dinner together. Specifically, the moment she'd opened the door. Never before had a woman caused his entire body to burn. Up close she'd been even more beautiful and by the end of the evening she'd had him tied in knots in the most sensual way. Any other man would think such an intense attraction to a woman wasn't normal. However, to him it was. He'd figured it would be that way when he'd found his soulmate, the woman destined to have a special place in his life.

Jaxon was well aware she had issues with accepting that place. Quite frankly, she didn't believe that place existed. The text messages he'd received from her before leaving Forbes pretty much confirmed it. One had thanked him for the roses and the other had turned down his invitation to dinner. She had then proceeded to tell him that she hoped he enjoyed the rest of his stay in Gamble.

If Nadia thought that was the end of them, she was mistaken. There was nothing stopping him from figuring out a different approach.

His thoughts shifted to the call he'd gotten from his administrative assistant advising him of Gamble's mayor's request to meet with him. A meeting had been scheduled for next week but he would have preferred scheduling time with Nadia instead.

He'd dismissed their sexual chemistry as one-sided until she had stood beside him while they'd discussed the huge family picture over her fireplace. That's when he'd felt it, not only the vibes coming from him but from her as well. And the chemistry had been there each and every time their gazes met during dinner. He'd known every time she'd looked over at him because it had resulted in him looking at her.

It didn't take him long for him to realize the reason she hadn't picked up on all those sexual vibes coming from him was because she'd been too busy trying to ignore those coming from her. That's when he'd decided to feed her the cake. Doing so had certainly turned up the heat, which was the very thing he'd wanted to happen. It had been the very thing that had prompted her to remove her blinders.

What he'd thought about most over the last three days had been the kiss they'd shared. It had been everything he'd thought it would be and more. Although it had been intense and invigorating, it hadn't been enough.

A few hours later he was back in his hotel room in Gamble. It was close to seven and he hadn't responded to the two text messages Nadia had sent him. Now he would.

Instead of texting her back he decided to call her. Picking up his cell phone he punched in her number. The phone rang several times and for a minute he thought perhaps she would not answer once she saw the call was from him. He was about to disconnect when she clicked on.

"Hello."

He pulled in a deep breath the moment he heard her voice. "Nadia, I got your messages. I'm glad you liked the roses."

She paused before saying, "They are beautiful. Thank you again."

"You are welcome. As for my dinner invitation, I'm sorry you've decided not to go out with me. I regret that what I said the other night scared you off."

She hesitated and then said, "Nothing about what you said scared me."

He couldn't help but smile at her strong denial. "Didn't it?"

"No. There was no reason it should when it's apparent you're living in a delusional world."

Undaunted by her words, he said, "That's your opinion. We could meet and discuss it further if you weren't so afraid to face the truth."

"Truth? There's no truth in what you're thinking, Jaxon. I don't like overconfident men."

That's what he'd been told. "You're getting a self-assured man confused with an overconfident one. I know what I want, and I want you. I've been up front with you. I don't like playing games with a woman any more than I like a woman playing games with me."

He could just imagine her glaring him down through her phone. "Anyway, you've made your decision. Have a nice night, Nadia."

"Wait!"

He took his time answering. "Yes?"

"I'll have dinner with you, and you'll see how unafraid I am of you. And you can decide on the place."

"Fine. I will do that and call you in a few days with the details. Goodbye, Nadia."

"Goodbye."

He couldn't help but smile when she ended the call.

Seven

Nadia stood in the same spot she had last week when she'd watched Jaxon arrive. Unlike then, when she hadn't known what to expect, she knew now. He was a nice guy although a delusional one. There was no other way for her to describe a man who'd told her, without as much as blinking an eye, that he intended to marry her. Regardless of the fact that other than the surface stuff, they knew nothing about each other. Then there was the reality that they weren't in love. In fact, the verdict was still out as to whether she would even consider them friends.

She'd heard from Rissa that he had met with the mayor yesterday. No one knew how that meeting went, although she had more than a hunch what was discussed. Nadia had no idea how much of an expansion Jaxon was contemplating and wondered would it be enough to help the job employment crisis the city would soon be facing. More than likely, Ravnel Technologies would be relocating a lot of their present employees and might not need additional staff. At least not to the magnitude the city was hoping for.

Thinking it was best to move away from the window, she did so. There was no need for her adrenaline to get revved up when he got out of the car. She would have more time to fully check him out later and hoped she could contain herself when she did so.

She quickly left the kitchen and moved to the living room with no intention of giving him the chance to knock. Grabbing her purse and shawl, she opened the door and stepped out on the porch, locking the door behind her. He had called a few days ago saying dinner plans had been finalized. When she'd asked where and suggested she just meet him there, seeing no reason for him to drive to her house to pick her up, he refused to do that, saying his definition of a date was the guy picking up the woman from her home and returning her there. He never did say where they were going.

She studied him as he got out of the car. He was talking on his cell phone and hadn't looked up to see her. Since he'd told her to dress casually, she'd opted for a skirt and blouse. It was her first time wearing the ensemble that she'd purchased earlier that year while shopping with her sisters in New York. Her sisters thought she looked good in them.

From the expression that appeared on Jaxon's face when he put his phone in his jacket pocket and glanced up and saw her, he agreed with her sisters. She thought he looked good, too, dressed in a pair of dark slacks, a tweed jacket and that black Stetson on his head.

He had stopped walking and stood there in a masculine stance that caused her heart rate to increase. The sun was going down behind him and the backdrop—orange and gold over the mountains—was a breathtaking sight that complemented a breathtaking-looking man. Seeing it before her eyes stirred something deep within her and she just couldn't understand it. She'd been raised around eye candy, ultrahandsome men, mainly the Westmorelands, and then there were the Outlaws. She would even say she'd met a few cowboys in town she thought were good on the eyes. But at that moment, the memory of any other man faded to black. Jaxon Ravnel was in a class all by himself. His lips curved into that killer smile that showed all his dimples as he began walking again.

Nadia drew in slow, steadying breaths and wished Jaxon's smile didn't affect her the way it did. Having a handsome man stare at you with male appreciation in his eyes was one thing. Throw a sexy smile in the mix and it was lethal. "Hello, Jaxon."

"Nadia. You look nice."

"Thanks. I hope what I'm wearing is appropriate for where we're going."

"It is. Are you ready to go?"

"Yes."

She wished he hadn't reached for her hand, leaving her no choice but to give it to him. The moment he touched it, goose bumps appeared on her skin. Suddenly, images floated through her mind, namely that of his arms wrapped tight around her as she'd kissed him as deeply and thoroughly as he'd kissed her.

He walked her to his car and opened the door. Releasing his hand, she slid onto the leather seat. She hadn't missed how his gaze had lowered to her legs when the hem of her skirt had inched up a little. "Is anything wrong, Jaxon?" she asked, after making sure her seat belt was securely fastened.

He moved his gaze to her face and his lips curved into a smile. One that sent flutters through her stomach. "No, nothing is wrong."

A short while later they had driven past downtown, where most of the popular restaurants were located. She glanced over at him, and evidently anticipating her question, he said, "Where we're going is a surprise."

"And what if I don't like surprises?"

"Then I'll make doubly certain you like this one."

When the interior of the car got too quiet to suit her, she said, "I understand you had a meeting with the mayor the other day."

He grinned and gave her a sideways glance. "Yes, that's right."

Was he going to tell her anything? When moments passed and he didn't, she figured he wouldn't. Then he said, "That was awful what happened to the Dunnings Financial Group. I understand a lot of people lost their jobs. However, I'm glad they got a good severance package."

"I'm glad, too, but unfortunately it doesn't extend to our school."

He looked at her when he brought the car to a stop. "What do you mean?"

She wished she hadn't said anything, but since she had, she might as well give him an answer. "Every year the school puts on this huge holiday play. This year a well-known movie director from Hollywood, who is a good friend of Pam's, is volunteering his time here. It will be the biggest production the school has put on so far and also the most expensive. Unfortunately, Dunnings was our major sponsor. Their bankruptcy pretty much left us in a bind."

"I'm sorry to hear that. Will you have to cancel the event?"

"I hope not. I'm working hard to find a replacement sponsor." She stopped talking when she looked out the car's window. "Why are we at the airport?"

He brought the car to a stop and smiled over at her. "Because we'll be dining on my jet."

Jaxon thought the look of surprise on Nadia's face was not only priceless, but it was also one of the most sensuous expressions he'd ever seen. The way her lips parted in an "oh" followed by her eyes lighting up and ending with a smile that spread wide across her lips. That smile went straight to his heart. Not that there had been any doubts about his feelings for her before, but if there had been, they had dissolved at that moment.

"You're kidding, right?" she asked him, her smile widening ever more.

"No, I'm not kidding."

When she realized he was serious, she rocked her body in her seat in a happy dance.

He threw his head back and laughed, loving her excitement. He hadn't been sure what to expect when he'd thought of the idea. "I guess that means you have no problem with flying."

"Heck no. I think the Denver Westmorelands shied away from owning a corporate jet because of what happened to their parents, but those Atlanta-based Westmorelands have no reservations about it. And flying is a way of life for those Outlaws in Alaska."

Jaxon knew that to be true. The Westmoreland triplets, Clint, Cole and Casey, were licensed pilots. And because of Alaska's road system, people living there owned more planes than cars. All six of the Outlaws owned planes. In fact, Garth, the oldest Outlaw son, was married to Regan, their company's pilot.

It seemed Nadia was in a good mood and he intended to take full advantage of her joviality. "Ready to go aboard?"

"Yes."

Now he was glad for all the special arrangements he had made. He had gone out of his way to impress her tonight. Getting out of the car, he came around on her side to open the door. This time he tried not to be so obvious when he glanced down at her legs. Taking her hand, he walked over to the plane, where his pilot and flight host were waiting. Introductions were made before he escorted her up the steps.

"My parents always had the company jet, and I had a Cessna since I rarely did international travel. But now that I'm in charge, I decided to get a jet that fit my needs. I've only had this one for six months," he told her when he saw her glancing around curiously.

"This is nice," Nadia said. "The only other time I've been on a corporate jet was during one of Charm's bridal showers. It was given to her in flight by Regan. We had so much fun during the three-hour flight. We never did land. The entire shower was held while we were in the sky."

"Who was the pilot that night?" he asked as he escorted her over to the seats. He would give her a tour of the jet later.

"A girlfriend of Regan's. Garth had volunteered but he was told no husbands or significant others were allowed on that trip. I'm glad. Things got pretty wild."

"Were there half-naked men on board?"

She threw up her head and laugh. "I'll never tell. Don't you know what goes on at the bridal shower stays at the bridal shower? I'm sure men have the same rule for the bachelor party."

"I guess they do." He was tempted to say not only was that the rule for a bachelor party but that had been the case for that poker tournament a couple of months ago as well.

Nadia sat in the seat facing him and they both followed instructions when the pilot told them to buckle up. She was deliberately looking everywhere else but at him. That was fine since he had no intentions of looking anywhere else other than at her.

"You have big plans for the weekend?" he asked, not just for conversational purposes but as a way to get her to glance over at him. She did so and when their gazes met, he felt it. He had a feeling she did, too. The attraction was stronger than ever. He was beginning to think that the more they were alone the more the sexual chemistry increased between them.

She looked over at him at the exact moment the plane began moving down the runway. "Not big plans. Normal chores that need to be done. What about you?"

"I'm flying home tomorrow. My parents like to see their only child every once and a while."

She nodded. "You're close to them?"

"Very."

"I heard they were nice."

He could tell by her expression that she regretted saying that because it meant his name had come up in a discussion she'd had with someone. Before he could ask who had told her that, she cleaned up her comment by adding, "I believe Paige mentioned she met them at one of Jess's fundraising dinners."

"She did. My parents are big on making financial contributions to their favorite political candidates. Now that they consider Jess, as well as Reggie Westmoreland, as family, they wanted to attend and do their part."

"That was kind of them."

"I have kind parents." He truly meant that. As long as he could remember they'd always been there for him, encouraging him to be his own man. The only thing they'd demanded of him was to always have respect for others, especially women. Now was not the time to tell her that he'd told his parents about her, and they were looking forward to meeting her.

When the plane had leveled off in the sky and the pilot indicated it was okay to move around, he unbuckled his seat belt and stood. By the time he had walked over to her, she had unbuckled her own and was standing as well. "You're ready to show me around?" she asked excitedly.

In all honesty, he wanted to do a lot more than that. Taking her hand, he said, "Yes, I am ready to show you around before dinner is served."

Eight

Nadia was impressed by everything she saw on Jaxon's private jet. From the thick rich carpeting to the smooth leather seats in his sitting room. However, what touched her most was the table set for dinner. It was just as impressive as any table in a five-star restaurant.

He introduced her to the chef, who was also on the flight. The food had tasted wonderful and she'd wasted no time letting the chef know. Dessert was banana pudding cake. Evidently Jaxon had inquired about her favorite dessert the way she'd done for him.

"I can't eat a thing more," she said, pushing back from the table. "Your cook outdid himself with dinner and so did you."

He chuckled. "I didn't cook."

"No, but you arranged all of this," she said, using her

hand to encompass the dining table. "A beautifully set table, great food, champagne and a delicious dessert, all the time while flying high in the sky. Things can't get any better than this."

In all honestly, that's what bothered her. She hadn't wanted to be impressed by anything he'd done tonight. She had decided tonight would be her chance to use any means possible to make him think twice about pursing any type of relationship with her. But whenever he gave her a warm smile, like he was doing now, she couldn't stop the desire flowing through her. Desire she knew he not only felt but reciprocated.

Why was the sexual chemistry stronger between them tonight than it had been at dinner last week? She figured that kiss had a lot to do with it. The same kiss she couldn't get off her mind. The kiss that had her licking her lips every morning and night, and a few times in between, to see if his taste was still there.

"Do you want to go in the sitting room to look out at the stars?"

She hesitated a minute before she said, "Yes, I'd love to."

"I think you'll love the view," he said, grabbing the bottle of wine off the table.

"I'm sure I will."

The sitting room had a beautiful leather sofa that faced a huge window. It was a beautiful night and the sky was clear and the stars appeared to be everywhere. They'd been in the air a couple of hours now and every so often the pilot would announce what state they were flying over. They were now in Idaho and would do a zig-zag across Montana before returning to Wyoming.

"Too bad Dylan is away on a concert tour and Charm is with him. Otherwise we could have dropped in to say hello," he said.

"That would have been nice," she said, easing down on the sofa. Charm owned her own Cessna and Dylan's ranch in Idaho had an airstrip. The flight distance between their ranch and Gamble was less than an hour. Charm would often fly into the Gamble airport, pick up Nadia and two of them would fly to Westmoreland Country.

Charm's husband, Dylan, was an award-winning singer and guitarist. He'd won another award earlier that year and had called Charm on stage while making his acceptance speech to introduce her to all his fans.

Nadia settled down on the sofa and was surprised when Jaxon came to sit beside her. She thought he would take the single chair across from her and quickly scooted over to make room.

"It's a beautiful night, isn't it?" he said, refilling their wineglasses.

"Yes, and you were right, I love the view."

"So do I."

She noticed he wasn't looking out the window but his gaze was on her. Was he flirting with her? The last thing she wanted was to send out an erroneous message that she was in any way entertaining the thought of what he claimed the other night. Namely, that he intended to marry her. Rissa thought she should at least be flattered, but she wasn't.

"So what do you see when you glance out the window?" she asked him.

He looked out the window and then back at her. "I see an array of beautiful stars dotting a dark sky and a quarter moon peeking out at them. Now ask me what I see when I look at you."

She wasn't sure she wanted to know as she felt the heat flowing between them. However, drawing in a deep breath, she asked, "So, what do you see?"

"A woman I want to dance with."

She lifted a brow. "Dance?"

"Yes. So will you dance with me?"

"Without music?"

"What makes you think that?"

She was about to say because no music was playing when he reached for the remote on the table. With a press of his finger, music came through speakers. Of course it would be a slow tune.

Standing, he reached out his hand to her. "Please dance with me, Nadia. I need to hold you in my arms."

She could make a comeback that she didn't need to hold him in hers, but the thought of having her body pressed to his while his arms were wrapped around her was too tempting to deny.

Placing her hand in his, he eased her to her feet and when he gently pulled her into his arms, she didn't hesitate. The moment her body pressed against his, it seemed everything woman inside of her went into overdrive. Instinctively she rested her head on his chest and inhaled his manly fragrance.

This was not supposed to be happening. She had

done her research, had looked up the top twenty ways to scare a man away. Yet she hadn't tried any of the suggestions tonight. She had been too impressed with sharing dinner with him thirty thousand feet off the ground to concentrate on anything other than him.

She needed to take a big pause and catch her breath. But not now. Not even tonight. Jaxon was in control, and she didn't want to fight against this. His looks, his aroma, his personality and the way he made her feel…

No matter what, she had to get a grip on reality. The last thing she wanted to do was encourage him in his nonsense that he would marry her one day.

"I love dancing with you, Nadia."

His low, husky and sexy voice sent her heart pounding. "Do you?"

"Can't you tell?"

If he was hinting at the fact that dancing with her had aroused him, then yes, she could tell. She wondered if he could tell she was just as aroused. Her breasts, as they pressed against his chest, felt sensitive. Could he tell her nipples had hardened? Were poking into him?

"Are you okay, sweetheart?"

She wondered why he used that term of endearment. She wasn't his sweetheart. And why had he even asked her that? Had she moaned and hadn't realized she had done so? Was he feeling the intense heat leaving her body and going to his? She lifted her head off his chest to look at him and wished she hadn't. The dark eyes staring down at her caused flutters in her stomach. "I'm fine, Jaxon, why do you ask?"

"No reason."

There had to have been a reason, but she knew better than to push the issue. She was smart enough to know when and how to operate on the side of caution. Tonight, she would ignore any endearments or sexual innuendos. Deliberate or otherwise.

The music stopped and then another tune began playing. She was going to suggest they sit this one out, cool things off a minute, but when he pulled her closer Nadia decided not to say anything at all. She liked the feel of the warm hard body pressed close to hers, the even breathing near her ear and the way he gently rubbed strong hands up and down her back. Point blank, more than anything, she wanted to savor the moment.

As if he had the ability to read her thoughts, he whispered, "I love holding you in my arms and will find any excuse to do so."

"Even by dancing?" She lifted her face from his chest to ask him while looking into his dark eyes.

"Yes, even by dancing. But it's just the beginning."

"The beginning of what?"

"Our courtship that will end in marriage."

Jaxon saw the flare of defiance that leaped into Nadia's eyes and wondered if she knew how beautiful she looked when she was filled with fire. His gaze then shifted to her mouth. A mouth he was tempted to kiss and devour.

"Why can't you get it through that thick skull that a marriage between us won't be happening, Jaxon?"

He shifted his gaze back to her eyes. "Mainly because I believe it will, Nadia."

She let out a frustrated sigh. "Why are you being so difficult?"

"Why are you?" he countered.

"I am not being difficult ,just realistic. I don't know how things operate in your world. Maybe the wealthy Ravnels of Virginia are used to doing things this way."

"What way?"

"Saying what they want and then getting it regardless of people's feelings, thoughts or pride?"

"That's not how my family operates, Nadia."

"Isn't it?"

"No."

"Well, that's how it seems to me." She pushed out of his arms and placed her hands on her hips. "What would make you think I'd want to marry a man who doesn't love me or one who I don't love? Did it ever occur to you that I might want a marriage where I know my husband loved me, and I wouldn't have to worry about..."

He frowned. "About what?"

"It doesn't matter."

Jaxon thought it did. The Westmorelands claimed that as far as they knew, Nadia had dated on occasion but had never been in a serious or exclusive relationship. Now he wondered if there had been someone they hadn't known about. Some man who had broken her heart?

"I think it does matter," he said.

"No, it doesn't."

He decided not to push the issue. "All right then. Let's talk about the issue of love. You don't think two people can fall in love with each other?" he asked, deciding not to admit he was already there. No need to bring that into the conversation when she wouldn't believe him.

"Yes, but they fall in love first and then talk about marriage and not the other way around, Jaxon."

"The reason I talked about marriage was because I wanted to be honest with you up front, to let you know my intentions toward you were honorable, Nadia. I am not a womanizer or a man on the prowl. I want you as part of my future."

"But you don't know me."

"I know you are a very beautiful and desirable woman. A woman who is deserving of a man who will love you, cherish you and make you happy."

"And you believe you are that man?"

"I know I am. All I need is a chance for you to get to know me and for me to get to know you better."

She shook her head. "What if once you get to know me you don't like me after all? But I discover I like you? All I can see is another heartbreak, Jaxon, and I won't go through something like that again."

Another heartbreak? He'd guessed right. At that moment the pilot asked them to take their seats for the landing. They had returned to Gamble. He inwardly cursed the timing. It was just as he'd suspected. Some man had broken her heart. Was it someone she'd met during the six years she'd been in college? Had it been someone she'd met after moving back to Gamble? One of those cowboys she'd gotten so uptight about?

He needed to convince her that they should spend more time together. It would only be then that she would believe he'd never break her heart. Instead of saying anything else to him, she left the sitting room to return to her seat in the cabin.

By the time he got there she was already buckled in and staring out the window. She didn't even look over at him.

After sitting down and snapping his seat belt in place, he glanced over at her. "Nadia?"

She turned from the window to look at him. "Yes?"

"I want to see you again. Spend time with you."

"I don't think that's a good idea."

He disagreed—he wanted to get to know her—but one thing he knew how to be was flexible. Normally, he wasn't one who liked changing the rules of any game, but for her he would. Apparently telling her up front that he wanted to marry her hadn't been a good idea. Yet he couldn't backtrack on it now or else she would think he really didn't know his own heart and mind.

"I'm not interested in anything other than an acquaintance type of relationship while you're in Gamble," she continued. "Of course when we're around the Westmorelands and Outlaws it can extend to one of friendship. There's no way we can avoid it being any other way when we're there."

He didn't like what he was hearing. "And if I don't want that kind of relationship?"

She frowned at him. "You don't have a choice."

She was wrong—he did have a choice—but he would let her assume she was calling the shots. "I will give you what you want."

"Thank you."

"However, I am open to you changing your mind at any time."

"I won't change my mind, Jaxon. Unlike some women, I don't need a man in my life."

He nodded. More than anything he was determined to make sure she did, and that man would be him.

Nine

"I would help you out if I could, Nadia, you know that. However, I just donated to the community's college scholarship drive."

Nadia released a disappointed sigh. "I understand, Marv. Tell Harriett and the boys hello for me."

"Will do. Goodbye."

"Goodbye."

Nadia disconnected the call and marked Marvin Booster's name off the list of possible sponsors for the holiday play. She, Marvin and his wife, Harriett, had gone to the same church as kids when their parents were alive. He owned one of the largest ranches in Gamble and was a big supporter of community projects.

She frowned when she saw the next name, Fletcher Mallard. Shaking her head, she marked through his name as well, refusing to call and ask him for anything. Fletcher had been Pam's fiancé years ago and swore Nadia and her sisters were the reason Pam hadn't married him. He would conveniently forget the lie he'd told to get Pam to agree to marry him in the first place. It was the lie Dillon exposed at the wedding in the nick of time.

Nevertheless, the man still wanted to blame Nadia and her sisters anyway. Unfortunately, he was wealthier now than before. His chain of grocery stores had grown and was in almost every state in the Midwest and still expanding. She'd also heard he was on his fourth wife.

She was about to pick up the phone to call the next person when the buzzer on her desk sounded. Pressing the button, she asked, "Yes, China?"

"Someone is here to see you. A Mr. Jaxon Ravnel."

A frown settled on Nadia's face. Why was Jaxon here? She hadn't seen or talked to him since that night he'd taken her to dinner on board his jet. That had been over a week ago. She would be lying if she said she hadn't thought about him because she had. More times than she wanted to.

Telling him there would only be an acquaintance-ship between them had meant no kisses and no holding hands. When he had taken her home, he had walked her to the door, told her how much he had enjoyed her company and made sure she had gotten inside the house safely before leaving.

"Ms. Novak?"

Releasing a deep sigh, she said, "Please show Mr. Ravnel in."

"Trust me when I say it will be my pleasure, Miss Novak."

Nadia rolled her eyes as she moved from behind her desk. She recognized that voice. It was the same one China used whenever one of the Westmoreland or Outlaw men arrived in town and would take her to lunch. She could understand a young girl of China's age getting all hot and bothered seeing such eye candy, and Jaxon was definitely that.

The door opened and seeing Jaxon again took her breath away. Literally. Why did he have to look so ultraenticing and mouthwateringly appealing in his business suit? Looking like the billion dollars he probably was. And why couldn't she control her gaze from roaming over him, appreciating how his muscles filled out that jacket?

"Jaxon," she said, moving toward him to shake the hand he'd extended. She had to fight back the reaction she felt the moment their hands touched. "It's good seeing you again."

Too late, she watched China's brow inch up in curiosity. Her administrative assistant had latched on to the word *again*, which meant Nadia and Jaxon had seen each other before.

"It's good seeing you again, as well, Nadia," he said with a smile that complemented everything about him. His masculine power and that virile strength were definitely radiating from him today.

Nadia glanced to China. "Thanks for escorting Mr. Ravnel to my office. That will be all."

Once China had left and closed the door behind her,

Nadia turned back to Jaxon. "And the reason for your visit?" she asked, offering him a seat in the chair in front of her desk.

"The reason I'm here, Nadia, is strictly business."

"Is it?" she asked, going back around her desk to sit down.

"Yes."

"And what kind of business is there that would bring you here?"

It was only after she'd taken her seat that he took the one she'd offered him. As usual he was displaying impeccable manners. She wished the way his slacks stretched across a pair of masculine thighs when he sat down didn't send her heart racing.

"An article will be appearing in the *Gamble Daily Tribune* tomorrow that Ravnel Technologies has acquired over fifteen hundred acres of land to expand our business here."

She couldn't help the smile that spread across her lips. For both him and the city. "Congratulations. That's a lot of land."

"Yes, it is. The city was instrumental in helping me acquire what I needed."

Nadia could just imagine. They probably saw it as a boom to Gamble's economy.

"Thanks for letting me know, but you didn't have to come all the way over here to tell me." In a way she wished he hadn't. When it came to Jaxon, out of sight, out of mind worked best. She'd managed to get by on her dreams of him at bedtime and memories of their one and only kiss.

"That's not why I'm here."

"Oh? Then what is the purpose of your visit?"

"To offer you a proposal. I decided to do so here first before moving on to some other entity."

Now he had her curious. "And what is this proposal?"

He leaned forward in his chair as if to make sure he had her absolute attention. There was no need for him to do that since he'd had it the moment he'd walked into her office. "Ravnel Technologies wants to replace the Dunnings Financial Group as the sponsor for this year's holiday play."

She didn't say anything for a minute because she was too stunned to speak. His company partnering with the school for the play would be wonderful. A prayer that was answered. A…

A thought suddenly popped into her head, and she looked at Jaxon. He was staring at her. For some reason she couldn't turn away and the thought that had taken root in her head began growing. She broke eye contact and looked down at the notepad on her desk and then back at him. He was still staring at her.

"Why, Jaxon?"

He lifted a brow. "Why what?"

"Why do you want to partner with Dream Makers Acting Academy? What do you think you're going to get out of doing so?"

Jaxon figured there were several answers he could give her. The main one being her idea of being acquaintances wasn't working for him and he was determined to make sure it didn't work for her either. The moment he had walked into her office, everything faded to black except her. Desire, to a degree he had never felt before for any woman, had rushed through him while he had taken in every single thing about her. Her dark slacks and pink blouse made her look feminine as hell, and her hair, a mass of locks around her face, highlighted her features and emphasized what a totally beautiful woman she was.

Now he was here and she was there, right within his radar, and he had come up with a plan that would keep her there. But he wouldn't admit that. Her question meant she suspected he had an ulterior motive for choosing this school to partner with. She was right, yet he would not only downplay her suspicions, but he also intended to eliminate them completely. He was a businessman and she'd never seen the business side of him before. Now she would.

"What exactly are you asking me, Nadia?"

She leaned forward and placed her elbows on her desk to rest her chin on her hands. Her eyes pierced into his, but he had no problem with it because his gaze was just as penetrating. "Does your decision have anything to do with me?"

He had to fight back telling her that everything had something to do with her. Instead, he said, "To be quite honest, it only pertains to you because you mentioned last week that you needed a sponsor for the play. My reason for deciding to replace Dunnings Financial Group has everything to do with my relationship to the Westmorelands and Outlaws. As you indicated the other night, you and I don't have a relationship, we have an acquaintanceship. I made it clear then, and I'm making it clear now, that I will abide by your wishes." He paused before continuing, "Ravnel Technologies likes to bond with the towns they become a part of. When we purchased that land in Forbes last year we partnered with the Boys and Girls Clubs there. Therefore, it would make perfect sense to align my company with an institution connected to a group I now consider as family."

He allowed a lull in the conversation to let what he'd said to sink in before adding, "If you have a problem with it, please say so."

"I don't have a problem with it."

He nodded. "The sponsorship I'm offering is strictly business. You will be required to periodically keep my company abreast of how things are going with the play. Will you agree to that?"

She stared at him and a part of him knew Nadia was stubborn enough to say no, she didn't agree. She had just that much nerve and was just that defiant. Seconds had almost ticked into a full minute before she said, "Yes, I'll agree."

"Good. My administrative assistant, Langley Easton, will be contacting you later today to complete the necessary paperwork and ask questions for the newspaper article."

"The newspaper article?"

"Yes. Sometime this week your local newspaper will announce my company's plans to build here. Whenever such an announcement is made, Ravnel Technologies uses that opportunity to assure the citizens of our commitment to the community by making it known what nonprofit organization we plan to partner with the first year. Typically, we rotate annually. Since this is almost the end of the year, it was decided that sponsoring the holiday play would work in our favor. In January, we will open it up so other local nonprofits can apply."

"I see."

He stood. "Do you have any other questions for me?"

"No. I don't have any questions."

"Like I said, Langley will be contacting you later today. However, at any time you can reach me at this number," he said, extending his business card to her.

"I have your number already."

"You have my personal number. This is my business number."

She took the card. "Thank you."

"Have a good day, Nadia." Then, without saying anything else, he walked out of her office.

An hour later Jaxon walked into his hotel room. He hoped what he'd told Nadia had squashed her suspicions about his company's motives for the sponsorship. He had finished ordering room service when his cell phone rang. He couldn't help but smile as he clicked on. "Dad. Are you and Mom back?" His parents had flown to Barcelona. No special occasion, just a two-week getaway. They did that a lot now that they'd both retired.

"Yes, we're back but not for long. Your mom wants to spend a couple of weeks in Toronto before the cold weather sets in."

Jaxon nodded. It was no secret that Ingrid Ravnel didn't like cold weather. She barely tolerated it. "I take it Barcelona was nice."

"Yes, it was. And I understand we've acquired more land."

"Yes, we have. It was a good deal. Like Forbes, they presented an economic development plan that will benefit the town and our company."

"That's good to hear." Although Jaxon kept his father in the loop, he appreciated that Arnett Ravnel never questioned his judgment about any business decisions. "And just so you know, Ravnel Technologies is sponsoring a holiday play being produced by the acting school here."

"What's the title of the play?"

"It's a Wonderful Life."

"That's one of your mother's holiday favorites. We can't wait to see it."

So, in other words, they would be visiting Gamble. Jaxon knew his parents. Ever since that day he'd shared with them that Nadia Novak was the woman he intended to marry, they'd been anxious to meet her.

He talked to his father for a few minutes more before they ended the call. He had time to shower before room service arrived with dinner. Getting into bed before nine was first on his list. If Nadia thought she had seen the last of him for a while, then she was mistaken.

Ten

"Did he really say that, Nadia?" Rissa asked, after taking a sip of her coffee and leaning forward in her chair. It was early morning and the two of them were sitting in Nadia's office, sharing coffee and chitchatting like they usually did. Nadia had just told Rissa what had happened yesterday with Jaxon.

"He didn't have to. Giving me his business card said it all as far as I'm concerned."

Rissa rolled her eyes over her cup of coffee. "Well, you did want him to leave you alone. Not that I thought he was bothering you. Telling a woman of his intentions to marry her is not a bad thing. In fact, I think it's romantic."

Now it was Nadia who rolled her eyes. "I don't agree and you're missing the point."

"Okay, what is the point?" Rissa asked, leaning back in her chair.

"First of all, the more I think about it, the more I get upset that Jaxon had the nerve, the very gall, to tell me of his plans to marry me. He probably only did it because some men have an entitlement complex. Benson thought he was entitled to me and so did Hoyle."

"And?" Rissa asked, as if she expected more.

"And once I put Jaxon in his place by letting him know I wouldn't tolerate his foolishness, he stopped."

Confusion lined Rissa's features. "But that's what you wanted him to do, right?"

"But he didn't put up a fight, which proves he wasn't serious about anything to begin with."

"You don't know that, Nadia."

"Yes, I do. Nobody can turn their feelings off like that. Granted, he hadn't said he felt anything for me, but still. It's obvious he no longer wants to marry me."

"And that bothers you, doesn't it?" Rissa asked, giving her an odd look. A look Nadia had gotten used to over the years. It was one of Rissa's analytical looks. There were times she thought her friend was wasting her time in the financial industry and should own a psychiatry office.

Nadia knew it was imperative that she made her best friend understand. "What I don't like is the thought of him being overconfident in thinking he could marry me and telling me such when he had no intentions of doing it."

Rissa chuckled. "Now you're being dramatic. You either want Jaxon to show interest in you or you don't.

You told him not to and he is following your request. Now you're upset about it. That makes no sense, Nadia, unless…"

"Unless what?"

"Unless…deep down you did like the thought of him wanting to marry you one day."

"That's ridiculous."

Rissa tilted her head. "Is it? You act offended that he took you at your word and is leaving you alone. Had he continued to pursue you, then you could have complained that you were being harassed. So, being the gentleman you say that he is, he is abiding by your wishes. Now the acquaintanceship has moved to a strictly business relationship and for some reason that is bothering you. I'd think you would appreciate him stepping in as a sponsor for the play. That's wonderful and takes a load off your mind."

"Yes, and I do appreciate it."

"So, what's the problem? What's the real reason your panties are in a twist?"

Nadia didn't say anything for a minute and then she said in a soft voice, "Whether or not I wanted him to pursue me or not, the moment I pushed back he moved on. That meant he wasn't serious about a future with me anyway."

Rissa smiled. "You like him, don't you?"

Nadia shrugged. "He was moving too fast. He was talking marriage and didn't even know me."

"Then you should have told him to slow down. Instead, you sent him away. Do you know what I think?"

Nadia didn't want to ask but figured her best friend would tell her anyway. "No, what?"

"That you like Jaxon more than you want to admit, and that you'll give anything for another kiss, another taste of his mouth, his tongue, the opportunity to be your first rumple between the sheets and—"

"Rissa!"

"Just keeping it real, my friend."

"I refuse to involve myself with a man who only wanted to connect himself with me because…"

Rissa lifted a brow. "Because of what?"

Nadia ran a hand down her face. "I honestly don't know."

Rissa stood after checking her watch. "Then maybe it's time you stop assuming and find out the answers. The real answers, Nadia. And how about taking a look in the mirror. You're beautiful. That's why he wanted to connect with you. You're not a bad catch and Jaxon Ravnel isn't either. Just so you know, the word is out and he's already at the top of every single woman's hit list in town."

After draining the last of her coffee and tossing the cup in a nearby trash can, Rissa smiled over at her and said, "See you tomorrow. Same place. Same time. However, I certainly hope you have a different attitude."

By the end of the day, Nadia was clearing off her desk and getting ready to leave when her cell phone rang. She smiled upon recognizing the caller. "Hello, Pammie." Calling her oldest sister by her nickname whenever they spoke was something Nadia hadn't outgrown.

"Nadia, I just heard the good news. I understand

Jaxon will replace the Dunnings Financial Group as the sponsor of this year's holiday play. That's wonderful!"

Pam was the second person to sing Jaxon's praises. Rissa had been the first. Nadia figured there would be others tomorrow when news of his company expansion to Gamble, as well as his being sponsor of the play, appeared in tomorrow's newspaper. His personal assistant, Langley Easton, had called and introduced herself. The woman sounded very professional and young.

That had prompted Nadia, out of curiosity, to check out Ravnel Technologies' website. Now she wished she hadn't. Not only was Miss Easton professional and young. She was also attractive and single. It said she had been Jaxon's personal assistant for a few years. Had the two ever dated? Been romantically involved? Why on earth did Nadia care if they had?

"Nadia?"

"Yes?"

"You are glad about it, too, aren't you? I'm sure you had everything under control as far as getting a replacement, but Jaxon has made your job easier."

"Yes, and I appreciate him doing so. But…"

"But what?"

Pam was the last person Nadia needed to tell about her complex relationship with Jaxon. But then, to be honest, she and Jaxon didn't have a relationship. That thought made her ask her sister something she had wondered about for years. "Pammie, at the time you met Dillon you were engaged to marry Fletcher. What made you fall in love with Dillon when you were promised to another man?"

Pam didn't say anything for a moment, and then said, "I didn't love Fletcher. Our marriage was to be one of convenience. However, I'd agreed to a sexual relationship since we both wanted kids. But I looked at my engagement to Fletcher as a business deal, which is why I wouldn't sleep with him before the wedding."

Pam paused and Nadia figured she was remembering that time fifteen years ago. "That day when you, Jill and Paige called me outside to let me know a man was there to see me, and I saw Dillon for myself, engaged or not engaged, the moment I gazed into his eyes I was not only attracted to him, but knew, if given the chance, I could feel more."

If given the chance she could feel more...

Nadia wondered if it could it be that way for her with Jaxon. "Why didn't you fight it? After all, you were engaged."

"Trust me, I tried. But there are some things you aren't equipped to fight. An attraction that could lead to falling in love is one of them."

"Did it scare you? Your inability to resist your attraction?" Nadia asked.

Pam chuckled. "It petrified me because I didn't know Dillon. I had just met him and he certainly didn't know me. Yet I felt things for him that I hadn't felt for Fletcher. I wasn't even physically attracted to Fletcher. With Dillon it was another story altogether. The sexual chemistry between us was strong."

Nadia would admit the same thing between her and Jaxon. There was something about him that stirred sensations deep within her each and every time they were near each other. Just dancing with him the other night had jarred her senses in a way they'd never been jarred before.

"The sexual chemistry between us was even stronger whenever we were alone," Pam cut into Nadia's thoughts to say. "I knew I was in deep trouble that day he returned to go through that trunk in the attic. We were at the house alone."

"Oh." Just like the night Nadia and Jaxon had been alone when she'd invited him to dinner. The same house.

"Is there a reason you're asking me these questions, Nadia?"

"No. There's no particular reason, Pammie. I just think you and Dillon make the best couple ever."

"Thanks. There was a connection between us that we were both trying hard to ignore, given the fact I was an engaged woman."

"What if Dillon had told you he wanted to marry you after you guys had only known each other a few days? Would you have broken things off with Fletcher to marry him?"

"No. Although I was attracted to Dillon, I didn't feel I knew him and he didn't know me. But then I'd agreed to marry Fletcher because I had thought I knew him when in essence, I didn't know him at all. I've discovered people can fall in love without fully knowing each other or knowing everything about each other. It has to start with something. I'm glad that once I discovered a connection between me and Dillon that I didn't fight it. And that connection between us, combined with a hefty dose of sexual chemistry, got stronger every time we saw each other."

Nadia took in everything Pam had said. Had Rissa been right? Had she overreacted to Jaxon's claim that he intended to marry her? She would admit she'd felt a connection to him that got stronger each time they saw each other. Did that mean anything?

"Well, I'll let you go, Nadia. It's time for you to leave for today, right?" Pam said.

"Yes. I was just wrapping things up."

"Have a safe drive home. And Nadia?"

"Yes, Pammie?"

There was a pause and then, "Nothing. Goodbye."

Jaxon opened the paper and saw that news of Ravnel Technologies' expansion into Gamble was all over the front page. His company's PR department had also arranged a slate of local interviews, and Langley had a list of other nonprofit projects his company intended to be a part of during the coming year.

Once he'd made the decision to expand his company beyond Virginia, he knew what that would entail, from strategy to execution. One of the first things to do was strengthen the company's presence in the chosen community. In Forbes, his company had hosted a fundraising event to raise money for a new building for the Boys and Girls Club. It was to be built on land that Ravnel Technologies had donated. Not only had they donated the land, but also would match all contributions made.

In Gamble, he would start with sponsoring the holiday play. He'd seen the budget but wanted Nadia to think bigger. No reason to host the event in the school's auditorium when there was a theater in town. He'd had Langley check it out already.

He had finished drinking his coffee and was about to go into the bedroom of his hotel suite to get dressed when his phone rang. It was his business line. Heat flowed through his body at the possibility it was Nadia. He picked up the phone, and saw the call was from his administrative assistant. "Yes, Langley?"

"Mr. Ravnel, I got a call from Sue Ellen Donovan, talk show host of *Good Morning Wyoming*. A show produced at a television station that's located in the valley between Gamble and Jackson Hole. The show not only broadcasts in those two areas but several other towns scattered about. She wanted to know if you're available one day this week to appear on her show. She's interested in why you selected Gamble for expansion."

The real reason, he thought, was a well-guarded secret. He'd done television interviews in the past but usually Paul Maloney, the person in charge of PR for the company, handled that sort of thing. "Is there a reason Paul can't do the interview?"

"Ms. Donovan specifically asked for you."

Jaxon rubbed his chin, feeling somewhat annoyed. "Did she?"

"Yes. She said it would have a greater impact if you did it. She thinks it would give the interview more community appeal. I told her in that case she should also invite Nadia Novak of the Dream Makers Acting Academy. That way the two of you could inform the viewers how Ravnel Technologies' move into the community will benefit Gamble and surrounding areas. Already your company has partnered with the academy to sponsor their holiday play. Personally, I think publicity for the school might boost interest in nearby towns, which will result in more ticket sales."

Jaxon smiled, liking the way Langley thought. It would also be a way for him and Nadia to share space, even if it was only on a stage at a television studio. "Since it's a community piece I agree that both Ms. Novak and I should be interviewed together."

"Does that mean you will do the interview?"

"Yes."

"I'll suggest that Ms. Donovan call Ms. Novak to invite her to join you on the show. I've checked your schedule and this Friday morning will work for you. It airs at ten."

"Make sure that date and time works for Ms. Novak as well. If not, I expect the station to be flexible with both of us."

"Yes, sir."

Jaxon hung up the phone thinking his day was off to a good start. Things could not have worked out more perfectly if he'd arranged it himself. He knew Nadia was still trying to figure him out. To fight what she'd felt, and, for whatever reason, she refused to lower her guard not even an inch. He knew before he could gain a place in her heart, he would have to gain her trust. That also meant she had to deal with whatever pain still lingered from a love that had gone bad. A love he had to somehow convince her hadn't been meant to be anyway.

His father had told him that it had taken his mother

almost a year to see the light. Jaxon wasn't sure he would last a year. He wanted Nadia just that much. He wanted her physically, sexually and all those ways in between. But he also wanted her for more than that. He wanted her to be a part of his life, the mother of his children, his partner in love until death do them part.

He had told Dillon he wouldn't break Nadia's heart, and he intended to keep that promise. However, the one thing Dillon and the others failed to realize was that if something went wrong, he might be the one who ended up with the broken heart.

Nadia returned to her office from lunch thinking that everyone in town must have read the paper's headlines. Rissa had brought her a copy with a huge smile on her face. No doubt she was hoping the bank she managed would get the Ravnel business account.

Settling in the chair behind her desk, Nadia was pleased that the newspaper had also mentioned that Ravnel Technologies would be the sponsor of this year's holiday play. She had just taken a file off her desk when her buzzer went off. "Yes, China?"

"Sue Ellen Donovan, of *Good Morning Wyoming*, Station WKJP, is on the line."

Nadia lifted a brow, wondering why Ms. Donovan would be calling. Earlier that year Nadia had reached out to the woman for an interview on one of their shows to promote the school's spring pageant. The woman had turned down the request saying the event wasn't important enough. Over the years, what had started out as a community awareness show was now only interviewing the rich and famous vacationing in the area. Specifically, on the ski slopes in Jackson Hole.

"Please put the call through, China."

"Okay."

Upon hearing the connection, Nadia said, "This is Nadia Novak. May I help you?"

"Ms. Novak, this is Sue Ellen Donovan of *Good Morning Wyoming.* We are excited that Ravnel Technologies will be expanding into Gamble and we understand your school will benefit. On Friday morning we will be interviewing Mr. Ravnel. Since we want this as a community piece, and it was announced that his company will be the major sponsor of your school's holiday play this year, it would be great if you could be a part of the show as well."

So now the show wanted to highlight something other than celebrities vacationing in the area? What a switch. "That sounds wonderful, and I would love to be on your show."

"Great. I'll see you Friday at ten."

After disconnecting the call, Nadia leaned back in her chair. She would take free publicity for the school any way she could get it. The students were excited about the news and that made her appreciative of Jaxon's company helping out. Specifically, bailing her out.

And he *had* bailed her out. He'd even admitted he'd selected the school not only because of the family connection, but also because she'd mentioned she didn't have a sponsor for the play. She would admit that was thoughtful of him. She would also admit something else. She did like him...a little. Her conversation with

Pam yesterday had helped somewhat. Then there were the memories of the words Jaxon had spoken to her weeks ago.

My intention, Nadia Novak, is to marry you.

She quivered each and every time she remembered them. His words had been precise and he'd said them in a deep, husky voice that had flowed from those sexy lips of his. The tone had been so smooth it had taken her a minute to respond. Although at first she'd taken what he'd said as a tease, it didn't take long for her to realize he was serious. Even when he shouldn't have been.

During their coffee and chitchat time this morning, Rissa had come down on Nadia pretty hard. Rissa had accused Nadia of always whining about what the men in the past had done to her and how much of a disappointment they'd been, of letting her past hurts and heartbreaks be the cause of her not having a relationship with a man. She'd gone on to say that Nadia would never find out if Jaxon was or was not the man for her without giving him a chance.

Well, it was a moot point now since all there was between them was business. Besides, one heartbreak had been enough for her. She wasn't ready to risk her heart on another. But what she *was* ready for was to be intimate with a man.

At twenty-eight it was probably past time and she probably would have eventually gone all the way with Hoyle if he hadn't acted like an ass about it. Like he thought not only was he entitled, but also that he was the best thing in her lifetime, as if she would be a fool to pass up the chance to roll between the sheets with him.

He was a typical male who thought his balls were made of gold. That was the type of man she wanted no part of.

So far Jaxon hadn't come across that way. Other than thinking that one day they would marry, he was an okay guy. Even when she'd told him they could not have any type of relationship, he had respected her wishes. However, she couldn't get their kiss out of her mind. Just the memory of it made her heart pump wildly in her chest and her mouth hunger for more.

For years she'd heard Rissa, Jillian and, more recently, Paige whisper about how wonderful it was to share a bed with a man. She'd even come home from college unexpectedly one weekend and walked into Dillon's house to the sound of Pam screaming all over the place. It didn't take long to comprehend they'd been screams of pleasure and not pain.

Her curiosity about the kind of pleasure that could make you scream was what had sparked her interest in Hoyle. Now, after sharing that kiss with Jaxon, her curiosity was not just sparked; it had been ignited. Maybe it was time for her to finally do something about it.

How would he handle her change in attitude of them going from acquaintances to just business to personal and intimate? Would he think she was fickle as hell? Probably. More importantly, would it bother him that she was still a virgin at twenty-eight?

Years ago, she'd overheard a conversation between the two Westmoreland cousins, Derringer and Riley, where they said the last kind of woman any man wanted to have in his bed was a virgin. Mainly because no man wanted to be a woman's first, and most men wanted an experienced woman in their bed. Because of Derringer's and Riley's reputations at the time, she'd had no reason to think they hadn't known what they were talking about. If that was true, then how would she handle what she definitely saw as a problem?

And another problem—Rissa had said the gold diggers around these parts would be honing their predatory skills on Jaxon. For some reason Nadia didn't like the thought. But then if Jaxon wanted to marry her like he claimed, wouldn't that give her an advantage over the other women?

How many times had Rissa said that Jaxon came across as the type of man who went after what he wanted? News flash! Nadia was that type of woman, and right now she wanted Jaxon. Not for anything long-term but rather for the short-term. She needed her curiosity appeased about sex once and for all to see what the hoopla was about.

Her approach to Jaxon had to be subtle. No man wanted to think he'd been targeted. That was another thing she'd heard the Westmoreland cousins say. A man didn't like being seduced. They preferred being the seducer. So how would that work for her?

Picking up the phone, she called Rissa. Her best friend should be on her way home from work now. Rissa picked up on the first ring and from the sound of it, she was in her car and the phone call was coming through by Bluetooth on her car's speakers.

"You're alone?" Nadia asked, wanting to make sure her kids weren't in the car with her.

"Yes, I'm alone. Why?"

"I have a question for you and I want it for your ears only. Just give me an answer, no inquiries, please. Will you do that?"

Rissa hesitated a minute, then said, "Yes."

Satisfied her friend would do what she said, Nadia asked, "How do you get a man to make love to you without seducing him?"

Eleven

Jaxon got out of his car and strolled up the walkway to Nadia's front door. She had left a message on his business phone last night while he'd been in the shower. She'd taken her car to the shop yesterday and it wouldn't be ready for today's trip to the valley. Nadia wanted to know if she could catch a ride with him. He had called her back and in the most professional voice he could deliver, he'd told her that yes, she could, and he would arrive to pick her up around eight.

To be quite honest, he'd been surprised by her call. Especially when her request meant they would be sharing the same vehicle to get to their destination. But then he figured since she was getting free publicity for the school and the holiday play she would tolerate anything or anyone. Including him.

The door opened and she stood there. She held his gaze and he held hers. Had it been just a few days ago when he'd seen her last? He should have been prepared but he wasn't. Now he couldn't help but zero in on everything about her. She was dressed in a two-piece business suit that made her look both professional and gorgeous to a degree that left him speechless. Her hair was pinned up on her head and twisted in a ball. Her makeup wasn't heavy; it was just enough not to overtake her natural beauty.

It seemed each and every time their paths crossed the sexual chemistry between them increased. Even now it flowed between them, and they both knew it and there wasn't a damn thing either of them could do about it. It was a raw physical force made up of her hormones and his testosterone that had taken over not only their minds but also their bodies.

The sound of his phone alarm going off broke the spell. He glanced away momentarily to pull it out of his pocket and turn it off. When he glanced back at her he saw the same sexual awareness in her features that he figured she saw in his. Only thing they could do was try and ignore it.

"Good morning, Nadia. Are you ready to go?"

"Yes. Just let me grab my coffee. Would you like a cup?"

If he said yes, that meant she would have to invite him in. That would definitely be a change from the last time he'd been here, when she'd been waiting outside on the steps with no need for him to come inside.

"Yes, if you don't mind. I wasn't sure how traffic

would be getting here this morning, so I didn't stop for coffee."

"No problem," she said, moving aside for him to come in.

He turned back to her when he heard the door close behind him. "You look nice."

"Thanks. So do you. And how do you like your coffee?"

"Black."

"Okay. I'll be back. I'm sure you want us to get on the road as soon as possible."

When she left and headed for the kitchen, he was drawn to that huge photo over the fireplace just like the last time he'd been here. That photo of her parents and sisters. This time he really studied it. She was the perfect combination of both parents. That's what he wanted for them. Him and her. Kids who would look like the both of them. He could envision a daughter with her eyes and smile; and a son who would have his height and mouth. It was a mouth his mom often referred to as the Ravnel mouth. She said that was one of the first things that drew her to his father. The shape of his mouth and the darkness of his eyes.

"Here you are."

He turned around and she was there, handing him coffee in a to-go cup with a lid. "Thanks. Cup's convenient," he said, accepting the coffee she offered. Their hands touched in the process and he felt a flutter in the pit of his gut.

"I keep a ton of them here. I have two cups of coffee

every morning. One before I leave here while getting dressed and another when I get to school, from Rissa."

"Rissa?"

"Yes, Marissa Phelps, my best friend."

He lifted a brow. "Your best friend is living in Gamble?"

"She's lived here all her life. We separated when I moved to Denver but we stayed in touch and went to the same college in Wyoming." She glanced at her watch and then at him. "I'm ready to leave if you are."

Yes, he was ready. The sooner they got out of this house the better. "I'm ready."

"Are you attending Cheyenne's surprise birthday party?"

Nadia glanced over at Jaxon. They were out of Gamble's city limits and were in the part of Wyoming the locals called the valley. It was the area between Gamble and Jackson Hole. Sparse towns were scattered about and most of the people were ranchers.

She nodded resolutely and said, "Yes, I plan to go. What about you?"

"Yes, I'm going. I wouldn't think of missing it."

She turned to look out the window again, at the objects they passed. Now they were on a two-lane road with very little traffic. The television station was in Valley Bluff, a small town between here and Jackson Hole.

Nadia thought about her conversation with Rissa yesterday. Needless to say, her best friend had given her an earful. According to Rissa, if a woman wanted a man and the man wanted her, then no seduction was needed. Just roll with the flow. She suggested that when

Jaxon returned Nadia home, she should invite him in. When he kissed her goodbye, she should let him know she enjoyed it. That sort of thing fired up a man's libido. A deeply aroused man could make you just as aroused as he was.

Nadia recalled how aroused Jaxon had been when dancing with her, and how aroused she'd gotten knowing he wanted her. Even now, while sharing car space with him, she was getting aroused. What on earth was happening to her? It was as if since she'd decided not to hold back where he was concerned, her body was yearning for what was to come. But what if he didn't want to make the switch from business to pleasure? What if he'd decided she wasn't worth the trouble and just wanted a platonic relationship between them?

What gave her hope was the strong sexual chemistry still flowing between them. So far they'd managed to keep up a steady stream of conversation, and she was glad of that. She'd taken the time to tell him of the excitement buzzing around town about his company's plans to expand in Gamble. A lot of people were wondering what type of positions would be available. He'd told her about the job fair his company planned to hold in the spring.

Jaxon also shared that they anticipated it taking a year and a half for the Ravnel Technologies' state-of-the-art complex to be built. In the meantime, they would be leasing space—namely six floors—in the Lesswick Building in town. She appreciated him sharing that much information with her.

He asked her about the play and mentioned it was

his mother's favorite for the holidays, and his parents looked forward to attending. She was glad to hear that and intended to make sure they got special seats in the front of the auditorium.

"I like Langley," she said truthfully. They had talked a few times and the woman seemed efficient at her job. But still, Nadia couldn't help wondering if Jaxon and the woman had ever been involved.

The car had come to a traffic light and he glanced over at her. "She keeps me pretty much on point."

"Has she been your administrative assistant long?"

"Around four years now. I hired her right out of college."

"She seems like a nice person and efficient in what she does."

"She is. That's the reason I hate losing her."

Nadia raised her brow. *Losing her?* "She's leaving?"

"Yes. Langley is getting married in June to Rick, her college sweetheart. He took a government job in Amsterdam, and she'll be moving there after the wedding."

Nadia didn't say anything for a minute as she inwardly admitted that she'd been jealous of the beautiful young woman, which honestly didn't make any sense. There was never a time she'd gotten jealous of any woman over a man. Such a thing just wasn't in her makeup. At least, it never had been before.

"I take it you've been interviewed by Ms. Donovan before," Jaxon said, cutting into her thoughts.

Nadia rolled her eyes. "Not hardly." At the strange look he gave her she decided to explain. "Although *Good Morning Wyoming* started off as a one-hour show to keep the viewers abreast of the things going on in the four communities it serves, a couple of years ago the producers switched gears."

"Switched gears how?"

"They switched their focus to celebrities who visited the area to ski and hang out in and around Jackson Hole. Would you believe Ms. Donovan turned me down each and every time I called to ask for time on her show?"

"That's a missed opportunity for her," Jaxon said, shaking his head as he moved the car forward when the traffic light changed. "I hear you're doing great things at the academy."

She figured Pam told him that but decided to ask him anyway. "You heard that from who?"

"The mayor and some others."

That made her feel good. "I'm convinced the only reason I got an invite to the show was because of you."

"Me?"

"Yes. It would make more sense to show what your company is doing to help the community by hearing from the first recipient of your company's kindness."

He didn't say anything, and she figured he'd agreed with what she'd stated. "We're here," he said. When Jaxon brought the car to a stop he glanced at his watch. "We're almost an hour early."

She nodded. "It's better to be early than late." Then after a moment she said, "I want to thank you, Jaxon."

"No problem since I was coming this way."

"No, I want to thank you for everything. For replacing the Dunnings Financial Group as the play's sponsor.

Although the students had faith in me to find a replacement. Unfortunately, they were wrong."

Nadia watched as he eased the car seat back to give himself more room to stretch out his legs. "No, they weren't wrong. You got a replacement."

She shook her head. "No, I didn't. Miraculously, you came to me."

He shrugged. "Does it matter?"

Yes, it mattered to her that this tall, ultrahandsome, broad-shouldered, sexy-as all-outdoors man helped her save face with not only the students but everyone involved in the play, including the community, which looked forward to seeing the performance every year. It was a time when the residents came together to support a good cause.

"It does to me."

He nodded. "Then I'm glad my company could help."

She didn't say anything. He hadn't said he was glad that he could help but that *his company* could help. Was that his way of reminding her that she'd made it pretty clear she didn't want any type of relationship between them? She'd made a shambles of things with Jaxon, and she knew it was up to her to undo the mess she'd made.

Sue Ellen Donovan was smiling into the camera. "Today our guests on the show are Jaxon Ravnel, CEO of Ravnel Technologies, along with Miss Nadia Novak, the VP of Development and Community Civic Engagement for the Dream Makers Acting Academy in Gamble."

Jaxon watched the camera switch from Ms. Donovan to zero in on him before shifting to Nadia. He saw how strikingly beautiful she was on camera. As far as he was concerned Sue Ellen Donovan's introduction of him took way too long. By the time it was finished everyone knew more about his family and their wealth than they needed to. She also harped on the fact he was single and a prime catch. He thought the statement was inappropriate and was tempted to say he was officially off the market because the woman he wanted to marry was sitting on stage beside him.

"Thank you two for coming and sharing information with our viewing audience," Sue Ellen Donovan said, reclaiming his attention. "First, I want to begin with you, Mr. Ravnel. I'm aware of your company's decision to expand in Texas as well as Wyoming. What made you choose Gamble?"

Of course he'd been expecting that question and provided the same answer he'd given others who'd asked. After instituting a plan for growth, it became a business decision to expand in other states. Mainly as a way to improve and further develop products and services.

Sue Ellen Donovan continued to ask questions so that his responses could fully explain the benefits in communities when big businesses made such a move.

She then turned her attention to Nadia. However, she only asked one question before moving her attention back to him. Then the woman's questions began centering on his private life, which annoyed the hell out of Jaxon. It became obvious that she was turning this into some sort of celebrity interview.

He saw the disappointment in Nadia's eyes. After he finished answering the last question Sue Ellen had asked, and she was about to ask him another, a rebellious Nadia spoke up and said, "I think it would be wonderful to tell the audience about the play the academy is producing."

Before the woman could say whether it would be wonderful or not, Jaxon agreed. "I think that is a great idea, Ms. Novak. After all, the purpose of this interview was to highlight what my company will be doing in the community and not focus on my personal life." He then turned to Sue Ellen Donovan. "Isn't that right?"

A chagrined expression appeared on the woman's face. "Yes, of course."

Nadia began speaking and Jaxon took in the richness of her voice as she explained things in a way that would get viewers excited about the event. She went into detail about how an acclaimed director from Hollywood had volunteered to direct the show. From Sue Ellen Donovan's expression it was obvious she hadn't known that.

He chimed in on occasion and told everyone how excited his company was to partner with the school as sponsor, and he shared the names of other charities his company was looking into sponsoring in the near future. At the end he mentioned his company would be setting up a job fair because he wanted to hire as many qualified individuals in the area as possible, in addition to relocating some of his own people.

Sue Ellen opened the network call lines and some of the viewers had questions about Jaxon's company, as well as the school's play. Some callers even made comments that it was great hearing about something else other than movie stars and they hoped the television

station did more such shows. Jaxon hoped the producers took that under consideration.

At the end of the show the production assistant rushed
on stage to remove the mics off their clothes. That's
when Sue Ellen invited Jaxon to lunch. It didn't go past
him that she didn't extend the invitation to Nadia.

"Thanks, but Ms. Novak and I have made plans for
lunch before returning to Gamble."

"Oh."

"I want to thank you for finally having me on your
show," Nadia said, giving Sue Ellen a smile that even
Jaxon could tell didn't quite reach her eyes.

Sue Ellen nodded, pulling a business card out of her
jacket. Handing it to Jaxon, she said, "I would love for
you to call me sometime. I'll be glad to tell you more
about the area and even show you around."

He took the card more out of courtesy than anything
else. "Thanks, I'll keep that in mind," he said, although
he had no plans to do so. He then turned to Nadia. "Are
you ready to go, Ms. Novak?"

She nodded. "Yes, Mr. Ravnel. I'm ready."

When they were buckled inside the car, he glanced
over at Nadia before starting the engine. "Where do you
want to go for lunch? You're more familiar with the area
than I am."

She gave him a smile that had his stomach churning with sexual need. "There's a great bar and grill in
the next town. It's owned by friends of mine and the
food is great."

"That sounds good," he said, putting on his aviator-style sunglasses. Although it was chilly outside, the bright sun was shining over the mountains.

He glanced over at her. "Are you in a hurry to return to Gamble?"

"No, why do you ask?"

"There are several stops I need to make before we head back." The truth of the matter was that he was in no hurry to get her back home.

"No problem. I'll call and let China know I'm taking the rest of the day off. I need time off anyway. It's been a while since I've taken any."

Now that he knew that bit of information, he was going to make sure she enjoyed today with him.

Twelve

After leaving the television station they had lunch at Gravel, a bar and grill owned by a college friend of Nadia's named Lilli. For years Lilli's parents had run the place and had recently turned it over to Lilli when they retired.

Jaxon placed his hand in the center of her back while they walked into the restaurant. His touch had an effect on her. All sorts of feelings rippled through her, and she was totally conscious of him as a man. And from the feminine looks they got when they entered, quite a few other women were aware of him as well.

She could tell Jaxon liked Lilli when they were introduced. Most people did. She had that kind of personality. He also liked Aaron, Lilli's husband. Since Aaron was originally from Norfolk, Virginia, the two had a lot to talk about, being from the same state.

Lilli had been Nadia's friend long enough to detect something between her and Jaxon, although she'd introduced him as a business associate. Had Nadia's interest in him been obvious? She discovered her answer when, after placing her order, she excused herself to go to the bathroom and deliberately cornered Lilli. "What gives, Lil?"

Lilli threw her head back and laughed. "You tell me, girlfriend. I can't wait until I talk to Rissa. Business associate, my ass. The sexual chemistry between you and Jaxon Ravnel is so thick I can feel it."

"It's not," Nadia scoffed.

"It is, too. I'm sure even Aaron felt it and he has a tendency to let stuff go over his head. Another thing I noticed is that Jaxon can't keep his eyes off you, so the desire isn't just coming from you, kiddo."

She hoped not. Otherwise, she'd been reading the vibes all wrong. But then she didn't have that much experience with men to read the signs Rissa had told her to look out for. She was well aware of the fire raging inside her whenever he glanced her way, gave her a smile or when he'd placed his hand at the center of her back. Returning to her table, she tried to stay composed but it was hard. Never had she been this taken with a man. Jaxon had the ability to short-circuit her senses.

She'd ordered a hamburger, fries and a strawberry milkshake. He had a brisket sandwich with sweet potato fries and a vanilla shake. Over lunch he told her how he'd recently gone into partnership with the Westmorelands' horse-training business. She had heard that from Paige but enjoyed listening to him tell her about it. She sat there trying to convince herself her enjoyment had nothing to do with the deep, husky sound of his voice. Nor did it have anything to do with how sensuous his mouth looked whenever it moved.

"How did your parents meet?" she asked, curious about the two people who'd raised him. She'd heard from Paige, who'd met them, that his mother was gorgeous and the epitome of a defined and elegant woman. She probably had more sophistication in her pinkie finger than Nadia had in her entire body.

He smiled at her question, and she immediately felt a quivering in the pit of her stomach. "Mom and Dad were the two most unlikely people to get together. He needed more land to expand the institute and she was president of this group whose sole purpose was to protect lands and natural resources from excessive development. Needless to say, they butted heads."

"I can imagine."

"I don't think you can. I still find it hard to believe at times. I understand back in the day Dad was a rather stern businessman who was used to having things his way. Mom was a tough cookie. At the time Dad was the most eligible bachelor in town and was known to dazzle most women."

Probably like his son, she thought. "So how did they come to a compromise?"

"I don't think they did. At the time she was a college professor at a community college in Dumfries. He thought she was the most temperamental, unmanageable, outspoken and sassy woman he'd ever met."

Nadia laughed. "She sounds like a woman I can truly admire."

"She was one he could admire, too. Dad says he fell in love with Mom the moment he walked into her office to give her hell. He was immediately taken with her because she was the first woman who didn't treat him like he was a prize catch. Instead, she treated him like he was a nuisance she was forced to deal with." He took a sip of his iced tea and then said, "Needless to say, less than a year after they met they got married."

Nadia nodded. "What was the outcome of the land your father wanted but she didn't want him to have?"

"Since the primary concern of her organization was the trees on the property that had been there for over one hundred years, Dad promised to build around them. Although that meant having the architectural plans redone, which was costly."

A short while later, after they'd eaten, Jaxon told her how much he'd enjoyed his meal. To her surprise, when they were leaving, he told Lilli and Aaron he would be coming back.

When they left Gravel, he reminded Nadia of the errands he had to make in Jackson Hole. They went to several men's shops looking for shirts and ties. He also purchased another Stetson. Last was a pair of boots. At first it felt odd going shopping with him but after a while it seemed like a natural act. He asked her opinion about several ties and bought the ones she told him she liked the best.

By the time they'd finished with all his shopping it was close to five o'clock and he suggested they grab dinner. They dined at a very elegant restaurant in Jackson Hole. The moment she walked into the Jagged Edge she recalled hearing about it from Cash Outlaw's wife, Brianna. This was where Cash had brought her for their wedding dinner. It was just as beautiful as Brianna had said. The restaurant was massive as well as impressive with a set of triple stairs that led to other dining areas, high cathedral ceilings and beautiful chandeliers.

Dinner had been delicious and instead of discussing anything personal, she'd asked him about what he'd said during Sue Ellen Donovan's interview. Specifically, those community projects he was adding to his agenda for next year. One conversation led to another and he shared with her his plans for his company. With the acquired land in Wyoming, he was finished expanding for now. His concentration would be on hiring the most qualified people to manage both the Forbes and Gamble expansions.

"I hadn't meant to keep you away so long," he said when they were headed back to Gamble. They had enjoyed conversing so much that neither of them had realized how late it had gotten. It was close to eight o'clock.

"That's fine. I enjoyed taking a day off work." And she truly meant it. What she hadn't added was that she had enjoyed spending the time with him.

"What in the world!"

She heard the startled astonishment in his voice, and then he pulled the car over to the shoulder of the road. She followed his gaze as he stared out the window and into the sky. She saw what had him so captivated. The Milky Way could occasionally be seen in this part of Wyoming.

It was known that the state of Wyoming was one of the only states in the country where an individual could enjoy the beauty of the universe. Over the years she'd seen planets, nebulae, a multitude of stars and galaxies. It was the best place for stargazing and most people around these parts owned telescopes. Tonight, you didn't need one. The sight before them was a spectacular view with clarity.

"I've never seen anything so beautiful."

She nodded, understanding completely. That was usually a person's reaction upon seeing the Milky Way for the first time. "On those nights when the skies were really dark, Dad and Mom used to gather us up in our pjs and drive us to Peake Row. It's the best place around here to see the Milky Way."

"Peake Row? I'd love to go there. And I'd love for you to go with me. You can even wear your pj's."

She turned to look at him and could see the seriousness in his gaze. He wasn't teasing. Clearing her throat, she said, "Thanks for the invite, but I'll pass."

She glanced back into the sky when suddenly a mass of red seemed to circle around the stars in the shape of an arrow. "My goodness!" Now she was the one with startled astonishment in her voice.

"What is it?" he asked, staring up into the sky and seeing the same thing that she did.

"That rarely appears, what looks like a huge ball of fire encircling a cluster of stars. It's beautiful."

"It is. Have you ever seen it before?"

"No." There was no need to tell him that around these parts there were some who believed if a couple saw it together, it was a sure sign of everlasting love. She was glad she wasn't one of those believers.

When the sky began getting dark again, he said, "I guess the show is over."

"Yes, I guess it is. It was beautiful while it lasted though."

An hour later they were pulling up in her yard. The floodlights from the house shone into the car and highlighted his features. "It's late but at least I got you back safe and sound."

"And I appreciate it," she said, flashing him a smile.

"I enjoyed your company," he said, opening his door to get out.

She watched him come around to her side of the car to open the door and wondered if he'd felt the sexual chemistry between them that she'd been feeling all day. She'd spent the entire day with him and had enjoyed it. When they reached her front door, she thanked him for the ride into Valley Bluff.

"Don't mention it. Are you sure you have a way to pick up your car tomorrow?"

"Yes. Rissa will be taking me. Like I told you, Steve's Auto Repair Shop is open all day on Saturdays."

"Okay. Flick the blinds when you get inside to let me know you're safe."

Nadia nodded, a little disappointed he hadn't asked to come inside. Would he kiss her goodbye? He was standing close but not too close. "I will. Thanks. Good night."

"Good night, Nadia."

Her key was in her hand and she turned to her front door. She heard his footsteps moving down the stairs and when she opened the door to go inside, she turned to look over her shoulder, certain he'd made it to his car by now. He hadn't. Instead, he stood on the last step. Their gazes met and held.

She was going to ask if anything was wrong, but couldn't. It was as if she was in a trance where her vocal cords weren't working. Nadia swallowed as she slowly turned back around to face him. She felt the pull, the connection, and all that chemistry Lilli had teased her about earlier that day. She also felt something else she couldn't explain.

Time appeared to drone on endlessly before he spoke in a low, deep voice. "You're killing me, Nadia."

She was killing him? Did he not know what he was doing to her?

"How?" she heard herself asking.

"Do you not feel it? All that chemistry? Have you not felt it all day?"

No need for her to play dumb. They were both adults after all. "Yes, I feel it and yes, I've felt it all day."

From his expression it was obvious her response had surprised him. He slowly began walking back to her. When he came to a stop in front of her, he asked, "Do you want to go inside and talk about it?"

Nadia nibbled nervously on her bottom lip. Was that what she wanted? Or did she want something more? Although she didn't believe seeing that sign in the sky had anything to do with love, maybe it was the universe's way of letting her know it was time to make one important move in her life. And if that was true, then why not make that move with him?

Wasn't that the advice Rissa had given her? To invite him in? The chemistry between them was hot and there was no doubt in her mind he had the ability to rock her world. But more than anything, she believed that unlike Benson, he wasn't the type of man who would break a woman's heart without caring that it might cause her pain.

"Nadia?"

Making her decision, she said, "No. I don't want to go inside and talk about it, Jaxon. I want to go inside and do something about it."

Jaxon followed Nadia inside and closed the door behind them. After she strolled to the living room, she kicked off her shoes. The heels weren't high enough to be considered stilettos, but had looked sexy on her legs nonetheless. His gaze focused entirely on her as she removed her jacket and began unbuttoning her blouse. "Don't you think we need to talk first?" he asked.

"No." She slanted him a cool yet decisive look. Determined. "But we do need to get the status of our relationship squared."

He watched as she finished unbuttoning her blouse. It hung open, revealing a sexy black lace bra. "Squared in what way, Nadia?"

"You said if I wanted to change the status of our relationship you'd grant me the courtesy of doing so."

He lifted a brow. "And are you doing so?"

"Yes. I want more than an acquaintanceship or a business relationship between us. At least for tonight anyway."

"Do you?"

"Yes."

If she thought this would be a single sexual encounter, a once-in-a-lifetime-thing for them, she was wrong. He'd engaged in casual sex before but he wouldn't do so with her. Never with her. Regardless of whether she accepted it or not, she was the woman who would be his future wife. Once they made love there was no turning back.

He slowly crossed the floor to stand in front of her. "So what do you want from me, Nadia?"

In her bare feet, she took a step closer and he immediately breathed in her scent. The same scent that had captivated him during the drive all day. The same scent that could send desire rippling through him whenever it flowed through his nostrils.

Jaxon took a sharp breath when she deliberately pressed her body against his. There was no way she couldn't tell he was aroused. Every cell in his body throbbed due to overloaded testosterone. Maybe he should warn her just how long it had been since he'd been with a woman. Not since meeting her more than a year ago and wanting her to be the only woman he made love to for the rest of his life. That meant his entire body was in a sexually deprived state.

She then leaned toward him, where their mouths were almost touching, and whispered, "I want one steamy night, Jaxon. I've never had one before, and I want you to give me one."

She'd never had one before? Questions flared in his mind. Was she saying no man had ever given her a night to remember? The Big O? Satisfied her to the degree she had expected? Or was she stating something else altogether? That she'd never…

The thought that suddenly entered his mind was way too much to imagine as a possibility. After all, she was twenty-eight. Then he stopped thinking at all when she leaned in closer and used the tip of her tongue to swipe across his lips.

He wrapped his arms around her waist and pulled her toward him and kissed her long, hard and deep. She wanted a steamy night and he intended to give her one.

Nadia sighed deep in her throat. Jaxon was giving her a kiss that topped any kiss she'd ever shared. It was a kiss that even made the first one they'd shared weeks ago seem tame in comparison.

He released her mouth to give her a moment to draw in a much needed breath before capturing her mouth again. The feel of his tongue dueling with hers stimulated her in a way she'd never been stimulated before. Tonight his mouth was greedier, more demanding.

Suddenly she pulled back, breaking off the kiss, parting her lips to draw in another deep breath, her gaze focused solely on him. She kept her gaze on Jaxon while licking her lips. Never had a man tasted so delicious. He stood there with his arms wrapped around her, giving her time to…do what? Slow down the rapid beating of her heart? The urgent throb between her legs? His gaze was as intently focused on her as hers was on him.

"You have beautiful lips, Nadia."

His words made her swipe her tongue across them, and she saw how his gaze followed the movement. "I think you have beautiful lips, too." She wasn't good at small talk. But then she wasn't good at flirting either.

In a surprise move, he slid his hands beneath her blouse to caress her back. It was the same spot he'd placed his hand several times today but now he was touching her skin. The moment he did so, something flared in his eyes and heat filled her completely.

Then, in an unexpected move, he swept her off her feet and into his arms. "Which way?"

"Upstairs. First bedroom on your right."

How he managed to maneuver the stairs while holding her firmly in his arms, she wasn't sure. But he did. After placing her on the bed, he leaned in and kissed her again. A jolt of sexual energy rushed through her body when their tongues began devouring each other.

When he finally released her mouth, he straightened and stared down at her. More heat than she could ever have imagined suffused her. She could only lie there, propped against her pillow, and stare back. No man had ever made her feel this way from a kiss. Desire was actually clawing at her and each breath she took caught on a surge of yearning so sharp it felt painful.

"I don't think you have any idea how much I want you, Nadia."

She had news for him. She doubted he knew how much she wanted him, too. Arousal coiled in the very core of her. She'd never considered herself an overly sexual being. Until him. Not in a million years would she have asked any man to give her one steamy night. However, she had done so with him.

"What's going on in that pretty little head of yours, Nadia? You aren't changing your mind about tonight, are you?"

She was surprised he'd asked. Most men would not have. They would have taken the ball she'd placed in their court and played it without caring that she might be having doubts. "No, I'm not changing my mind."

He nodded and the serious expression on his face eased into a smile. "In that case, whose clothes come off first? Yours or mine?"

Knowing her answer would seal her fate, a fate she was looking forward to, she said, "Yours. More than anything I want to undress you, Jaxon."

Thirteen

Nadia's words did something to him. They fired up his libido even more. Undressing him was just one of the things he wanted her to do to him. "Then come undress me."

His heart kicked up a notch and his erection pressed hard against the zipper of his pants when she eased off the bed and slowly walked over to him. He couldn't help noticing just how uneven her breath was with every step she took. From the first, he'd thought her to be sexy as hell. That hadn't changed. Although after tonight her place in his life still might be unclear to her, at least it would be a start.

And speaking of a start…she looked unsure about where and how to begin. Those earlier thoughts he'd had regarding her experience level returned. But then it honestly didn't matter. He would gladly introduce her to everything any other man had fallen short in doing.

He stared down at her and she stared up at him. Her beautiful chocolate-brown eyes held a level of innocence he hadn't expected. Then, as if the look in his eyes motivated her, she pushed the jacket from his shoulders and began unbuttoning his shirt. His heart rate increased with every button she touched. Moments later, when she eased his shirt from his trousers and it hung open, she seemed transfixed with his chest.

"I love a man with a hairy chest, Jaxon."

He was glad to hear that. "What else do you love about a man?"

She switched her eyes from his chest to his face. "I love a man who cares enough about his health to stay in shape. You have nice abs as well."

He chuckled at that. "Thanks. I think you have nice abs, too."

She lifted a brow. "You've never seen my abs."

"Yes, I have."

"When?"

That wasn't hard for him to recall. "The weekend I was in Westmoreland Country for Bane's second set of triplets' first birthday. You were getting out of their swimming pool." The image of her in that two-piece bikini had permanently fried his brain. She had looked just that hot. "You looked sexy as hell."

"You liked what you saw, did you?" she asked, tracing a slow path up and down his chest.

He couldn't stop the sharp breath that escaped his lips. "I most certainly did. I liked it a lot."

She tilted her head and looked at him questioningly. "Yet you never showed any sign of interest."

Since he'd promised not to mention marriage again, he wouldn't tell her that he'd decided the day they'd been introduced that she would be his wife. "The interest was there, Nadia. I'm just not a man who likes rushing into anything. That's not my style."

Nadia didn't say anything to that. Instead, she lifted her hands to push his shirt off his shoulders. Then she lowered her hands to his belt, but not before again tracing a path through the hair on his chest. She'd obviously been serious when she said she liked a hairy chest.

Jaxon was trying hard to keep his control in check when she unbuckled his belt and eased it from the loops. He almost stopped breathing when her hands went to his zipper to slide it down. Because of his erection, her doing so wasn't an easy task. He glanced down and watched her, saw the determined look on her face and hoped like hell she didn't ask him to suck it in. There was no way he could.

When she'd finally slid the zipper all the way down, she looked up at him and met his gaze with a huge smile of accomplishment on her face.

"Now what?" he asked, thinking just how much he loved her.

"Your shoes and socks have to go before I can tackle your pants and briefs."

"Okay," he said, thinking he definitely didn't have a problem with her tackling anything when it came to him.

Easing down on the bed, he removed his shoes and socks as she watched him intently. When he stood back up, she was there, reaching out her hand for the waist-band of his slacks. "Maybe I shouldn't tell you this," she said softly, "but I like how you dress. With your suits. Makes you stand out as the businessman that you are."

He chuckled. "You mean you don't prefer seeing me in jeans and a Western shirt?"

She glanced up at him. "I've seen you dressed that way in Westmoreland Country, and I liked it, too. But there is something about you in a suit and Stetson. Especially when you don't wear a tie. I like the open-shirt look."

She would say that after he'd purchased three new ties that day. "Because of the hairy chest?"

She smiled. "Precisely."

He wondered if Nadia realized she was giving him too much information. However, he had no intention of telling her that, but he would file it in the back of his mind for future use.

Jaxon ceased thinking when she eased his slacks down his hips and legs and stooped to assist while he stepped out of them. When she stood back up, she stared at his middle. He was in a pair of black briefs and the size of his erection couldn't be helped. He wanted her just that much.

"Now for that last piece," she said in a somewhat nervous tone. The last thing he wanted was for her to get cold feet now.

"I'm all yours, Nadia." He meant that more than she would ever know.

She glanced up at his face from staring at his groin

and then took a step toward him. He watched with bated breath as she eased down the last piece of his clothing.

For the longest time she stared down at his aroused shaft. It was as if she was seeing a man—up close and personal—for the first time. That niggling thought he'd forced to the back of his mind earlier tried to make its way to the forefront yet again. He pushed it back.

Then as if she pulled herself out of a trance, she shifted her gaze to other parts of him. With a huge smile on her face, she met his gaze and said, "Well, I guess I'm finished."

He smiled back and said, "Not quite."

Not quite? Nadia figured a dumbfounded look had to be on her face. Finding her voice, she decided to ask. "What else is there?"

Instead of answering, he leaned down and picked up his slacks to pull something out of one of the pockets. He opened his hand to show her what he had. Condom packets. Several of them. "Oh."

"You want to do the honors, Nadia?"

She arched a brow. He had to be kidding. Although she was sure some women might not have a problem doing such a thing, she did. She wouldn't know where to start. And the thought of holding him in her hand while figuring out a condom was too much to think about. Even now his erection jutted proudly from a dark thatch of hair. Why did the sight of it make her want to reach out and run her fingers through those curls?

"Nadia?"

She raised her gaze to him. He was waiting for her response. "Thanks, but I'll let you do it."

"You're sure?"

"Positive."

He nodded and she stood there and watched him. When he finished, he glanced back at her. "Now it's my turn."

Nadia swallowed. She had gotten so caught up in watching him sheath himself that she couldn't comprehend his words. "Your turn?"

"Yes. It's my turn to undress you."

Not wasting any time, he pushed her blouse from her shoulders. Then he unhooked the front clasp of her bra, which made her breasts spill out. "Your breasts are beautiful. So damn shapely," he said, staring at them.

It was on the tip of her tongue to say they were also real. "Glad you like them."

"I'm going to prove just how much I like them in a moment. There aren't any limitations tonight, right?"

She blinked at his question. "Limitations?"

"Yes. You want steamy and I want to make tonight as steamy for you as it can get."

His words had heat gathering in the area between her legs. "There are no limitations, Jaxon."

"Good."

He finished undressing her by removing her skirt. Crouching down in front of her, he lowered her black lace panties down her legs and then remained there to stare at her feminine mound. It was as if he was fascinated by it, and she knew why. Although she wasn't sexually active, she wanted to look pretty down there regardless. That was why she routinely got a French bikini wax with a little artwork thrown in. The curls left down there were in the shape of a heart.

"That design is beautiful," he said, standing back on his feet.

"Thanks."

"And just so you know, Nadia, tonight will be a night of pleasure for the both of us. Especially for you."

She tilted her head to look up at him. Did he know about her virginity? "Why especially for me?"

"Because you deserve a man cherishing your body while making love to it."

His words touched Nadia. Her first time with a man was playing out how she'd hoped, how she'd fantasized it could be. She'd always wanted her first to be some-one who wouldn't rush things. Someone who'd want to pleasure her, and Jaxon just said he would.

Her breath took on a different pattern when Jaxon's gaze moved from her eyes down her naked body—head to toe—before returning to the juncture of her thighs.

Feeling emboldened, she took a couple of steps to him and wrapped her arms around his neck. Doing so made them skin-to-skin, hard to soft.

She whispered, "I'm ready for the Jaxon Ravnel experience."

Fourteen

The Jaxon Ravnel experience?

No woman had ever termed making love with him that way, Jaxon thought. Coming from Nadia, he would take it. Not only would he take it, but he would try like hell to make it an experience she would never forget. It took more than great sex to bind a woman to a man and vice versa, but at least it was an explosive connection.

Sweeping her into his arms he carried her over to the bed. By the end of the night, she would be his physically. He would continue to work on her mentally by having them get to know each other more, showing her how good they could be together and making sure she fully understood the impact she had on his heart and the place he had designed for her in his life.

After placing her on the bed, he joined her there.

Pulling her into his arms, he zeroed in on her mouth for a kiss. More than anything, he wanted to not only give Nadia intense pleasure, but he also wanted them to savor the night so she'd want plenty of steamy nights with him. The kiss was long, deep and passionate. It fired up everything inside of him and, from the sound of her moans, it fired her up as well.

Simultaneously, his hands were all over her. His fingers touched areas on her body he intended to give his full concentration to later. Right now, his focus was on her mouth and her taste. From their first kiss he'd found her flavor addictive and mind-blowingly delicious. He could kiss her all day or every chance he got. Holding back and not kissing her good-night when he'd brought her home after dinner on his jet had been the hardest thing he'd ever had to do.

Finally, he broke off the kiss and stared down at her. Her lips glistened, and he lowered his head to lick the wetness from them with the tip of his tongue. After licking and nibbling around her mouth a while, he licked toward her neck. From there he licked his way to her breasts and took a swollen peak into his mouth. He heard a whimper escape her lips as he sucked harder. Like he'd told her, she had beautiful breasts. They were the perfect size and shape. When he'd removed her bra to reveal them, sensations ripped through him. It had taken everything he had to hold himself in check. He'd never considered himself a breast man. Of course he liked looking at them and sampling them on occasion. But he'd never wanted to gobble up a pair like he was doing to Nadia.

Then he eased his finger between her legs. He began to shamelessly stroke her there while he devoured her breasts. Her feminine scent got to him, arousing him in a way he hadn't thought possible. It was then that he knew it was time to go further south. Shifting his body, he pulled away from her breasts and moved down to her stomach, licking and nibbling. Her skin was soft, delicate beneath his tongue, and the taste was incredible. He figured if her skin tasted this awesome, he could just imagine how tasty the area between her legs would be.

"Jaxon…"

Although her thighs opened when he'd placed his head between them, the way she'd said his name made him think no other man had gone down on her before. He glanced up and saw how she was looking at him with a mixture of want, need and curiosity. He knew then he would take his time, feast on her properly, to ensure this part of lovemaking was something she enjoyed.

He lowered his head and went to work. Grabbing hold of her hips, he eased his tongue inside of her. He loved the moan she made; he'd made one as well. She was so damn delicious. Her delectable flavor seemed to send his tongue into a licking frenzy. Locking his mouth to her feminine mound while holding her hips tight, he began devouring her. She grabbed his head to hold him to her. Such a thing wasn't needed since he had no intention of going anywhere. Never had his tongue been so eager to satisfy a woman.

He knew from the sudden jerking of her body that she was climaxing, but he refused to pull his mouth away. He kept it there while his tongue enjoyed the taste of her feminine juices. They invigorated him, filled him with a craving the extent of which he'd never felt for a woman. After lapping up as much of her as he could, he pulled his mouth away and looked up at her.

The satisfaction on her face touched him, sent sensuous shivers all through his body. She had enjoyed it as much as he had, and he was glad. Now it was time for the union of not only their bodies, but also their minds and souls.

Taking a deep breath, which included a whiff of her scent, he moved to ease his body over hers. While holding her gaze firmly with his, he slowly entered her. He knew the moment his earlier suspicions were confirmed. He was going where no man had gone before.

He was humbled and honored to be Nadia's first. Although she might not know it or accept it, she belonged to him in every way a woman could belong to a man. At twenty-eight he wasn't sure why she'd waited but she had and he would be the lucky guy. The only guy.

Their gazes held and as he stared into her eyes, he felt the same degree of desire he'd felt when he'd first met her, the same desire he felt whenever he was close to her. Now they were as close as two people could possibly be. All he could do was stare down into her beautiful face. With her hair spread out across the pillows, her features were even more striking. If it was possible to fall in love with her even more, at that moment he did.

He moved again and she widened her legs as if to welcome him in. When he had pushed his way inside her to the hilt, he asked, "You're okay?"

Reaching up, she wrapped her arms around his neck. She smiled and said, "Yes, I'm okay."

"Good, because I'm about to give you the ride of your life, sweetheart."

And he meant it.

Something inside of Nadia flared to life when Jaxon began thrusting. And when he growled low in his throat, every hormone inside of her sizzled as if she was burning alive from the inside out. She felt it in every pore, nerve and pulse. And then there was the sound of flesh slapping against flesh and the way his gaze held hers as if daring her to look away. She couldn't.

He managed to go deeper and deeper and she wondered how her body was keeping up with his urgent demands. She'd begun moving her body as well; she couldn't help but respond. Her body throbbed in areas it never had before.

Then there was the feel of his pubic hair rubbing against hers. It seemed everything surrounding them was on overload. His manly scent seemed to envelop her and when he leaned in to nibble on her earlobe, the feel of his hot breath near her neck made her heart skip a beat.

Each time he made a downward thrust, her feminine muscles tightened and tried holding him in while her hands glided up and down his naked back. Was this what made her sisters wear such satisfied smiles whenever they talked about their husbands' abilities in the bedroom? Now she fully understood what she'd been missing by not doing this with a man. But a part of her knew that it might not have been this good, this overwhelming, this hot with any other man but Jaxon. For reasons she didn't understand, they connected on every level.

Suddenly, he moved his mouth from her ear to her lips at the same time he used his hands to lift her hips to a more secure fit while moving inside of her. This kiss was hotter than any they'd ever shared. It was a full contact, wet-tongue kiss that made her head reel and her senses spin. And when his tongue captured hers, she clamped his face with her hands while returning the kiss with the same hunger and need he was plowing into it.

Then she felt it. It was as if every roll of his hips, every hard thrust into her body and the mind-blowing kiss had prepared her for this. It felt like a sexual explosion tearing her body apart with pleasure. She pulled her mouth from his and let out a scream as she felt her body splinter into a thousand pieces. Each piece filled with frissons of fire and passion.

Then she heard him holler out her name at the same time his body jerked hard while he continued to pound inside her, hard and deep. That pushed her into another orgasm. She welcomed it, needed it and desperately wanted it. She clenched her inner muscles around him tighter and knew he was giving her all he had. Yet she wanted more. Arching her back, her inner muscles clamped down on him, trying to draw everything out of him. She was determined to receive it all.

And just like she wanted, it happened for the third time. And she screamed yet again.

* * *

"Nadia?"

She forced open her eyes, feeling drained and depleted of all strength. Meeting Jaxon's gaze she forced a single word from her lungs. "Yes?"

"I need to go into the bathroom and come back to take care of you."

"Take care of me, how?"

"Last night was your first time and if I don't put you in a tub of warm water, you're going to be sore tomorrow."

She was glad that once he'd discovered she was a virgin he hadn't stopped making love to her. "I'm not ready to move just yet. Besides, I won't be too sore. I ride a lot."

He chuckled and tenderly kissed her lips. "Yes, sweetheart, but tonight you weren't the one doing the riding."

That was true but as far as she was concerned, it didn't matter. She wasn't ready for their bodies to separate, which was why her legs had a firm grip across his back. He couldn't go anywhere until she released him. "I liked it and want to do it again."

Seeing those lips she loved ease into a smile made her pulse rate increase. "I don't suggest we do that."

"Why?"

"It might make you even sorer."

"I'll chance a little discomfort for another few rounds."

He lifted a brow. "Another few rounds?"

"Yes. Now that I have you where I want you, I'm not ready to let you go." Too late she realized what she'd said and knew how her words could be misconstrued. She quickly added, "What I meant is that this is all new to me and I wondered how it would be. Now that I know and I like it, I'm wondering what took me so long to try it."

"Not that I'm complaining, but what did take you so long?" he asked, nuzzling his lips near her earlobes again.

Since he'd been her first, a position most men didn't want, and he hadn't made a fuss about it, she did owe him some sort of explanation. "I'll tell you, but not tonight. I want you again, Jaxon."

He stared down at her and she could feel him expanding inside of her. "I need to change condoms."

She knew he probably should, especially after hearing how Maverick had gotten Phire pregnant. But still. "Maybe the next go-round. I'm not ready for you to come out of me yet. Just so you know I am on the pill and I'm safe."

He stared at her and then said, "I'm safe as well."

A smile touched her lips. "Then there's no reason for us to worry about a condom, is there?"

He pushed back a lock of hair that had fallen in her face. "You sure?"

"I'm positive." Tonight in his arms, while he was here in her bed, she felt feminine and safe. She also felt desired. His aroused body attested to that. Then there was that hum of lust that had infiltrated her brain, making her want more of him. She wanted to know how it felt for him to release his semen inside of her. Tonight, he had introduced her to something her body had never done before and she had enjoyed it immensely. Maybe a little too much. She would have to worry about that later.

She had asked for one steamy night and she was definitely getting it.

Fifteen

Jaxon came awake to the brightness of the sun coming in through the window and the sound of Nadia's even breathing. She was still sleeping while cuddled in his arms. He could definitely get used to waking up each morning this way. He couldn't imagine anything better than being in bed with the woman he loved, holding her close after a night of lovemaking.

He hoped like hell she'd be able to walk today but she'd gotten just what she'd asked for. He'd given her fair warning. However, she'd refused to take heed. He had removed the condom after their first lovemaking session but hadn't put another one on. The feel of being skin to skin with her had driven his own need to have her over and over again. Each and every time their bodies joined, he'd loved her that much more. It had been before dawn this morning when they'd finally drifted off to sleep wrapped in each other's arms.

As he lay there staring up at the ceiling he wondered what today would bring. Would she regret what happened last night? Ask him to leave? Assume last night was one and done? Had last night been only about lust for her? That meant it was up to him to show her the difference between lust and love. She might not love him now, but there was no reason for her not to love him eventually. He would have enough love for the two of them until she did. In time she would see that their lives were entwined, and he would never hurt her.

There was a knock at her front door. He glanced at the clock on her wall and wondered who would be paying her a visit before nine in the morning? Hell, it would be just his luck for one of those Westmorelands or Outlaws to be here. She'd said they were known to drop in unannounced.

When the knock sounded again, she stirred in his arms and then slowly opened her eyes. He knew the exact moment she brought him into focus. He tried to prepare himself for what was to come. She hadn't asked him to spend the night; it just happened that way. He wondered if she'd remember how many times her legs had held his body hostage.

She continued to stare at him as if trying to recall why he was there. Then it seemed as if she remembered and the recollection made her smile. He released a relieved breath. "Good morning, Nadia."

"Good morning to you, Jaxon."

She sounded like she was in a good mood and then

she proved she was by leaning over and brushing her lips across his. Before she could move back, he took over the kiss, deciding to show her what a real good-morning kiss looked like. He captured her mouth and exploited it for all it was worth and for him, it was worth everything.

The knock at the door sounded again. Louder this time. Jaxon reluctantly pulled his mouth away from hers. However, out of necessity, he licked around her lips and asked, "Do you normally get visitors this early?"

She licked around his mouth as well. "It's probably Rissa. She was supposed to take me to pick up my car this morning. I should have called her. Since you're here you can take me. At least if you don't mind."

"No, I don't mind."

"She's probably seen your car and figures you're still here since I'd told her I would be catching a ride with you to the television station yesterday."

He nodded. "Do you have a problem with her knowing I spent the night?"

"Heck no." She eased out of bed. "I would call and tell her to go away but my cell phone is downstairs." It didn't seem to bother her that she was standing there naked. "I'll grab my robe and let her know you'll give me a ride to the repair shop. And you might as well put on some clothes, too. She'll want to meet you."

"Then I can't disappoint her," he said, getting out of bed and not missing how her gaze traveled the full length of his body. There was no need to ask if she liked what she saw. All during their lovemaking last night she'd kept saying she did.

"I'll go downstairs before she calls the police to report you've done harm to me and gotten rid of my body. Rissa's husband, Shayne, is a US Marshal and her mind gets carried away at times."

Jaxon could certainly arrest Rissa's fears about him getting rid of Nadia's body. And speaking of that body, he decided to ask, "How do you feel this morning? Are you sore?"

His question made her blush. "I'm fine, Jaxon. Of course I'm sore, but the best way to work out soreness is to keep the muscles moving."

He nodded. "May I use your bathroom to freshen up?"

"Sure and there's a toiletry bag beneath the vanity you can use."

"Thanks."

As Jaxon headed for the bathroom, he was glad Nadia had no problem letting her best friend know he'd spent the night. As far as he was concerned, that was a good start.

"Please wipe that silly-looking grin off your face, Rissa," Nadia said, stepping aside to let her friend enter her home.

"Well, it took you long enough to open the door and with your robe on and probably wearing nothing underneath, what am I to assume?" Rissa replied with a smirk on her face.

"I don't know, you tell me," Nadia said, closing the door.

"Well, the one thing I can assume is that you're no longer a twenty-eight-year-old virgin."

Rissa didn't know just how right she was about that. "I won't say."

"You don't have to say with all those passion marks on your neck. I'm surprised you can still walk this morning."

In a way Nadia was surprised, too. Her body was sore but she felt wonderful. "You're a smart woman, Rissa. You saw Jaxon's car out front. After the second knock, you should have kept moving, knowing I would call you later."

"Are you kidding me? You wanted me to miss seeing a huge smile on your face so I can gladly say I told you so?"

Nadia shook her head. For years Rissa had tried telling Nadia what she'd been missing by not engaging in an intimate relationship with a man. Rissa had accused Nadia of letting Benson win by not getting over what he'd done while they'd been in college.

"Well?"

Nadia glanced over at Rissa. "Well what?"

"I want to see that morning-after smile. The glow is there but I want to see the smile. No way will I believe Jaxon Ravnel didn't put a smile on your face." Rissa then glanced around. "Where is he, by the way?"

"Upstairs, and if it will get you to leave, here's my smile." Unashamedly, Nadia gave her friend a huge, wide smile. The widest she could make.

Rissa laughed. "I knew it!" She gave Nadia a big hug. "I knew the two of you were meant to be together and—"

"Whoa. Hold up." Nadia shook her head. "Now

you're talking nonsense," she said, lowering her voice to a hushed tone. "Jaxon and I are not meant to be together. Last night was one and done. Nothing has changed. It's back to the way things were before."

Rissa rolled her eyes and responded in a hushed tone as well. "I hate to tell you but that's not possible."

"And why not?"

"Your body knows him. It will want him. It will need him."

"That's rubbish. I don't want nor will I need any man, Rissa," Nadia said.

"You'll see and when you do, don't say I didn't warn you."

Nadia waved off her words. "Whatever."

"Well, since I've seen your smile I'll leave now and—"

"I hope you're not leaving on my account," a male voice said behind them.

Nadia and Rissa glanced around to see Jaxon walking down the stairs. At least he was dressed in his slacks and shirt. Why did he have to look so darn sexy this morning?

Seeing Rissa staring at him as if in a daze, Nadia leaned over and whispered, "Remember, you're a married woman."

Rissa snatched her gaze from Jaxon to look at Nadia with a sheepish grin and whispered back, "I'm trying hard to remember."

Shayne was a good-looking man. But Nadia had to admit, there was good-looking and then there was goody-looking. This morning, Jaxon was not only goody-looking; he was sexy, sensual and salacious.

They watched him come down the stairs. Nadia didn't know Rissa's thoughts but she definitely knew hers. *What a man, what a man…* This morning he was jaw-droppingly handsome. Just the thought that last night she had gotten as much of him as he'd gotten of her made goose bumps appear on her body. Even now her gaze was glued to the zipper on his pants as she remembered everything. Every lusty, hungry moment of last night.

When he came to a stop in front of them, Nadia made introductions. Then Jaxon said, "Rissa, I'm happy to meet you. Nadia has told me a lot about you."

Nadia lifted a brow. Had she? She mentioned that she and Rissa were best friends and had been since they were kids, but that was all. She figured he was just being kind…as usual.

"Thanks and welcome to Gamble. I understand your company is expanding here."

"That's right," he replied with that killer smile. "Will you be joining us for breakfast?"

Breakfast? Nadia wondered what made Jaxon assume he was staying for breakfast. "Rissa has a lot to do today and was just about to leave," she said, taking her best friend's arm and leading her toward the door.

"Yes, that's right. I was about to leave. It was nice meeting you, Jaxon."

"Same here, Rissa."

When Nadia closed the door behind Rissa, she turned to Jaxon, ready to light into him about his assumptions about breakfast or that he might be hanging around, period. Maybe she needed to make it clear to

him that last night was one and done. She was about to
open her mouth when he lowered his lips to hers.

She knew what was about to happen but didn't want
to stop it. Jaxon was seducing her and she was letting
him. He began torturing her mouth the way he'd done
several times last night. After ending the kiss, he nibbled her lips from corner to corner and then used the
tip of his tongue to lick around the lines of her mouth.
When she made a breathless sigh, his tongue eased inside her mouth once again, took hold of her tongue and
began an intimate, sensual duel.

If that wasn't enough, she could feel his erection
pressed hard against her middle and the more they
kissed, the bigger he got. Then suddenly, she was swept
into his strong arms as he moved in the direction of
the stairs.

Jaxon had a good idea just what Nadia had expected
when he'd swept her into his arms to take her back upstairs. When he entered her bedroom, he hadn't placed
her on the bed but kept moving to the bathroom. Once
there he removed her robe before placing her in the
warm sudsy water he had prepared for her.

"A good soak will help those sore muscles," he said,
crouching down beside the tub.

"And what will you be doing while I'm soaking?"

He smiled and pushed a wayward lock from her face.
"I'm going to the hotel to shower and change. Then I'll
be back to take you to get your car. By then it will be
lunchtime. Will you have lunch with me?" He knew
to ask rather than to assume. The last thing he wanted

was for Nadia to think he was calling the shots. He was beginning to know her well and the one thing she disliked was a man assuming he had any rights as far as she was concerned. So far everything she'd gotten was what she had asked for.

"Thanks for the invitation, but I have things to do today and I'm sure you do, too."

If she thought that was her way to get rid of him, she was sorely mistaken. He would give her space but he had no intention of leaving her alone completely. Last night was a game changer for them. He'd never known any woman who was more sensual, more uninhibited, more open to trying new things. He'd never forget the moment he realized she was still a virgin. His chest had expanded along with his shaft, knowing he was the first man to go inside her.

Once they'd established that she was on a reliable form of birth control and they both were safe healthwise, he had dispensed with the use of the condom. Each and every time he'd come inside her he'd experienced an earth-shattering orgasm. Hell, he'd lost count of how many times they'd come. They'd even hit multiples a few times. There was no doubt in his mind that he had placed his stamp all over her. Evidently, she hadn't yet seen those passion marks on her neck, not to mention other parts of her body. She now belonged to him as much as he belonged to her.

"Is there anything you need me to do before I leave?"

She lifted her chin. "Of course not. In fact you didn't have to do this. I could have filled my own tub with water."

"I know, but I liked doing it." And before she could say anything, he leaned in and brushed a kiss across her lips. "I'll be back in an hour."

"I can call Rissa to come back and take me to get my car."

Standing, he said, "I want to take you. Besides, earlier you said Rissa had a lot to do today. Whereas, I have plenty of time."

She frowned. "Well, I hope you don't plan to get underfoot by thinking last night meant anything."

Jaxon had news for her. Last night had meant everything. "Are you normally this grouchy in the mornings, Nadia?"

Her frown deepened. "I'm not grouchy."

"Yes, you are. While soaking, you should not only work out the soreness but also the grouchiness. I'll see you later."

He heard what she said when he walked out of the bathroom. Walker Rafferty had said he'd never heard Nadia curse. Jaxon just had, and his ears were still blistered.

He chuckled as he went down the stairs. Before it was all over, she would probably be inclined to say even more curse words. Nadia was headstrong, opinionated and had no problem stating how she felt about any given topic. She'd done so last night. She liked being in control and for a while he'd let her. He wouldn't change a thing about her. But he would straighten her out on a few things. He was a permanent part of her life and the sooner she accepted that fact the easier things would be for the both of them.

Sixteen

Nadia didn't lean back to relax in the water until she heard the sound of the front door closing and locking behind Jaxon. She couldn't help licking her lips. The man had more sensuality in his lips than some men had in their entire body.

And speaking of his body...

Granted she'd never been in the presence of a naked man, but she couldn't imagine one with a more trim and fit body than Jaxon. She had studied his physique like an architect would study a blueprint. Taking in the solid muscles that seemed to be everywhere. Even his coffee-colored skin tone had seemed to glow beneath her bedroom light.

And he was so well endowed. The thought of that particular body part being inside her most of the night, giving her pleasure, made her shiver at the memories. And when he'd placed his body above hers and stared down into her eyes, every inch of him had been compelling. She drew in a deep breath at the delicious and tantalizing memories. There was no reason to worry about her bathwater turning cold since the heat from her body was definitely keeping it warm. Jaxon Ravnel had touched her in the right places and had made a lasting impression on her while doing so.

And that was the crux of her problem. She didn't want any man to make a lasting impression on her. But she couldn't refute the fact that he had. Jaxon had made her first time special. Way too special. Both mentally and physically. He had made it worth the wait. And for some reason that was a sore spot even when it shouldn't be.

She should be elated he had given her such tender, loving care. He'd even run bathwater for her in deference to her well-being. How many men would do such a thing? Some would not have hung around until morning. There were some who wouldn't even invite a woman to their home for the night, preferring to always go to hers. She would eye-roll any woman who allowed such a thing.

A short while later she eased out of the tub to get dressed. Jaxon said he would be back in an hour and there was no reason not to believe him. There was a lot about him she was trying to figure out. Did he see their relationship changing or did she just assume he did?

Earlier, when he'd invited her to lunch and she'd declined, he hadn't given any pushback. It was as if it hadn't mattered to him one iota if she accepted his lunch invitation or not. And last night, she'd been the one to tell him she wanted to change their relationship just for that night. Did his nonchalance mean anything?

As she slid into her jeans she wondered if she was overthinking the situation. All they'd had was last night. But what if he wanted more? Was he pretending he didn't want more to throw her off kilter? She pushed such a thought from her mind. Jaxon said he was a man who didn't play games with a woman and there was no reason to assume he was doing so now.

Exactly on the hour there was a knock on her door. Giving herself one last look in the mirror, she quickly moved down the stairs to open it. Nadia was glad the weather was cool so it wouldn't look odd for her to be wearing a scarf. The last thing she needed was for anyone to see all those passion marks on her neck. It was bad enough Rissa had seen them.

She glanced through the peephole. It was Jaxon all right and like her, he was wearing jeans and a Western shirt with the top three buttons undone.

Was that on purpose since she'd told him she had a fetish for chest hair? If so, it was working. She could recall last night when she had dragged her fingers through it, buried her face in it. Her thighs quivered at the memories. And as if he knew she was watching him, he smiled. Dang. That smile would be the death of her.

Drawing in a deep breath, she opened the door without asking who it was. No point since he'd known she'd been watching him. "Jaxon, I'm ready and you look nice," she said, grabbing her purse and jacket without inviting him inside.

"So do you and I like your scarf," he replied as he waited for her to lock the door behind her.

"Thanks." Although she thanked him there was no doubt in her mind that he knew why she was wearing one.

They walked side by side down the steps to his parked car. Forever being a gentleman, he opened the door for her. "Thank you, Jaxon."

He smiled down at her. "You're welcome, Nadia."

She frowned when he closed the door to walk around to his side of the car. Why were they acting so formal with each other? This was the same man who had undressed her last night. The same man she had undressed. The man she'd given her virginity to, and who in the span of fourteen hours had taught her more positions for lovemaking than she'd thought were possible. He had packed a lot into those hours and she had no complaints.

When he got in the car, before starting the engine, he glanced over at her with concern on his features. "Still sore?"

She was about to tell him he was asking her something too personal but then pulled back. Hadn't she just thought they were acting formal with each other? For that reason, she decided to answer. "I'm fine, Jaxon. What about you? Are you sore?" She figured that question would shut him up. They were now discussing her inexperience versus his experience.

"Yes, in fact. I tried some positions with you I've never done with other women."

Yeah, right. "You could have fooled me. You seemed good at everything you were doing."

"Only because it was you."

She rolled her eyes. Did he honestly expect her to believe that? Deciding to change the subject, she said, "If the invitation is still open, I'll have lunch with you."

"Okay," he said, starting the car and driving it out of the yard.

Nadia didn't think he sounded all that enthused about it. "If you'd rather I didn't, then…"

"The invitation is still open, Nadia, and I would love for you to join me for lunch. However, I've made after-lunch plans."

"Oh."

"I'm going horseback riding."

"Horseback riding?"

"Yes. I understand the Ellerey Ranch arranges activities like that."

"They do, and they have some beautiful horses," she said.

"That's what I heard and you're welcome to join me if you like. You did say you can ride a horse, right?"

Did he not believe her? "Yes, and I recall saying I was pretty good at it."

"If you say so."

"And that's what I meant," was her retort.

Nadia wished he hadn't mentioned he was going to the Ellerey's ranch. Immediately, thoughts of Clementine Ellerey, the granddaughter of old man Ellerey, flashed in her mind. Twice divorced at thirty, the woman was known to be a man-eater. It didn't help matters that a lot of men around these parts thought she was absolutely gorgeous. Well, maybe she was. But that was no reason to deliberately sleep with someone's boyfriend or husband just because she could, if rumors could be believed. Clementine had a reputation around town and not a good one. More than likely, she would be at the ranch, especially if she got wind that Jaxon was coming. Well, Nadia had news for Clementine. Not on her watch.

Nadia turned around in her seat to face Jaxon as he came to the gate that led off the Novak Homestead. "I'd love to join you, and I can't wait to show you how well I can ride."

After picking up Nadia's car, Jaxon followed her back home. Then they had lunch at a restaurant on the outskirts of town that, in his opinion, served the best BBQ ribs he'd eaten in a long time. When they reached the Ellerey Ranch two horses were saddled and ready for them to ride.

For some reason the man's granddaughter, a woman who looked to be in her late twenties, had saddled the second horse for herself. She'd assumed Jaxon would want company and had invited herself to go riding with him. Why she'd thought such a thing when he didn't even know her, he couldn't say.

It didn't take long to figure out what she was about and he wasn't having it. He let her know that Nadia would be his riding partner. From the way she'd glared at Nadia it was obvious the woman hadn't liked that too much. Not that he'd given a royal damn.

As soon as Nadia was seated in her saddle, she had taken off and he'd chased after her. It didn't take long for her to prove she was the expert horsewoman she'd claimed to be. Not that he'd doubted it for a second. He liked ruffling her feathers. He had enjoyed racing across the valley with her and then trotting along several paths.

"Oh, look," she called out and slowed her horse.

His gaze followed to where she was pointing. A fawn was caught between the fencing. They brought their horses to a stop and Nadia was off before Jaxon could help her down. She rushed over to where the baby deer was crying for its mother.

"Poor thing," Nadia said, glancing around.

"We need to untangle it and set it free," he said. "It's my guess the mother is around here somewhere, probably watching and hoping we don't do her baby any harm. I need to grab a pair of gloves from the saddle bag."

When he returned, he saw Nadia smoothing the animal with calming words and it was no longer crying. It took them working together to untangle the fawn only because the animal was skittish and frightened. Once they had set it free, the fawn took off. Up in the distance they saw it was joined by the mother and then both animals skedaddled into the woods.

"Well, that was our excitement for today," Nadia said, smiling.

"There's a lake over there. We might as well rest the horses and let them take a drink," he said.

Going back to the horses, they grabbed the reins and walked toward the lake. "When Dad was alive there were a lot of horses on the Novak Homestead," Nadia said, leaning against a tree. "We had to sell them all when he got sick since money was needed. That's when I lost my horse. He was one of the ones we had to sell."

Jaxon nodded. This wasn't the first time she'd told him how she and her sisters had made sacrifices when their father had taken ill. Sacrifices they had been glad to make so their father could get the best medical care. The first night Jaxon had shared dinner at her place she'd told him how Pam had returned home after giving up acting. Jill had to stop her riding lessons. Yesterday, on the drive to Valley Bluff, they'd passed a dance studio and she told him Paige had been taking dance classes there until their father had gotten too sick for her to continue. Now, Nadia had told him she'd given away a horse that had meant a lot to her.

"What was your horse's name?" he asked, leaning against a tree opposite her. The fading sun highlighted her features. They were the same beautiful features he'd stared down into last night while making love to her.

"Cocoa. I named him when he was born because he was the color of rich, dark cocoa. He was the best horse a girl could ever have, and he was beautiful."

"I bet he was."

"I have a picture of me at eleven sitting on his back. It was the last one Cocoa and I took together."

Jaxon recalled seeing the framed picture on a wall in her bedroom. He could hear the sadness in her voice. It was sadness he wished he could take away. Deciding to change the subject, he said, "I wonder where this lake leads to."

Nadia told him the history of the Ellerey Ranch and

how Jamie Ellerey was the descendant of one of the town's founders. She then told him more of the town's history and how her great-great grandfather had been one of the first to settle in the area as well. While she was talking, he wondered if she would consider living somewhere else. Or was she pretty rooted here since returning after living in Denver all those years? Gamble was the type of town that could grow on you. Everyone he'd met had been hardworking and friendly. That's why he knew if Nadia preferred living here permanently, then he would, too. His home would always be with her.

"What's the deal with Ellerey's granddaughter? I take it the two of you know each other."

Nadia nodded. "I've known Clementine all my life. Her father was old man Ellerey's only child and I understand he was a real decent man. When Clementine's parents were killed in an avalanche during a ski trip, old man Ellerey raised her alone. She was only three and needless to say he spoiled her rotten. She's always been a pain in everyone's side. Even as a kid. I'd hoped her attitude had improved when I moved back years later but it hasn't. She has this entitlement complex. She believes she's entitled to anything or anyone she wants."

Jaxon had gotten that same impression.

"I'm sure you noticed how beautiful she is," Nadia added.

Yes, he'd noticed. "I'm a man who believes inner beauty is just as important as outer beauty. Even more so." There was no need to add that he'd dated a number of women who'd had the looks of a goddess but possessed hearts of stone.

"It's time to get back, Jaxon."

He glanced at his watch. It had gotten late and he hadn't been aware so much time had passed. "I enjoyed today with you, Nadia." No need to tell her again how much he'd enjoyed his night with her, too. He had pretty much proved it last night.

She didn't say anything for a minute and then stated, "And I enjoyed being with you today, too, Jaxon. But nothing has changed."

"You're wrong about that. Everything between us has changed after last night." He wouldn't waste his time saying that as far as he was concerned last night sealed the deal. "I was your first," he added.

"But that doesn't mean you'll be my last."

"That's how I intend for it to be."

A frown appeared on her face. "Don't tell me you're the male version of Clementine with an entitlement complex."

"I won't tell you that, but I will tell you this," he said, crossing the distance separating them. "I don't make it a habit to have sex with virgins. In fact, I never have before. I could have stopped things before I finished the deed, but you know why I didn't?"

"Of course I know. The same degree of lust that consumed me also consumed you."

"Lust had nothing to do with it for me. It was love."

Her eyes widened. "Love?" She threw her head back and laughed. "Oh, that's rich. Weeks ago, you said you wanted to marry me when you didn't even know me. Now today you want me to believe you've fallen in love with me? Really?"

He glared at her. "Yes, really. I fell in love with you the moment we were introduced."

She frowned and glared back. "That's not possible. Besides, I don't want any man to love me or want to marry me."

"That's tough because I do and I will." Before she could say anything else, Jaxon leaned down and planted his mouth on hers.

She didn't pull away. Instead, she wrapped her tongue around his the same way she'd done last night. Somehow their mouths always mated in perfect unity. An intense flare of heat consumed his entire body while he held her in his arms and continued to kiss her like he never wanted to stop. She might be mad at him but it was obvious she wanted this kiss as much as he did.

What was she afraid of and why?

When he finally released her lips, he stared into her eyes, which had a look that all but said she couldn't believe she had let him kiss her and that she had kissed him back. Her next words proved it. "We should not have done that."

He tilted the Stetson back from his eyes to gaze down at her. "Everything we've done or are doing was meant to be, Nadia."

The glare was back in her eyes. "I disagree. I'm ready to go, Jaxon."

"Okay, but there's something I want to ask you first."

"What?"

"Who hurt you?"

She broke eye contact with him to look away and then she looked back at him. "I don't know what you mean."

"I think you do. There's a reason you hold yourself back."

She threw her head back and laughed again. "Hold myself back? What about last night? If anything, I let myself go."

"Yes, and it took you twenty-eight years to do so. I want to know what man broke your heart to make you not want to fall in love again. Twenty-eight-year-old virgins are rare these days."

"That's none of your business, Jaxon."

"That's where you're wrong. Every single thing about you is my business, Nadia."

Jaxon watched an angry Nadia walk over to her horse. After mounting it, she glanced over at him. "No, it's not. I don't want or need a man in my life."

"Well, I want and need you in mine, Nadia."

She glared at him before nudging her horse and taking off racing across the field.

Nadia was quiet on the drive back to the Novak Homestead. Jaxon thought about engaging her in conversation but decided against it. He'd said his piece so he let her stew. But anger or no anger, he could still feel the sexual chemistry surrounding them in the confines of the car. In a way, he really shouldn't have been surprised. If nothing else, last night proved just how combustible they were. How well connected. For her, it might only have been lust, but for him it was love.

When he brought the car to a stop in front of the house, she got out without waiting for him to come around to open the car door for her. "Don't bother. I can see myself inside."

Ignoring what she said, he got out anyway and walked a few paces behind her. He shouldn't be noticing, but he liked the way her jeans shaped her backside and loved the sashay of her hips when she walked. The woman couldn't help being sexy no matter what she put on her body or took off of it.

When she reached the door and unlocked it, she did glance over her shoulder to say, "Thank you."

"You're welcome and flick the curtains or open the blinds to let me know you're safe inside. And Nadia?"

She slowly turned to him. He hadn't even come up the steps to the porch. Instead, he stood back. He knew if he got too close, he would want to pull her into his arms and kiss her. "I meant everything I said about my feelings for you. I love you and have from the moment we were introduced. If you change your mind about me, about us, then you know how to reach me."

He watched her go inside and closed the door. He didn't move off the steps to return to his car until she had flicked the curtain.

Seventeen

Nadia jumped when Rissa snapped her fingers in front of Nadia's face. She hadn't known her best friend had even moved out of the chair. Nadia frowned. "What did you do that for?"

Rissa returned to her chair in front of Nadia's desk. "To get your attention. You've been zoning out on me since I got here. Do you want to talk about it?"

She was about to tell Rissa that no, she didn't want to talk about it. Rissa had been trying to get information out of Nadia since the moment she'd arrived. However, the teasing glint in Rissa's eyes had been replaced with concern. She heard it in her friend's voice and saw it in her face.

Other than her sisters, Rissa knew Nadia better than anyone. If she could feel Nadia was out of sorts, then her worry was justified. Nadia was not one to let a man get under her skin. Yet Jaxon had done so.

"Jaxon and I argued."

Rissa nodded her head as if not surprised. "The two of you have been at odds since he told you he wanted to marry you. I thought you guys had declared a truce or something since you slept with him Friday night."

"It's gotten worse."

Rissa lifted a brow. "How?"

"Now he thinks he's in love with me."

Rissa stared at her for a moment and then asked, "He actually told you that?"

"Yes. It was when we'd gone riding at the Ellerey Ranch on Saturday. We were at the lake letting our horses rest and he said he loved me. He also said he felt entitled to me because he was the first guy I slept with."

Rissa frowned. "Did he really say that?"

"No, but that's the way he acted."

"Or is that the way you took it, Nadia? I know you. And the one thing I do know is you have a tendency to make a mountain out of a molehill."

When Nadia didn't say anything, Rissa leaned back in her chair and studied her. "Why do I have the feeling you aren't telling me everything?"

Probably because she wasn't, Nadia thought. She hadn't told Rissa of her unusual feeling of jealousy when she'd seen a picture of Jaxon's administrative assistant on his website and how relieved she was when he'd said the beautiful woman was getting married. Nor had she told her how she'd deliberately gone horseback riding with him just so Clementine Ellerey wouldn't get her clutches in him.

"I'm getting jealous where Jaxon is concerned."

Rissa raised a brow. "Jealous in what way?"

She then told Rissa of the two situations and when a smile spread across Rissa's lips, she asked, "Why are you smiling?"

"Because you're not a woman who makes a habit of getting jealous over a man. That could only mean one thing."

"What?"

"You care for Jaxon Ravnel more than you're admitting to me and, more importantly, to yourself."

"I don't want a man in my life. Especially not him."

"Why not him?" Rissa asked with a sheen of curiosity in her eyes.

Nadia inhaled deeply as she struggled to say the words to make Rissa understand. "Because Jaxon is too good to be true. Everybody likes him. I told you how he exposed that man who was deceiving the Outlaws. He didn't have to do that, but he did. Now the Westmorelands and Outlaws think he's a swell guy. Even all the women in the family like him."

"All the women but you." Rissa hadn't stated it as a question.

"I don't dislike him."

Rissa chuckled. "Heck, I hope not after all that bumping and grinding the two of you did Friday night and early Saturday morning."

Nadia shrugged. "Women have been known to sleep with men they don't like."

"Not most women and definitely not you." Rissa finished the last of her coffee and tossed the cup in the trash can at the side of Nadia's desk. "But I still don't understand. Why are you afraid of getting involved with Jaxon? Do you think he will play you like Benson did?"

"Of course not."

"Then what is it, Nadia?"

"I'm not his type. He should be interested in a woman with grace and refinement. One full of sophistication."

"That's utter nonsense. If Jaxon says he loves you and wants to marry you then that means you are the woman he wants. Besides, worrying about if you're Jaxon's type might be the least of your problems, Nadia."

"What do you mean?"

"You know Jaxon. Your mouth knows him. Your tongue knows him. In other words, your entire being knows him. I bet you spent this weekend remembering how good things were with him. How the real thing was better compared to your dreams. How he knocked all your fantasies right out of the ballpark."

Nadia rolled her eyes, refusing to admit everything Rissa said was true. "You act as if Jaxon will become an addiction."

"It's a good chance he might. Maybe he already is. I think you've fallen for Jaxon, but you're fighting it like hell."

Nadia sat straight up in her chair. "I don't love Jaxon."

Rissa waved off her words. "You can deny it all you want but the signs are there. Anytime you mention his name your eyes light up. Your breathing changes. Personally, I think it's wonderful that he loves you and wants to marry you and has told you so. How many men are that up front with a woman?" Rissa then glanced at her watch and stood. "I gotta leave now to get to work on time. Remember I'll be out of town the rest of the week on that business trip to San Diego. However, if you need to talk, I'll just be a phone call away."

Nadia nodded, knowing this issue with Jaxon was something she had to figure out for herself.

It was past six on Thursday when Nadia finally left the academy for home. Usually, she didn't work so late but Langley had called with the budget for Ravnel Technologies' sponsorship. It was more than she and her staff had anticipated. Definitely a lot more than the Dunnings Financial Group had agreed to give them. Langley even mentioned that Jaxon had suggested using the local theater instead of the high school's auditorium. Additional funds would be allotted if she chose to do so.

She had immediately liked the idea and had called an impromptu meeting with her staff to see what they thought. Everyone got all excited. They couldn't wait to share the news with the students tomorrow.

Jill and Paige had called before Nadia had closed up her office. Both were excited about the surprise party for Quade Westmoreland's wife, Cheyenne, this weekend and wanted to know when she'd be arriving. When she'd told them she had just purchased her ticket that morning, Paige asked why she hadn't caught a ride with Jaxon on his plane. Saying he probably would not have minded since he would be attending the party, too.

She'd told Paige there was no way she could have

imposed like that. What if he was bringing a date? Jill agreed with Nadia and said although Jaxon had never brought a woman to any of the family's functions before, that didn't mean he would never bring one. After all Jaxon was single and good-looking. Paige still thought it shouldn't be an issue. All Jaxon had to do was to tell his date that Nadia was nothing more than a family friend.

Nothing more than a family friend...

She hadn't yet told her sisters how her relationship with Jaxon had taken a turn since that time she'd invited him to dinner. In a way, she was glad she hadn't shared the news since she and Jaxon were back to not having a relationship at all, although according to Jaxon, he loved her and wanted to marry her.

She would admit she wasn't as shocked now by what he'd said as she had been on Saturday. That had been five days ago. Since then she'd done a lot of thinking. Rissa had been right. Nadia was falling for Jaxon.

It had taken her five days and sleepless nights to finally accept that. She had thought a lot about him since Saturday and now it was Thursday. She missed him and constantly replayed in her mind the time they'd spent together. She also replayed in her mind the dinners they'd shared, both at her home and on his jet.

However, more than anything she thought about that day last year when they'd been introduced. She had been attracted to him from the start and, according to him, he'd been more than attracted. He claimed he'd fallen in love with her. Could she believe that? Hadn't he said at lunch that day that his father had fallen in love with his mother the same way?

She'd also heard about such things happening to a couple of the Westmoreland men, like Bane. He swore he'd fallen for Crystal when he'd come upon her walking home from school. He hadn't hesitated to turn his motorcycle around and introduce himself. And Dillon claimed he'd fallen in love with Pam even though she'd been engaged to Fletcher. Could she believe such a thing happened to Jaxon?

Getting into her car, she started the engine. As she drove out of the parking lot, she thought about what she'd seen that night when they'd viewed the Milky Way. She hadn't mentioned it to Rissa because her friend was one of those believers and would have sworn that was the sign Nadia needed that she and Jaxon were destined to share everlasting love. Were they?

I meant everything I said about my feelings for you. I love you and have from the moment we were introduced. If you change your mind about me, about us, then you know how to reach me.

Why was she remembering Jaxon's words now? Why had she thought of them a lot this week? Why was her heart beating so fast? And why was she getting off the exit that would take her to Jaxon's hotel? It was one of the newest hotels in the city and she'd heard it was one of the fanciest. When it was first built it had seemed out of place in a ranch town. However, now it fit. More importantly, it fit a man like Jaxon.

She pulled into his hotel and parked her car. Why was she here? Would he be upset that she showed up unannounced? She couldn't worry about that now. The one thing she did know was that she missed him and more than anything she wanted to see him.

Jaxon was about to order room service when he heard the knock at his hotel room door. He frowned, hoping like hell it wasn't Clementine Ellerey. The woman had had the audacity to come to his hotel room a few days ago. He'd opened the door, but of course he hadn't let her in.

He'd tried telling her in the nicest way that he wasn't interested. When it seemed his words were falling on deaf ears, he'd had to be frank. She wasn't his type and he would appreciate if she left him alone and moved on and not invite herself to his hotel room again. Ms. Ellerey hadn't liked that one iota and threatened to ruin his name in town by saying he'd sexually harassed her. There had been no doubt in her mind the townspeople would believe her over him. After all, she was a hometown girl and that meant something in Gamble.

He was glad he'd anticipated she would make such a move, after that stunt she'd tried on Saturday and after hearing Nadia's opinion of her. Saturday night he'd called Martin Lockley, the man who handled all his security, to run a check on her. He'd gotten Lockley's report first thing Monday morning and it was rather colorful and informative.

There were four men in Gamble she was currently sleeping with behind their wives' backs. When he'd told Ms. Ellerey everything he knew about her and assured her he wouldn't hesitate to share the report with the good people of Gamble if she carried out her threats, she quickly left.

He glanced out his door's peephole. It wasn't Clementine Ellerey but was the woman who'd been on his mind constantly since parting ways with her on Saturday evening. That had been five days ago and although he'd missed her like hell, he'd wanted to give her space to think about all he'd said. Things he had no intention of backing down on.

Had she come to give him another piece of her mind or was she here because she believed what he'd said? As if she knew he was staring at her, she stared back and sensations ripped through him. He had to breathe slowly for air to flow through his lungs.

Opening the door to his suite, he didn't bother to ask what she was doing there. It didn't matter because he was glad to see her. "Hello, Nadia."

"Hello, Jaxon. May I come in?"

As far as he was concerned, she could come in and stay and never leave. "Yes," he said and stepped aside for her to enter.

She was certainly getting a different reception than the one he'd given Clementine Ellerey. But then this was the woman he was deeply in love with. The one he wanted more than anything to share his life with. She looked good in her plaid pencil skirt, earth-tone suede knee-high boots and matching suede jacket.

He shoved his hands into the pockets of his pants. Otherwise, he would be tempted to reach out and pull her into his arms. Desire between them was always intense, heated and charged. Tonight, it seemed even more so. Sexual chemistry dominated the air they shared, like usual. They stood staring at each other, feeling it shimmering around them.

The moonlight filtering through the curtains seemed to fill the room with an ethereal light that bathed her in a radiant glow. Maybe it was his eyes, but she appeared even more beautiful tonight than ever before. The room seemed electrified. He was convinced all it would take was a touch to send sparks flying.

"I want to thank you for that suggestion you made for the academy to hold the play at the theater in town," she finally broke the silence to say.

He nodded. "You didn't have to come all the way over here to thank me, Nadia."

"I know. That's not the only reason I'm here."

"It's not?"

"No. I felt the need to talk to you about something, Jaxon."

He wondered what she wanted to talk about. Just her being here in his hotel suite was causing heat to stir in his groin. More than anything, he needed to keep his control in check. "Okay, come into the sitting area. We can talk there," he said, leading the way. His suite was spacious, but at the moment it seemed way too cozy.

"Please have a seat," he said, offering her the sofa. When she moved around him, her hips accidentally brushed against his. Suddenly, like a magnet, their bodies connected, and he drew her to him and lowered his head to hers.

Eighteen

The moment Jaxon's lips touched hers, Nadia felt energized, mesmerized and totally captivated. Automatically, her arms went around his neck and her body pressed hard against his. She felt him; there were just some things a man couldn't hide and a full-blown erection was one of them.

And now he was kissing her the way she wanted. The way she needed. It always amazed her how his tongue could work its way around her mouth, eliciting hers to participate and duel in the most sensuous way. Every bone in her body felt completely enthralled. Whenever he kissed her, she was incapable of holding back. He made her feel things she'd never felt before, and all from a kiss. But she knew tonight they would share more than a kiss. The reason she'd come was to talk, but she had no problem getting this first. Like him, she needed it now. Talking would come later.

When he swept her into his arms without breaking the kiss, she tightened her hold around his neck. He wanted her and she wanted him. Something else she knew now with all certainty was that she *did* love him. The moment he had opened the door and she'd looked into his face, she'd known. The face she had dreamed about for over a year, the face that belonged to her fantasy man. She could not fight emotions she'd been too afraid to face any longer.

Jaxon broke off the kiss when he placed her on the bed. Then he stepped back, held her gaze and began removing his clothes. Likewise, she began dispensing with hers. No words were spoken. None were needed. Their kiss had told them everything.

"I've missed you," he said in a deep, throaty voice.

She was about to tell him that he'd known where to find her, but didn't. She had needed the space, the distance and the longing. She was even glad Rissa had been out of town on that business trip. Nadia's feelings for Jaxon were something she'd needed to figure out for herself, and she had.

Staring deep into his gaze, she said, "And I missed you, too. I'm here now and so are you."

He nodded. "And that's all that matters."

Moving closer to the bed, he pulled her into his arms and she went willingly. Together they fell back onto the mattress with their lips joined. She doubted she would ever tire of being kissed by him. His kisses were always mind-blowingly hot.

Moments later, he broke off the kiss, and in a surprise move, he shifted his body so she was on top of him. At the questioning look he must have seen in her eyes, he said, "Tonight, I want you to ride me. After seeing you on a horse I know how good you are at it."

She smiled down at him. "I plan to do my best."

Jaxon quickly concluded that if Nadia got any better she would kill him. She was riding him right into another orgasm. The third for the both of them. She would come and he would follow like clockwork. It was like she hadn't gotten enough of him any more than he'd gotten enough of her. How long would they keep this up? Probably until neither had strength to do anything else.

With each and every upward thrust from him, she would grind her hips against his in a way that had an abundance of liquid heat coiling in his erection. He gazed up into her eyes and what he saw took his breath away. He didn't see lust-filled eyes but ones full of something else. But then, maybe he was seeing what he wanted to see and not what was really there.

All thoughts fled his mind when the sounds of Nadia's moans reached a high peak. Just the thought that she was riding him with the expertise she'd ridden that horse on Saturday made his breath rush from his lungs. She continued to take him inch by incredibly sweet inch.

Now her hips were coming down faster and harder. Every cell in his body was set and ready to explode the moment she did. She was still tight and he could feel her body tighten even more and pulse around him. And each time she came down on him their gazes caught and locked. He cupped a hand across her bottom, loving the feel of the movement she made every time their bodies connected.

"Jaxon!"

Then it happened. An explosion that plunged them into sweet oblivion. When she came downward on him again, he dragged his tongue over her face, licking the moisture that had accumulated there. Another shudder of pleasure tore through them and this time it was him who yelled out her name.

"Nadia!"

Waves of pleasure shot through every part of him and then detonated on glorious impact. He knew that for as long as he lived every time they came together would be burned into his memory as well as his heart. When her body collapsed on his, he wrapped his arms around her and held her tight. Unable to hold it back, he whispered. "I love you, Nadia."

She went still and then lifted her head off his chest and looked into his eyes. "And I love you, too."

Then she closed her eyes and slept.

Nadia came awake to the feel of someone's tongue licking across her face. Slowly opening her eyes, she met Jaxon's gaze. He was no longer in the bed with her but was sitting on the side of the mattress next to her. When she reached out to him, he pulled her into his lap and gave her a kiss that she felt all the way to her toes.

When he released her mouth, he said, "Did you mean what you said?"

She knew what he was asking and nodded. "Yes."

She drew in a deep breath and with it came the scent of their lovemaking that was still very potent in the room. "There is so much I need to tell you, Jaxon."

"Okay, but we need to eat first."

"Eat?"

"Yes, I ordered room service. I don't know about you, but I'm famished."

She was hungry, too, since she hadn't eaten since lunch. She glanced over at the clock on his nightstand. "It's after ten?"

"Yes. We've been busy."

She couldn't help but smile. That was an understatement. He stood with her in his arms and placed her on her feet. "Do I need to run warm bathwater for you or are you okay?"

"I'm okay." Nodding, he went to the closet and grabbed one of the hotel's complimentary robes. It was a match to the one he was wearing. "I don't have a problem if you want to walk around naked, but I figure we need to give our bodies a rest while we eat."

She totally agreed. As soon as she slid into her robe, which he helped her do, he swept her back into his arms and carried her out of the bedroom to the dining area, where a table for two was set up. Complete with candles and wineglasses. Several bottles of champagne sat chilling in an ice-bucket.

"The table setting is beautiful. But what's with the champagne? You do know I have to go to work tomorrow, right?" she said, when he placed her in her chair.

"You sure you don't want to play hooky?"

"I want to but I'd better not. Besides, I'm getting off

early tomorrow to pack and fly to DC tomorrow evening for Cheyenne's surprise birthday party."

"Cancel your flight. You can fly with me on my jet. I'm leaving tomorrow as well."

"What time?"

"Whenever you're ready to go. My time is your time."

"Thanks." She uncovered her dishes and smiled. "This looks delicious," she said of the steak and potatoes on her plate.

"It is. I've had it before and the chef here is pretty good. I believe you will enjoy it."

She did. Over dinner she told him how excited her staff was about his sponsorship and how a special assembly was scheduled tomorrow morning where it would be announced that the venue for the play would be the theater instead of the high school's auditorium.

"I can't wait to see the student's faces." She reached across the table and squeezed his hand. "Thank you."

He smiled at her. "I was happy to do it." He glanced at both their empty plates. "Are you ready for our talk now?"

She nodded. "Yes, I'm ready."

Not wanting Nadia too far away from him, Jaxon gathered her into his arms, carried her over to the sofa and sat down with her in his lap. "Now tell me what we need to talk about, sweetheart."

It took her a minute to speak, and he figured she was collecting her thoughts. That had to be the reason she was looking down while fidgeting with the buttons on her robe. Finally, she said, "His name was Benson

Cummings. I met him at the University of Wyoming the second week of class. I immediately liked him since he seemed like a nice guy. It only took me five months to find out what a total ass he was when it was discovered he was keeping a journal of all the freshmen girls he'd slept with or planned to sleep with. I was on his to-do list. Not only that, he had the date by my name and his friends were going to video us doing it." She paused. "I was hurt since I honestly thought he liked me as much as I'd liked him. I had fallen hard for him, Jaxon."

"So what did you do about it?" he asked her when she got silent, looking back down at the buttons on her robe. He was fighting back the anger he felt for what the guy had done and had planned to do.

She lifted her head to gaze into his eyes. "What do you mean what did I do about it?"

Jaxon fought back a smile. Those innocent-looking eyes staring into his weren't fooling him any. She was a renegade, a rebel and a hellion. She would not have let that Cummings guy get away with anything. "Just what I asked, Nadia. What did you do about it?"

She went back to fidgeting with the buttons again. Clearing her throat she said, "Well, there was that time we emptied twenty-five bottles of chocolate syrup into his car and then dumped several bags of live ants in there as well."

Jaxon's eyes widened. "Who were 'we' and where did you get bags of live ants?"

She looked back up at him and smiled. "We, meaning me, Rissa and Lilli. And as for the live ants, it just so happens that one of the agricultural labs on campus was working on several ant farms. We got them from there." Nadia paused and said, "Then there was that other incident."

"What other incident?"

"The one that got him expelled from school."

Jaxon was almost too afraid to ask what Nadia had done to make that happen. "Tell me about it."

"We found out he was sneaking girls from another campus into his dorm room for pot parties. The kind that ended up being orgies. The security guy on campus got an anonymous tip about it and Benson, his roommates and several others were caught red-handed. All naked as the day they were born."

"I guess you were the one who provided the anonymous tip."

"Of course." She laughed and he couldn't help but laugh as well.

"Cummings never traced his misfortunes back to you?"

"Nope. I played the innocent. Besides, he had over twenty girls' names on that list. It could have been any of us out for revenge."

But it was you, he thought. Good for her. "And because of him you were cautious about getting serious about any guy again?"

"Yes. But years passed and when I moved back to Gamble, I decided to have an open mind. Especially with so many good-looking cowboys around here. The first one I met was Hoyle Adams. Like Benson, he seemed nice enough. He asked me out to the movies, and I enjoyed myself. He seemed to be a perfect gentleman. So I invited him to dinner one evening."

"And?"

She frowned. "And he thought the dinner invitation was really a sleepover. Imagine my shock when he went out to his truck for his overnight bag while I was in the kitchen getting dessert. He honestly thought he was spending the night. I tossed him and his overnight bag out the door."

He fought back a grin. "No wonder you went off on me that night I asked about inviting a cowboy to dinner."

"Yes, that was the reason." She got quiet and then said, "Just so you know, Jaxon, I was attracted to you from the first. But I thought it was one sided since you weren't paying me any attention. I didn't want to make a fool of myself so I deliberately avoided you."

"Like I told you, I was trying to play it safe by not showing my interest in you immediately. The last thing I wanted was one of my Outlaw cousins or the Westmorelands to challenge me to a fistfight for getting out of line with you."

She chuckled. "They would not have done that. If anything, they would have warned you away from me. They know how I can be at times."

"I take it you never told them about Cummings."

"There was no need. I handled it."

She most certainly had. "Is there anything else I need to know?"

She turned around to face him and wrapped her arms around his neck. "Nothing other than I meant what I said in bed. I love you. I fought it. I kept telling myself I couldn't love you because we didn't know each other. I even convinced myself it was just lust, but I was wrong."

"And when did you realize you were wrong and it was more than lust?"

"Tonight. The minute you opened the door. Seeing you again put a lot of things in perspective. I had missed you so much and it had only been five days. I wondered how I would handle it if it had been five weeks, five months or five years. That's when I knew I loved you, Jaxon."

"And I love you, sweetheart. And I meant what I told you that night. I intend to marry you one day. Granted, I hadn't planned to tell you about my plans that soon, but I felt I had to be honest with you. I didn't want you to think all I was interested in was sex."

She smiled. "It was hard to believe you were serious since most men run away from marriage."

"Not me. My parents set good examples for me to follow."

"Are you sure about me? I'm not a sophisticated or refined kind of woman."

"Trust me, you're the kind of woman I need, want and desire."

"And speaking of desire…" she whispered against his lips. "What will it take for you to give me one more steamy night?"

"All you have to do is ask."

"Well, I'm asking, Jaxon."

He stood with her in his arms and headed for the bedroom.

Nineteen

Nadia knew the moment her sisters Jill and Paige arrived at Cheyenne Steele Westmoreland's birthday party, which was being held in the nation's capital at the Saxon Hotel. The huge ballroom of the luxurious hotel was beautifully decorated with balloons and birthday streamers. Nadia had seen her sister Pam when she first arrived a short while ago.

To say Cheyenne had been surprised about the party was an understatement. Quade had told her they would be attending another joint fundraiser for his two senator cousins, Reggie Westmoreland and Jess Outlaw. She hadn't suspected a thing and the look on her face when she'd entered the ballroom to discover the party was in her honor was priceless.

Nadia thought it was good seeing so many Westmorelands and Outlaws together. If anyone found it odd that Jaxon was always by her side, they didn't mention it. However, several women in the family did give her curious looks. The men did not, and she thought that was rather strange.

She braced herself when she saw Jill and Paige make a beeline straight to her. None of her sisters had a clue about her and Jaxon. She hadn't had a chance to pull them aside to tell them anything yet.

After greeting everyone in the group standing around Nadia, Paige and Jill gave their sister a hug. "When did you arrive in town?" Paige asked.

"I got in early today." No need to tell her that her plans to arrive yesterday had been waylaid when instead of helping her pack like he claimed he would do, Jaxon had kept her on her back in bed. But then she'd kept him on his back a few times as well.

"That's why we couldn't reach you. You were probably in the air," Jill surmised.

"Probably. I caught a ride with Jaxon on his jet."

Both women shifted their gazes to Jaxon and smiled. "Thanks for getting her here. Does that mean you didn't bring a date?" Jill asked.

Jaxon lifted a brow. "A date?"

"Yes. We had suggested early in the week that Nadia catch a ride here with you, but she was worried you might be bringing a date and didn't want to impose," Paige said.

Jaxon smiled back. "Oh, I see. And to answer your question, yes, I brought a date. In fact, I brought the woman I intend to marry as soon as she's ready to tell me yes."

Nadia noticed several people around them had their eyes and ears on Jaxon and she knew why. He'd never mentioned being in a serious relationship with anyone. "Really?" Paige said, smiling brightly.

Jill's and Paige's gazes searched the group surrounding them before glancing around the room. They then turned their gazes back to Jaxon. "Where is she? We can't wait to meet her," Jill said.

A huge smile spread across Jaxon's lips. "She's standing right in front of you." He wrapped his arm around Nadia's waist before leaning in to brush a kiss on her lips.

"What! When! How!" Her sisters' squeals of excitement caused others to look their way. Then others came over to join them to hear the details.

"Don't tell me you and Jaxon pulled a secret affair like me and Aidan," Jill said, grinning from ear to ear.

Nadia chuckled as she leaned back against Jaxon. "There was nothing secret about us, trust me. None of you were in Gamble to get into our business."

Paige was about to make a comment when suddenly Clint Westmoreland, who was standing in the group, exclaimed, "Who the hell is that guy that just walked in?"

Everyone turned toward the entrance of the ballroom. It was Chance Steele, one of Cheyenne's cousins, who answered, "That's Dominic's best friend, Matt Caulder. They were raised together as brothers. Do you know him?"

Before Clint could answer, his brother Cole and his sister Casey, along with their spouses, walked up. Nadia noticed that the same shocked look that was on Clint's face was on his siblings'. His sister Casey asked Clint in a deep, emotional voice. "Do you see that guy's face, Clint?"

"Yes, I see it."

Now everyone was curious as to what was going on. Nadia studied the guy who seemed to be in his midforties and who she thought was very handsome and distinguished looking.

"Hey, while you're all interested in the guy, I want to know about the young woman with him," Alisdare Westmoreland said. "Is that his wife, girlfriend, sister or daughter?" Nadia could only assume Alisdare, who at twenty-nine was single and worked as a FBI agent, was hoping it was one of the latter two.

"The young lady with Matt is his daughter," Sebastian Steele, another one of Cheyenne's cousins, said. He turned to Clint. "Why the interest in Matt? What's wrong with his face?"

Clint glanced over at him and said, "Nothing, other than it's the spitting image of our Uncle Sid, and we want to know why."

It was after midnight when Jaxon opened his hotel room door and stepped aside to let Nadia enter. Thanks to Dominic everyone attending Cheyenne's birthday party was given complimentary accommodations. Jaxon had upgraded to one of the larger suites on the other side of the hotel for privacy.

A lot of celebrating had been going on, not just for Cheyenne's birthday but once news got around that the Westmoreland triplets—Clint, Cole and Casey—had found their long-lost cousin, the son of Sid Roberts, the legendary rodeo star and renowned horse trainer. Matt Caulder had never known the identity of his biological father, but that night he learned that Sid had hired someone to find him, and they'd looked for him for years, but they never found him. Everyone was excited when the triplets' father, Corey Westmoreland, had welcomed Matt to the Westmoreland family as an honorary member. In a shocking move, Bart Outlaw had done the same.

Jaxon was glad that since accepting his relationship to the Westmorelands, Bart was doing a better job of connecting. Jaxon's Outlaw cousins thought Bart's marriage to Claudia had a lot to do with it and Jaxon would agree. Bart could still be his ornery self at times but these days he was more hospitable and sociable. Jaxon's parents had even invited Bart and Claudia to Virginia over the summer, so his mother could visit with her cousin Bart. The two couples got along wonderfully.

"It was a great party, wasn't it?"

Nadia's words cut into Jaxon's thoughts as he leaned against the closed hotel room door and watched as she kicked off her stilettos. She had worn a short and sexy dress that showed what a great pair of legs she had. "Yes, it was. There were quite a number of revelations tonight. The one that really took me by surprise was Quade and Cheyenne's announcement that they're having another baby," Nadia said. "Their triplets are in their early teens. But they'd always said they wanted other kids. It will be funny if they have another set of triplets like Bane and Crystal."

"Well, according to Quade they aren't worried about

it. If it happens, it happens," Jaxon said, moving away from the door. "And what do you think of Quade's father James's announcement that he's located more Westmorelands?"

Nadia chuckled. "From the cheers that went up around the ballroom, I think everyone was happy and excited about it. James is considered the genealogist in the family. I understand he's been on the trail of those particular Westmorelands for a while. Ever since it was reported in a national newspaper some years back that the wife of some man with the last name Westmoreland had given birth to quadruplets."

Jaxon smiled as he came to stand in front of her. "I'm sure that was the first clue there might be a connection."

"What?"

"Multiple births. It seems such a thing runs rampant with the Westmorelands and Outlaws."

Nadia threw her head back and laughed. "You noticed?"

"Can't help but notice. I think Adrian and Aidan get a kick out of fooling me every time. I still can't tell them apart."

She reached up and wrapped her arms around his neck. "Maybe one day I'll let you in on the secret as to how to do that."

He leaned in and nibbled around her lips. "Promise?"

"Um, yes. A number of people were surprised to discover we're together. Mostly the ladies. The men, however, didn't seem surprised. Would you care to explain that?"

He leaned back and stared down at her. "They weren't surprised because they knew I intended to marry you."

She lifted a brow. "And just how did they know that?"

"I told them when we were together at the poker tournament in Westmoreland Country."

"That was in August. Three months ago."

"I know," he said, smiling. "I knew from the first that you were the woman for me. Am I the man for you, Nadia?"

She lifted up on tiptoes to brush her lips across his and whispered, "Yes, Jaxon, you are definitely the man for me."

"Good." He then swept her into his arms and carried her to the bedroom. He placed her on her feet beside the bed. Stepping back, he reached for the duffel bag he'd placed there earlier and retrieved a small white box. Kneeling on one knee in front of her, he said, "If you believe that then will you marry me? Will you share my life, my name and my babies as my wife?"

Tears filled her eyes as she nodded and said, "Yes!"

Jaxon slid his ring on her finger, stood and pulled her into his arms. "You have made me a happy man, and just so you know, my parents knew about my intentions as well. I talked to them earlier and they want you to know they are excited to welcome you to the family."

"Oh, Jaxon," she said, wiping away the tears that had appeared in her eyes as she gazed down at her ring. "It's beautiful. I'm so happy."

"So am I, sweetheart. So am I."

He then leaned in and captured her mouth in his.

Epilogue

Nadia's heart nearly stopped when saw Jaxon standing beneath the beautifully decorated gazebo that overlooked Gemma Lake. It was a beautiful day in June and it was her wedding day. Jaxon had wanted a Christmas wedding, but she had talked him out of that. So much was already on her plate with the holiday play, and she wouldn't have time to plan the type of wedding she'd always wanted. Besides, she'd always wanted a June wedding.

For the time being, he had moved into the house on the Novak Homestead with her. He'd been kept busy with getting everything set up for the expansion of Ravnel Technologies into Gamble. The weekend following Cheyenne's birthday party, he had flown Nadia to his home in Virginia. She had fallen in love with his ranch immediately and couldn't wait to move there after they married. His parents had been awesome and were happy for them. She knew she was blessed to be getting such wonderful in-laws.

She glanced around at all the people in attendance—family, friends and some of Jaxon's business associates. Alpha, Riley's wife, was the event planner in the Westmoreland family. Everything was beautifully decorated in colors of pink and black. Her sisters and the women in the family thought Nadia had gone loco when she told them of her decision to break from tradition and wear a black wedding dress instead of a white one.

The one person who thought it was a great idea was Jaxon's mother. She had worn black on her wedding day and offered Nadia her wedding dress to wear. It was beautiful and the moment Nadia had tried it on she thought it embodied elegance. Made of intricate floral lace appliqués and embellished with over five thousand beads and sequins. She especially loved the illusion plunge bodice and lace-trimmed keyhole back. The soft, sweeping skirt had a double slit that would swish with her every step.

Once she'd explained to them a black wedding dress symbolized the bride's undying love and commitment to her husband until death do them part, they understood. And when they saw her in it for the first time, they cried. Now seeing how Jaxon was staring at her let her know she'd made the right decision because he knew what wearing the black wedding dress meant.

"You're ready, Nadia?"

She glanced over at the man who would be walking her down the aisle and smiled. "Yes, Dillon. I'm ready."

And she was. She loved Jaxon and was looking forward to sharing the rest of her life with him. She smiled as she strolled closer to him then looked over at her twenty bridesmaids, who were pretty in their beautiful pink gowns. Pam was her matron of honor and Jaxon's father was his best man. The groomsmen wore black tuxes with pink shirts and black bow ties.

Anyone who hadn't known of Nadia's plans to wear a black wedding dress were first sending choruses of "What?" around the room. And then those choruses were replaced with oohs and ahhs... She glanced at her mother-in-law, who winked at her, and she winked back. Her mother-in-law was silently telling her she looked beautiful. Nadia felt beautiful.

When they reached Jaxon and the minister asked who was giving her away, Dillon spoke up and then placed her hand in Jaxon's. Nadia leaned over to kiss Dillon's cheek and said, "Thanks for everything and thanks for marrying Pammie and making us a part of your family."

She then turned to Jaxon and smiled. Just like her wedding dress signified, he was the man she would love for the rest of her life.

"And where are you taking me, Jaxon?" Nadia asked as he held her hand.

"To my barn."

He glanced down at his wife of less than twenty-four hours. After the wedding and reception, instead of flying straight to the Maldives, where they would spend a two-week honeymoon, he had flown her to his ranch, where he wanted to present her with her wedding gift.

They had changed out of their wedding attire and were both wearing jeans. He doubted she would ever know how he felt the moment he'd seen her on Dillon's arm. Just knowing he was married to the beautiful woman by his side filled his heart with joy.

"Did I tell you how beautiful you looked in your wedding dress, Nadia?"

She smiled up at him. "Yes, but I'll never get tired of your compliments, so keep them coming."

He threw his head back and laughed. Both the wedding and reception, which had been attended by over three hundred people, had gone off beautifully. "What's up with Sloan's best friend Redford St. James and Leslie's best friend, Carmen Golan?" Jaxon asked.

Nadia chuckled. "So you noticed? Well, Carmen let it be known at Sloan and Leslie's wedding a few years ago that she's going to be the woman who ends Redford's womanizing ways. Redford doesn't intend for that to happen since he loves his life just the way it is. Usually, he tries to avoid Carmen, but it seems there was no such luck at our wedding."

"He might be avoiding her, but I denote some interest on his part," Jaxon said.

"Yes, but it's I-want-to-bed-you interest and not I-want-to-wed-you interest. The latter is what Carmen wants."

They stepped into his huge barn and when Nadia saw what he intended for her to see, she released a loud squeal. "Cocoa!"

She then raced over toward the horse. By the time Jaxon joined her she looked at him with tears in her eyes. "How did you find him? Cocoa was sold sixteen years ago," she said, hugging the huge stallion. It was obvious the horse remembered her as well.

"It wasn't easy. Luckily Pam knew the people he was sold to. Zane was able to track him down for me. Over the past sixteen years he's had four owners and each one used him as a stud horse. Zane was able to locate his present owner, a rancher in North Dakota. He didn't want to part with him until he saw how much I was willing to pay. And seeing the look on your face just now made buying him back worth it."

"Thanks so much. I want to go riding."

"You will but not with him, with me."

He knew the moment she'd figured out what he meant. Releasing the horse, she turned and wrapped her arms around his neck. "That can be arranged. When do we leave for the Maldives?"

"Anytime after breakfast in the morning."

Nadia's smile widened. "In that case, I want a wedding night we will always remember. And I have no problem doing the riding."

Jaxon grinned. "Tonight, we will both ride. I plan to make our wedding night as steamy as hell."

When he swept her into his arms, she said, "Another steamy night is just what I need."

He then carried her out of the barn toward their home.

* * * * *

Dear Reader,

Your opinions are important to us. So if you'll participate in our fast and free "One Minute" Survey, YOU can pick up to four wonderful books that WE pay for when you try the Harlequin Reader Service!

As a leading publisher of women's fiction, we'd love to hear from you. That's why we promise to reward you for completing our survey.

IMPORTANT: Please complete the survey and return it. We'll send your Free Books and a Free Mystery Gift right away. And we pay for shipping and handling too! *← We pay for EVERYTHING!*

Try **Harlequin® Desire** and get 2 books featuring the worlds of the American elite with juicy plot twists, delicious sensuality and intriguing scandal.

Try **Harlequin Presents® Larger-Print** and get 2 books featuring the glamourous lives of royals and billionaires in a world of exotic locations, where passion knows no bounds.

Or TRY BOTH!

Thank you again for participating in our "One Minute" Survey. It really takes just a minute (or less) to complete the survey… and your free books and gift will be well worth it!

If you continue with your subscription, you can look forward to curated monthly shipments of brand-new books from your selected series, always at a discount off the cover price! Plus you can cancel any time. So don't miss out, return your One Minute Survey today to get your Free books.

Pam Powers

"One Minute" Survey

GET YOUR FREE BOOKS AND A FREE GIFT!

✓ Complete this Survey ✓ Return this survey

▼ DETACH AND MAIL CARD TODAY! ▼

1 Do you try to find time to read every day?
☐ YES ☐ NO

2 Do you prefer stories with happy endings?
☐ YES ☐ NO

3 Do you enjoy having books delivered to your home?
☐ YES ☐ NO

4 Do you share your favorite books with friends?
☐ YES ☐ NO

YES! I have completed the above "One Minute" Survey. Please send me my Free Books and a Free Mystery Gift (worth over $20 retail). I understand that I am under no obligation to buy anything, as explained on the back of this card.

☐ **Harlequin Desire®**
225/326 CTI G2AF

☐ **Harlequin Presents® Larger-Print**
176/376 CTI G2AF

☐ **BOTH**
(225/326 & 176/376)
CTI G2AG

FIRST NAME

LAST NAME

ADDRESS

APT.#

CITY

STATE/PROV.

ZIP/POSTAL CODE

EMAIL ☐ Please check this box if you would like to receive newsletters and promotional emails from Harlequin Enterprises ULC and its affiliates. You can unsubscribe anytime.

Your Privacy—Your information is being collected by Harlequin Enterprises ULC, operating as Harlequin Reader Service. For a complete summary of the information we collect, how we use this information and to whom it is disclosed, please visit our privacy notice located at https://corporate.harlequin.com/privacy-notice. From time to time we may also exchange your personal information with reputable third parties. If you wish to opt out of this sharing of your personal information, please visit www.readerservice.com/consumerschoice or call 1-800-873-8635. Notice to California Residents—Under California law, you have specific rights to control and access your data. For more information on these rights and how to exercise them, visit https:// corporate.harlequin.com/california-privacy.

HD/HP-1123-OM

HARLEQUIN Reader Service —**Here's how it works:**

Accepting your 2 free books and free gift (gift valued at approximately $10.00 retail) places you under no obligation to buy anything. You may keep the books and gift and return the shipping statement marked "cancel." If you do not cancel, approximately one month later we'll send you more books from the series you have chosen, and bill you at our low, subscribers-only discount price. Harlequin Presents® Larger-Print books consist of 6 books each month and cost $6.80 each in the U.S. or $6.99 each in Canada, a savings of at least 6% off the cover price. Harlequin Desire® books consist of 3 books (2in1 editions) each month and cost just $7.83 each in the U.S. or $8.43 each in Canada, a savings of at least 12% off the cover price. It's quite a bargain! Shipping and handling is just 50¢ per book in the U.S. and $1.25 per book in Canada*. You may return any shipment at our expense and cancel at any time by contacting customer service — or you may continue to receive monthly shipments at our low, subscribers-only discount price plus shipping and handling.

USA TODAY bestselling author **Naima Simone**'s love of romance was first stirred by Harlequin books pilfered from her grandmother. Now she spends her days writing sizzling romances with a touch of humor and snark.

She is wife to her own real-life superhero and mother to two awesome kids. They live in perfect domestically challenged bliss in the southern United States.

Books by Naima Simone

Harlequin Desire

Her Best Kept Secret
An Off-Limits Merger

Billionaires of Boston

Vows in Name Only
Secrets of a One Night Stand
The Perfect Fake Date
Black Sheep Bargain

HQN Books

The Road to Rose Bend
Christmas in Rose Bend
With Love from Rose Bend

Visit the Author Profile page
at Harlequin.com for more titles.

You can also find Naima Simone on Facebook,
along with other Harlequin Desire authors,
at Facebook.com/HarlequinDesireAuthors!

Dear Reader,

The legend of the brooch is working its magic again! Or is it? Dun-dun-duuuun. Oh wait. This is romance. Of course, there's a happily-ever-after! But oh, the journey there. Sigh.

The second and final book in the girls' trip duet brings Tatum Haas and Bran Holleran's love story. Confession time: I have a thing for widowers and widows. I love writing all the angsty emotion and then their eventual return to joy. Tatum Haas loses her fiancé on the eve of her wedding. Not quite a widow, but close enough. Still, complicating her grief is the swirl of scandal that surrounds his death. And when a sexy older man enters her life, she's drawn to him despite his being a client of her family's business and the heartbreak and loss that has made her more than a little skittish about any romantic entanglement. But she can't deny her desire for Bran, even though it may cost her more than she could possibly know.

Passion, love and secrets abound in *An Off-Limits Merger*! I hope you fall in love with Tatum and Bran!

Happy reading!

Naima

AN OFF-LIMITS MERGER

Naima Simone

To Gary. 143.

To Connie Marie Butts.
I'll miss you forever
and love you longer than that.

Prologue

Tatum Haas laughed, reaching for the bottle of Riesling and refilling her near-empty glass. The happiness inside her resembled the golden wine. Light. Sweet. Perfect. She'd been waiting for this night since her first meeting with Mark Walker at one of the endless fundraiser galas that demanded Tatum's attendance because her mother sat on the committee. That event where they'd met, though, had been different. She'd found the man who would change her life forever.

Yes, that night—and all the wonderful, sweet and romantic evenings and days following—had led her here. To the evening before she would finally be Mrs. Mark Walker.

She couldn't contain her smile as she lifted her glass for another sip.

Everything was…perfect.

"I know what that smile means," said her best friend, Nore Daniels. "You're either thinking about Mark or this right here…" Nore teased, picking up her fork and diving into the decadent plate of seafood pasta in front of her.

Tatum grinned.

Still chuckling, Nore jabbed her fork in the direction of the hotel suite door. "You're the only one with a key to the suite, right? Dara will sense you having fun, or—" she gasped dramatically "—eating a carb, and your soon-to-be mother-in-law will bust up in here and shut this down. That woman can sniff out joy like a great white smelling spring breakers on a beach. And the result is the same. Carnage."

Tatum shouldn't laugh; it only encouraged Nore. And Dara Walker would be her mother-in-law as of tomorrow. But hell, Nore wasn't wrong. Dara had been over-the-top with the preparations for the wedding. And this girls' night with her best friend and maid of honor had been her only respite—or escape.

"No worries. There's only one key to this room. And I might've told everyone we're staying at the Four Seasons instead of The Liberty." Tatum picked up her fork and twirled the pasta around the tines before slipping the food into her mouth. And closed her eyes on a hum. "This is obscenely good." She dug back into her plate. "That it's damn near the first thing I've eaten in a month without Mom watching me probably has something to do with it."

How sad that at twenty-eight and almost a married woman, Tatum felt *pasta* was her form of rebellion.

She shrugged, as if she could dislodge that irritating, disloyal thought.

"Sneaky. I like it." Nore squinted at her. "And your mother is a lovely woman, but she doesn't know shit if she's trying to make you starve yourself. You're gorgeous just the way you are."

Tatum smiled. "Mark believes that, too."

"I adore Mark," Nore said, "but the most important thing is *you* know that."

Tatum stretched an arm across the table and squeezed her friend's hand. "I do. I promise."

And this summed up why they'd been best friends since college. Through ten years, living in different states and all the other messes life had thrown them, nothing could diminish the friendship and love they shared.

"Oh before I forget." Nore jumped up from the couch. "Be right back." She raced from the living room, disappeared into the bedroom they were sharing for the night and reappeared a couple of minutes later carrying a small white box wrapped with a silver bow. "For you. I hope you didn't think I forgot."

Tatum softly laughed, accepting the present. She didn't need to lift the lid to know what lay inside. Delight bubbled inside her. "I didn't think you would," she murmured, removing the bow and then the top. "I'm not going to lie. Wearing this is one of the things I've been most looking forward to about tomorrow."

During a girls' trip that summer, Nore had dragged Tatum to a pawn shop with the intent of selling the engagement ring from Nore's jerk of an ex-fiancé. Instead,

Nore had spotted this gorgeous and unique brooch. Gold and silver were molded into tiny delicate flowers of turquoise, pink and ruby red, and diamonds and seed pearls dotted the petals and vines. They created a border around a stunning portrait of a woman. While a wide-brimmed hat hid most of her features, her back and regal profile were visible, as was the smooth light brown skin of her cheek, mouth, chin and elegant neck. It was definitely a statement piece, and her best friend had taken one look at the Victorian brooch and bought it as a wedding gift for Tatum. Her something old *and* new.

"What're you doing?" Nore laughed as Tatum pinned the jewelry to her sweater. "Isn't it some kind of bad luck to wear that before your wedding day?"

"Please." She waved off Nore's question, brushing a finger over the enamel portrait. "Something this beautiful and with such a romantic legend attached to it couldn't be bad luck." Tilting her head, Tatum grinned. "So tell me again how it's just a fairy tale?"

Nore rolled her eyes but nothing could hide the happiness that emanated from her as if a beacon shone from under her skin. "All right, so maybe the legend isn't sentimental bullshit. I mean, could someone make an argument that finding the brooch and me meeting and falling in love with Joaquin was purely coincidental? Sure. But you know what, Tate?" A soft smile curved Nore's mouth. "How we came together? How we pushed through? It's been nothing less than magical to me. So, yes, I'm a believer in whatever enchantment or love that brooch holds. And I also believe it's found its rightful place with you."

Tatum traced the jeweled flowers, thinking of the beautiful tale attached to the piece. According to the saleswoman, the daughter of a Barbadian Parliament member had traveled with her father to London. Once there, she'd fallen in love at first sight with an English baron. The two lived and loved for many happy years and he'd had the jewelry piece commissioned as a symbol of his love for her. Because of that devotion, the story claimed whoever possessed the brooch would experience the same kind of love. They would find their soulmate, and though the path would be troubled, they'd ultimately find a lasting, true love.

"Thank you, Nore. This means the world to me. And so do you."

"Nope." Her friend shook her head, wagging her finger. "No, ma'am. You're not going to have me up here crying and looking haggard tomorrow. Feelings. Ew." Nore scrunched her nose. "Hell no, I—"

The peal of Tatum's cell interrupted Nore, and still grinning, Tatum picked it up, glancing down at the screen. She barely contained her grimace when Dara's name filled the caller ID. Her mother-in-law-to-be must've figured out Tatum and Nore's disappearing act.

Preparing herself for the upcoming nice-nasty tirade that only a society maven could deliver, Tatum pressed the answer button and lifted the phone to her ear. "Hi, Dara," Tatum greeted, smothering a laugh as Nore rolled her eyes. "I'm so sorry about the hotel mix-up—"

"Tatum."

Everything in her went still. As if a primal part of her recognized that something important had happened. But also that the "something" would be earthshaking. Life altering. And her brain was granting her one last moment of normalcy before her world shattered around her.

"Tatum," Dara repeated, her voice huskier, still trembling.

"Yes. I'm here."

Nore's gaze sharpened, a frown drawing her dark eyebrows together.

"Honey, I need you to come to Mass General as fast as you can, okay?"

Tatum's pulse spiked, and acidic fear flooded her mouth. If the mention of the hospital hadn't sent her heart racing, then the *honey* from Dara Walker would've—the reserved older woman never used endearments.

"Dara," Tatum whispered. Then swallowed, tried speaking again, but her voice didn't emerge any stronger. "What's wrong? Is it...?" She couldn't voice it. Because that would make this burgeoning nightmare real.

"It's Mark, Tatum," Dara said, confirming Tatum's biggest fear.

Her nightmare.

"No." Tatum shook her head as if Mark's mother could see the gesture. As if the motion, the objection would somehow unravel Dara's words. Make them untrue.

"Please, Tatum. Get here as fast as you can. He's in surgery, but I don't—" Her voice cracked.

"I'm on... I'm..." Tatum's suddenly dry throat wouldn't allow her to finish the sentence.

Nore reached out, plucked the phone from Tatum's stiff fingers.

"Hi, Dara. This is Nore. What's going on?" She paused,

her worried golden-brown gaze fixed on Tatum. Alarm flared in her friend's eyes as she listened to Mark's mother. "Don't worry—I'll get Tate to the hospital. We'll be there in ten minutes. See you soon."

Sheer panic propelled Tatum to her feet. She shot out of the chair, gripping the edge of the table to steady herself, and Nore grasped her elbow.

"I got you. You go to the door and the elevators. I'll be right behind you with your shoes, coat and purse. Right behind you, Tate." With a gentle but firm shove, Nore pushed her toward the suite door.

Tatum didn't remember leaving the suite or arriving at the hospital. The next couple of hours passed in a blur of low voices, dread, anxiety and confusion. She and Nore sat in a small private waiting room along with Mark's and Tatum's parents, as well as her sister, Mia. Maybe Dara called them, or even Nore had on their way to the hospital. Tatum had ceased to be aware of anything but the fear that wrapped around her lungs in a brutal, suffocating grip.

Please, God, let Mark be okay. Please let him live. I can't lose him. Not when we're just about to start our life together. I didn't get to say I love you to him...

Surging to her feet, she scrubbed her hands up and down her arms. Just as she paced to the window, a low voice spoke from the other side of the room.

"Mr. and Mrs. Walker?" A petite Black woman in scrubs and a surgical cap approached Dara and Leo, her lovely features calm, composed.

Mark's parents rushed over to the doctor, and Nore appeared at Tatum's side while her parents formed a steady wall on the other. *Go over there*, a voice screamed inside her head. *Go be with them.* But she couldn't move.

"Yes." Leo Walker curved an arm around his wife's waist.

"I'm Dr. Jennifer Danner. I operated on your son." She met the Walkers' gazes, and the compassion in the doctor's eyes ripped a hole in Tatum's chest even before she continued speaking. "I'm sorry. He didn't make it. Your son suffered massive brain injury from a ruptured brain aneurysm. We tried everything we could to save him but he's gone. I'm very sorry."

A horrific wail rebounded off the walls of the waiting room, and Dara collapsed in Leo's arms. That terrible, agonized sound echoed in Tatum's head, her chest, her belly. Her own knees liquefied beneath her.

Time ceased to matter, ceased to exist. There were only those two words.

He's gone.

He's gone.

The pain ripped through her.

He's gone.

He's gone.

"Oh fuck."

Nore's stunned yet furious whisper sliced through the smothering blanket of grief. Blinking, Tatum stared at her friend's dark frown as she peered at the cell in her hand. Her tongue couldn't move to ask her what was wrong, but just as she thought the question, Tatum noticed her sister peering at Nore's phone, shock suffusing her expression as well. And when Mia glanced at Tatum, uncharacteristic pity in her dark gaze, grief temporarily shifted to dread.

Her cell vibrated in the pocket of her cardigan, and for a moment, Tatum considered not looking at it. Nothing good waited for her on that phone. Yet, her numb fingers closed around the steadily humming cell.

A social media notification with Mark's name underneath it. God, that hadn't taken long. But they couldn't know he was de— They couldn't know *that* yet since they'd just received the news, right? No, all they could report was he'd been rushed to the hospital...

She pressed her thumb to the screen.

"Tate, no. Don't—" Nore grabbed her hand.

But it was too late.

Funny.

Just seconds earlier she'd believed the pain pulsing through her like a raw, open wound was the worst pain she'd ever experienced. She'd been wrong.

TheSpilledTea, a popular social media–based tabloid company, had been thorough.

Pictures of Mark on a gurney.

Images of his parents, of Tatum and Nore arriving at the hospital.

But it was the story underneath that sent her spiraling into agony.

Mark Walker, heir to one of the largest communications corporations in the country. Fiancé to Boston socialite Tatum Haas.
Anonymous 911 call by mysterious woman.
Found naked and unresponsive in hotel room.

Eve of wedding.
Obvious signs of sexual tryst.

No. She hadn't believed a more brutal pain than loss existed. But when a woman discovered the man she loved, the man she'd been prepared to devote the rest of her life to had spent his final moments inside someone else... Well, she understood two things in that moment.

One, she'd been fooling herself. She'd never experienced true agony until now.

And two. When your heart had been betrayed and broken, that so-called thin line between love and hate evaporated.

Oh no. Fuck that thin line.

Hate and love were so inextricably melded, she couldn't separate one from the other.

But hate...

Hate had an edge.

One

Ten months later

A. Armani suit. Wool.

   B. Barbara Harrington. CEO of Mouton Publishing.

   C. Cartier watch. Panthère de Cartier, to be exact. A twenty-thousand-dollar price tag.

   Tatum scanned the throng of guests crowded into the gilded ballroom of the historic hotel as she unhurriedly wound a path through them. Huge crystal-and-gold chandeliers were suspended from the cathedral ceilings, reflecting light off the many jewels adorning hair, ears, necks, even dresses. Narrowing her eyes, she swept her gaze over the ringed balconies high above the floor. Satisfaction whispered through her.

D. Denise Jacobs wearing a Dior gold-and-pearl collar necklace. Two points on that one.

Tatum had become somewhat of a pro at this alphabet game she played at social events. What had started as a method of surviving the torturous appearances her parents insisted on had turned into a fun challenge. Once or twice, she'd even reached *Z.* It seemed pathetic that this had become her idea of a good time. But after the last ten months of blocking out the whispers, the gossip, the humiliation and pain, she didn't care how sad her coping mechanisms were. Whatever worked to get her through these evenings and back to the sanctuary of her home. So, she'd cling to her game.

E. Emerald green cocktail dress. Okay, that was weak…

"Did they ever figure out who he was screwing in that hotel room when he died?" a not-so-hushed voice asked behind Tatum.

Ice slid through her, and it required every bit of her battle-scarred but iron-strong control not to flinch. Or turn around and find out the identity of the avaricious gossiper.

"No. And it's been almost a year since he died. You'd think they would've discovered *something* already. It's damned hard to keep a secret for long in this city," another woman said with a chuckle.

"Well, I *did* hear that was *far* from his first affair. Apparently, he'd been a bit—" a small laugh partially covered by a delicate cough "—popular."

The second woman scoffed. "Especially with other men's wives, if what people are saying is true. Maybe that's why the 911 caller was never found. If I was cheating on my husband, I wouldn't come forward either. Can you imagine *that* conversation with the police?"

A delicate hand grasped Tatum's elbow and gently but firmly pushed her forward.

"Since I was raised with you, I know you were taught it's rude to eavesdrop," Mia drawled, steering Tatum away from the conversation. "Especially when you're ear-hustling on two little bitches who don't have the manners or common sense to even look around and see who's listening."

"How else am I supposed to know what people are saying? We were also taught that knowledge is power," Tatum said, her conversational tone belying the bitterness, hurt and…helplessness swirling inside her with no outlet. Well, grabbing champagne glasses from the passing server and smashing them to the floor would be an outlet, but not a constructive one. And that would be breaking her parents' cardinal rule.

Do not make a spectacle.

Or rather, even more of one.

Because apparently, being the would-be bride of a man who had died bare-ass naked during sex in a hotel suite the night before his wedding was the very definition of a spectacle.

And yet, they kept making her attend these social gatherings, trotting her out in public as if the demise of her engagement—no pun intended—was a spectator event.

Tatum was the local fair rolling into town; every time she walked into a room, a giddy and greedy excitement traveled through the crowds. Her pain, her shame, the remnants of her pride seemed to be the most popular ride.

"Now you're being deliberately obtuse. I swear, sometimes I think you're punishing yourself by listening to that bullshit," Mia snapped.

Tatum waved off her younger sister's theory, scoffing, covering the brief ache tightening her chest. How could she explain that witnessing the gossip was her own form of rebellion? Her small way of recapturing just a small piece of the power she'd lost ten months ago in that hospital waiting room? Confronting those women or walking away would've smacked too much of running. But standing there, letting the gossip strike her skin, absorbing the tiny blows...

Yes, it sounded silly—confident, sexy, gave-zero-fucks Mia wouldn't understand. And because they'd never been as close as sisters only two years apart should be, Tatum didn't attempt to explain it.

It was times like this when she really missed Nore. Her best friend would've simply got it...got her.

"I'm not a masochist, Mia," Tatum assured her. "Blame our parents. This is why they have me here. Less punishment, though, and more inoculation. The more I'm exposed to the stares and comments, the less sensitive I am. Builds up my immune system."

Mia glanced at her, the corner of her lip curled in a faint sneer. "You take such satisfaction in playing the victim."

Tatum's footsteps stuttered, and she slowed to a halt,

her gaze centered on her sister, studying the same dark eyes their mother had bequeathed to them.

No, she and Mia didn't share a tight relationship, but since Mark's death, Mia had been less abrasive and more compassionate, even her defender in some situations, such as the one she'd just tugged Tatum away from. But then, there were other occasions when Tatum could almost believe… She shook her head.

"You know, I can't decide if you're mad at me or mad on my behalf. Because I haven't done anything to deserve that remark," Tatum murmured.

Mia huffed out a breath and glanced away, a tiny muscle flicking along her jaw. After a moment, she looked back at Tatum. "Look, I'm—"

"Girls, we've been looking for you," Regina Haas announced, approaching them with a smile and a warning glint in her eyes.

And as soon as Tatum noticed who accompanied her mother and father, the meaning behind that cautionary gleam became clear.

Leo and Dara Walker.

Dammit.

"It's a crush in here. Which is great for the Hearts and Hope Foundation," Tatum smoothly said, referring to the children's cancer organization that would receive the funds from the evening's donations and silent auction. Shifting her attention to Mark's parents, she forced her lips into a smile. "Hello, Leo and Dara. It's wonderful to see you."

Dara moved forward to clasp Tatum's arms and brush

a kiss on each of her cheeks. "You, too, Tatum. We've missed you."

To the casual listener, the older woman's voice carried a warm tone, but Tatum caught the subtle note of censure. A band around Tatum's chest tightened as if someone were turning a screw, and the muscles in her face trembled from the effort of maintaining her smile.

"I'll take the blame for that." Her father settled a hand on her back. "Having Tatum in the office has been a godsend and I've been monopolizing her time."

Why should she apologize for carrying on? For not dedicating her life as a shrine to Mark's memory?

Immediately on the heels of that thought, guilt crept through her. It wasn't that she didn't still care about Dara and Leo. How couldn't she? They'd been in her life as long as Mark had. But after... They'd expected her to grieve like them. But she couldn't. It was impossible. While they had lost a beloved son, Tatum had lost the man she'd loved, learned of his cruel betrayal, been abandoned to suffer the consequences of his actions. Yes, she grieved, but her feelings were much more... complicated.

She reached for the brooch she'd pinned at the bottom of the deep vee of her neckline, grazing her fingertips over the cameo. It was the first time she'd worn it since...that evening. Why had she decided to wear it tonight of all nights? She couldn't explain. To persuade herself she was over her pain, her grief? That she wasn't defined by her past?

It was an epic fail.

"That's understandable. Dara has accused me of

throwing myself back into work as a way of coping with…" Leo cleared his throat.

And only the flash of sadness in his eyes prevented Tatum from commenting that she actually enjoyed her position at BayStar Media, that it wasn't just busywork to avoid thinking about Mark.

Constantly biting her tongue and pretending to be broken over a man who hadn't given a single, solitary damn about breaking *her*—it chafed.

And she was developing rug burn.

"I was going to call you this week, Tatum," Dara said. "Leo and I have decided to create a foundation in Mark's honor. We're offering scholarships and paid internships at MassComm to incoming college students in the Boston area."

"That's wonderful," Tatum murmured.

And it was. For the students benefiting, the opportunities would be invaluable.

Dara smiled. "I'm glad you think so. We're hosting a ceremony and dinner in a couple of months to announce the foundation. We debated holding it on the anniversary of Mark's…passing, but Leo and I think this will be a chance to commemorate such a solemn and painful time with something positive and hopeful. I believe Mark would've approved." Dara's smile trembled a little. "We would love if you would attend as our guest speaker. No one knew Mark better than you, and it would mean so much as the woman he loved and as the person who loved him if you'd speak on his behalf."

Tatum stared at Dara, stunned.

Did she…? She couldn't really expect…? There was no way she…?

As she shifted her gaze from Dara's expectant expression to Leo's steady look, Tatum's belly constricted around a terrible, painful ache. Yes, Dara did expect Tatum to get up in front of hundreds of people and pretend that Mark hadn't ripped out her heart, that she hadn't suffered the embarrassment over the last ten months… Pretend that Mark had been a loving, devoted partner when everyone in that room would know the truth…

They expected her to lie to cover Mark's reputation even if it cost her what precious little remained of her own.

Heat rolled through her, streaming up her chest, neck and face. She forced her hands to remain straight at her sides when her fingers almost curled into fists. With her light brown skin, she couldn't hide the slashes of red that stained her cheekbones. It'd been one of her mother's greatest despairs that Tatum had never learned to control her face as every good socialite should. And right now, her face probably shouted *hell no*.

"Of course she will. It's so kind of you to ask." Her mother rushed into the silence to assure the Walkers. "Just let us know when the dates have been firmed up and we'll all be there."

"If you'll excuse me, please." Tatum didn't offer a reason for leaving; she lacked the mental or emotional bandwidth to conjure one up, and she doubted *this is some bullshit* would do. Besides, she couldn't even utter that. Not when she could barely *breathe*. Turning on her stiletto, she walked away from the small group and wound her way through the crowded ballroom, no destination in mind.

Anger propelled her forward. Anger at her parents, at the Walkers—at fucking *everyone*, including herself.

Stop being this pawn on their chessboard. Do *something.* Say *something. Find your backbone.*

Backbone. She locked down the caustic chuckle that abraded her throat. What a joke. At some point in the past months, she'd lost that as well as the strength she'd always believed to be one of her prized qualities. Maybe she'd buried her spine in the ground with Mark. Along with her pride. Along with her trust in people…in her judgment. In her herself.

Dammit.

She should've stayed home tonight.

She should've…

Shaking her head, she increased her pace, her footsteps keeping time with the desperate beat of the pulse pounding in her head.

There was no point in thinking about should haves. Just as there was no point in wishing she could turn back the hands of time and open the eyes she'd willfully kept shut.

No matter how desperately she wanted to, she couldn't outrun this mess.

Mark had given her no choice but to outlive it.

Two

What the fuck did I do to deserve ending up here?

Bran Holleran held his thin cigar between his finger and thumb, clamping it between his lips. Squinting his eyes, he puffed on it, the chocolate and Jack Daniel's notes swirling over his tongue. He savored them before blowing the smoke out into the cool late-September night.

Was it rude to be out here on this deserted balcony when the social event he'd been invited to attend by the investor he was in Boston to woo—yes, woo, dammit—was inside? Yes. Rude as hell. But was he ready to reenter that ballroom thick with people who reeked of money, blue blood and condescension?

No.

This shit wasn't him.

Galas. Tuxedos. Diamonds that cost more than his whole house. Ten-thousand-dollar plates.

Yeah, he was cofounder of Greer Motorcycles Co., the high-end motorcycle manufacturer, and a multimillionaire in his own right. But none of that changed who he remained at heart—a man whose passion was building custom motorcycles and riding them on long stretches of road. A man who'd rather have a thick rare T-bone steak and a cold beer than a lump of fish eggs on a cracker and a glass of wine.

Yet here he was. In Boston at some high-society party instead of back in Seattle, Washington, either in his office or at Greer's factory working on a new custom build. Logically, he understood why he'd been chosen to come here instead of Joaquin Iverson, his friend and cofounder. Joaquin had recently become engaged, and his fiancée's event-planning company was also based in Seattle. It'd made more sense for Bran, who didn't have any personal attachments and could work long-distance, to temporarily relocate cross-country.

Still didn't mean he wasn't asking God whom he'd offended to end up in his version of hell.

Lifting the cigar to his mouth again, he closed his eyes. He didn't smoke often, but the indulgence helped him relax, and right now, surrounded by all these people with their fake high-pitched laughter, mind-numbing small talk and cardboard food with too many sauces, he needed to *relax*.

Fuck. He had a whole month of this.

He puffed harder.

The striking of heels against stone alerted him to the

end of his solitude before he heard the sensual, husky notes of a woman's voice. Irritation flashed through him, but so did something else. Something edgier, darker that became even more restless and insistent as that throaty voice drew closer. He couldn't even catch the words, but he didn't need to. That voice...

Pure sex. The kind that got so hot and sweaty you had to throw the covers off so they didn't get twisted up around you. The kind that permeated the room with its own perfume.

Plucking the cigar from between his lips, he stared hard at the shadow that drifted toward him. His gut clenched, hard.

Anticipation.

This eagerness usually only wound its way through him when he sat down and prepared to work on a bike. Until this moment, as he stared into darkness, he'd believed nothing could compare to that.

Damn, he'd been wrong.

"Is it so inconceivable to think, for just one moment, that I don't want to live my life in the past? That I want to move on and not be your son's fool, pathetic fiancée for the rest of my days?" A growl rumbled out of her, and it echoed in his chest, in his gut. Lower still over his awakening cock. Disgust flickered inside him. He was forty years old, for God's sake. Not a wet-behind-the-ears kid whose dick bricked up with the slightest turn of the wind. Yet, he didn't move as she continued with her tirade, oblivious to her fascinated audience. "The audacity of me to hope my life would be my own? Dammit, you know this is your fault. Maybe if you'd put your foot down, and oh I don't know, placed your needs ahead of someone else's for once, like they do, you'd be free, if not happy. God, what would that feel like?"

A sigh whispered on the air, and the woman moved out of the shadows to the edge of the balcony, into the direct beam of the moonlight.

Goddamn.

Emerald green slid over a tall, slender frame with curves his palms itched to track. The dress should've been demure—it covered her from shoulder to wrist and draped to the floor with a small train in the back. His younger sister, Dani, who owned a bridal shop and had drilled a few dress details into his head, called the design a mermaid style. But when the woman turned toward him, all thoughts of *demure* jumped over the edge of the balcony—along with his ability to form coherent thoughts.

A deep vee plunged between her small, perfect breasts, displaying golden brown skin from the elegant column of her neck to well below her breastbone. Unlike most of the women back in the ballroom, she only wore a glittering pair of earrings. Not that she needed more jewelry. All that gorgeous skin would've rendered even the Hope Diamond gratuitous.

A silver belt accentuated a small waist and the flare of her hips. Impossibly long legs pressed against the dark green material, and both his cock and his imagination would have to be on permanent vacation not to stir at the thought of those limbs wrapped around his waist—or his head.

She shifted, and he dragged his gaze up the beauty of her body to her— His breath lodged in his throat. *Damn.*

If her body was stunning, her face... He slowly lowered his cigar so nothing could obstruct his view. Her face was a work of art.

A glimmer of recognition flashed inside him, but it winked out like an extinguished flame under a ruthless wave of lust. Lust and awe.

Delicately arched eyebrows over thickly lashed almond-shaped eyes. Cheekbones high and sharp. A proud, patrician nose with a very faint smattering of freckles across the bridge that prevented it from crossing over into arrogance. A graceful jawline he suspected could turn stubborn. And a wide, lush mouth that shouldn't have him ordering his cock to stand down like he was a horny-ass teenager. He was too damn old for that shit. Too damn old for *her*, given that she couldn't have been older than twenty-five or so.

His gaze lingered on the full, sensual bottom curve of her lip.

Apparently his dick ascribed to the "age is just a number" school of thought.

"This is ridiculous," she murmured, almost too low for him to catch. "I must be just as ridiculous."

"I don't know. I've been called worse." The words escaped him before he realized he'd intended to speak.

"Oh my God." Her body jerked, and she snapped her head in his direction. Her hand flew to the base of her throat. "What the hell?"

He brought his cigar back to his lips and puffed on it, blowing smoke out several seconds later, then continued as if she hadn't spoken. Or wasn't staring at him in wide-eyed shock. "I've been called worse," he repeated. "Done worse. You out here talking to your-self might seem, well…questionable to you, but other people may consider it normal behavior and a healthy way of working through your issues."

He didn't know who was more surprised—her or him. He and Joaquin were such great friends and busi-ness partners because they communicated through mo-torcycles, monosyllabic words and grunts. It was their love language. Neither one of them indulged in—or needed—lengthy conversations with one another. They weren't built like that.

Bran definitely wasn't. He didn't talk much, or tease. Didn't flirt. Even before Roma, he hadn't been that guy, but *after* his ex-wife, whatever inclination he'd had to try and behave differently had gone scorched earth by his divorce.

Yet here he stood in a shadow-enshrouded balcony talking to a stranger and toying with flirting.

And his only excuse was *her*.

Like a living flame, burning bright against the dark night, she seemed to *seethe* with emotion. And he was a kid warned away from a hot stove, longing to touch that fire. And only once his skin had been licked by its heat would he know to back away…or crave its bite again.

"It's also rude to cut in on other people's private con-versations," she bit out. "Even if it's with themselves."

A bark of laughter barreled up his chest, but with ef-fort he shoved it back down. Because that made no damn sense. It was funny as hell, though. Which served to spike an unwanted curiosity about the stunning woman before him. Right alongside that inconvenient lust.

A combination that any man who thought with his brain rather than his dick would run away from.

"Rude?" He shrugged. "Maybe." He cocked his head. "But then, I was here first. So technically, that means you're violating my space. If you want privacy, there are other balconies where you can have a one-on-one argument. Given what I saw of this place, you have about ten more to pick from."

She frowned. Even as she glared at him, his body tightened in anticipation that had him feeling like his skin had shrunk on his extra-large frame.

"You're looking like you want to jump, baby girl." He brought his cigar back to his lips as he delivered the warning on a low silken murmur. "And the way I'm feeling right now, I might be in the mood to catch you. Be sure that's what you signed up for, though. Don't let the suit fool you."

Her soft catch of breath caressed his ears, stroked over his chest—and lower. Though he couldn't quite detect the color of her eyes, the slight widening of them and the parting of her lips denoted her shock. At his words? Probably. Just looking at her—her beauty, flawless body, clothes—and the company she kept behind them in that ballroom, he seriously doubted anyone had ever dared to speak to her as he'd just done.

Hell, had anyone ever dared dig their hands in that long, thick hair that fell over her shoulder in a perfect dark sheet? Pull on it, tug her head back and mess up that immaculately applied lipstick until it stained both of their mouths and skin?

No. He'd bet his 1973 Norton Commando 850 that

none of the men back there sipping their champagne and ogling the waitstaff had ever given that to her.

"Excuse me?" she whispered. "Don't let the suit fool me?" From one instant to the next, her frown cleared and a smile curved her plush mouth. And no one could've missed the edge sharp enough to draw blood. "Well, would a trash can do? It seems like that would be a better fit for your manners. Especially since you obviously believe it's okay to disrespect me."

He'd been right. Touching that flame didn't have him wanting to back away.

He stepped closer.

Again, she wasn't quick enough in concealing her reaction, and she retreated a step before drawing up short. That delicate but stubborn chin hiked up, and apparently not satisfied, she recovered the ground she'd given up. And he glimpsed her eyes for the first time.

It could've been the moonlight that made the brown appear almost black, but somehow he doubted it. And as he stared down into those damn-near-bottomless depths, he found himself battling the urge to retreat, to stumble back a step before he dove into her with a recklessness that was completely alien to him.

Her gaze lowered from his, skimmed over his face, beard, not betraying a blink at his long hair pulled back into a bun before taking in the black-on-black Tom Ford suit. When she returned her regard to him, her dark eyes didn't reveal her thoughts, and for the first time in more years than he could remember, he cared about a stranger's opinion. Because if it wasn't about a bike he designed or manufactured, he usually didn't give a fuck.

But now, staring down into a pair of inscrutable brown-black eyes, he did.

And that unnerved him more than he cared to admit.

"Disrespect you?" He exhaled, turning his head so he didn't blow the chocolate-flavored smoke in her face. Arching an eyebrow, he said, "That was an invitation and a disclaimer. You're the one in a mood, baby girl. I was just letting you know I might want to indulge it. If upfront and honest talk offends or scares you, then that would be a 'you' problem. Because again—" he jerked his chin to the side, indicating the space around them "—my balcony first."

Yeah, he was being deliberately…provoking.

And if he were honest, it surprised him. True, he did possess a blunt a manner, but this? Something about her… He wanted to poke, prod. See if she would hide behind that icy, polite demeanor with the nice-nasty edges or slip and allow him to see more of that fire.

He didn't come here—to this event, to Boston—for this. To tease some mysterious, unknown woman on a dark balcony. A woman he wouldn't see again after tonight. He didn't come here to wonder what those perfectly manicured nails would feel like biting into his bare shoulders or back. To discover if those eyes would grow even darker with lust.

To wonder if that flash of fire he'd glimpsed would burn just as bright, as hot if he sank hard and deep inside her…

Yes, no doubt about it, he was being deliberately provoking. But to what end? Her emotion?

Or her lust?

Because fuck him, if he didn't want both.

Not that he had anything against a one-night stand with a gorgeous woman. Hell, that pretty much summed up his relationship history in the last seven years since his divorce. But as much as he hungered to find out how that throaty voice would sound wrapped around his name as she screamed in orgasm, an equal amount of disquiet crept through him.

There might be a man who could fuck her and walk away without being greedy for another taste.

He had the sneaking suspicion that man wouldn't be him.

She closed her eyes and drew in a breath, and again, a niggling sense of familiarity flickered in the back of his skull. Did he know her? Had they met? Couldn't have. No way in hell he would've forgotten her.

She pinched the bridge of her nose, shaking her head. "No. Just…no." She lowered her hand and opened her eyes, wrinkling her nose. "An invitation? To what? Maim you? Because that line can't possibly work. What self-respecting person has fallen for it?"

"Not a line." He shrugged a shoulder and set his cigar on the ashtray resting near the stone ledge. "Just offering you an outlet. And the chance to place your needs first, as you claim you have a problem doing." Sliding his hands in the front pockets of his suit pants, he murmured, "Just from the observation of a random eavesdropper, there isn't anything foolish or pathetic about you. I can't speak on the 'fiancée' part, though."

Pain glinted in her eyes so brightly, he couldn't have mistaken it for anything but what it was. And the sight of it pierced him like the heel of her stiletto to his chest, cutting off his banter and his breath.

"Hey, baby girl—" he said, voice low, shifting closer to her.

"Don't call me that."

She probably meant to snap at him. But the words emerged as a low rasp.

"Okay," he said, deliberately softening his voice. Instead of backing away like he should, he leaned against the stone railing, studying her, seeking to defuse the situation and extinguish the hurt in her gaze. "What should I call you, then? What's your name?"

Her lips parted—whether to give an answer or to tell him to go to hell, he didn't know—but he didn't get the chance to find out. At least not from her.

"Tatum, I've been looking all over for you."

This woman he recognized as soon as she stepped through the wide French doors, and as soon as Mia Haas said, "Tatum," that nagging sense of familiarity finally clicked into place.

Tatum Haas.

The best friend of Joaquin's fiancée, Nore.

The daughter of the man Bran was in Boston to see as an investor in Greer Motorcycle's newest model.

Well, damn.

A wide pit yawned in the bottom of his stomach, then stretched higher toward his chest. In the emptiness echoed disappointment and the shadow of loss. He shook his head and straightened, stepping away from the woman who'd gone from pure temptation to off-limits in the blink of an eye.

Yeah, who was he kidding? She was still pure temptation.

"Ms. Haas, it's good to see you again," he said, turning to Silas Haas's other daughter, the one he'd met in Seattle. The beautiful young woman had attended the launch party for their first electric model, the KING One, months ago. And later, when Bran and Joaquin had taken the first meetings with BayStar about a possible investment for their new line of cost-friendly motorcycles, Mia had sat in on them. He nodded at her now. "How're you doing?"

"Well, Mr. Holleran. But please, it's Mia." She smiled, and he noticed the resemblance between the two women. Both shared the same eyes and bone structure, although Tatum stood a couple of inches taller and Mia boasted a slightly curvier frame. And Mia's mouth didn't put him in the mind frame of sin, sweat and begging. "Since you're in Boston for the foreseeable future," Mia continued, "and we'll be working together, I hope I can call you Bran."

"Of course."

"I take it you two know each other," Tatum said to her sister, not looking at him at all.

For some reason, he wanted to grasp her chin and turn her head toward him, force that almost-black gaze to him.

But that was foolishness, too, for several reasons.

Didn't stop his fingertips from tingling, though.

"We do," Mia said. "Mr. Holleran, or Bran," she corrected herself with a soft chuckle, "is one of our newest clients. BayStar is investing in his company, Greer Motorcycles. I'm surprised Dad didn't mention it to you."

If he hadn't been watching Tatum so closely, he might've missed the slight clenching of her jaw. But he didn't miss it. And though it fell under the category of "not my business," he couldn't help but wonder what that was about.

"Well, Mr. Holleran." Tatum turned to him, her mouth stretched into what she probably would mistakenly label a smile. He, on the other hand, knew bullshit when he saw it. Especially when it sounded like she'd swallowed glass. "It would seem like we aren't really strangers."

"Not at all," he said. "Some might even consider us in-laws." He tilted his head, his regard falling to the brooch pinned to the bottom of the plunging vee between her breasts. "I should've recognized that, if nothing else. It's a distinctive piece. Nore Daniels wore it the first time we met at my best friend Joaquin Iverson's birthday party."

Tatum blinked, confusion clouding her eyes. But a moment later, realization dawned.

"You're—" She shook her head, frowning. "No, that's not possible. We would've met long before now."

"Not really. The first time you visited Seattle after Nore and Joaquin met is when they were…"

Tatum snorted. "I believe what you're trying not to say is when Joaquin fucked up."

"Yes, that." No point in defending his friend. Joaquin had screwed up but thankfully he'd pulled his head out of his ass before it'd been too late. "And since then

Nore has flown out here to see you. Sorry, I didn't recognize you."

"Yes, well, Tatum's had quite a lot going on lately, which is why the rest of us have circled the wagons, so to speak. Not that we mind. That's what family is for, after all." Mia moved forward and slid her arm through his. "Which reminds me, Tatum," she continued, glancing over her shoulder at her sister. "Mom and Dad sent me to find you since you abruptly ran off. Dinner and the silent auction are about to start."

"You two go ahead. I'll be right behind you." Tatum waved her hand, her voice even, as devoid of emotion as her face.

And he hated it.

This wasn't the woman he'd been sparring with for the last twenty minutes. He wanted her back, not this solemn version with her fire banked.

But it wasn't just that.

It didn't sit right with him to walk away with Mia and leave Tatum alone. There was something—a tension, a rigidity—that had entered their space, entered Tatum since her sister had joined them on the balcony. And though he only possessed a barely there connection to Tatum through mutual friends, and their initial meeting had contained more vinegar than honey, he couldn't leave her behind.

"We'll wait." He removed his arm from Mia's. "When you're ready."

Mia stiffened, but he ignored it, his attention focused on Tatum. She, in turn, stared at him. An emotion flickered across her face, but it appeared and disappeared before he could crack its meaning. Not that he spoke fluent Tatum Haas.

Not that he cared to.

Shit. Lying had to be bad for the digestion.

"I wasn't aware I required an escort," she snarked, then jerked her head toward his cigar, which still smoldered on the ashtray. "You don't want to forget to put that out and take it with you."

"It's a cigar, baby girl, not a cigarette. You don't 'put it out.' You allow it to die out gracefully."

"That doesn't sound pretentious at all. And I told you don't call me that."

The bite returned to her voice, and satisfaction hummed under his skin.

"And you never gave me a name to call you in its place," he reminded her, and her full mouth firmed in annoyance. What did it say about him that he enjoyed it? "Are you ready to go in together, or are we hanging out here longer?"

An emotion gleamed in those dark eyes and once more he had to check the overwhelming urge to pinch her chin, tilt her head back and study that gaze, mine it for all its secrets.

But experience had taught him the brutal lesson of giving in to impulse. Once a person had his life dragged from one end of hell and back, he heeded every warning.

And Tatum Haas was a walking, breathing caution sign wrapped up in a neon red alert. The blinking kind.

Fucking danger ahead.

That chin he'd imagined cupping lifted, and that reserved mask slid back into place. "Pity is not on the dinner menu for this evening. I don't need or want yours," she coolly informed him, then strode past him and her sister.

The aloof socialite veneer was impeccable. And he might've believed it and felt put in his place if he hadn't glimpsed those eyes.

Yeah, they betrayed her hurt and ruined the whole charade.

"You'll have to excuse my sister," Mia said as he watched Tatum disappear back inside the ballroom teeming with people. "I promise you we all really do have better manners." She laughed softly. "She's had a tough year—"

"Yes, I get that." Glancing down at her, he nodded. "You said dinner's about to start? We should probably get in there so you can get to your table and I can find mine."

"Oh. Uh—" she gave her head a slight shake "—yes, you're right." A frown flirted with her brows before her expression cleared, and she recovered with another smile. "We should head in."

Mia probably wasn't used to being interrupted or, given her beauty, men not hanging on every word she uttered. But Bran didn't want to hear what she had to say about her sister. Yes, he was very aware of just how "tough" Tatum's year had been. Her best friend was engaged to his. Of course, Joaquin had shared some of the details with him.

But getting the story from Mia—or anyone here—smacked too much of gossip. Didn't matter that she was

Tatum's sister. And not only had he outgrown that shit when he graduated high school, but there seemed to be something else he couldn't quite put a finger on...

He lifted a shoulder and moved forward, mentally shaking off that nagging sense of...whatever. He was here in Boston to lock in his investor and oversee a couple more opportunities for their new model.

That was it.

Not to meet or engage in dangerously flirtatious banter with prickly younger women who talked to themselves.

Not to imagine how said prickly younger woman looked midorgasm. Especially when she was the daughter of the investor he needed.

And definitely not to entangle himself in a ménage with him, her and the ghost of her dead fiancé.

No. The sooner he got his business handled and got out of Boston, the better.

Three

Monday mornings were a torture all their own, especially precoffee, but being summoned to her father's office—still with no coffee—tipped this one over into a special level.

Grinding her teeth, she studied the steadily rising numbers of the elevator as it carried her to the executive floor. Not that she minded seeing her father; she loved Silas Haas and had been a self-admitted daddy's girl from the time she'd been born. But ever since Mark's death, there'd been an indefinable change in their relationship. As if when he looked at her, he didn't quite know what to make of her. Like Mark's infidelities and death had tainted her, irreversibly changed her from the daughter he'd once known and left him with…her. And Silas seemed to be out of his element in how to handle her. So he'd opted for wavering between kid gloves and tough love and her mother went with ignoring the entire episode.

Was it any wonder Tatum's stomach had decided to make a jailbreak for her throat?

She had no idea which version of her father she'd encounter this morning.

Both of them saddened and irritated her.

She didn't need to be "handled." She needed... She needed them to see her as a person and not a scandalous tragedy.

The elevator slid to a stop and the doors opened. Sighing, she stepped onto the floor that housed all the offices for the senior-level executives of BayStar Media. *One day*, she promised herself, surveying the closed heavy oak doors with their embossed gold doorplates and individual assistant desks guarding their sanctuaries. A conference room with floor-to-ceiling windows, a large table with mounted tablets and surrounded by leather chairs, and a huge screen occupied one side of the area. And at the end of the corridor sat the corner office of BayStar's CEO and the grandson of the founder, Silas Haas.

As she approached her father's closed door, his executive assistant, Brenda, glanced up from the computer screen on her desk.

"Good morning, Tatum." She smiled, the blunt ends of her sleek blond bob brushing her jaw as she nodded. "You can go on in. He's expecting you."

"Thanks, Brenda." Before Tatum headed in, though, she reached into her purse and removed a small paper bag, then set it on the top of the desk. "Here you go. For Ryan and his new collection."

The other woman's lips rounded in an O as she accepted the gift. While other ten-year-old boys might be consumed with video games, cartoons or sports, Brenda's little boy loved to collect. Everything from book series to trading cards—if they caught his attention, he collected it. Right now, he was focused on gathering a key chain from every state in the US.

"What's this…?" Brenda removed the Washington State–shaped key chain with landmarks engraved on it, including the Space Needle and Mount Rainier. She grinned, her green eyes bright. "Tatum, you didn't have to do this."

"Of course I did. When Dad told me about Ryan's newest collection, I had my best friend go right out to the store, buy me a key chain and mail it to me. Tell him I need a picture when it's complete."

"I definitely will. Thank you again. He's going to love it!"

"You're welcome." With another smile, she continued toward her father's office, trying to hold on to that bit of joy. She had a suspicion she'd need it.

After a couple of raps on the closed door, she waited several seconds before twisting the knob and entering. Her father sat behind his massive, ruthlessly neat glass-and-chrome desk, glancing up when she stepped into the room.

He welcomed her with a smile before standing and rounding the desk, arms outstretched, and the band constricting her chest loosened a fraction. If he'd called her here to drop some kind of bomb, he probably wouldn't have greeted her with such warmth. Silas had always been an affectionate parent but also a firm one when required. Still, this side of him reassured her that she wouldn't face bullshit this morning.

Thank God.

Maybe she could get that coffee now.

"Good morning, Tatum. You look well. How're you doing?" He met her halfway across his cavernous office, gripping her upper arms and pulling her into a quick embrace, then brushing a kiss over her cheek.

"Good, Dad. I can't complain. How're you?"

He stroked a hand down his blue-and-gray-striped tie and his thick, muscular stomach. Big and wide-shouldered, he more resembled the linebacker he'd once been for Notre Dame than a CEO. Silas remained in shape, and Tatum had inherited their height from him.

"Fine, fine. Have a seat." He waved toward the couch, table, armchairs and service station loaded down with a coffee urn, cups and saucers and smaller sugar and cream pots. "We're just waiting on your sister."

Tatum arched an eyebrow as she strode toward the sitting area and the nectar of the gods, otherwise known as coffee. No one could ever call her a morning person, and she owned it. A couple of minutes later, she stirred liberal amounts of cream and sugar into the fragrant brew and lifted her gaze to her father, who sat behind his desk once again.

"Any hint on what this impromptu meeting is about?" she asked, raising her cup to her mouth for a careful sip.

"Patience, Tatum. Y'know, your mother and I—"

"Almost named me that, I know." She laughed at the family joke that her parents had teased her with so many times because she lacked that particular virtue. Carrying her cup and saucer, she sank down onto the couch. "While we're waiting on Mia, I've been meaning to ask you—"

"Sorry, I'm late," Mia announced, breezing into the office. "Traffic is terrible this morning." Smiling at her father, she strode toward Tatum and dumped her purse and bag on one of the armchairs before approaching the service station. "Can you catch me up on what I missed?"

"I waited on you to arrive to start," their father said, a note of disapproval in his tone.

Frowning, Tatum slid a look at Mia, who appeared unbothered, her attention focused on pouring coffee. If Tatum's impatience was a Haas joke, then Mia's inability to arrive anywhere on time was another one. So why did her father seem annoyed? Hell, by now they all cushioned time into anything involving Mia.

"If you two are ready, I'll begin." He joined them, claiming an armchair across from Tatum as Mia lowered to one adjacent to the couch.

"BayStar has an investment opportunity with a high-end motorcycle manufacturer based out of Seattle. Mia, you're already familiar with Greer Motorcycles, and Tatum, from what I understand, Nore is engaged to one of its owners. From a business aspect with BayStar, we've been in talks with Joaquin Iverson and Bran Holleran for months about investing in a new line they're about to launch—their second launch of a new model within a year."

He passed Tatum and Mia a tablet each, and on the screen was a report on Greer Motorcycles, the company's history, solvency and a summary of the investment proposal.

She lifted her cup of coffee for another sip, hiding anything her face happened to betray at the sound of Bran's name. Stunned didn't begin to cover the blast of ice that had hit her when Mia mentioned Bran being a client of BayStar's. Tatum would've remembered it if her sister had talked about him before. Just as she remembered every single detail having to do with Bran Holleran.

Unbidden, her mind drifted to him, the cofounder of Greer—she knew this as she'd read a short bio on him. The perfunctory facts neatly summed him up: forty years old, custom bike builder, twenty years' experience in his field, owner of one of the best custom-build companies in the southern US before he collaborated with Joaquin Iverson to establish Greer.

The black-and-white details in no way captured the charismatic, sexual gut punch that was Bran Holleran.

Even now, a shiver danced down her spine as a vision of him from Saturday night wavered in front of her. A wave of heat poured through her like fresh lava. She gritted her teeth against the rush of warmth, but it was pointless. Just as trying to not think about the man was pointless.

Bran Holleran hadn't just gotten under her skin. He'd crept into her mind and taken up residence.

Like a damn squatter.

When he'd stepped out of the shadowed corner and into the moonlight, she'd been struck senseless. That hadn't even happened when she'd met Mark, and up until the moment she'd laid eyes on Bran's striking features, Mark had been the handsomest man she'd seen.

Handsome.

Could she get more bland?

Handsome didn't begin to describe the wide, strong brow, or the stark, almost harsh cheekbones and jawline. Or the bright blue of his gaze that incongruously reminded her of fire under heavy, dark eyebrows. Didn't start to cover the bold slash of nose some could've called hawkish but she labeled domineering. Definitely didn't properly describe the carnal delight that was his mouth. God…

She downed more coffee but it didn't stop another wave of heat swamping her. Just the thought of those firm, wide lips bordered by that thick salt-and-pepper beard had her fighting not to squirm.

What would that facial hair feel like brushing over her skin? Over her breasts? Her inner thighs? Would it be abrasive and leave a burn behind, reminding her he'd been there? Or would it be soft, a silken caress like gentle fingertips?

Clearing her throat, she refocused on the present… and not on the ache pulsing between her thighs.

"That's not a red flag?" she asked her father. "Two launches in a year could be a sign of them expanding too fast."

"If this was another company, maybe. But not them.

And they're two entirely different products. One was their first electric motorcycle and this one will cater to a different demographic. And you have their numbers in front of you. Greer doesn't *need* our investment to roll this out, but they want it in more of a partnership. We can offer them money as well as the resources that come with BayStar Media. And Greer is a sound investment for us."

"And if I may add," Mia interjected. "Between the two founders, they bring a combined thirty years' experience in the motorcycle industry—twenty years with Bran and ten years with Joaquin Iverson, and that's not counting the number of years Joaquin spent racing bikes. They know their industry and client base. And in the decade Greer Motorcycles has been in operation, they've grown to a multimillion-dollar business. They've been all custom builds until now. And they're seeking to move into mass production with this new line. Just from the research I've done, I believe they can do it successfully, and BayStar would profit as an investor."

"All true, and I agree with you." Silas nodded at Mia, then looked at Tatum. "Mia mentioned you met Bran at the fundraiser Saturday night."

Annoyance glimmered inside her, and she resisted glancing at her sister. Logically, her sister relaying that Tatum bumped into Bran shouldn't have bothered Tatum. It shouldn't have struck her as Mia tattling or trying to get in their father's ear. Shouldn't have…

But it did.

And she hated that.

"Yes, we did. And we spoke briefly," Tatum admitted. "Definitely not long enough to cover a new partnership with BayStar."

Her father nodded. "That's fine. You'll be rectifying that in the future." He paused. "Because I'm placing you over this investment project. And you will be the liaison for BayStar while Bran Holleran is in Boston."

A beat of silence pounded in the office, and Tatum didn't know who was more shocked: her or Mia. Blinking, she stared at her father, then looked at Mia, who gaped at Silas as well.

"Dad, I don't understand." Mia shook her head. "What do you mean?"

"I'm sorry, Dad, I'm not sure I understand," Tatum said at the same time, objecting with her sister but for different reasons.

Mia because she obviously felt blindsided, and Tatum because she didn't want this responsibility. More specifically, she didn't want to have anything to do with Bran Holleran.

"Just what I said. Tatum, you will take point on the Greer Motorcycles account." He leaned back in his chair and set his tablet on the side table next to him. "Everything you need to know to catch you up to speed is in what I just sent you. Including the marketing projects we have set up for Greer so far. It's going to be your responsibility to use our resources to secure more for this investment. You'll report your progress directly to me."

Overwhelmed. As she stared down at the tablet, the date on it blurred. For a moment, she considered dropping the device to the floor and power walking from her father's office.

Since Mark's death, Silas had treated her like his glorified intern, keeping her close, doling out tasks but not allowing her to stray too far from under his wing. There was a marked difference in how he treated Mia, her younger sister, like a competent, capable employee, and Tatum, like a broken bird he didn't trust to leave the nest.

And now, he'd thrust her out.

It was what she'd wanted; she'd hated his coddling. But...yes. Overwhelmed.

"Hold on, Dad, please. Just hold on." Mia scooted to the edge of her chair, holding out a hand, palm up. She loosed a short, sharp chuckle. "You can't be serious. Greer Motorcycles is my account."

"If Mia already started working on this—"

Her sister threw Tatum a narrow-eyed glare. "I don't need you to defend me," she snapped.

Well, hell. She'd been trying to side with her. They wanted the same thing, after all—Tatum off this account and Mia back on it.

But, as always, Mia tended to see Tatum as the competition, sometimes even the enemy, rather than an ally. Her sister took sibling rivalry to another level. Always had, even though Tatum had wanted nothing more than to be close to her.

"I've made my decision," Silas said, voice flat, final.

Yet Mia refused to let it go.

Slashing her hand through the air, she insisted, "Dad, I did all the legwork and research on this project. I flew out to Seattle to attend the launch of the KING One and to meet with Bran and Joaquin. I already know this deal, so it doesn't make sense that you would just remove me from it."

His eyes hardened. In one moment to the next, he changed from Silas, their affectionate and protective father, to Silas, decisive and sometimes ruthless CEO of BayStar Media.

"As an employee of BayStar, you did what was requested and required of you. But not once did I say you would take lead on this deal. I asked you for research and to accumulate information, that is all. You took it upon yourself to fly out to Seattle and hold an initial meeting with Greer and informed me after the fact. Just as you attended their launch just weeks after—" Silas shot a swift look at Tatum before returning his attention to Mia "—after everything that occurred. That was inappropriate and I certainly didn't ask you to go. But again, you did so on your own."

"Only because I noticed Greer Motorcycles on your agenda for discussion with the board and I decided to take the initiative. As you've taught us."

"If you'd believed I would've agreed with your actions, you would've been up front with me beforehand, Mia, not after. That includes the meeting you took with Joaquin and Bran, placing me in the awkward position of having to pretend I'd known about it all along. I don't operate that way. And if you weren't my daughter, you would've been fired. Too many times you've acted like a lone wolf, and I won't reward bad behavior."

He turned once more to Tatum, and pinned her with a steady, hard stare.

"You're heading this deal. The fact is, Tatum, everyone—our employees, the board, shareholders, the public—needs to see you are more than this…incident with Mark. That you can not only handle this responsibility as an officer in this company but that you can successfully close the deal. This is the opportunity for that."

Hurt shimmered inside her. Hurt and a humiliation so deep it seemed grafted to her cells. A humiliation that didn't belong to her but had become hers all the same.

"This is bullshit," Mia hissed.

"Tread carefully, Mia," Silas snapped.

"No." She bolted to her feet, her body nearly trembling with outrage. "I've worked on this deal, but now I'm being kicked off because *she*—" Mia flung a hand in Tatum's direction "—has a PR problem? Like I said. This. Is. Bullshit."

After snatching up her bag and purse, Mia stalked out of the office and slammed the door behind her. Tatum didn't move, the reverberation of the noise and her sister's anger vibrating through her. Her heart pounded against her sternum and the beat filled her ears.

"Dad," Tatum murmured. "Why're you doing this?"

"I explained my reasons." He rose from his chair and crossed the room to his desk. "Your sister will get over this. In the meantime, you should have all the information you need to get rolling."

"Mia is not just going to get over this, Dad. And I can't say I blame her. This isn't fair. Not to her. Not even to Bran Holleran or Joaquin, who are probably comfortable with her as the representative of BayStar—"

"You need this. Do you understand me, Tatum?" he asked, stopping in front of his desk and turning around to meet her gaze, his own as uncompromising as his tone. "You. Need. This. Professionally and personally. You went through a serious upheaval this past year, but you know as well as I do that people are sympathetic for five minutes. Then they start looking at you. What did you do? What's wrong with you? And because you've never addressed it, speculation has only increased, not diminished."

Anger and pain speared through her, and she sucked in a breath. "None of what happened with Mark is my fault," she said, hating that her voice shook. "And I can't control how people look at or think about me."

"No, it wasn't and no, you can't. And none of it is fair, Tatum," he murmured.

She bit the inside of her cheek to stem the flow of words. Words that would've been vitriolic and undeserved had she yelled at him not to "handle" her. Not to treat her like she was this fragile thing that would shatter at the slightest harsh comment.

Unbidden, her mind flew to Bran Holleran. He hadn't treated her like that. He'd spoken to her with a rawness in that rough-road voice that had made her feel substantial, grounded…whole. There'd been nothing careful or curated about his speech. He just hadn't given a fuck, and it'd been…liberating.

Exhilarating.

And it was that exhilaration that had her nervous to

be in his company. Some women might be thrilled to have the sweet song of excitement buzz through their veins, hum under their skin.

But most women hadn't been so burned by a man that the thought of trusting one with anything again— her body, her feelings or, God forbid, her heart—ranked up there alongside cuddling with a homicidal shape-shifting clown.

"But," her father continued, dragging her attention back to the here and now, "at the risk of being cliché, life isn't fair. Even less when you're a woman and a very convenient and visible target for a man's failures. So as wrong and burdensome as it is, the challenge to change the narrative falls on you. And I have to own part of the blame in this. I've treated you more as a daughter than an employee, and that's how people have come to view you. But if you're honest, Tatum, you haven't fought too hard to come from under my wing. You've become comfortable. Too comfortable, even though both of us know you're capable of taking over my job if you wanted it."

"That's not tr—" she automatically objected, but when her father arched an eyebrow, the protest died on her tongue. She frowned. Had she been complacent? *Yes.* The answer shimmered in her head, whisper soft but definite. "I can see why you'd say that. I did sit back and lick my wounds, and maybe I let it go on too long. But I've never been satisfied with leaning on you or letting you coddle me, Dad. I've never been content to sit on my behind and collect a check without earning it."

"I know that, Tatum. No one knows that more than

me." He paused and his gaze switched to a picture on his desk. She couldn't see it from her position on the couch, but she didn't need to. Her father'd had the framed photo of his family—her mother, her and Mia—sitting on the desktop for as long as she could remember. "Now's your chance to show everyone else. To prove it to everyone else."

He slid a hand into his pants pocket and rubbed the other over his head. "I had also planned on telling this to you and your sister together, but since she left..." He frowned, shooting a glance at the closed office door as if Mia still stood there. "I guess I'll have to find her later and share this with her. But Greg Mendahl is retiring at the end of the year. I will be promoting someone from within to the position of chief operating officer, and I would like that to be one of my daughters. Both of you have worked for this company full-time for years and interned since you were teens. You've been here longer than Mia, but as unfair as your sister believes I am, I also can't just give you the position based on that. Especially when she's been kicking ass here at BayStar these last few months. Do you even want the position, Tatum?"

"Yes, of course."

She didn't need to think about her answer. Some little girls imagined being models or actresses or doctors. She'd only wanted to work with her father at her family's company and continue the legacy of her great-grandfather. Tatum *enjoyed* her job.

She refused to allow Mark's death—no, Mark's *betrayal*—to steal another dream from her.

"Of course I want the position," she repeated, her voice stronger, more certain this time.

"Good." He nodded, a gleam in his dark brown eyes. "I've already contacted Bran Holleran and told him to expect your call."

She returned his nod, not allowing her expression to reveal the trepidation twisting inside her. Just the thought of seeing the tall older man with the piercing blue eyes and big body had an avalanche of emotions crashing through her.

Nerves. Irritation. Fear.

Excitement.

The last two she resented like hell.

Because once again, her future depended on a man. A wild card.

And she didn't like it.

She didn't like it at all.

Four

Damn. And he'd thought Seattle traffic was bad.

Bran shook his head as he hit the lock button on his key fob and strode up one of Beacon Hill's famous cobblestone streets. Not only had he hit afternoon lunch traffic but he'd also circled the block six times looking for a place to park in this historic Boston neighborhood.

At any other time, he would've slowed his pace to take in the stately brownstones with their flower boxes, iron gas lamps and grand architecture from the turn of the century. Whenever he visited a new city, he loved to tour the corners and areas that made each place distinct. And this one, where history seemed to emanate from the brick of the streets and buildings, was one of those areas. But he couldn't today. Not when he was already five minutes late for his appointment. And something told him the person waiting on him not only valued punctuality but would be looking for anything to strike a mark in his con column.

He shook his head as he passed an array of antique shops, cafés and boutiques on Charles Street and approached the Italian restaurant Tatum had suggested for their lunch. To say he and Tatum Haas had started out on the wrong foot would be akin to saying the Bermuda Triangle was a lost and found section.

As he stepped inside, scents of oregano, basil and thyme greeted him, and he couldn't help inhaling the delicious aromas deep into his lungs. His stomach growled in approval. He scanned the restaurant, surprised at its emptiness. Given the location, the elegance of the place and the promise of the scents emanating from the kitchen, he would've expected the restaurant to be bursting at the seams with people. Had he mixed up the time or the location?

"Good afternoon, sir. Are you Mr. Holleran?" an older man in a black suit and white shirt asked, walking up to him.

"Yes." Bran scanned the vacant area once more. "I'm supposed to meet Tatum Haas here."

The other man nodded and swept a hand to his right. "Yes, sir. She's already arrived. If you'll follow me."

Several moments later, they entered a private dining room that could've been borrowed directly from the movie set of a Tuscan villa. Stone walls, antique lamps, terra-cotta tile, and pots of red and purple flowers had him longing for another trip back to the country of his grandfather's birth. But as beautiful as the setting might be, nothing could divert his attention from the woman rising from the circular table that could easily sit ten or twelve people.

He'd only seen her in evening wear but she looked just as stunning in a simpler royal blue wrap dress. With her long dark hair pulled back in a high ponytail, nothing hindered her refined features from view and he studied the beautiful face that had been haunting him the last couple of days…and nights. He'd halfway convinced himself the depth of those dark eyes, the sharpness of her perfect cheekbones and the prurient lushness of her mouth were his imagination or a trick of the shadows.

The joke was on him.

"Mr. Holleran," she said in that smoky voice that seemed damn near inappropriate for daytime hours. She glanced away from him and smiled at the older man next to him. "Thank you. We're ready to begin now."

"As you wish." The maître d' dipped his head in acknowledgment. "I'll send your server in now."

Tatum lowered into her seat and Bran settled into a chair across from her.

"Thank you for meeting with me on such short notice," she said.

"Of course." He nodded. "But is what we're about to discuss so top secret you had to rent out the entire restaurant?"

She arched an eyebrow, and he found himself waiting, *anticipating* the retort she would deliver. Trading barbs with this woman was better than some of the best sex he'd ever had.

"While I can assure you BayStar Media considers you an important client, closing a restaurant to speak with you isn't really necessary." She picked up the glass of water on the table and sipped from it before continuing. "But since the owners here are longtime friends of the family, they allow us to use their restaurant for lunch meetings before they open for the evening. They have excellent food and it's one of the most popular places to eat in Boston. I thought you might appreciate experiencing one of our attractions even while we're working."

The words were pleasant enough, but that proper tone with its sprinkling of icicles... It told him if he didn't like her choice, he could choke on it.

Why that had lust thickening in his veins, he couldn't explain. Before now, he'd never cottoned to that opposites attract bullshit. But now? Comparing her smooth, buffed edges to his rougher ones... Her upper-crust, champagne and caviar background to his blue-collar, beer and steak fries one... Her aloof reserve to his don't-give-a-fuck approach... Yeah, they were as different as night and day. Yet, no woman had stimulated his mind and his body like Tatum Haas. Not even his ex-wife.

And since he would be working closely with Tatum on a project that meant expansion in another direction for his company, that "stimulation" was not a good thing.

On the contrary. It meant, he'd either keep his dick in his pants or he was fucked. And not in the way that part of his anatomy was used to.

"I'm appreciative," he said, picking up the wine list. As if that signaled their server, he appeared at the table, and they placed their drink requests. A Riesling for her, and a Sam Adams for him. "I don't know any other way to be, so can I speak freely?"

Because nothing about her escaped his notice, he caught the slight tensing of her body. And the very deliberate loosening of it.

"Yes. If we're going to be working together for the length of time you're in Boston, I think we should be honest with each other."

"Is this—" he waved a hand back and forth between them "—going to be a problem?"

"I'm not sure what you're referring to by—" she mimicked his gesture "—this."

Cocking his head, he studied her. "What happened to honesty?"

"I can assure you I'm perfectly capable of handling Greer Motorcycles' account."

"I didn't imply you aren't. The question on the table is do you *want to*."

Her full lips firmed for a moment before she nodded. "Yes. I wouldn't be sitting across from you if I didn't want to be here. Believe me, Mr. Holleran, this investment with Greer is as important to me as it is to you."

Well, that was telling. Not as important to BayStar Media, but to *her*.

"Okay, then," he conceded, although he was far from satisfied with her answer. "How about we start with you calling me Bran."

After a brief hesitation, she nodded. "Fine. And please call me Tatum."

She paused, leaning back as their waiter returned with their drinks. They took a couple of minutes to place their lunch orders, and then she returned her attention to him. The impact of that dark gaze struck him like a kick to the chest. He lifted his beer to his mouth, but the cold alcohol did little to alleviate the lick of heat curling and twisting low in his gut.

She's a good ten years younger than you, at least, he reminded himself. And she was no doubt still grieving her dead fiancé. From what Nore had mentioned, the two had been very much in love. Hell, even if Tatum wasn't his business liaison with BayStar, she still remained too young and in love with a ghost.

He didn't need those fucking complications.

"I've read Greer's biography and a little about Joaquin Iverson and yourself. Can you tell me more about the company and the new line of motorcycles you'd like us to invest in?" she asked, lifting her wineglass to her mouth.

Even Moses appearing before him and wielding a stone tablet of commandments couldn't have stopped Bran from watching those lips part around the glass rim. Never in his life had he wanted to trade places with a wine flute, but damn. Here he was.

Tightening his grip on the bottle in his hand, he sipped more of the alcohol and immediately wished for another beer. It might take a few to get through this meeting.

"As you probably know, we've been in business for ten years, almost eleven now. Joaquin, who was one of the top professional racers, had already been a customer of mine when he approached me about starting a high-end motorcycle manufacturing company. I owned a smaller custom-build business at the time and step-

ping into this larger arena was definitely higher risk—
especially since the majority of new companies don't see
profits for years—but that's life," he said with a shrug.
"And neither Joaquin nor I have ever played it safe, so I
decided to join him. We have an excellent team around
us and we managed to turn Greer into a multimillion-
dollar business. We recently launched our first electric
model, and the sales have been outstanding so far. We've
been beyond pleased with it and the customer response."

Her fingers drummed against the bowl of her glass,
and it momentarily distracted him. It wasn't possible,
but he swore he could feel the pulse of that touch on his
chest, his abdomen...and lower. He shifted in his seat,
fighting the urge to reach across the table and cover her
hand with his to stop the movement.

Or to tangle those slim, elegant fingers with his
longer, thicker ones and savor the differences between
them before lifting each fingertip to his mouth and ac-
quainting it with his lips, his tongue.

Shit.

He'd asked her if it was going to be a problem working together.

He should've been posing that question to himself.

"Can I ask why Greer is rolling out two new motorcycle models back-to-back? I'm a layperson who freely
admits she doesn't know anything about bikes, but is it
fiscally sound to do this? Are you afraid of oversaturat-
ing your client base?"

"That's a good question." He folded his arms on the
table and leaned forward. "And the answer is no, we're
not, simply because the customer who will or has bought

a custom build from us or purchased the KING One isn't the same client who will purchase this newer model." Her eyes brightened with interest, and the delight of discussing his passion warmed him. "Until now, every motorcycle we've manufactured has been a custom build, meaning the client contacts us, discusses what they specifically want in their bike and, after it's completed, we deliver it. Because we work so closely with our customers, we manufacture anywhere from two to three hundred bikes a year. But this newest model will be different. Not only will it be our first cost-friendly line, but it will also be mass-produced. This is a new direction for us but Joaquin and I both agree that between the quality of our product and the name recognition behind Greer Motorcycles, it will be a success."

"Hold that thought." Tatum turned to the chair next to her and picked up a tablet, then started tapping on the screen several times. "Have you considered an ad campaign surrounding the…" She frowned slightly. "What is the name of the new model?"

He held up a hand and shook it back and forth. "We've been going back and forth on a permanent one. The KING One was easy—we named it after Joaquin's father. But we've tossed around a couple. For now, we're leaning toward the Greer Rocket."

"No."

He blinked. Shock rippled through him. He stared at the top of her head as she tapped something else into her tablet. Hell, she hadn't even bothered to look up when she dismissed the name for *their* bike.

"Excuse me?" he asked.

"I said, no." She finally raised her head and met his gaze, and even though annoyance whipped through him, a part of him still found the wrinkling of her nose adorable.

Damn. He was in a professional meeting. He had to leave adjectives like *sexy*, *beautiful* and *adorable* at the fucking door.

"What do you mean 'no'?"

"No offense, and I'm sure all of you at Greer know your business, but that's a terrible name."

He stared at her. "When someone says 'but,' what they really mean is forget everything I said before 'but.' Now I'm about to tell you what I really think."

"I watch *Dr. Phil*, too," she drawled then tilted her head. "Of course, you're old enough to remember when he was on *Oprah*."

He snorted. "So you're not only insulting the professionals' choice of name for their product but you're taking potshots at my age. Nice." He tipped his chin toward her tablet. "Just tell me what problem you have with the name while I order you a glass of milk to go with lunch."

The corner of her mouth kicked up, and so did his temperature.

"I'm sure you have your reasons for the Rocket, but since we agreed on honesty between us, I hear that and think of a vibrator."

Holy shit.

Somehow, he managed not to choke on his tongue or fall out of his seat. But no way in hell could he prevent the barrage of erotic images from bombarding his head. Her, gorgeous brown skin dewy with sweat, long hair a dark tangle haloed around her head, eyes closed, body straining…

Kill. Me. Now.

He couldn't unsee that image. Especially with the word *vibrator* seeming to echo in the room as if it had been shouted in a wind tunnel.

"Excuse me?" he croaked.

She shrugged a slim shoulder, seemingly oblivious to the arousal she'd detonated like a bomb. "Sorry. Not sorry." She held up a hand as if stopping him from speaking. *As if I could speak.* "And I know what you're getting ready to say. A motorcycle is called a crotch rocket. But other than being really obvious and unimaginative, the name will draw more smirks than praises."

He tipped his beer bottle up, taking a long, *long* sip.

"Well then, what do you propose?" he finally asked.

"So glad you asked." Smiling, she flipped the tablet around and showed him an image of the prototype he'd sent over to her father and sister. "Tell me what you see when you look at this."

"A standard bike powered by a 399 cc, air-cooled, two-valved single-cylinder engine with a fuel injection that provides amazing response practicality. It's light and compact and is well suited to both beginner and experienced riders. It's also the perfect bike for a custom build. So a client can add customizations if they'd like."

She nodded. "Okay, my turn. Do you know what I see?" Flipping the tablet, she peered down at the screen. "A really kick-ass-looking bike. Ooh. And it's shiny and black. Looks fast. Vroom." He barely managed to swallow his bark of laughter as she glanced back at him, that eyebrow arched once more. "What name can we come up with that crosses the divide between all the cool details you just provided and my 'vroom'?"

"I'm guessing you have one?" He waved a hand, gesturing that the floor was hers.

"As a matter of fact, I do." She smiled, setting the tablet down on the table. "Greer Motorcycles presents The Gauntlet. A gauntlet protects, shields and is essential to armor. That's the message you want to send your customer. It's a steady, reliable bike that will protect you on the road, an essential addition to your collection. But also, it's a challenge to all of the established motorcycle manufacturers that your new line is coming for their spot and their clientele."

Goddamn.

She was good.

"Well?" She dropped her hands to her lap, her shoulders straightening. No, bracing. Did she expect him to reject her suggestion? Did she doubt herself? "What do you think?"

"I think I should call Joaquin and let him know our model has a new name."

Her lips slowly curved upward into a wide smile, and the delight there gleamed in her dark eyes. Once more, all the air escaped his lungs, driven from them by shock. And desire.

God, that smile.

As if a hand pressed against his chest, he leaned back in his chair, pinned by the beauty and power of it. Was this really the first time he'd seen her smile?

Yes. The answer came, swift and certain. Because if he'd been on the receiving end of *that* before, he would've not only remembered, but would've been doing everything in his power to elicit its reappearance.

Clearing his throat, he reached for his beer again and then offered up a little prayer of thanks as the server entered the room with their food. Maybe if he stuffed his mouth with veal parmigiana, there'd be fewer chances of him uttering something stupid—and too revealing.

Like how her smile should either be outlawed or canonized because no one should wield a superpower like that.

Or how the joy lighting those brown-black eyes had him greedy to see what lust would do to them. Darken them until her gaze appeared almost obsidian? Or brighten them even more until they burned him with their heat?

Then… Then he remembered why she probably didn't smile as much. Why he'd glimpsed more hurt and barrenness in her gaze than joy.

When a person lost their partner to death—even under the worst of circumstances—it left wounds, scars. An emptiness that was impossible to fill. He should know; he'd had a front-row seat to that kind of mourning after his stepfather died. It'd been four years, and his mother still hadn't wholly recovered.

He needed to keep that at the forefront of his mind. Remember that he hadn't arrived in Boston to get involved in any kind of entanglement. Especially when it seemed like both of them carried so much baggage they rivaled a damn airport.

"I'm glad you like it." She picked up her fork and cut into her lasagna. "So my father mentioned other opportunities you're looking into while here. Do you need our assistance with any of them?"

For the next forty minutes, they ate and conversed about the deal to have their motorcycle featured in a movie filming in Boston the following week. It would be great promotion and a chance for millions of people to view their newest model before it even rolled out.

As they finished up their meals, their waiter returned to remove the empty plates and replace them with two big slices of cheesecake covered in strawberry sauce and fruit. Like with her meal, Tatum dug into the dessert with relish and appreciation. And her low hum of pleasure vibrated over his skin, beneath it. Damn, did anything this woman do not strike him as fucking hot?

"What happened to your sister?"

Her fork hovered above her food, her gaze lifting to his. As if a door shut, those eyes that had been so bright with interest only seconds ago became shuttered, closing him out of her thoughts.

"I'm not sure what you mean," she said, that cool note returning to her voice.

"Until the call from your father, I was under the impression Mia would be handling the deal with Bay-Star. Is there a reason behind the abrupt change from her to you?"

She set the eating utensil beside her plate and straightened until it seemed her spine fused with the chair back.

"No reason other than Silas preferred I take over. If you have any questions, I'm sure he'll be willing to answer them for you. But I doubt he would've placed someone inept over this account when closing it would be extremely beneficial to both you and BayStar."

Her tone remained even, neutral. And not a curl of her lip, a flare of her nostril or a flicker of emotion in her eyes betrayed her. Yet something...

The subtle stiffness of her shoulders.

The slight hike of her chin.

Her hands, which had been on the table, were now under it, out of view.

Funny how he noticed those tiny details when before now, he'd only paid that close attention to motorcycles. They were more interesting and less bothersome than people.

But Tatum Haas was proving to be different from most "people."

"Are you this prickly with everyone or am I special?" he asked.

For a moment, she didn't reply. But then her eyes briefly closed and she turned her head to the side. When she finally returned her gaze to him, the inscrutable expression had disappeared and the faintest hint of a smile curved her mouth.

"I'm a little scared to admit that it might be with everyone." Shaking her head, she said, "I apologize. I do want to see this investment happen. I think there's something special here for both Greer and BayStar."

Bran nodded and debated whether or not to bring up the elephant in the room that they both seemed determined to waltz around.

What the hell. He mentally shrugged. He'd never been much of a dancer anyway.

"If any of this is due to Saturday night, we should have a conversation to clear the air."

"Yes, we got off on the wrong foot." Tatum picked up her fork again but didn't resume eating the dessert. "But that's in the past. It doesn't affect the here and now."

The hell it didn't. His encounter with the fiery, combative woman on the balcony had flipped a switch in his body, and he'd been inconveniently fascinated since then. And this aspect of her—the sharp, creative businesswoman—only deepened that absorption. Deepened the need winding its way through his veins straight to his cock.

No, he might not act on that grinding lust, but he couldn't deny its existence either.

He had control of his dick, though, not the other way around. And he would be damned if he allowed an attraction—he had to snort at that anemic description—to derail his purpose in being here and working with her.

"Good." Then because a disconnect obviously existed between his brain and mouth, he murmured, "Do you want to talk about why you're prickly?"

"No." Her answer, flat and definite, came immediately and carried a whole lot of *shut this shit down* behind it.

Yeah, he heard the message as clearly as a shout and would heed it. He caught something else, too. Her pain. Her anger.

He'd been through a rough and ugly divorce. And while the end of a marriage could be compared to a death—of a relationship, a certain lifestyle, a dream—it wasn't the same as an actual death. This woman bore the scars of losing not just her future and the man she'd loved but the man she'd believed him to be.

If working together on a deal that was crucial to his company's expansion wasn't enough reason not to become involved with Tatum Haas, then playing second fiddle to a memory—that was a battle where there could be no winners.

No, he'd stay here for the month needed to settle business for Greer. Then he'd leave for home, where he belonged.

Now if he could just get his cock to cooperate.

Which would be easier if he stopped staring at that beautiful temptation of a mouth. Or those soulful almost-black eyes. Or the sleek fall of her hair. Or the slim yet tight curves of her body.

Shit. He just needed to stop looking, period.

Tatum flattened her hands on either side of her dessert plate and studied them as if they held answers. Finally, she lifted her head and met his gaze, and a small fissure zigzagged through the resolutions he'd just cemented in his head. His grip tightened around his fork, but that measure of control didn't erase the desire to feel her soft skin beneath his fingers. To sweep his thumb over those cheekbones and somehow erase the shadows from her eyes.

Fuck.

Thoughts like that belonged to a younger man tasting his first sting of love. Not to him, an older divorced cynic with more miles and experience than a 1984 Harley Davidson Shovelhead.

"Mia mentioned you would be in Boston for the next few weeks, and we'll no doubt communicate often. But it would be best if we kept our interactions strictly professional. It's…simpler that way."

Though he'd already arrived at the same conclusion, irritation crept through him.

"That won't be a problem," he said. Forking up cheesecake and fruit, he steered the conversation back to the newly christened Gauntlet. Right where it belonged. "I'm supposed to be on the set of the movie next week…"

No. Not a problem at all.

Five

"There you are," Nore greeted Tatum from the laptop screen. Her best friend sat on her couch, legs curled under her, popcorn in her lap and glass of wine on the coffee table in front of her. In other words, ready for their monthly Movie Night. "I thought I was going to have to start calling your phone off the hook to hunt you down."

Tatum laughed, sinking to her own sofa. After breaking open a microwave bag of cheese popcorn, she dumped the snack into a bowl she'd brought into the living room. Picking up her own glass of wine, she toasted her friend. Though they were literally on opposite sides of the country, they had a standing "date" every second Thursday night of the month—Movie Night.

After Mark died, Nore had let Tatum miss a couple

of their get-togethers. But she hadn't let Tatum get away with that for long. On the third month, Nore had flown to Boston, invaded Tatum's house and didn't leave for a week. Much like Tatum had done for Nore when her friend had been going through a rough time with Joaquin.

That's the kind of friendship they shared.

And it'd helped to ground Tatum, keep her sane during one of the darkest periods in her life.

"Now, you know I was going to be here. Can't have you jumping on another flight to see me. Hell, I might not get you out of my house next time." Tatum grinned and dumped a bag of M&M's into her popcorn.

"Please. You love when I come visit." Nore waved her hand and then leaned forward, squinting at her through the screen. "Daaamn, woman! A whole bag of M&M's? All right, this is obviously an emergency. Movie Night can wait a few minutes. What's wrong?"

"Why does something have to be wrong just because I'm indulging in a few snacks?"

Nore tilted her head, and her skepticism reached through the laptop. "In college, I came back to our dorm room to find you eating a bag of sour cream 'n' onion chips with mini Snickers thrown in. That's when you found out Lawrence Collins had been seen taking another girl to his room at a frat party not hours after declaring his undying devotion to you. Several years ago, you tore up a pint of strawberry ice cream with chocolate chip cookies and Twix mixed in. A coincidence that you'd discovered your ex Richard had kissed Mia at your family's annual July Fourth party? I think not. And then, what about—"

"Fine." Tatum scowled at her friend, holding up a hand to stop Exhibit C. "You might have a small point."

"Small?" Nore snorted. "I'll let you have that one. But just go ahead and spill. Who's the man—and why the hell didn't I know there even *was* a man?—and what did he do?" She jabbed a finger at Tatum. "And later we're really going to dive into how we, as women, need to stop being emotionally out of control over another person and letting it manifest in binge eating. That shit is old. If you want to eat your weight in snacks because that's just what you feel like doing or because it's fucking Monday, great! Awesome! Do you and I'll probably join in. But allowing someone else that control? Nope. We're done with that, sis." She inhaled and blew it out. "Okay, that's me getting down off my soapbox. Now. Dish. And no judgment because that's not what we do either."

The need to object rose inside her. But she couldn't lash out at her friend or even tell her to mind her own business. Because Nore was right; Tatum couldn't deny it. And it took a true friend to tell her the truth and hold up a mirror so she could be the best possible her.

Didn't mean she wasn't going to eat this bowl of popcorn, though.

"The reason I didn't mention a man is because there isn't a man—at least not how you're meaning." At Nore's squint, Tatum huffed out a breath. "Bran Holleran is here in Boston," she said by way of explanation.

"Yes." Nore drew the word out. "I thought I men-

tioned he would be out there for a few weeks? Joaquin told me they approached your company for an
investment opportunity and Bran is out there to finalize
that, among other things, for their new motorcycle." She
shook her head. "But what does that have to do with—
oh. You and Bran?" she asked, leaning forward. "How?
What? When? Was it *good*?"

A bark of laughter escaped Tatum and she leaned
back from the barrage of questions, holding her palms
up. "Wait a minute, wait a minute." She chuckled again.
"First, there isn't a me and Bran. We met last weekend
at a fundraiser and let's just say that was…memorable."

"How memorable? 'Fond memory that gives you
fuzzies' memorable? Or 'Hey, future kids, your mom
had a hot dirty past and she regrets nothing' memorable?"

"Nore. Seriously."

"What?" She shrugged, lifting a hand of popcorn to
her mouth. "I love Joaquin with all my heart but that
doesn't mean I'm blind. The man is sexy as hell with
that salt-and-pepper hair and beard, striking blue eyes
and big body. He's *Roadhouse* Sam Elliott meets *Sons
of Anarchy* Charlie Hunnam. Tell me I'm wrong."

Nope, she wasn't wrong. And as an image of Bran
at the restaurant table—that tall frame sprawled in his
chair like a king on a throne—flitted across her mind,
her body cosigned the sentiment. Bran Holleran wasn't
just sexy—he exuded sex. With each syllable drenched
in that deep rough-and-tumble voice with its hint of the
South. With each shift of those wide shoulders and each

stride of his long, powerful legs. With every movement of his wide, carnal mouth.

With every too-incisive, too-knowing stare of those beautiful, bright blue eyes.

"Yes, he's a good-looking man," Tatum conceded with a straight face. "But mostly he just gives me the urge to take off my shoe and break a heel going upside his head with it. And you know how much I love my Manolo Blahnik stilettoes. The truth is our meeting was more along the lines of *Ten Things I Hate About You*."

"You do realize those two end up together in the end, right?"

"Nore." Tatum groaned then laughed. "We are not Heath Ledger and Julia Stiles. More like Tom and Jerry," she muttered. "But anyway, we totally rubbed each other the wrong way. Only after, do I discover he's here in Boston because of BayStar. That's not the end of it, though. Dad removed Mia from the account and assigned me to it. So now I'm working directly with Bran and it's..." She frowned, her mouth twisting.

"Uncomfortable?" Nore supplied.

"Yes." She huffed out the answer. "And that might be a bit of an understatement."

"Why? Because you two exchanged some sharp words?"

"Yes. No." Tatum frowned. "I don't know."

Nore didn't immediately reply, but Tatum could practically feel her regard through the laptop screen.

"What?" Tatum pressed her friend. "You're usually not one to be at a loss for words or hold back. Just say what's on your mind."

Nore blew out a breath. "Okay, here's the thing. I'm usually not a proponent of you being uncomfortable, but right now? I'm thankful for it. Other than work, you haven't shown much interest in anything—or anyone. And if Bran is making you feel, *period*, then I'm all for it. I don't care if it's anger, irritation or homicidal tendencies. Wait." She scrunched up her nose. "Maybe I do care about the last one. I couldn't come visit you in jail. It's such a depressing place."

"Nice to know your concern has its limits," Tatum drawled. "And I love you, but I'm not remotely interested in getting involved with Bran or any other man. I don't think I need to explain why."

"It's been almost a year, Tate," Nore murmured. "And I'm not saying there's a time limit to grief. But I also hate to see you a prisoner to the pain and anger of Mark's death. He's still controlling you from the grave."

Silence echoed between them, and Nore's words ricocheted off the walls of Tatum's skull. Like an accusation. Or a revelation.

Again, she yearned to deny her friend's words. But she couldn't. There were some days she felt *consumed* with powerlessness and resentment. Overwhelmed by it. Especially when others wouldn't let her forget that she would always be Mark Walker's Jilted Fiancée. Or Mark Walker's Almost But Not Quite Widow.

Closing her eyes, she pinched the bridge of her nose. "I think..." she whispered then trailed off.

"You think what? You know you can talk to me about anything and it stays here, Tate," Nore reminded her.

Opening her eyes, Tatum sighed but instead of meeting her friend's gaze, she stared at her untouched glass of wine. "I think," she softly began again, "if I just knew everything. If there weren't any more secrets. He lied and left me in the dark the entire time we were together. And now that he's gone, I still don't have the truth. I continue to play the fool because, in a way, he's still lying to me. If I knew…" she repeated, then shook her head.

"What will it change, Tate?"

"For once, I'll feel like I have control over my life. I won't sit here every day with my stomach in knots waiting for the other shoe to drop and blow my life to pieces again. If I know everything—Why did he treat me like this? How long was it going on? Who was the other woman?—then I won't continue to feel like a blind idiot who chose a man who didn't choose her back."

"Babe." Nore sighed and set her bowl of popcorn next to her. "You need to acknowledge that you might never discover the answers to those questions. And then you're going to have to find a way to be okay with that. Mark being unfaithful wasn't a reflection on you. It speaks more about his lack of character than yours. Yes, I hate to speak ill of the dead, but I won't lie either. You are and never have been a fool. And anyone who says differently? Fuck 'em."

Laughter bubbled up inside Tatum, momentarily lightening the weight on her chest. "I hear what you're saying, Nore. I honestly do, and I'll try. But contrary to popular opinion, getting under a new man isn't always the answer to getting over the old one."

"So don't get under him—yet." Nore grinned. "All

I'm saying is if you're so busy focusing on the past and holding on to it, you'll never be free for whatever or whoever comes into your life." Nore tilted her head. "You still have the brooch, right?"

Tatum tried not to roll her eyes…and failed.

"Oh God, Nore, please don't start that." She shook her head, picking up her glass of wine. "Yes, I have the brooch, and I'm holding on to it because my best friend bought it for me as a gift. But my well for believing in fairy tales has run completely dry."

Nore squinted at her. "Oh so when I had it, you believed in the legend. But now you don't?"

"The night you gave it to me, my fiancé died and I discovered he'd been a manwhore our entire relationship. So no, I don't believe in it."

"Have you ever stopped to consider that maybe—just maybe—Mark wasn't the true love you were meant to have? That your real soulmate is still out there?"

No, she hadn't considered that. And though the story attached to the brooch was romantic, she'd meant what she told Nore. Legends, fairy tales… They belonged to other women, not her. More importantly, she wanted no part of them. It'd been the stars in her eyes that hadn't allowed her to see the lies right in front of her.

No. She'd never put herself in the position to fall for another man's lies again.

Mark had taught her a valuable lesson.

Never give everything to someone else and risk having nothing left but shattered pieces of herself. She couldn't afford to repeat her mistakes. Next time she might not have anything left to pick up. And she refused to be that weak woman again.

"How about I make a deal with you?" Tatum held up her glass toward the screen. "If my soulmate comes along, you'll be the first to know."

Nore held up her own glass. "I'm going to hold you to that. Then I can intervene before you provide him with a dissertation on why soulmates don't exist."

Laughing, Tatum lifted her wine to her mouth for a deep sip. "I wouldn't give him a dissertation. Now, maybe a three-page, single-spaced essay…"

Snorting, Nore set down her glass and grabbed her bowl of popcorn, moving it back to her lap. "Let's get this movie going. But be warned." Nore jabbed a finger at her. "I'm not done with you."

"You wouldn't be my best friend if you were."

Six

Bran stood outside the metal fence with black netting. He scanned the crowds that had gathered in the area, but didn't spy a specific lovely face. Glancing down at the watch on his wrist, he noted the time. Still about ten minutes before the time he'd given Tatum. And she could've hit traffic on her way out to Weymouth from Boston. No doubt it was even thicker as she approached The Hangout, the huge former fighter jet hangar behind him that had been transformed into a soundstage for the blockbuster movie that had just started filming.

An electric charge seemed to fill the air, emanating from the people hoping to catch a glimpse of one of the stars or some of the action behind the fence. Hell, he couldn't blame them. He didn't get starstruck easily, and yet excitement hummed through him at being a part of this Hollywood magic, even if peripherally.

Just as he started to glance at his watch again, he caught movement out of the corner of his eye. And the buzz in his veins jacked higher. Shit. That didn't bode well. But he didn't glance away from the slender woman striding up the street with a confidence that had his gut knotting with arousal. His heart drummed out a sonorous rhythm, one that echoed in his cock. Heat surged over his skin, and the soft breeze of late September did nothing to cool him. Because this particular warmth wasn't due to the outside temperature.

Damn.

It'd been a little over a week since he'd last seen Tatum and his body reacted as if it'd been years. No. Didn't bode well at all.

Stuffing his hands in the pockets of the black hoodie he wore under a dark blue blazer, he walked forward, meeting her halfway. It was either that or continue ogling her like a creep.

She's eleven years younger than you. When she was a junior in high school, you were getting married.

He silently repeated the reminder like a mantra. A warning. His ex-wife had been five years younger than him, and the longer they'd been married, the more that age gap had widened.

"Tatum," he greeted, sweeping a glance down and taking in her dark red wide-legged jumpsuit that accentuated the sleek lines and sensuous curves of her lithe frame. "Good to see you again."

"You, too."

She stretched out her hand toward him and his stomach tightened. Damn. He'd been trying to avoid touching her for a sense of self-preservation. Reluctantly, he clasped her hand in his, and the press of her smaller, softer palm to his larger, rougher one... Yeah, it shouldn't have been sexual. But it was. He couldn't help looking down at their hands and imagining how it would be with their bodies aligned together, his larger frame wrapped around her more slender one. The need to cover her, surround her...protect her clawed at him.

As soon as possible, he dropped her hand and returned his to his hoodie.

"I'm sorry about running late. Finding parking around here was terrible. I didn't count on that," she said. "I noticed all the crew parking signs and didn't want to risk getting towed."

"No problem. You're good." He turned and fell into step beside her as they headed back toward the entry point. "I appreciate you taking the time out of your day."

She shrugged. "It's only a half-hour drive. And besides—" she tilted her head toward him, smiled "—it's not every day I get invited to an actual movie set."

"True." He arched an eyebrow. "And of course, you get to see your investment for the first time," he added, tone dry.

"Oh of course. There's that." The corner of her mouth quirked. "Speaking of our investment... Have you spoken with Joaquin about changing the name of the motorcycle?"

"Yes, I did as soon as we finished up our lunch." He couldn't contain his smile as he thought back on the video call with his partner and friend. "His exact words were, 'Well, damn. Can we hire her?'" As Tatum laughed, he forced his gaze not to linger on her pretty mouth. "I guess you can say he was for it. Our new model is officially called The Gauntlet. The changes in marketing and design are being implemented right now."

She didn't reply but her soft smile might as well as have shouted her delight and pride. Inside the pocket of his hoodie, he balled his fist, his nails pricking his palm. Nice try, but the tiny bite of pain didn't erase his need to trace that full bottom lip.

Damn, he wanted to feast on that smile.

Minutes later, they entered the gate with their passes, and Bran led her across the lot toward the former hangar. Trucks and steel construction containers occupied the perimeter of the property. Crew and staff strode to and from the building, and the set appeared to be its own small town.

Breaking his own rule about touching her, Bran set a hand to the small of her back, and he ground his teeth at the blast of heat that punched him in the chest and slid its way through his body.

"We have permission to visit the set today but I wanted to take you over to the trailer first and let you see The Gauntlet up close," he explained, guiding her toward one of the trucks.

"I would love to," she said. "I don't think the notes I read included how your new model ended up being included in an upcoming film. Other than the obvious promotional reasons, it must be exciting for you to see your product on the big screen."

"Yeah, it is. And after twenty years in this business, I didn't think I'd be able to experience another first."

"You're lucky," she murmured. "I experience new firsts all the time."

He glanced down at her, but she didn't look up at him or elaborate on that enigmatic statement. A part of him wanted to stop right in the middle of the lot, turn her toward him and demand an explanation. Tell him about the subdued note in her voice.

Give him names, times and locations so he could handle every person who dared cause the thread of pain in those words.

But he'd stopped going around beating up people on behalf of others in grade school. No, wait. High school. In his defense, though, when Michael Wheeler decided to put his hand on Bran's sister's ass, the football player had pretty much asked to have his own ass delivered to him.

Mentally shaking his head, Bran refocused on their conversation.

"This way." He jerked his chin toward a trailer on the right side of the lot. "You asked how we managed to get our motorcycle in the movie. It's a case of who I know. Which for me happens to be someone with the casting company. They were looking for certain cars to rent and they also needed a motorcycle for a chase scene. She'd been a longtime client of mine, and I'd built several motorcycles for her. So when she called and asked about one for the film, it was the perfect opportunity."

"Longtime client?" she asked. "Is she from the South, too?"

He slid her a glance. "If you're going fishing, at least let me give you a rod."

"Fine." She held up her hands. "Busted. But can I point out that a gentleman would've just answered the question instead of calling me nosy?"

"Well, there's your answer. I never claimed to be a gentleman." He smirked at her low snort. "And no, as far as I know, Tracy is LA born and bred. And I'm from Georgia. Although I haven't lived there for at least a decade. My mother's still there, though."

"Really? Your mother?" she echoed, surprise ringing in her voice.

"Yes, I do have one of those," he drawled. "Contrary to the bio on Greer's website, I didn't spring from a god's skull. That's just a press release."

"A good one, too, although I thought the picture of you in full armor was a bit much."

"Shit. I told marketing that might be a little over-the-top."

Their gazes met. And they grinned.

But in the next instant, the air between them grew charged, electric, and their wide smiles ebbed then disappeared.

"You should do that more often," he murmured.

"You do realize how condescending it sounds for you to tell me I should smile more, right?" she asked just as softly.

They'd come to a halt in the middle of the lot, and for him, they could've been the only two there. That's how focused, no, *consumed* he was by this woman.

"I heard it as soon as I said it, and I apologize. It does

sound incredibly patronizing." He paused. "Still, I'll say I hate why you've probably lost that smile."

She didn't reply, but her mouth firmed. Surprise and another more enigmatic emotion flickered in her eyes before she glanced way from him. *Dammit.* Why had he mentioned the death of her fiancé, even peripherally? To insert distance between them? To remind himself *why* he needed to insert that distance? Both?

As he dragged a hand over his head, his fingers bumped the bun on top of his head. There could've been a less clumsy way of him doing that without causing her pain. *Asshole*, he hissed at himself.

"There's the trailer," he said, dipping his head toward the truck containing Greer's new model. "I let them know we're on our way."

Fifteen minutes later, he wheeled the motorcycle down the ramp then popped the kickstand, halting it in front of Tatum.

"This is it," he announced proudly. Maybe even a little reverently. "The Gauntlet."

"It's beautiful. Can I?" Tatum's hand hovered over the handlebar.

"Of course."

With a nod, she stroked a palm over the chrome panel and the seat. He felt that touch over his skin, his chest, his ribs, his hip. Struggling not to shift and fidget under the oddly sensual action, he switched his attention back to the motorcycle, taking his time to catalog and scrutinize every detail, ensuring nothing was amiss.

"It's bigger than I imagined," she said with a low huff of laughter. "More… I don't know, sexy, if that's a thing."

Yeah, it was.

"I can't speak for all riders, but for me it can be sexual having all that power between your legs and being in control of it. There's the absolute freedom of it, too. Nothing but you and the elements. The wind pressing against your skin and roaring in your ears like a lover. Yeah, it can be sexy as hell."

Her lips parted, and her tongue peeked out to slide over her the bottom curve. What would she do if he reached across this bike, cupped the back of her neck and captured that mouth with his own? Traded her moan for his? Part of him was willing to say *fuck it* to every reason why he shouldn't.

"So." She cleared her throat, grazing her fingers over the seat again. "In the file, the model is black. But this is red. I remember you telling me they would all be mass-produced the same."

"They will be. But one great feature is they're the perfect basis for custom builds. Like this one. Take a look." He pointed out elements on the bike. "The Gauntlet has good bones, and specifically for the movie, we added lower superbike-style bend handlebars as well as a tuck-and-roll seat and trunk. We then streamlined the rear fender a bit and have the red paint on the panels. It has amazing torque and power. I test-drove it myself, and it's an incredibly smooth ride." He swept a hand over the immaculate chrome.

"You really love what you do, don't you?" Tatum asked, and he didn't need to look at her to catch her smile; he heard it in her voice. Although, hell, he really liked looking at her.

And the sight of her lips curved in pleasure was just so damn pretty.

Still… He fought not to fidget under the warmth in her eyes.

"I know you're now the president of your own company but looking at you with the motorcycle, hearing you talk about each and every detail…" She shook her head. "No one could miss your joy, your passion for it. You really love the art that goes into building and designing a bike."

"I do. Each one is its own challenge and accomplishment."

She studied him, and this time he surrendered to the need to avoid her inspection. God, a woman over a decade his junior had him ducking his head like a boy half his age. Who was he again?

"I read that you used to own your own custom-build business. You probably don't have as much time to be hands-on with Greer as you did then," she said.

"Most of my time is spent in the office rather than the garage or warehouse. But I still approve every design because you're right. It's a matter of pride."

"But you miss it."

"I miss it," he softly admitted. "Owning a small business is different than running a larger company. Less… intimate, although I can name almost all of our employees and consider several of them close friends. But yeah, I do miss getting my hands dirty. If I didn't have my own collection of bikes, I'd probably go a little crazy." He jerked his chin toward her. "And you?"

She tried to control her flinch. The movement was almost imperceptible, but Bran noted it.

"And me what?"

"You brought up passion and joy. What's yours? Working for your family's company? I've heard you're good at it."

A sardonic caricature of a smile twisted her lips, and he instantly detested it. That didn't fit, didn't belong on her.

"Really? Who told you that? Nore?"

"No." He crossed his arms over his chest. "Your father, actually, as well as several of your coworkers and employees. They admire and respect you. Why would you think they don't?"

"Did I say that?" she asked, voice tight.

"Yes, Tatum, you did."

A tense quiet descended between them, taut and so fucking loud with her denial, her pain, her...*screams*. They rang in his ears.

"Just say it," she whispered. "Ask me."

"Tell me," he whispered back. "I don't want to hear it unless you willingly tell me."

"Maybe..." Her lips flattened and her jaw clenched. After a moment, she continued, her voice a shade lower. "I'm already this figure either to be pitied or condemned. A cautionary tale or a salacious piece of gossip. Maybe I don't want to be either with you. Maybe I just want to be who I was before my life imploded."

She's not yours to comfort.

His mind understood that, but his body ached to do differently. His hands tingled with the need to cup the back of her neck and slide into her hair. His chest itched to have her pressed against it. His thighs tensed, ready to brace her negligible weight against him, embrace her strength and absorb it into his own.

He gave his head one short, hard shake then lowered his arms to his sides.

"And who were you before?" he asked.

She blinked, as if surprised by the question. For a long moment, she met his gaze then dropped it to the motorcycle, tracing a finger along the curved handlebar. What did it say about him that the stroke shivered down his rib cage?

It said he was in deeper shit than he cared to acknowledge.

"I was a successful businesswoman who didn't doubt her purpose. A professional who inspired confidence because I was confident. A woman who knew she was loved and desired and cherished the security of it. A woman who had the world at her fingertips."

She inhaled a breath, lifting her head. And it was a good thing he didn't know where her ex-fiancé was buried because he might go dig him up, kill him, then drive him six feet deep again. For causing that pain in her almost-black eyes, the bastard deserved it.

Loosing a short, jagged laugh, she pushed her long hair over her shoulder, then straightened those same shoulders. As if she were shrugging on emotional armor, her reserve seemed to settle piece by piece. The hike of her chin, the subtle shifting of her body away from the motorcycle and him, the smoothing of her expression.

And he resented every slight alteration that enclosed her behind that impenetrable wall of ice.

"Betrayal by someone who is supposed to love you doesn't strip away the core of you," he quietly said. "Does it beat you down until you're fucking screaming for mercy? Does it make you question every decision you've ever made and have you wondering if you can trust yourself, much less anyone else? Hell yes. But change who you are at the very core of your being? No. We don't come out the same—but shit, when people are in accidents, they don't either. They're scarred, in pain and need to go through rehab to relearn everything they once did so easily. It's the same thing when someone violates your faith in them and puts your whole worldview on its ass. But underneath all the bullshit, you're still you. Scars and all."

"You said 'we,'" she murmured.

He frowned. "What?"

"You said, 'We don't come out the same.' Like you personally know what it is to be changed by betrayal."

Her mask slipped—just enough for him to catch. And if he hadn't, he might not have answered her question. But if tearing back the curtain on his own past would punch a bigger chink in that steely armor... Yeah, he'd do it.

"I've been married. And divorced." He dipped his chin. "You don't go through that and not come out on the other side without some bruises."

She stared at him, and he glimpsed the curiosity in her eyes.

"Just say it," he said, returning her words from moments earlier. "Ask me."

Her lips parted, and though he didn't enjoy delving into the bloody wreckage that had been his marriage, his gut tightened as he prepared to do just that. For her.

"I—" She frowned and, bowing her head, removed her phone from the pocket of her jumpsuit. "Sorry, I need to take this." She tapped the screen and then held the cell to her ear. "Hey, Dad." Tilting her head, she slightly turned away from Bran. "Yes. I'm in Weymouth with Bran Holleran. We're visiting the movie set." She pinched the bridge of her nose as she listened to whatever Silas Haas said on the other end of the line. "This can't wait?" she asked, and it sounded like the question came through gritted teeth. "Dad, I'm not—" A pause. "Fine. I'll be there in an hour or two." Pause. "No, it cannot be sooner since I have to drive back to Boston... See you soon."

Bran cocked his head. "Change of plans?"

Annoyance and something else—something murkier and complicated—flashed across her face.

"Yes." She shook her head. "I'm sorry, Bran. An... emergency has come up and I need to return to Boston." Glancing down, she once more touched the seat of the motorcycle then dropped her arm. "Thank you for introducing me to The Gauntlet. I think Greer has a great product and I'm even more excited about this project."

"I'm glad." He studied her, taking in the taut line of her jaw. "Everything okay?"

She smiled, and he had to swallow his growl at the phoniness of it. Again, he strong-armed down the urge to take that pretty mouth. This time to erase the blasphemy curving it.

"Yes, just something I have to see to. But—" she waved a hand over the motorcycle "—do you think it would be too much trouble to take stills of this model? I'd love to include them in my presentation to the board of a customized version of The Gauntlet. Show its versatility."

"I can arrange that."

"Great." Nodding, she said, "I really do apologize for leaving so suddenly. It's rude at best and unprofessional at worst. If…"

She trailed off, and his chest burned with anger at whatever in that phone conversation caused the strain that damn near vibrated from her.

"You don't owe me an explanation, Tatum."

Her lips twisted, and how sad that this hard, self-deprecating curl seemed more honest than the smile she'd just given him.

"Yes, I do, but thank you for not requiring one." With a soft sigh, she circled the motorcycle and strode off in the direction of the gate.

For several long moments, Bran stared after her, watching her elegant figure walk farther and farther away. He hadn't been privy to that phone conversation, didn't know exactly what had been said to cause the sudden switch in demeanor from wary but open to closed off and defensive. Didn't matter to him.

What did matter was he had to grab a hold of the handlebar, grasp a physical reminder of why he'd traveled to Boston. Business. An investment. Company growth.

Not to protect a beautiful but lonely woman from whatever harm she was heading toward.

No. He wrapped his hands around both handlebars and released the kickstand.

His business might be *with* Tatum Haas, but she *wasn't* his business. He'd leave the superhero shit to the directors of the film.

Besides, in the end, who would save *him* from *her*?

Seven

Hell had been depicted as a lake of fire.

Or a land of flames and brimstone.

Even a bottomless obsidian pit.

For Tatum, hell was a dinner party.

A dinner party with polite, well-mannered guests, laughter as tinkling and bright as the cutlery, and free-flowing wine that led to freer-flowing tongues.

Regina Haas didn't need a reason to host a get-together. *Oh Meghan Markle and Prince Harry are being fabulous again over on IG? Dinner party to celebrate!*

Tatum smothered a sigh, peering down into her half-empty glass of wine. Apparently, a side effect of Merlot was bitchiness. Huh. That probably wasn't included on the label.

She loved her mother; God knew she loved her mother.

But they'd never been as close as mother and daughter should be. Regina was all beautification committees, fundraiser boards and country clubs. And Tatum was a Netflix-and-chill workaholic. She swore the proudest she'd made her mother was when she'd become engaged to Mark. And now that Tatum was a not-quite-jilted-but-definitely-disgraced almost bride, they'd returned to that limbo of being related but having no idea what to say to each other.

Which explained Tatum's presence at yet another torturous dinner party where, by not-so-happy coincidence, she would end up sitting next to an eligible bachelor. That she stayed and didn't complain was the bone she threw to Regina for being the stain on their family reputation and the punishment she inflicted on herself for... Hell, she could take her pick.

"I don't know what that wine's said to offend you, but I think I'll pass."

An electric current charged through her, and she stiffened under the shock of lust. Dammit. Without her permission, her lashes lowered, and she inhaled the intoxicating scent of chocolate, oak and sex. Pure, raw, wild sex.

Only one man possessed that scent.

And even though it'd been three days since she'd last savored that particular aroma—three days since she'd left him to be dragged back into her past—it had the power to set her ablaze.

Damn, she should be running in the opposite direction. But like any prey trapped in the sight of a powerful, sleek beast, it was much too late for that. Besides, if she were honest, she wasn't entirely sure she wanted to flee.

But she was entirely certain she desired to be caught. More wine.

Lifting the glass, she slowly turned around and met Bran's bright blue eyes. And pretended her breath didn't snag in her throat.

"Hello, Bran."

"Tatum." His gaze dropped to her glass. "I usually count on the alcohol to get me through shit like this, but it doesn't seem to be helping you. So maybe I'll pass up the wine and request the hard liquor."

"Smart move. Especially since Mom invited Colleen Howell. Sweet lady but she's at the bottom of her second martini. By the time dessert is served, she'll have offended every marginalized community and explained exactly how this world is going to hell in a handbasket. Spoiler alert. If it were up to her, we'd all be extras in *The Handmaid's Tale*."

He blinked then cocked his head. "Where I'm from, we don't usually combine 'sweet lady' and 'racist' in the same sentence. And we for damn sure don't invite them to sit down and break bread."

She snorted. "Well, welcome to my world, where the only thing more rude than being a racist is confronting one and making them feel uncomfortable about their bigotry."

A frown creased his brow and once more he glanced down at her glass. "Exactly how many of those have you had?"

She heaved a sigh and took another sip. "Not enough."

When his frown deepened, she admitted, "Two. And counting."

A corner of his mouth kicked up and the heat swarming through her veins added to the effects of the alcohol. She almost braced herself against his wide chest, but at the last moment, she caught herself and tightened her grip on the glass stem.

Maybe drinking around this man wasn't the wisest decision. His singular potency reduced her to a lightweight.

"Well, it looks like I need to catch up. Especially if you're going to be dropping truths all evening, I'm going to need it." He lowered his head, so she had an up close and personal view of the black striations in his blue eyes. His minty breath ghosted over her cheek, and holy... Please, God, let that moan have echoed in her head instead of aloud. "For the first time I'm looking forward to this evening."

He straightened and gestured toward the circling waiter, and even the flick of his fingers had her gulping down the remaining wine in her glass.

What was it about him that had her so...fascinated?

The thick, long dark hair he'd bound in a tie at the back of his head? The coarse yet neat beard sprinkled with strands of gray? The sensual dichotomy of bold, craggy facial features and a plush mouth? The big, wiry body that radiated strength and power? She was no stranger to good-looking men. Men with flawless beauty that seemed almost otherworldly. But that didn't pertain to Bran Holleran.

Even in a perfectly tailored navy blue suit that fit his

frame as if he'd been stitched into it, he exuded a carnal, corporeal *roughness* that spoke of virility, sexuality, dominance.

In other words, Bran Holleran was so damn *touchable*.

"I've been thinking about you the last few days," he said after requesting a whiskey from the server. "Is everything okay? You mentioned an emergency when you left."

She swallowed, battling back the wave of nausea that crashed into her. She set her empty glass down on an end table, the fruity Merlot suddenly too much.

Emergency. Anger roiled inside her chest, spreading like destructive flames. A scream tickled the back of her throat, but as she did with all her emotions when it came to Mark, his lies, his death, his parents, she swallowed it down. The "family emergency" had turned out to be Mark's mother finally cleaning out his apartment and calling her parents to send Tatum over as emotional support. She had slowed down communicating with Dara and Leo months ago. It might have been selfish. It might have made her cold and unfeeling in their eyes. But for Tatum's own sanity she had distanced herself. And after the other day, she should've stuck to her resolution. But she'd caved to the pressure.

And now she paid for it.

"Fine." She tipped her head back to meet his gaze. "Everything's fine."

"Liar."

Shock tripped through her at his blunt accusation. Shock and an electric charge of pure lust.

What the hell?

"Excuse me?" she rasped.

No man—not even Mark—had ever been so direct and bold with her. Whether out of manners, the weight of her last name or the money that backed that name, the men of her acquaintance had always been unfailingly polite…at least to her face.

Maybe they just didn't care enough to be so flatly honest.

Mark hadn't.

God knows she would've rather had his honesty than his perfect manners any day.

As the reverberation of that truth shook her, Bran cocked his head. "Are you lying as a way of telling me to mind my business? Or has 'fine' become a habit?" Eyes narrowed, he shook his head. "I can't tell which one."

"Stop it." She hated that it emerged as a plea.

Almost hated *him* for it.

But if she'd learned anything about Bran in the last couple of weeks, it was that his hard exterior reflected a laser focus that could be intimidating or exciting when pinned on her. At this moment, those bright blue eyes elicited a desperation inside her.

Desperation for him to cease this emotional full court press.

Desperation for him to continue pressuring her, to make her answer. To make her lance a wound that threatened to poison her.

A wound that everyone else in her life pretended not to see.

"Okay, Tatum. I'll back off." Just as relief and disappointment flooded through her in equal measure, he murmured, "For now."

"Bran, I'm so glad you could make it." Mia approached them, and with a smile that could only be described as sultry, she set a hand on Bran's muscular upper arm. A bristling tension invaded Tatum, and damn, that wasn't good. Not good at all. "It's wonderful to see you again."

"Hello, Mia," he greeted, turning and at the same time dislodging her hand from him.

Whether the move had been intentional or not, a fierce satisfaction whistled through her. That and another razor-sharp slice of relief. She could try to deceive herself but the sour slide of jealousy through her belly wouldn't allow it.

She detested seeing her sister intimately touch Bran.

The stark, terrifying realization had Tatum edging away from him mentally and physically. From them both.

Or she tried to.

The big hand at the middle of her spine prevented her from moving.

Mia's gaze dropped to where he was touching her, and her mouth tightened at the corners. Her sister cut a glance at Tatum, speculation gleaming. A denial rose to Tatum's tongue, but she swallowed it down. What was the saying about a guilty man running when no one pursued him? Besides, it would be a lie.

There was nothing professional about the arousal pulsing inside her like a beacon.

"We haven't seen that much of each other since

you've been in Boston," Mia said, returning her attention to Bran. "How're you liking our city so far?"

"It's beautiful. I'm still working remotely from my hotel room, but outside of that, I've done a little exploring. I even took one of the guided tours. There's a lot of history here."

"Guided tours?" Mia chuckled, and Tatum stiffened, recognizing the edge to it.

Her sister, with her beauty and charismatic personality, dominated attention and a room. But the flip side of that meant she could sometimes be a mean girl when she felt challenged. Tatum had been sliced by that acerbic wit more than a few times. And as Mia slid an amused look in Tatum's direction, she prepared herself to be on the receiving end of her sister's sharp tongue once again.

"Tatum, really?" Mia shook her head, giving Bran a rueful smile. "You have to forgive my sister. It's been a while for her, so she's probably forgotten things like hospitality and client care. But no worries. I'll have a packet of sights, events and entertainment sent to your hotel. We can also arrange for an employee from Bay-Star to accompany you, if you wish." She shrugged a bare shoulder. "And of course, you still have my number. If you'd prefer to have someone familiar tag along rather than a stranger, don't hesitate to call. I'd love to introduce our city to you."

Tatum stared at her sister, disbelief and more than a little hurt seizing her in an ironclad grip. She could barely move—hell, *breathe*.

You have to forgive my sister. It's been a while for her...

Mia's words reverberated in Tatum's head, growing louder with each ricochet off her skull, drowning out the hum of chatter in the room. With Tatum being older by just two years, there'd always existed some sibling rivalry between them. Not on Tatum's part, but from the time they were young Mia had believed they were in some kind of competition.

If Tatum made the honor roll, Mia had to hit the dean's list.

If Tatum joined the cheerleading team, Mia had to be captain.

If Tatum earned the position of senior vice president at BayStar, Mia had to aim for the same but in a shorter amount of time.

Still, Mia had never undermined Tatum in front of others. Had never deliberately hurt her.

Had definitely never thrown her under the bus. What the hell? Why would she...?

Oh you know why.

She only had to take one look at her sister's face, at her body language. At the soft smile that carried a hint of invitation, the gleam of admiration in her brown eyes. At how she canted her petite, slim frame toward Bran.

Mia wanted Bran. At the very least, she was attracted to him.

Oh God.

Tatum's stomach bottomed out. Dread and another darker, far more complicated emotion rushed in to fill the void. She deliberately flattened her hand against her outer thigh, determined not to press her palm against that strange, awful ache in her belly.

Part of her grappled with the need to shift away from Bran. He was her client, dammit. *Her client.* Didn't matter that just one look at his bold, almost harsh features and soft, wide mouth detonated an explosion of heat across her nerves.

Didn't matter that when he gazed at her with those electric blue eyes, she glimpsed something Mark and the circumstances of his death had stolen from her.

Desire. Hope.

Or maybe she was just projecting.

The fact that she wanted to hold on to that desire, clutch that hope as if it were an endangered species, blared a visceral warning to avoid him—that gaze, his touch, his fucking scent—at all costs.

Yet… She didn't move. Didn't shift away when the smart, wise thing would have been to put the length of the room between them. Because something more desperate than her fear resided deep inside her, restless, insistent. Ravenous.

"Thank you for the offer," Bran said with a nod. "But I actually enjoy exploring a city on my own."

Disappointment flickered in Mia's eyes, but she still maintained her smile, though Tatum noted the slight strain around it.

"Well, know the offer stands." Mia switched her attention to Tatum. "The Walkers have arrived. Mom wanted to make sure you spoke to them."

It was Tatum's turn to force a smile. "Great. I'll go find them in a few minutes." Or not.

Annoyance vibrated through her. Her mother hadn't thought of giving her a heads-up that Dara and Leo would be attending tonight? Of course she hadn't. Just like her mother had pressured her father into calling Tatum about helping Dara and Leo clean out Mark's place, her mother had exhibited quite clearly whose side she fell on when it came to this whole shit show called Tatum's Life. No, Tatum wouldn't be marrying their son, but Regina Haas didn't want to lose the social or business connections. Didn't occur to her mother that constant contact with Mark's parents inflicted a pain on Tatum that left her scarred.

"Just a warning," Mia continued. "Dara was telling Mom about that foundation they're creating…and how you haven't returned any of her phone calls or made time to discuss the ceremony." She arched an eyebrow. "You might want to start thinking up an excuse—or escape route—now."

With a small smirk, Mia walked off, and though Tatum wanted to snatch her sister up and demand to know her problem, she instead scanned the room, doing exactly what Mia suggested. Searching for an escape route.

God, she was such a coward.

"This foundation must be secretly funding crimes against humanity."

"What?" Tatum startled. She'd almost forgotten Bran still stood behind her.

No, that was a lie.

"I said this foundation must be up to no good if your reaction to your sister's announcement is anything to go by. Here." He gently encircled her wrist, lifting her arm and pressing his glass of whiskey into her hand. Wrapping her fingers around the glass, he said, "Drink. You look like you need it more than me right now."

She should've balked at the command. She damn sure shouldn't raise the whiskey to her mouth.

But she didn't balk…and she did drink. And she imagined that even as the bold, smoky flavor hit her tongue, she could taste his specific flavor underneath the nut and caramel notes. A shiver danced through her as she thought about her mouth covering the same place his had touched. And as the whiskey burned a path to her stomach, she briefly closed her eyes, savoring the heat.

When she lifted her lashes, her gaze crashed into his. The blue seemed to crackle with an inner fire, and its flames licked at her breasts, belly…her clenching sex.

God.

The damp flesh between her legs spasmed even as her nipples beaded.

Was he aware of how he stared at her? Like he could consume her in huge greedy bites and return for a second serving.

Screw it. She took another sip of whiskey.

"What's wrong, Tate?"

His use of the nickname only Nore used jarred her. And unlike the familial affection Nore elicited, the sound of the shortened version of her name on his lips had a whirlpool of need eddying low in her belly. Because she could imagine him whispering the nickname in her ear as he surrounded her, covered her…pushed inside her.

She considered lying, brushing off his question and

then finding an empty corner where she could avoid him and the Walkers. That had become her MO when she couldn't brazen out a situation, after all. Hide, as Mia had mockingly accused.

So yes, she should've followed that tried-and-true method.

Instead, when her lips parted, the lie didn't emerge. The truth did.

"The Walkers," she began, haltingly at first, but after a deep breath, the words tumbled out, damn near tripping over one another. "The Walkers are Mark's parents."

His face remained impassive but she caught the slight softening around his mouth and in his eyes. "Okay." His gaze roamed over her face before meeting her eyes again. "You don't get along with them?"

She huffed out a breath that abraded her throat.

"If only it were that simple. No." She shook her head. "I think I might prefer it if they hated me," she murmured then loosed a low chuckle. "That sounds terrible, doesn't it? But that's how I feel sometimes—terrible, heartless. Because only a terrible, heartless person would rather their almost in-laws despise them than be this…lodestone for their son, for their grief, for the expectations. No one has guidelines for how I should feel toward the people who would have been my mother- and father-in-law if not for their son being caught with his dick hanging out in a hotel room. Literally."

Her chest rose and fell. But God, if it didn't give her a small measure of relief saying it aloud.

Bran shifted, placing his big, hard body between her

and the rest of the room, shielding her from curious stares.

"Drink again, baby. Finish it." He nudged the side of the tumbler with a bent finger. "Then go get your coat, leave and wait for me outside. I'll make your excuses to your parents."

"What?" she rasped, blinking up at him.

She'd heard his words but didn't fully grasp their meaning.

"Go on and finish that, Tate." He nodded toward the drink and then waited until she did as told. As the alcohol spread its warmth through her, he removed the glass from her hand and set it on the table beside her empty wine flute. "Now go." He jerked his chin in the direction of the living room entrance. "I'll be right behind you."

"I don't understand—"

"It's obvious you want to be here as much as I do. Except I hate this pretentious bullshit and you appear to be here under coercion or out of duty—which are two sides of the same coin to me. So I'm about to go find Silas and let him know that you weren't feeling well and I'm dropping you off at your house. Head out now so it'll only be me lying." When she didn't move, still too stunned that he was honest to God attempting to *rescue* her, he cupped her hip and squeezed. *"Go, Tatum."*

The contradictory kindness and firm command shattered her numbness, and her body moved as if guided by his instruction, even before her mind settled on obeying. She didn't stop to speak to anyone or to grab her coat, all of her attention focused on the front door and the quiet and freedom beyond it.

She craved it, could nearly taste it, and her eyes stung from the relief that coursed through her as she opened the door and stepped out into the night air. She didn't flinch or shiver against the cool breeze, too relieved to feel it. Eventually, she'd have to answer to her mother for skipping out on this dinner party, and it wouldn't be pretty. But right now? Right now she couldn't find it within herself to care. Not when for at least one more night she could shrug off the weight of grief, of shame, of imagined responsibilities.

Tonight she could be free, unburdened.

Behind her, the front door opened and then a large hand pressed to the small of her back. She didn't need to glance over her shoulder or inhale his scent to identify him. The ripple of lust undulating down her spine announced who stood behind her, who touched her.

"Where's your coat?" Bran asked, and moments later his sports jacket covered her, enveloping her in warmth and his sweet, earthy scent.

"I didn't want to stop and get it," she murmured, lifting her hand to grasp the lapels of the jacket and tug them closer.

Not because she was cold. No, because she wanted to sink farther into this sensory embrace.

"Ready to go?" He replaced his hand on her back.

"Yes," she said, descending the stairs. But because she had already thrown caution to the wind tonight and wildness sang in her veins, she tipped her head back and met his bright gaze as she stepped off the final stair. "But I don't want to go home."

He studied her for a long moment, then slowly nodded as if he'd come to some sort of decision.

"Okay, I'm game. Where would you like to go? This is your city, not mine." He tilted his head, and she tried and failed to prevent the shiver that worked its way through her at his hooded gaze. "Take me to your favorite place in Boston."

Back out now. Don't do this. Abort mission.

"I can do that," she whispered.

Damn.

Eight

"This is your favorite place in Boston?"

Bran surveyed Rowes Wharf, taking in the lights reflecting off Boston Harbor's dark water. Their perch on the low wall provided a great view of the huge arch over the waterfront as well as the marina, restaurants and a floating stage. At a little after eight, people were gathered in the restaurants, but only a few brave souls sat at the tables and chairs outside. It was cooler out here so close to the water but Tatum, still wearing his sports jacket, didn't seem to feel it. From the small smile that curved her pretty mouth, she didn't appear to feel anything but relaxed.

Good.

His chest constricted, and he curled his hands tighter around the edge of the wall.

He didn't need to close his eyes to conjure up an image of Tatum's beautiful features pulled tight with pain. Her sister's words had struck a nerve, but it'd been that verbal hemorrhaging of words—of truth—that compelled him to take her out of her parents' home.

He'd spent enough time with Tatum to realize that any one of those guests catching a glimpse of her vulnerability would probably be her nightmare. Hell, surprise had rippled through him when she unloaded all of that in front of him. Surprise, followed closely by a fierce surge of protectiveness. The same protective urge that had insisted he wrap her in his own clothes when she stood on the front stoop in nothing but the beautiful body-conforming off-the-shoulder dress. Even if just for a few brief moments she'd allowed him to see the Tatum Haas behind the curtain. To see her stripped-down, bare, exposed. And he didn't take that lightly. Not with this woman.

Silas had seemed to accept the story of Tatum being ill and needing to leave. But Bran could admit to himself that even if the older man had argued, nothing would've stopped him from taking Tatum out of that home.

He didn't care to analyze why.

"It's one of them," Tatum answered his question. "I also love Boston Common but it isn't too smart to go there after dark." She lifted her take-out coffee cup that he'd bought on their way out here. After a careful sip, she tilted her head back, eyes closed. That same faint smile played with her lips, and Bran slid his hands inside the front pocket of the hoodie he'd pulled on in lieu of his jacket. He fisted his fingers but they still tingled with the need to trace the line of her full bottom lip. "But I've loved coming here since I was a little girl when Dad chartered a yacht for my mom's birthday. This sounds silly now, but the wharf reminded me of Atlantis. Like a separate country floating on water. I had a pretty big imagination back then."

He scanned the waterfront again, this time viewing it through the eyes of a child.

"I can see that," he murmured, wanting her to continue talking.

She chuckled and for the first time that night, it sounded genuine. Satisfaction winged through him.

"Then the arch seemed like the gateway to another world, and I suppose a little of that wonder still exists. That, the water, the ships… It's like here, all things are possible. You can sail off, visit different places, be someone different, and never return if that's your choice. Or you can leave for a little while and always return home. It's a place of choices and possibilities." She loosed another of those soft rolls of laugher, accompanying it with a shake of her head. "I'm going on and on and probably sounding too fanciful for a grown woman."

"What does being an adult have to do with it? It's a shame that more of us don't maintain that whimsy or imagination."

She arched an eyebrow, a glint of amusement in her dark gaze. "You're a little too old to believe in mythical cities. Do you believe in Santa Claus, too?"

He shrugged. "I haven't seen any concrete evidence proving Atlantis doesn't exist. And back off Santa. He's a global treasure."

Her smile widened, and she shifted her attention back to the water and the marina. After several moments of silence, her soft sigh drifted on the night air.

"Are you going to ask me?"

Bran didn't pretend to misunderstand her. "No," he said, voice blunt. She switched her regard from the waterfront to him. "This—" he waved an arm toward the water "—isn't about quid pro quo. If you want to talk to me, fine. I'll listen. But if you want to debate the existence of Nessie next—which by the way, is real—or just sit here in silence, that's fine, too."

She stared at him, her lips slightly parted.

"I'll give you Nessie," she said, voice a little hoarser. Clearing her throat, she nodded then fell silent again. "Please ask me," she softly requested.

He studied her, the desperation threading through her voice there in her nearly black eyes.

Please ask me.

The three murmured words echoed in his head, a loaded appeal. There was too much he wanted to know about Tatum. And in this case, knowledge wasn't power. It would be his weakness, his downfall. The more he discovered, the harder it would be to preserve the distance he so needed with her. Curiosity mated with the hunger and lust twisting in his gut...

Yeah, a smart man knew mixing business with pleasure when he would be leaving in a matter of weeks was a destructive move. He shouldn't ask her anything. Shit, shouldn't be out with her in the first place.

But here he was.

And even as every self-preserving instinct within

him roared in disgust, he asked, "What happened with your fiancé?"

A visible shiver racked her, and he almost—almost—rescinded the question. But she'd requested this of him, which told him she *needed* this. Needed to lance this festering wound. So he waited.

"He died from a ruptured brain aneurysm on the night before our wedding day. I'll never forget sitting in that hospital waiting room, receiving the news that the man I loved was no more. He was gone. I would never hear his deep voice, his laughter. Never inhale his scent. Never be touched by him again."

She fell silent once more, clasping the edges of his jacket, pulling it tighter around her as if trying to sink into the dark blue material.

"I'll also never forget that just minutes after finding out I'd lost my fiancé, I discovered the paramedics had found him unresponsive and naked in a hotel suite. From the condoms in the room, both used and unused, it was obvious he hadn't been there alone. The night before he was supposed to stand up in front of our family and friends and pledge his fidelity to me, he'd been fucking another woman."

Her eyes briefly closed, and pain flickered across her face, momentarily tightening it. But then she lifted her lashes, and the stark, naked hurt in her eyes had him fisting his hands harder. Touching her wasn't only inappropriate but it might also stop her from talking. And he sensed talking was what she needed more than comfort.

"It would've been one thing to hear the news in private, that the man I'd been loyal to had betrayed me.

But I didn't. I discovered it through media outlets and on social media. Apparently, a call had been placed to 911 by an anonymous woman, and we assume she was the person he was with that night. My grief, my pain, my anger—it was all on display for public consumption. I couldn't even mourn him properly because I couldn't—can't—figure out a way to separate the man I'd loved from the man who betrayed me in the most cruel, hurtful way possible. Then there were the reporters, cameramen and keyboard warriors scrutinizing my every move, every expression, every word. If I didn't say anything or didn't cry, I was a coldhearted bitch and deserved him cheating on me. If I did show emotion, I was weak, crying over a man who obviously didn't love me enough to stay faithful. And then there was Mark's parents."

The confession poured from her in an unimpeded stream. Hurt, anger and, yes, grief throbbed in her voice, and it confirmed what he'd suspected all along. She still hadn't gotten over Mark Walker. There was too much emotion there, too much confusion left unresolved. While he sincerely doubted Tatum would intentionally hurt another person, anyone she became involved with would bear the weight of the baggage she carried.

Fuck, he hurt for her.

"Tell me they don't blame you for his actions," he said, voice sharper than he intended.

She crossed her arms over her chest. "No, they don't. As inconceivable as it sounds, it might be easier if they did. Don't get me wrong, I fully understand that they lost a son—their only son. And God yes, they should grieve, should be in pain. But they're his parents. I'm the woman he betrayed, lied to, humiliated. Their emotions are more clear-cut than mine. But they expect me to mourn as they do, to be his loving, devoted fiancée in life and death. And it's impossible. But they can't see that or don't want to face it. They've ignored how he hurt me, and want me to ignore it, too."

"Is that where this foundation that Mia mentioned comes in?"

Nodding, she loosened her arms and gripped the edge of the low wall, subtly rocking back and forth.

"Yes. At the fundraiser gala a couple of weeks ago, they announced to me and my family that they were starting a foundation in Mark's name, where they would offer scholarships and internships at their company to graduating college students. They asked me to be the guest speaker." She huffed out a sound caught somewhere between a rough exhale and a jagged laugh. "Be Mark's voice as his loving fiancée."

Damn. Even though he'd never met Mark's parents, that didn't prevent annoyance from pricking him. Of course, he sympathized with them—how could he not?—but they were either oblivious or willingly blind to the burden and pain they inflicted on Tatum.

"Are you going to do it?" he asked.

"No. I don't know." She swept a hand over her hair. "My mother already accepted on my behalf before I had a chance to say yes or no. I probably will."

He frowned, twisting to face her more fully. "Why?

I can tell you don't want anything to do with it. You're not obligated to his parents."

A half smile quirked the corner of her mouth, and instead of humor, it possessed a shitload of self-deprecation.

"You're frustrated with me. I can hear it in your voice," she murmured. "Not that I can blame you. I'm frustrated with myself. But the Walkers own Mass-Comm, and they're one of BayStar's business partners. That's why my parents were so thrilled about our relationship. It would've been like the merger of two media empires. And even though Mark's gone, they want to retain that connection. My father for business reasons and my mother for social. And no, I didn't ask for any of this, but they are on the receiving end of the embarrassment and unwanted negative attention because of me. So in a way, I am obligated to mitigate the damage. That's my responsibility."

"You mean your penance."

She sucked in a breath, and her chin snapped up as if he'd delivered a verbal blow. Blinking, she stared at him for several seconds.

Then breathed, "Yes."

"So you're paying the price for someone else's crime, and you're okay with that?" He didn't wait for her answer but pressed on. "Who in your life led you to believe that your feelings, your thoughts, your *heart* are expendable? Your voice, *you* are just as important as the man everyone lost. Just because you're alive and available, *tangible*, doesn't depreciate your life. And if they—your family and Mark's—can't see it, then that's their issue not yours. And no way in hell should you take on that burden. You're only responsible for you. Your man fucked up. Fucked up bad. He just so happened to die and escape the consequences of his cowardly behavior. Last I checked, reparations for screwing around have never been in anyone's will. So why the hell should you be expected to inherit his debt?"

He ground his teeth, trying to extinguish the anger flickering in his chest like flames.

"You're really upset. For me," she whispered, and the note of awe in her voice only stoked those flames.

Reaching out, he broke his own rule about touching her and cupped the back of her neck. He drew her forward as he leaned in, meeting her halfway. His nose nearly bumped hers, and he could taste the hint of coffee and hazelnut on her breath. Without his permission, his fingers flexed against the side of her throat. It wouldn't take much pressure to guide her forward the negligible amount to take her mouth and see if her kiss delivered on the promise of that taste.

"No," he ground out. "I'm not upset. I'm pissed. You. Did. Nothing. Wrong. And fuck whoever would try to make you believe you have to clean up the mess your ex made and left behind."

"I don't think we're supposed to speak ill of the dead."

"Fuck that, too," he said bluntly. Her eyes slightly widened, but he continued, "Dead or alive, I'm calling you out on your bullshit. And for him to screw around on you—betraying your trust is bullshit. So he can get it, too."

"He can get it, too?" A smile slowly curved her lips

then spread into a full-out grin. "You know you're cute when you're defending my honor."

"I'm forty fucking years old. I'm not cute."

"I don't think the two are mutually exclusive."

They stared at one another, and he couldn't stop himself from stroking his thumb up and down her neck. This close, he didn't miss her shiver at his touch. And damn if that tremor didn't ripple down his own spine… and over his cock.

He leaned back. Away from her. Away from temptation.

"Thank you," she murmured.

"You don't need to thank me for telling you the truth."

"I'm not," she said. "I'm thanking you for tonight. For…" She glanced at the water. "This. Thank you for this. It's…"

"You're welcome," he said.

She tilted her head, and those nearly black eyes roamed over his face.

"What? Just ask me what you're thinking." He could read the question in her gaze.

"Why did you—I hate to say *rescue me*, because I've never been some damsel in distress. Although lately…" She shoved a hand over her hair again, and he wanted to replace her fingers with his, feel the slide of the thick dark strands.

"Lately what?"

"Not important." She waved a hand, and when she gave him that forced, fake smile after he'd already witnessed the beauty of a genuine one, he almost growled a warning to her. "So why did you take me out of there tonight? Not that I don't appreciate it," she assured him, "but you were willing to lie to my father—your potential investor and business partner—to do it. Why?" she pressed.

"Because the people who should've noticed you were hurting didn't. So I did what they couldn't or refused to do."

She probably tried to control her flinch but didn't succeed. Neither did she conceal the spasm of emotion that crossed her features. He didn't mention either; her pride wouldn't thank him for saying anything.

Shaking her head, she murmured, "Why do you—"

"Care?" he finished for her. "That you even have to ask that pisses me off even more." His mouth twisted into a snarl that echoed in his head. "I have no doubt you can rescue yourself, Tate—something tells me you've been doing it a long while. And most people enduring what you have this past year would've broken. But that doesn't mean you can't loose the reins of control and let someone claim them. Doesn't mean you can't lean on them and allow them to bear the weight. That doesn't make you weak. It just makes you human."

"Is that what you did tonight? Give me someone to lean on?"

He studied the gleam in her eyes, the sinking of her teeth into her bottom lip, the unconscious lean of her body toward him.

Fuck.

Hot desire pounded through him, knotting his stomach, throbbing in his dick. His thighs tightened against the primal ache, and he inhaled a low, deep breath. But fuck if her sultry scent, which reminded him of sun-warmed sands and perfumed skin, didn't permeate his nostrils, his throat, his lungs.

"You're asking the wrong question, Tate," he said, and there wasn't a damn thing he could do about the gravel roughness to his voice. "You leaning on me, loosening some of that control… It isn't about me giving that to you. It's about you accepting what I'm offering. That's why you could never be weak. You had—and have—all the power."

"We're still talking about this evening at the dinner party, right?" she whispered.

Did she know her gaze dropped to his mouth? Lingered there?

Did she have any idea how close she was to having him showing her what he could do with his mouth?

No, to both.

She couldn't. Otherwise she wouldn't continue to sit there with him, with all that vulnerable soft heat in her eyes.

He would be the worst kind of asshole if he crossed the space separating them and took those slightly damp lips, introduced her to his tongue, to the greed barreling through him like a storm-whipped wind. No, he couldn't claim to have been the best man in all his forty years.

But tonight… Tonight he'd aim to be.

Goddammit.

He slowly stood, stretching his hand out to her. And the anticipation howling inside his head couldn't have been a clearer warning that touching her—even an innocuous palm pressed to palm—was a mistake.

But one he was willing to make.

Tatum stared at his hand for a long moment before she slid hers over his.

Yeah. Mistake.

He locked down the moan crawling up his chest and into his throat. Damn, if he didn't feel that soft caress down his chest, his abs and wrapped around his flesh. Touching this woman, whether it was her hand, the small of her back or her vulnerable nape, foretold a danger he should heed.

But apparently, experience didn't equal wisdom. Because as he gently pulled Tatum to her feet, none of the warnings and admonishments he'd given himself mattered. Not when her scent called to something wild in him. Not when her slender, wickedly curved body brushed his. Not when those dark brown eyes issued an invitation her mouth would deny.

"I should get you home," he said instead of answering her loaded question. Especially since he couldn't definitively state that his response would've been *yes*.

"Right. It's getting late." She nodded, slipping her hand free of his grasp, turning away.

But not before he caught a glimpse of the rueful twist of her lips. Yeah, she hadn't missed his avoidance. And as he followed behind her along the wharf, he shook his head.

Sometimes retreat didn't mean cowardice.

Sometimes it presented the wisest course of action.

He'd keep telling himself that, and hopefully soon he'd believe it.

Nine

Tatum stared at the contents of her walk-in closet as if the array of dresses, pants and blouses were the Riemann hypothesis instead of her options for Sunday brunch at her parents' place. Honestly, she'd rather sit down and attempt to solve the Millennium Prize Problem than attend the weekly meal with her family.

She winced.

Guilt crept through her, but she couldn't deny the truth. Ever since she'd disappeared from the dinner party on Friday night, her mother had been blowing up her phone, vacillating between passive-aggressive comments about ungrateful children to outraged criticism for embarrassing her—and leaving her dinner party unbalanced. Her father hadn't called at all, which portended a more ominous conversation.

Oh yes, she couldn't *wait* for brunch.

Sighing, she grabbed a pair of eggplant-colored high-waisted pants and a lavender lace shirt before she could change her mind. About the outfit and brunch. While her parents' chef would be serving roast beef as the entrée, Tatum knew she would be the main course.

Because the people who should've noticed you were hurting didn't. So I did what they couldn't or refused to do.

Bran's words from Friday night haunted her, and as she closed her eyes, his voice gained volume and speed in her head. Part of her wanted to dig that…that indictment out of her brain. To erase it as if it never existed. Because it charged her parents, Mia, the Walkers with not just leaving her out there exposed and unprotected, but maybe with being complicit in inflicting the hurt.

Then there was the other side of her that embraced it. Inside—so deep inside—something unfurled, reaching for those words, for him. Because he'd *seen*. He'd called a thing *a thing* even when she'd been afraid to say it. Felt guilty for thinking it.

But his bald, frank manner hit her as both intimidating and liberating.

And wholly addictive.

Like the man.

Exhaling a breath, she slid a hand over the back of her neck, recreating his hold on her, attempting to recapture the hot brand of it against her skin. Molten heat flowed through her at the memory. Now, like then, her breasts swelled, nipples tightening. She lowered a hand to her belly, pressing against the ache there, the same ache that had been there Friday night. Her thighs tightened against the heavy beat of arousal between her legs…assuaging it, stirring it? She curled her fingers, refusing to alleviate that needy pain.

Because stroking herself, making herself come to the memory of her client remained a step she wasn't willing to take.

Or was afraid to take.

Maybe. Because every encounter, every minute with him seemed to weaken her resolve.

Dropping her arm, lest she surrender to temptation, she exited her closet and tossed her clothes on her bed.

As she shrugged out of her robe, her cell phone rang on her bedside table. She side-eyed it for a moment. Had to be her mother ensuring she didn't plan on skipping brunch. Resentment flared in her chest but instead of smothering it like she usually did, she allowed it to kindle, her hurt blowing air on it.

Just for a moment. Then she squelched the rebellious, disloyal emotion and strode over to pick up the phone. Surprise struck her, and she blinked, peering down at the screen as if the name there would change.

No matter how long she stared, though, it remained the same.

Finally, she answered the call, lifting the cell to her ear.

"Hello," she said, her heart's rhythm filling her ears.

And yet Bran's "Hello, Tatum," clearly cut through the white noise. The sound of his deep rumble of a voice moved through her in a sinuous glide, leaving electricity in its wake.

Sinking to the edge of the bed behind her, she tightened her grasp on the phone. "Bran, this is a surprise. Is everything okay?"

"Yes, everything's good," he said. "You've just been on my mind."

She closed her eyes, ordering her body to stand down. Demanding her heart not jump in that juvenile way. Fear slunk into her chest, winding around her ribs. The last time the traitorous organ in her chest did this exhilarant trilling, she ended up with not just a broken heart, but a broken *world*. She couldn't trust her instincts. And yet…

And yet she didn't reprimand him for talking to her in such a personal way.

Didn't end the call.

If she were honest with herself, that ship had sailed the moment she'd walked out of her parents' house Friday night.

"I don't know if that's a good or bad thing," she murmured.

"Good," he assured her, and the low, dark rumble of *good* had her teeth sinking into her bottom lip to hold back a moan. "I want to show you something. Are you busy?"

"Right now?" She glanced around her bedroom as if the *something* had materialized there. That twisting spiral of excitement was a bad sign. "Today?"

"Yes, to both," he said, humor in his tone. "Are you free?"

No, I'm expected at brunch with my family in an hour.

The reply sat right there on her tongue. All she had to do was speak it. And she would because spending any more time with Bran outside of BayStar's office or in a professional setting was plain foolish. Not to mention, she couldn't just flake on her parents, no matter how much the thought of facing their disappointment had her belly in knots...

Who in your life led you to believe that your feelings, your thoughts, your heart *are expendable?*

Again, more of Bran's words returned to haunt her and a burst of frustration and...and helplessness mired with anger and pain echoed in her chest.

Did she consider her feelings, her basic needs of protection, acceptance and understanding expendable?

God, yes.

The answer blared loud and clear in her head. In her soul. When did she prioritize her own desires, her comfort? Her...joy?

Now. That's when she started. Now.

Even if it was just for this one time.

"Yes, I'm free," she said, throwing caution—and common sense—to the wind. "What do you have in mind?"

"Don't worry, you'll see. Just wear something comfortable and warm. I'll be there in half an hour."

"Half an hour!" she objected. But she was objecting to herself because he'd ended the call. And staring at the screen only wasted precious minutes of the time she had to get ready. "Dammit," she muttered, tossing the cell to the mattress and leaping to her closet.

Twenty-eight minutes later, she descended the stairs of her brownstone to the first floor and the foyer. Just as she moved off the last step, the doorbell rang, and for the briefest moment, she stiffened, her stomach fluttering like a whole net of trapped butterflies.

She couldn't see through the solid wood door but only one person could be standing on the other side.

Inhaling a deep breath that did nothing to calm the storm brewing inside her, she approached the door and opened it before reason could convince her otherwise. Though she knew Bran would be waiting on her stoop, the impact of him still propelled the air from her lungs.

She'd seen him in a flawlessly tailored suit, in business casual pants, shirt and jacket. And he'd been beautiful in all of it. But in this—in a black leather jacket, a black T-shirt, faded blue jeans and scuffed motorcycle boots—he was stunning. A visual and elemental blow to the senses.

Her fingertips itched to trace the craggy lines of his face thrown in sharp relief by the thick dark and gray strands secured at the back of his head. Instead, she shifted back from the door and waved him inside.

"Hello, Bran. Come in. I just need to grab my jacket."

"Thanks." His blue gaze swept over her thick cream sweater, black jeans and knee-high riding boots as he stepped into the house. "You look perfect."

"Thank you." She rubbed her hands down the front of her thighs. "You didn't give me much direction other than comfortable and warm. So…" Her hands fluttered, and dammit, she was babbling *and* fidgeting. *Stop talking and move*, she silently ordered herself. "I'll be right back."

Leaving him in the foyer, she headed down the hall

to the closet. A minute later, she returned, shrugging into a hip-length camel-colored leather jacket.

"Ready," she announced, and Bran's gaze shifted from scrutinizing her foyer to her. Once more, she fought not to fidget under that steady, unwavering stare and barely won the battle.

"You have a lovely home," he said.

"Thank you." She turned, surveying the space and attempting to view it through his eyes.

"It's...you."

She jerked her regard back to him, surprise whispering through her. "Thank you. Again," she murmured. "I'm a little afraid to ask what that means," she half joked.

Only half. Because part of her really wanted to know what he saw when he looked at her home. And the other part... Well, she feared he saw too much. And that he would be right.

"It's elegant, beautiful and thoughtful. It's clear every piece has been chosen carefully. But it's also comfortable. That living room is just that—a *living* room. I wouldn't be afraid to sit on the furniture. It looks like you not only actually use it but enjoy it."

She'd been right to be afraid. Vulnerability crept over her, and she almost patted her chest to make sure her flesh still covered her bones and heart. She hated this sense of exposure.

And yet she couldn't deny the bloom of pleasure that radiated from behind her rib cage, spreading wide.

Unlike some people did, when she'd bought the brownstone, she hadn't rented out the ground floor or upper level. Nor had she hired an interior designer. Mark hadn't understood it, and often told her she was wasting time and her efforts when she could easily hire someone to do the job faster. But this was her personal haven, her sanctuary. She'd selected each piece that graced the walls and occupied the floors and corners. From the dove-gray chaise longue under the George Inness landscape in the foyer to the custom bookshelves and reading nook in the living room, they all had been handpicked by her. And yes, enjoyed by her.

"It seems like your talents are wasted on custom design for motorcycles and should be focused on being a mentalist." She tossed out the nonchalant, teasing comment as she moved toward her front door, not willing to analyze his theory or how it affected her. "Ready to go? I can't deny I'm curious about where you're taking me."

He studied her for a long moment then dipped his head and followed her out of the house. Once she locked the door, he cupped her elbow and guided her down the front steps.

But she drew up short on the bottom one, her lips parting in shock.

"What…? Are you…? You can't…"

A low chuckle rumbled from the man next to her.

"I'm sorry. I didn't catch any of that." He continued striding over the sidewalk to the curb—and the motorcycle parked there. "But if I have to guess, I'm going with, this is The Gauntlet in the so-called flesh. Yes, I intend to take you on a ride on your potential investment and oh yeah, I'm very serious. Did I get it right?"

He arched an eyebrow, a smirk tugging the corner of his mouth.

"Yes, you covered it all." She flicked her fingers toward the motorcycle she'd seen on the movie lot. "You don't really expect me to get on that, do you?"

He slowly nodded. "I do. How else to fully judge the product you're considering financing? If you're going to stand up in front of your board and talk about The Gauntlet, then you have to experience it."

"Using reason isn't going to get me on that bike," she muttered, crossing her arms and glaring at him and the motorcycle.

"Tatum." His soft tone carried a note of steel. "Come here."

That voice shouldn't work. That dominant order should have her rebelling, not moving her feet in his direction. Yet moments after he commanded it, she stood in front of him, tipping her head back to meet his bright blue gaze.

"I would ask you if that usually works, but here I am, right in front of you, showing that it works," she grumbled.

He bent his head, lowering it until his lips grazed the rim of her ear. "Which one are you really scared of, Tate? Riding the bike or that you might actually enjoy riding the bike?"

A shiver rocked down her spine as she emotionally shrank away from his question. He was almost correct. She was afraid she might enjoy riding the bike with *him*. And because she couldn't allow him to guess that, she hiked her chin up and stepped closer to the bike.

"Sorry to disappoint you, but neither."

"I could never be disappointed in you, Tatum," he said, and while she reeled from that murmured admission, he removed a matte black helmet from the bike's trunk and moved in front of her.

Still speechless, she stood, unmoving, as he fit the gear over her head and then instructed her on how to mount the motorcycle. After she perched on the seat, he threw his leg over, his big body sitting in front of her. He freed a helmet identical to hers from the handlebars, covered his head with it then glanced over his shoulder.

"Ready?"

"Yes," she lied.

"Hold on to me," he ordered.

And the moment she'd craved and dreaded arrived.

Craved because she got to wrap her arms around him, press her chest and abs to his wide back...her sex to his firm, gorgeous ass.

Dreaded because she got to wrap her arms around him, press her chest and abs to his wide back...her sex to his firm, gorgeous ass.

Once she did this, there was no turning back. There was no forgetting how hard, solid and warm he felt. There was no unimagining how that hard, solid and warm body would press hers into a soft mattress.

After slowly sliding her arms around his trim waist, she locked her fingers and pressed them against the ladder of his abdomen. *Damn*. She'd never been more painfully aware of another person in her life.

The motorcycle roared to life and, *holy...* Behind the helmet, she closed her eyes and her lips parted on a gasp. She'd never sat on a washing machine stuck on the spin cycle, but *oh God* this delicious hum between her legs *had* to be why that activity remained so popular.

Bran eased out from the curb, the speed sedate over the cobbled road and onto Charles Street.

This isn't so bad. Not bad at all.

Then about ten minutes later, he exited onto the interstate and...

"Oh my God!" Her scream echoed inside the helmet, joining the thunderous pounding of her heart.

"You good?" Bran shouted, the wind carrying his question back to her.

"Oh my God!" she yelled again, and he laughed, long and loud.

Her laughter joined his.

The world flashed by them in a Technicolor blur, the wind a muted howl through the helmet and an almost sensual pressure against her body. And the power... On this great, rumbling machine, holding on to this equally strong beast of a man, she harnessed power, wielded it and walked the fine edge of becoming its casualty.

Teetering on that threshold was emboldening, terrifying...

Exhilarating.

Roaring down the highway, no cage of iron, chrome and glass between her and the elements, she could understand why some people chose the road and their motorcycles as a way of life.

The farther Boston grew behind them, the lighter her chest and shoulders became. And as the landscape changed from urban to farmland and forests, the weight of worries, responsibilities and duty sloughed off like a rough, too-tight, ill-fitting skin. Bran slowed and exited the interstate toward Taunton. Tatum took in the Taunton Green, the city square, as well as a couple of parks and historic buildings.

After a short break to stretch their legs—okay, *her* legs—they left Taunton, winding their way back through more countryside until their surroundings shifted once more as they neared South Boston.

"Castle Island?" she yelled minutes later, grinning as Fort Independence appeared in the distance.

Bran nodded, and she shook her head, still smiling. It'd been years since she'd been to the attraction on the shore of Boston Harbor. It was a little too cold for swimming at the beach, but the site also contained a playground, a gift shop, a food court and a wonderful ice cream parlor. Visitors could also tour Fort Independence, one of the oldest fortified sites of English origin in the US.

Delight raced through her as Bran parked in the designated area and cut the motorcycle's ignition. He dismounted, his thick thigh muscles bunching under the faded denim, and she swallowed a sigh at the sensual display. Sliding her hand into his outstretched one, she climbed off the bike, her own thighs trembling after riding for so long.

"You okay?" he asked, not releasing his clasp on her hand.

"Yes, I'm fine."

Only then did he reach out and remove her helmet. And though she could've done it herself, she allowed the gesture. He'd taken care of her, from unknowingly aiding her escape from an uncomfortable brunch to this joyous experience, to ensuring she was comfortable with several minibreaks during the ride... Bran had protected and pampered her. He'd given her a peace and respite she hadn't realized she so desperately needed.

And thank God it wasn't over yet. Because she didn't want to return home and have this day end. Not yet.

"Is this one of your tourist adventures?" she teased as he secured the helmets to the motorcycle.

He shrugged but humor gleamed in his blue eyes. "Sue me. I'm a cliché." He jerked his chin toward the entrance. "C'mon. One of the last tours is about to start."

For the next forty minutes, they walked around the huge fort and the grounds. Tatum didn't listen to their guide, knowledgeable as she was, as much as watch Bran listen to her. He was so attentive, seemed so captivated by the stories and facts the older woman relayed. That intense, focused expression shouldn't have been so hot, but damn, it was. She couldn't help envisioning how he employed that same focus and intensity when he slid inside a woman, when he dragged a scream of pleasure out of her.

Okay, maybe staring at him wasn't such a good idea. Old gray stone. Yes, a much better visual. Definitely safer.

"You enjoyed that," she said as the guided tour ended and their group scattered, some to explore on their own, and others no doubt headed to Sullivan's for lobster rolls and ice cream.

"I did. I'm a bit of a history buff. Always have been.

The love of it was one of the things my family and I shared. Growing up, we didn't have a ton of money, but every summer we decided on a city or town and we'd load up in the car, my dad would hitch the trailer with his bike—and later mine—to the back and we'd take off. The only requirement for our destination was it had to be historic. We'd visit all the different sites, do a couple of ghost tours. A Holleran vacation wasn't complete without a ghost tour." A smile softened his firm, wide mouth. "Those are some of my best memories."

"That sounds amazing," she murmured, strolling toward the fort's exit. "So you and your family—you're close, then?"

Yes, she was fishing, and to herself at least, she could confess to a hunger for any information not included in his bio or his BayStar dossier.

"We are. My father died four years ago—"

"Oh, Bran, I'm so sorry," she murmured, setting a hand on his forearm.

A muscle flexed under her palm, and he covered her hand with his, squeezing slightly. "Thank you. It's been rough, especially for my mother. They were married for thirty-eight years when he passed. She's still adjusting to a life without him."

He was quiet for a moment, a slight frown creasing his brow, but then he gave an abrupt shake of his head, and his expression cleared.

"Even though I've been in Seattle for a decade now, Mom and my sister Dani come out to visit me pretty often. It's not as regularly as I'd like, but Dani owns a bridal shop, so she can't just up and leave. But I go home to see them, too. And then we call each other several times a week. We all make an effort to keep in touch."

"That's how Nore and I are with each other. We call all the time but we also have monthly video chats set up."

He snorted. "I know about your movie nights with Nore. Joaquin ends up hanging out with me so he doesn't accidentally overhear something he shouldn't. Hearing you two debate the career longevity of Manuel Ferrara and his contribution to film might've scarred him for life."

"What?" She held up her hands, shrugging. "You mean to tell me Joaquin has a problem with his wife watching porn?"

"Hell no," he said, a half grin quirking the corner of his mouth. "He had a problem listening to his precious Nore and her proper friend describe said porn star's best moves and rate them one through ten. One being vanilla and ten being 'holy shit I think I just got pregnant with octuplets.' Your words, a direct quote, I believe. My poor friend. I think he lost some of his innocence that night."

Tatum barked out a crack of laughter and couldn't stop. She halted in the middle of the walkway, clutching her stomach. Wiping a tear from her eyes, she steadied herself against the fence as her hilarity eased.

"In my man's defense, though, he fully supports his fiancée watching porn. He's just firm on not hearing you two discuss it."

"That's fair." She snickered. "Wait until I tell Nore—"

"Oh no you don't." Bran jabbed a finger at her. "That

was told to you in the utmost confidence. She doesn't know about that and it's going to stay that way."

Grinning, Tatum heaved an exaggerated sigh and tipped her head back. "All right, *fine*. But she's my best friend. One of our rules is we don't keep secrets from one another."

"Yeah, well, I broke a code telling you that, so you'll keep this one," he warned.

He narrowed his eyes at her, and she held her hands up to her chest, palms raised.

"I said fine. I just want it known I'm doing this under duress." Too bad her wide smile belied that accusation. She pushed off the fence and started walking again, and Bran fell into step beside her. She slid a look at his strong profile highlighted by his thick salt-and-pepper beard. "Nore has mentioned you before, and while I knew you and Joaquin were business partners and pretty close, I didn't think you were best friends. Not like me and Nore."

"Joaquin is a good man, and I'm lucky to call him friend. He got me through one of the toughest periods of my life. Stuck beside me when not many people would've," he murmured.

"Your father's death?" she asked.

Bran glanced down at her, and pain flickered in his bright eyes. Her fingers tingled to touch him, to offer him comfort like he'd given her on the wharf. She hesitated, the small tic along his jaw a warning that she heeded.

Never would she have attributed the word *brittle* to Bran. And she still couldn't. But staring into his face with the shadows clouding his gaze, smooth skin pulled taut over his sharp bone structure, his wide mouth flattened into a grim line and that tiny muscle continuing to jump at his jaw...

He appeared to be a man on the edge of a break.

Inexplicably, she feared touching him would trigger that event. So she kept her hands to herself. Though a primal instinct deep inside cried out for her to do just the opposite.

"Yes, he supported me when my father died, but that's not what I mean. He stood by me through my divorce. And by rights, he didn't have to—hell, shouldn't have. Not after the damage my personal life wreaked on Greer, especially in our infancy. You don't fully understand the depth and scope of someone's love and loyalty until you've fucked up so bad others have walked away. And that person sticks. Not because of a contract. Not because of a business. Because they believe in you, trust you when they have every reason not to."

A thick trepidation gathered in her chest. For him, not herself. Nothing about his words suggested this story was a happy one.

"If you want to talk to me, fine. I'm here and I'll listen. But if you want to debate why I scored Manuel Ferrara's doggy style a solid eight or just sit here in silence, that's fine, too."

He blinked, and some of the shadows evaporated from his eyes as she threw his offer from Friday night—albeit the porn version—back at him. His mouth softened, losing some of the tightness at the corners.

"I can honestly say that might be the best offer I've received in a long time. At least in the last five years."

"Tell me, then," she whispered.

He turned, curled his fingers around the top of the fence as if he needed something solid to hold in this tumble back into his past. Then he lifted a hand and gestured toward her, beckoning her closer.

"Come here, Tate," he said, his voice low, rough, like it traveled over churned-up road. "Please."

She could no more resist his request or that tone than she could resist his earlier invitation to join him for the day. Something inside her was weak, vulnerable when it came to this man, and later, she would find a way to shore up her defenses against him. But not now.

She took his hand, and a moment later, he maneuvered her so she stood in front of him, her back to his wide, hard chest, his long arms caging her on either side. His chin brushed the side of her head, his mouth moving against her hair. The need to spin around, wrap her arms around his waist and bury her face in his jacket, inhale his scent yawned wide inside her. She longed to transfer her strength to him, as silly and impossible as it sounded. But this wasn't about her; it was about him. So she remained facing away from him, understanding without being told that he didn't want her to see him as he relayed this tale.

"We met when I was twenty-seven and she was twenty-two. Not only did I marry a younger woman but I was a total cliché and married an employee. Roma worked in my shop, and not long after she was hired, we started dating. We'd only been together two months before we eloped. To Vegas." His humorless chuckle, heavy with self-deprecation, brushed the top of her ear. She closed her eyes, hating the sound of it. "At first, we were happy. She quit working after we married, which I didn't mind. My mother didn't work outside the home. She was a homemaker. And my parents were full partners in their marriage. If that's what Roma wanted, then I was fine with it. But I soon discovered she didn't want to work outside the house—or in it. I offered to pay her tuition if she wanted to go back to college and complete her degree but that didn't interest her either. Only one thing did. Shopping."

Damn. She didn't need a crystal ball to foresee where this was headed. Glancing down, she stared at his hands and the knuckles blanched from his tight hold on the railing. She covered his hands with hers, intertwining their fingers. Her belly dipped when his lips grazed the rim of her ear, her hair. Keeping her emotional distance from this man was proving to be a hopeless endeavor.

"I owned my own business. I was successful. And when Joaquin and I decided to start Greer, we planned on the company being even more successful. And it was. But those first few years were building ones, and even with the capital we raised and our own fund we invested, they were tight. But that didn't stop Roma from spending. Every day, I'd return home from work and there would be bags littering our room and another bedroom that she used for her closet. Of course I'd heard about that kind of thing before, but seeing it, experiencing it? That was some shit. And no matter how many times I'd sit her down and talk to her about budgeting, it didn't stop her. Soon, we were in debt. Deep in debt."

He loosed another of those grating chuckles, shaking his head. The sound scraped over her senses, her skin and, screw it. She tried to turn around, look at him, but he stiffened his arms, caging her between his body and the fence.

"No, let me get this out. And I can't do that if you... If you're—"

"Okay, Bran," she whispered. "Whatever you need."

He pressed his forehead against the crown of her head for several moments, and they stood there, silent, the ripples of the lapping water in the harbor, the hum and laughter of people in the distance the only sounds.

"I grew up poor," he continued quietly. "Yeah, we had road trips in the summer, but there were times when grilled cheese and tomato soup was on the menu three times out of the week because it was lean at Dad's garage. I knew what it meant to go without because Mom had to make a choice between bills for that month. So money isn't that big a deal to me. But the other things..." He shook his head, and she braced herself for those *other things*.

"I don't know if it was a maturity issue, but she became resentful of the hours I spent working, which, admittedly, had increased after founding Greer. But I'd been attempting to build a life for us, and when she felt ignored or neglected, she wouldn't just spend money, she'd also come to the office and cause chaos by accusing me of cheating with our employees, verbally abusing the female staff by taking out her anger with me on them. She acted out in a bid for my attention, but the people around me were the casualties. Some of the employees she targeted quit. We lost a couple of early business contracts because her antics got back to them. Joaquin should've ended our partnership then. Hell, I would've. But he didn't. He not only kept me on as his partner but he also remained my friend, my brother as I made the hardest—and yet not the hardest—decision in my life. I ended my marriage."

"Bran, I'm so sorry," she said.

It struck her that she'd said the same thing about the loss of his father. But in a way, wasn't it another kind of death? She should know. She *did* know.

"Don't be. I gladly paid half my worth to divorce her. Money well spent."

Jerking her grip free of his, she spun around and tipped her head up to look into his face. Somewhere in the back of her mind, she conceded she was only able to look at him because he allowed it. That knowledge should not have sent a curl of heat twisting low inside her, but it did.

A grim smile curved his mouth and Tatum shook her head, lightly thumping a fist against his chest, right over his heart.

"Don't do that," she said. "Don't dismiss that relationship like it didn't impact you. Like it didn't have good, even happy moments. It's those moments that made the demise of the marriage hurt. Just because it ended ugly doesn't detract from the joy. I think the joy, the hope—they are why we're so angry when it falls apart. Because the love should've been enough to make it work. But we don't live in snow globes or pretty glass castles. Love and beautiful moments don't make a relationship. They aren't enough to sustain a marriage."

"Is this your version of a pep talk? Because if it is, you suck at it." He arched an eyebrow and rubbed the pad of his thumb over her cheekbone. The innocuous caress echoed in her sex, directly over her clit, and she trembled. Damn, even when he insulted her, this man did it for her. "You're too young to be this cynical."

"Not cynical. I'm only telling you what you already know. And it has nothing to do with age. Deliberately sabotaging the career, livelihood and dreams of the person you're supposed to love and support is a character flaw. I'm sure she had legitimate complaints—you working too many hours, probably not paying enough attention to her when you were home, being a man— but she chose an illegitimate way of reacting to those issues. Instead of sitting you down and telling you about yourself, she destroyed your finances, your stability and your future. Yes, she was immature. But she was also a fool."

Anger burned through Tatum, and right on the heels of it streamed embarrassment at her vehement defense of him. Damn, she should mind her business. Seriously, who was she to judge, when her own relationship had been such an epic failure? If anything—

The soft brush of lips over hers snatched her from her thoughts, and she gasped. Heat blasted through her from that barely there kiss but, oh God, it damn near rocked her back on her heels. Unable to help herself, she touched the tip of her tongue to her bottom lip and tasted him. Tasted his addictive earthy flavor. She smothered a moan. From the way his gaze dropped to her mouth and narrowed, she almost believed he heard that aborted sound.

"Why?" she whispered, and his scrutiny lifted to meet her eyes.

"Why what?" he asked and the growl in his voice rasped over her skin like calloused fingertips.

"Why did you…?" Instead of completing the question, she pressed her fingers to her mouth.

"I can give you the answer that wouldn't send you running scared or I can give you the truth that will damn us both. The choice is yours."

He stepped back from her, as if granting her physical space to make her decision. And she appreciated it. His scent, his intense gaze, his big frame surrounding her—they clouded her brain, permeated her senses until her head swam, full of *him*.

Her heart battered her rib cage, and the wet flesh between her legs pulsed with a heavy, aching beat, casting its vote. Her sex was all on board Team Truth, but her head… It threw warning after warning, reminding her of what happened the last time she'd let her guard down and trusted a man.

Reminding her she couldn't trust *herself*.

"The first answer," she murmured, shifting backward until the fence poked into her lower back. "Give me the first answer."

He studied her, and it bordered on intrusive. Or maybe that's just how it felt because she wanted to remain hidden from him, feared he would perceive just how much she secretly craved his truth. The self-destructive part of her longed to be damned. By him. With him.

God. What did that say about her?

"Thank you," he finally said, pinching her chin and tilting her head back even farther. Every part of her—her breath, her blood, her damn soul—stilled, waiting. For his next words, his next touch…the next brush of his mouth. "I kissed you as a thank-you for listening, for making me feel safe. For not judging me even though I acted like—" a quick smile lifted the corner of his mouth "—a man. Thank you, Tatum."

"You're welcome."

He cocked his head, and stepped forward, claiming the space both of them had inserted between them. From one second to the next she went from inhaling fresh air with a hint of rain to chocolate, oak and sex.

"When or if you want to know the other answer, call me. Come to me. But be ready for the truth, Tatum."

His stare kept her pinned in place for several long, taut moments. A sense of foreboding slid along her veins, flooding them. And underneath, electrifying, was excitement. Cruel, foolish excitement.

Moving back, Bran jerked his chin.

"You mentioned something about ice cream?"

Ice cream? He seriously expected her to just go eat ice cream after he turned her inside out with that ominous warning? But she said, "Yes."

"Have you ever had Sullivan's?"

"No, but I'm very much looking forward to it."

Their gazes caught again. Were they still talking

about the restaurant? She didn't know…and was too much of a coward to ask.

"Well, let's go get ice cream then," she murmured.

She pushed off the fence and started down the walkway, and Bran fell into step beside her. Relief should've been her companion as they headed toward the building housing the food court. But it wasn't. Instead, frustration and disappointment weighed on her like an indictment.

She'd made the right decision, the responsible decision, for herself and for her family. So why did she feel like she'd let herself down in her desperation to run toward the sensible and safe thing?

Ten

Bran aimed the remote at the mounted television, turning it on. Two news anchors conversed but he paid the program little mind. All he needed was noise to dispel the quiet in his hotel suite. Funny how he'd never really minded the quiet before. Especially after Roma left, he'd learned to value it. After all the arguing and screaming, he'd equated quiet with peace.

But after spending the day with Tatum, talking with her, hearing her laughter, her shouts against the wind while on the back of his motorcycle—yeah, it was too quiet. Instead of comforting, it suddenly seemed suffocating.

Tapping the volume button, he filled the room with the chatter of the weatherman forecasting rain tonight and a cold front predicted for tomorrow. Good thing he'd taken Tatum on that ride today because Monday would've been too cold.

And you would've missed having that beautiful body curved around you and her hands branding your skin.

He couldn't even tell his subconscious to shut the hell up because it was right. Even now, he could feel the phantom heat of her breasts against his spine, her fingers and palms pressed to his chest and abdomen, searing him through his jacket and shirt.

It'd been the ride from hell and one of pure, undiluted pleasure.

Having Tatum on the back of his bike had been only one of his fantasies. The other...

Setting the remote on the glass coffee table, he scrubbed a hand over his face, but it did nothing to dispel the images flashing across his mind like the dirtiest movie reel. Twisted sheets around tangled limbs. A slender, sleek body arching tight over him as he gripped curved hips. Long, toned arms and legs wrapped tight around his neck and waist. Perfectly manicured fingernails denting his shoulders...

Giving his head one hard shake, he grabbed a cigar and matches off the table and strode across the sunken living room. He climbed the one step into the dining area with its long table and eight tall-backed chairs. The opulence of the suite rolled right off him as he crossed to the French doors that led to the balcony. After twisting the knob, he stepped outside and within moments had the lit cigar to his lips. Puffing on it, he swirled the chocolate-and-whiskey flavor in his mouth before blowing out the cloud of smoke. He squinted at the view of downtown Boston, but the usual calm when he relaxed with his cigar didn't fill him.

Not when thoughts of the day tracked through his mind.

Fuck that. Thoughts of Tatum.

He stared down at the lit end of the cigar, not seeing the red embers. Instead, he saw the joy on Tatum's face as she removed his helmet. Heard her delighted scream as he revved the bike's engine and took off down the interstate. Inhaled the woodsy, citrus scent from the back of her ear as he rubbed his chin against her thick, long strands. Felt the comfort and heat of her body as he caged her between his chest and the fence.

Damn, he should've never thrown down that dare. He'd screwed himself with that move. Now all he could do was torture himself with images of what could've happened between them if she'd said yes. Because that's what her asking him for the truth surmounted to—her saying yes to them returning either back here or to her home. No, she'd done them both a favor.

Just as he brought the cigar back to his lips, a knock sounded on the suite door. He narrowed his eyes on the balcony doorway as if he could determine from there who would be bothering him at this time of night. Hell, who would be bothering him, period. He only knew a few people in Boston, and none of them would be here.

Sighing, he set the cigar on an ashtray and strode back inside. Curling his hand around the knob, he pulled the door open.

"Yeah—Tatum?" He transferred his grip from the knob to the frame, his fingers aching in protest at the tight hold. "What're you doing here?" he unintention-ally growled.

"I…" She blinked, her fingers twisting in front of the same jacket she'd worn earlier. As if becoming aware of the tell, she glanced down then dropped her arms to her sides. "I'm sorry to drop in on you unannounced. If it's a bad time…"

She started to turn, but before his mind had even is-sued permission, he grasped her lower arm.

"No." He jerked his hand back and tunneled his fin-gers through his hair, briefly fisting the strands be-fore lowering his arm to wave her inside. "No," he repeated. "It's fine. Please, come in." She hesitated, and he couldn't blame her. Not with how he'd just spo-ken to her. But he stepped back and dipped his chin. "Tatum. Come in," he repeated, voice lower, and damn, he tried for softer. But couldn't be certain he achieved it.

Still, she slowly nodded then entered and he clenched his jaw as her scent assailed him. If he had half a brain, he'd order her to leave. Nothing good could come from the thickening of his cock just from one good hit of her. But he, who'd learned the hard way not to be impul-sive, didn't tell her to exit. Instead, he closed the door and followed her farther inside the suite, studying the proud line of her shoulders and back, the subtle yet sen-sual sway of her hips.

He was fucked and he hadn't laid one finger on her.

Tatum paused beside the dining room table, survey-ing the elegantly appointed rooms. In the last few years, this kind of luxury had become his norm. But no matter how many zeroes in his net worth labeled him a millionaire, the young kid from small-town Georgia would always reside inside him, and that part would never get used to opulence. Though he currently stayed in one of Boston's most expensive five-star hotels, a small voice couldn't help reminding him how much money he'd save in one of those chain motels across town. All he needed was a clean bed, a shower and a working TV.

He shifted his scrutiny from the suite to Tatum. Now, she belonged here, in these surroundings. Nothing about Tatum Haas said chain hotel. Her skin deserved to grace only the highest thread count Egyptian cotton sheets. Only the best food prepared by top chefs should cross her lips. Only the best view of the city should greet her every morning.

Another reason he should escort her out of here. He could give her pleasure if she allowed him—give it to them both—but the man she needed, the man who'd enjoy galas and dinner parties, the man born of her world… That could never be him. And more importantly, he didn't want to be that man.

"Beautiful place," she said, finally turning to look at him.

"It is." He crossed his arms over his chest. "What're you doing here, Tatum?"

She slid her hands in the pockets of her jacket then swept one hand over her dark hair. The jerky movements relayed her nerves, as had the hand twisting at the door.

"Do you want something to drink?" he offered, because shit, he could use one. And it looked like she could, too. "Water, wine, scotch?"

"Scotch, please," she said, and he didn't miss the relief in her voice.

He nodded. "Why don't you take your jacket off? Unless you plan on having that drink and then running?"

A smile flirted with her mouth. With a silent, fierce curse, he pivoted, stalking toward the built-in bar in the living room. If it felt like he was running away from her and his obsession with that mouth, well... That's because he was running away.

Once he'd set two short glasses on top of the bar, he poured two fingers of scotch each from the crystal decanter and, inhaling a deep breath, turned. Tatum had removed her jacket and stood next to the couch. He approached her, offering her the drink. Their fingertips brushed as she accepted it, and he put a stranglehold on the groan that clawed up his throat.

Yeah. He should've definitely shown her the door.

Sipping the scotch, he welcomed the burn and studied her over the rim.

"You good?" he asked.

"Yes, thank you."

"Do you want to pretend we're talking about the scotch?"

Another of those smiles played with her lips and she shook her head. "I don't think I'll ever get used to how you speak to me," she murmured.

He frowned, lowering his glass. "Have I offended you?"

"No." She shook her head again and took a healthy sip, not even wincing at the potency of the alcohol. "On the contrary. Whatever is on your mind, you speak it.

Is some of it blunt and a little shocking in its frankness? Yes, but that's also why it's so…refreshing. I'm used to barbs wrapped in compliments. Insults gifted in pleasantries. The truth so entangled with lies that it's impossible to tell one from the other. Whether you're delivering praise, criticism or an opinion, it is what it is. And that's rare."

"That's sad." And no, he didn't speak all of what was on his mind. Especially with her. He would be in a shitload of trouble if he did.

"It is, isn't it?"

"Is that why you're here?" he pressed, because dammit, she *still* hadn't answered his question. And though he suspected the reason, he needed to hear it from her. Hear it in that sex-and-moonlight voice. "You're here for the truth?"

Lust ignited inside him, having already been at a simmer since he'd opened the door to her on the other side. He locked all his muscles against the onslaught of it, willing her to laugh off his question.

Willing her to give them both what they needed but, goddamn, had no business taking.

"Yes, that's why I'm here."

Fuck.

Her answer stroked down his chest, his clenching abdomen, his throbbing cock like a seeking hand.

"Give me the truth you didn't earlier today. The one I was too scared to ask for. I want it now."

"What's different between now and then? What changed?"

"You're stalling," she softly accused, taking another

sip of scotch. "And I might've been scared before, but it's you now. *You're* scared to answer *me*."

He didn't—couldn't—deny either allegation.

"What changed, Tate?"

She chuckled, and the smoky sound was molten heat in his blood. Gone was the nervous, fidgety woman who'd shown up at his hotel room door. She'd been replaced by an assured temptress, confident in not just herself but the obvious hold she had on him. Was he glimpsing the Tatum she'd been before her fiancé's death and infidelities had dented her heart and confidence?

The person he'd come to know—the smart businesswoman, vulnerable woman—was irresistible to him. And this version?

This version left him speechless and breathless.

"I shouldn't savor this, but I can't lie. I am." She stared down into her glass for a brief moment. "All this time, I thought it was only me feeling a little terrified, off-kilter and uncertain. But it isn't only me. You're right there with me. Tell me I'm lying," she demanded.

"You're lying," he said, partly just to see what this Tatum would do.

And partly because conceding that she was right— that she terrified him, left him standing on uneven ground—threatened to put him right back in the place he'd been seven years ago when he'd been powerless to stop the shitstorm shaking up his world.

Yeah, she scared him that much.

"I do believe this is the first time you've lied to me," she murmured. And smiled. "Good."

He didn't need to ask what she meant by that; he'd given himself away. So he remained silent. And just watched, fascinated and more than a little wary as she set her tumbler on the end of the coffee table and approached him, not stopping until only a breath of space separated his chest from hers.

"I came over here because I was sitting in my big, empty, too-quiet house trying to convince myself that being there was what I wanted. That it was the right thing to do and the right place to be. That it was safe. But the longer I sat there with the silence and the loneliness, what was right, safe became less and less important. I've always done what was expected of me, followed the rules my entire life. And where has it gotten me? Alone, afraid and quiet. For once, I wanted— *want*—to be selfish. I want to be loud."

If her admission hadn't snatched the air from his lungs, those nearly black eyes with their steady, unwavering stare would've. She stood emotionally naked before him. Shame crept inside him. Because he'd been too afraid to do the same.

He stepped back.

And stripped off his T-shirt.

Her soft gasp brushed against his bare chest as he moved forward, reclaiming the space he'd placed between them. He cupped her cheek with one hand and the whimper that escaped her damn near triggered one from him. Her lashes fluttered, and he bent his head, brushing his lips over the lids before trailing a caress over her cheekbone.

"You want the truth? I don't know if you do because I don't want it." He pressed a kiss to the skin just below her ear, absorbed the delicate shiver that trembled through her. Swallowed a hiss of pleasure as she gripped his waist, her palms against his naked skin. "From the moment you stepped out on that balcony, I've fantasized about you. Wondered if all that fire, all that attitude you threw would burn me alive if I ever got you under me…over me. Fantasized about being on the receiving end of that mouth, those teeth. Fantasized about you marking me with both."

He shifted his hand from her cheek to her head and burrowed his fingers in the thick strands, savoring her hair sliding over his sensitive skin. This time, he didn't hold back his groan. He gave that to her in return for her whimper. "I have no business saying this to you, and you have no business listening. You should tell me to go to hell and walk right out of this room. Because I'm going to be a complete asshole and put the weight of it on you. Because left up to me, I'm picking you up, wrapping those long mind-fuck legs around me and taking you into that bedroom. And not to discuss. Not to talk. We're going to fuck until both of our bodies give."

Her quick, heavy breath broke against his collarbone, and he knew her answer before she uttered a word.

"I don't want to talk either." She lifted her lashes, met his gaze. And the lust in those dark eyes—*damn*. "Fuck me," she whispered.

As if those two words snapped the threadbare restraints on his control, he did just as he promised. Bending down, he cupped the backs of her thighs then stood, hiking her into his arms. Without prompting, Tatum embraced him with her legs, her arms locking around his neck. He spun around and stalked toward the bedroom, desperation and lust lending him a focus that he'd only experienced with motorcycles.

"Wait."

Though every nerve ending screamed in denial and his cock throbbed in protest, he stopped. Searching her face for any sign of doubt, of discomfort, he waited as she requested.

"You're not the only one to dream," she whispered, threading her fingers through his beard, scratching her nails along his jaw. He gave her another moan because goddamn, it felt good. *She* felt good. "One kiss," she said, her gaze dropping to his mouth. "Can I have just one kiss before we—"

He crushed his mouth to hers.

She'd never have to beg him for this. Not when he craved it so bad his fucking toes ached with the need.

And that first taste… God, his knees almost buckled and took both of them to the floor. Sweet. Heady. And immediately addictive. Just one hit. That's all he needed to know he would always hunger for this particular flavor. *Her* flavor.

Her lips parted for the thrust of his tongue, and he took full advantage. Diving deep, he sucked and licked. Dueled and danced. The more he had of her, the more he tasted, the more moans she gave him, the more he needed, demanded.

It might've been a mistake giving in to her. The odds of them making it to the bedroom had severely decreased. And he didn't care. With the lust roaring in his ears, pumping in his veins, he'd take her on this floor and thank God for each rug burn.

She jerked her mouth away from his, and he wasn't too proud to admit he chased her. But she buried her face in his neck and muttered, "The bedroom. Please."

He didn't need any further encouragement. Within moments, he entered the dimly lit space and laid her on the mattress and followed her down. Then taking her mouth again. And again. And again. By the time he lifted his head, her lips were swollen and wet from his and they strained and rocked against each other. Hell, if she weren't still fully clothed and he didn't have his sweatpants on, he would be buried inside her, finally discovering for himself if the clasp of her sex was as tight as his imagination assured him it was.

Cradling the back of her neck, he helped her sit up. Fisting the bottom of her sweater, he tore it over her head and dropped it to the floor behind him. A black lace bra cupped her perfect small breasts, and he bent his head to sip from her flesh. One of those whimpers he was already addicted to echoed in his ears as she tangled her fingers in his hair, holding him to her. Urging him to taste more, take more. Or maybe he was just projecting. Either way, he accepted the offer.

Opening his mouth over the firm flesh, he reached behind her and unhooked the bra then peeled it down her arms. Satisfaction and need coursed through him as he molded her breasts to his hands, squeezing and plumping. He licked a path to her nipple and sucked her deep and hard, drawing on her, circling the beaded peak with his tongue. She arched into him, pressing her flesh into his mouth. Her hands scraped his scalp, his shoulders, his back, restless, urging. On a hum, he switched to the other breast, his fingers tugging and tweaking the damp tip as he again lost himself in her.

Her hips jerked, writhed. Tatum spread her legs wide, cradling him between them, grinding her sex against his abdomen. Damn, he wanted that hot, wet flesh against his skin. On his fingers. In his mouth.

Need and urgency bombarded him, and he sprang off the bed. Bending down to scatter kisses down her torso, he gripped the button on her jeans. He paused, glancing up at her, waiting a moment. If this wasn't what she really wanted...

"Please," she whispered.

A groan rushed through him as he knelt on the floor, removed each boot and then stripped her jeans down her legs. With a finger hooked on each side of her black lace underwear, he drew them off as well, slower, revealing her like a gift. And she was just that. A beautiful gift he'd never expected and damn sure didn't deserve.

"Bran," she breathed, her thighs tensing under his palms. She slid her own hands down her legs to tangle her fingers with his.

He shook his head. "Tell me to stop or move those hands, baby." He grazed the back of one hand with his lips. "The choice is yours."

After a moment, she dropped her arms to the mattress. Her body shook as she slowly widened her legs, and he could feel the effort it took for her to deliberately relax. He rewarded that trust with a hot open-mouthed kiss on her inner thigh.

As he inhaled deeply, her intoxicating musk filled him, and his stomach cramped with hunger. God, he just needed to satiate it. Or he could try. Fuck, he wanted to try.

Palming her thighs, he spread her wider and buried his mouth against her sex. Her sharp cry bounced off the walls, resounded in his ears, echoed in his chest, his gut. The sounds were almost as delicious to him as the succulent flesh under his tongue, his lips.

With a growl, he devoured her, attempting to get his fill, but even as he lapped at her clit, stroked a path between her swollen folds, he knew it was in vain. He could never get enough of her taste, of that small bud of nerves flinching and swelling under his hungry licks, of her liquid desire in that tight, hot channel. No. He was destined to become a fiend over her.

Pursing his lips over that engorged nub, he sucked even as he slipped two fingers inside her, groaning at that smooth, slick clasp. She quivered around him, and fuck, his dick pulsed, already feeling those tiny spasms over his own flesh. He reached down and fisted himself, trying to alleviate some of the pressure so this didn't end before it began. But he miscalculated. With her in his mouth and his fingers buried inside her, his hard grip only propelled him toward orgasm.

"Get there, baby," he growled, licking her, circling her clit with the tip of his tongue. He thrust inside her, harder, faster. Curling his fingers, he rubbed her, grinding his knuckles against her feminine lips. "Give it to me."

With a long, low moan, she came, her sex gripping

him in a chokehold. And he almost followed her. Taking several precious moments, he continued to stroke and rub, giving her the full measure of her release. But as soon as she slumped back against the sheets, he slid free and stood. And removed his sweatpants. After quickly grabbing a condom from his wallet on the bedside table, he ripped the foil package open and rolled the protection down his cock. Later, he might be embarrassed over the slight tremble in his body as he climbed over her. Later, he might deny the twist of anxiety in his gut as he kneed her legs farther apart and hooked her knee over his hip.

Later, he might ignore the small prayer he raised up as he notched the head of his cock between her soaked folds.

Later, later, later...

Right now, though, he admitted she shook him. He admitted being inside her scared and thrilled him.

He admitted this was important to him.

Threading his fingers through her hair, he smoothed it away from her face, fisting the strands. Unable to *not* kiss her, he took her mouth, and she didn't avoid him. Didn't shy away from tasting herself on his tongue and lips. And God, that was sexy as hell.

"On you," he said, trailing a kiss over her cheekbone to her ear. "When you're ready."

"Inside me, Bran," she whispered, her hands tangled in the hair at his nape. "Now."

He didn't need any further encouragement. Thrusting, he buried his cock deep inside her, and despite his best effort, a groan ripped free of his chest. God*damn*.

It was like diving into the sultriest sauna and the most refreshing pool of water. How had he gone…?

He cut that thought off, clenching his jaw.

Sex, he reminded himself, pressing his forehead to hers, eyes squeezed closed. It's sex. Amazing, fucking soul-tearing, mind-altering sex. But still…

"Tate? Baby," he growled. "On you," he reminded her. If the too-tight clasp of her core hadn't alerted him that she struggled to accommodate him, the quivering of her slick muscles and the fine tremble in her legs would've. "Tell me when I can move."

"One minute," she rasped, her arms tightening around him. "One minute."

"No hurry, baby."

Oh fuck, he was going to die. But he'd go happy.

He sucked the delicate line of her jaw and nipped before tracing a path down her neck and sipping from the shallow bowl in the middle of her collar bone. With a hum of pleasure, he kissed her again, lowering his hand and cupping one of her beautiful breasts. Shaping it. Squeezing it. Rolling her nipple.

Her hips rolled, pulsing, and lifting his head, he asked—begged, "Ready, Tate?"

"Please, yes," she moaned.

"Thank God."

She chuckled, but it ended on a gasp as he withdrew and drove forward again.

"Again," she breathed. "Oh my God, again."

He obliged, pulling free of her silken grip then powering back in. She sucked him inside, squeezing him, working him. How had he gone forty years without knowing this kind of pleasure? Rearing back, he hiked her thighs over his legs, cupping her ass, holding her steady for his hard, quick thrusts. Her cries poured out of her in a nonstop stream, and he accepted each one as a challenge to fuck her more, harder, bury his cock higher, deeper.

"Bran. I'm—" She gasped, and before she could finish the warning, her sex clamped down on him, rippling over him, milking him.

She came, hips writhing, body shaking, and on a gritted curse, he fell over her, one hand flattened next to her ear and the other still cradling her thigh. He pistoned into her again and again and once more before erupting and following her into a desperate, powerful orgasm. Electricity crackled up his back, nailed him in the back of the neck then traveled back down to sizzle at the base of his spine and even in the soles of his feet.

As he tumbled forward, gathering Tatum close and pressing his nose to the crook of her neck, he had one thought.

He'd fucked up.

Because once wouldn't be enough.

Eleven

Déjà vu.

Sighing, Tatum glanced down at her phone, glancing at the text message she'd received climbing into her car. Her father "requested" her presence as soon as she arrived at the office. Something told her that Monday was about get a lot Monday-er.

This impromptu meeting was about business or her ditching brunch yesterday. At the moment, she didn't feel equipped to discuss either.

The elevator slid to a halt, and the doors opened. Striding out, she barely managed not to wince at the unfamiliar twinges in her thighs…and the flesh between them. Heat poured through her with each reminder of the night before. Of the man responsible for the soreness. And those were the invisible souvenirs. This morning, as she showered, her fingers had glided over the smudged bruises on the insides of her thighs, on her breasts. Without her permission, her fingers lifted and glided over the one on the curve of her breast and hidden under her dress. She flushed.

"Woman, get it together," she muttered under her breath.

She'd snuck out of Bran's hotel before the sun rose, leaving him in the sheets they'd tangled together. That had been more difficult than she would've believed; a part of her—a large part—had wanted to stay in the king-size bed with him, his big body curled around hers. Because that craving had yawned so wide and deep inside her, she'd hurried out of there like Lucifer himself had been snapping at her ass. And not sexy Tom Ellis Lucifer. But the big horned fire-and-brimstone baddie.

Coward move, yes. At the moment, had she felt like she was running, if not for her life, then for her self-preservation and sanity? Yes.

So she could be excused.

But the joke was on her. Because she escaped the hotel room but couldn't outrun her body. Or her mind, where memories from the night before replayed like a movie reel.

Shoving those thoughts to the back of her mind as she approached her father's office—because it was bad form to have a meeting with her dad while thinking about the hottest sex ever—she smiled at Brenda.

"Good morning, Brenda," she greeted the executive assistant.

"Good morning to you, Tatum." She smiled and nodded her head toward the office door. "Your father and sister are already in there."

"Thanks." Still smiling, Tatum kept it until she turned around and then frowned.

Her father hadn't mentioned a meeting with her and Mia. If this was about yesterday, why would her sister need to be in attendance? After giving his door a quick rap, she waited until he called out then entered.

"Morning, Dad." She closed the office door as Silas and Mia both looked in her direction—he from behind his desk and Mia from the armchair in front of it.

Why did she get the feeling she'd just interrupted something?

Stop being paranoid, she immediately berated herself. It was her father and sister, not coworkers gossiping around the watercooler—if they had a watercooler.

"Hey, Mia," she said, her voice not betraying the disquiet gelling inside her belly. "Dad, I hope you have coffee ready. It's already a Monday," she teased, crossing the floor to the vacant armchair next to her sister.

"Coffee's over there." He dipped his chin in the direction of the sitting area, but Tatum didn't turn and glance over there, much less rise from her seat. Call it a survival instinct, but she didn't feel like she could remove her attention from either her father or sister. And God, that sounded plain awful. But she still didn't look away from them.

"Thank you." She paused and crossed her legs, flattening her hands on the arms of the chair. "What's going on?" Her twisting stomach wouldn't allow her to beat around the bush.

"What happened with brunch yesterday?" her father asked in return.

Seriously? This was the office. He was calling her on the carpet about missing a meal. They couldn't have done this by phone call? Though she'd suspected this might be the reason behind the early-morning meeting, it didn't annoy her any less. At some point during this past year, she hadn't just been viewed as broken but her parents had also started treating her as if she were nine instead of twenty-nine.

And yes, she was partly to blame because she'd been so mired in her own anger, pain and grief that she'd permitted it. But this had to stop. *Had* to stop. The coddling, the admonishments, the ambushing, the pushing... When did *she* get to push back?

"Dad." She inhaled a breath and slowly, deliberately released it. "I love you and Mom, but I explained to you both yesterday why I didn't come over."

"You said something came up," he said, templing his fingers under his chin, his dark gaze narrowed on her.

"Yes, and it did."

"On a Sunday?"

"On a Sunday," she repeated, and a tense quiet descended on the office when she didn't offer a more detailed explanation.

Finally, Silas sighed. "Tatum, I'm not sure what's going on but I'm concerned."

She tilted her head, frowning. "Forgive me, Dad, but I'm truly confused. You're concerned because I missed one family meal? At the most, it's rude to cancel at the last minute, but a meeting that smacks of an intervention? That's a little extreme."

"First, disappearing during your mother's dinner party Friday night and having a client take you home. No word from you on Saturday. Then you cancel yesterday, and when your sister went by your house to check on you, you weren't home. Not Friday evening or Sunday," he said, and even though his voice remained calm, she couldn't miss the accusation and disappointment there.

"Okay, let's talk about it, Dad," she said, leaning forward, propping an elbow on her knee. She met his gaze with her own, her heart thumping like a wild thing behind her breastbone. "Truth? I didn't become ill Friday night. I was anxious, frustrated and uncomfortable in the home where I should've felt safe and welcome. Instead, once again, you prioritized business and appearances over my well-being, my concern, my simple *feelings*, and invited Leo and Dara Walker."

"Are you serious, Tatum?" He scowled, flipping his hands up, and though her father would never speak it, the gesture clearly read, *What the fuck?* "Do you really expect me to end a business arrangement because of…Mark's death? That's ridiculous, immature and unprofessional."

"No, I don't expect you to end your business relationship with them. But I do expect and deserve loyalty. Keep it business—deal with them here in the office or in professional settings. But always inviting them into spaces I consider safe is a violation of our relationship. It would be one thing if their purpose was MassComm.

But every time, without fail, they pressure me to remain in the role of Mark's fiancée, unwilling to see how it tears me down. But if they either can't or are unwilling to see it, you and Mom do. You know what it does to me, and yet you continue to place me in that position because of *business*."

The silence in the room roared in her ears, echoing the frantic pounding of her pulse and heart. Her chest rose and fell on her rapid, agitated breaths, and she struggled, but finally won, to bring it under control. She refused to give her father the ammo of accusing her of being "emotional."

Even though, goddammit, she was emotional. If parents not protecting their child but opting to throw her to the wolves didn't call for *emotion*, than she didn't know what did.

"It's been almost a year, Tatum," he murmured, and she hated the compassion in his eyes.

Resented it.

She'd needed his compassion the first time the Walkers asked her to speak at Mark's funeral when the betrayal and pain had been fresh. She'd needed his concern when he'd called her, pressuring her to go over to Mark's old apartment to help clean it out and be dragged down a memory lane that had been all lies. She'd needed his protection when they'd impressed upon her again to speak at their foundation in his honor.

She'd needed her father, her parent. And he hadn't been there.

But Bran had. He'd shielded her from her parents' demands, their expectations, their thoughtlessness.

He'd done what none of her family had in almost a year, as her father had pointed out.

"We can't be responsible for wrapping you in cotton, Tate," Mia said, backing their father. So this was the side her sister had chosen today. It'd wavered over the months, flip-flopping. "You can't avoid them or anyone else, for that matter. Life is going on while you're stuck in the past."

"Stuck in the past?" Tatum loosed an abrupt, dry chuckle. "That's the problem, isn't it? I'm trying to move forward but I'm not allowed. And Dad—" she shifted her gaze back to her father "—if you can't even say what happened, how difficult do you think it is for me? 'Mark's death.' He didn't die in a car accident or have a heart attack. He had a brain aneurysm and died naked in a hotel room while screwing a woman that wasn't me, the fiancée he was supposed to marry the next morning. The fiancée he'd been cheating on for months, possibly our entire relationship. Those are the facts. No one—" she slid a hard look at her sister before returning her regard back to Silas "—gets to determine how I deal with it."

"Does part of you 'dealing with it' include becoming involved with a BayStar client?" he asked, his voice softer but no less demanding.

Shock shoved her back against the chair. Ice splintered inside her chest, and she couldn't move. She stared at her father, vocal cords encased in a deep freeze.

What…? How…?

"Answer me, Tatum. Are you—" he paused, his lips

firming into a grim line "—intimately involved with Bran Holleran?"

"Why would you ask me that?" How did he know? Or was he only fishing for information? Either way, she couldn't admit the truth. Not…right now. Guilt flared inside her, yet she didn't avoid his gaze, but met it. "Tell me what this is really about. I miss a Sunday brunch and suddenly I'm called on the carpet for what, exactly?" She tilted her head. "Sabotaging an account or attempting to acquire it by getting on my back? That's a big leap isn't it?"

"The fact is I've heard of…concerns about his demeanor toward you. And with you being in a vulnerable position—"

"Oh this is great." She leaned her head back and barked out a harsh laugh. "Dad, either you believe me capable enough of working in this company and possibly one day helming it or you don't. The only thing riding a fence gets you is splinters in the ass."

"Now just a minute," he snapped, flattening his palms on his desk and leaning forward. "I'm your father—"

"Here, you're my employer," she snapped back. "And tell me one thing I've done to jeopardize this account. One act of impropriety. Name it."

He glanced at Mia, and it was fleeting, but Tatum caught it. And understanding dawned. So bright and clear, she narrowed her eyes on her father then Mia.

"Oh I get it now. The source of the *concerns*." She arched an eyebrow and smiled and didn't try to soften the sharp edges of it. No, those edges reflected the jagged points of hurt in her heart. "How about you confide in me, Mia, instead of carrying tales to Dad? What is it about Bran Holleran that worries you?"

Mia sighed, rolling her eyes as if exasperated by Tatum and the discussion. "I just mentioned to Dad how he was a little handsy Friday night—"

"Handsy?" Tatum snapped, scrolling through her memories to the night of the dinner party. "In what way?"

"Tatum, stop being so obtuse. He touched your back—"

"And you touched his chest," Tatum shot back. "So if he was inappropriate, what were you?" Mia's lips parted, but Tatum shot up a hand, halting her next words. "Next, Mia—because that's bullshit and you know it—what is the rest of your evidence that is so dire it facilitated this *meeting*?"

She fought to grab a hold of her temper, but she suspected this was less about concern over any potential predatory advances and more over their rivalry. Both professional and personal. Mia was undoubtedly still angry about Dad removing her from the account. And… And Tatum hadn't forgotten the way her sister had looked at and touched Bran. With familiarity and more than a little interest.

There was an agenda here. And it was all Mia's.

"I came by your house Friday night after dinner to check on you and drove over on Sunday. You weren't home either night. And when I tried calling you and Bran, neither of you answered. I doubt that's just a co-incidence," she sneered.

"Oh so we've taken to doing drive-bys on each other?

While your concern is certainly—" Tatum's lip curled in a mocking smile "—touching, I can't help but wonder why you dropped by my house when you haven't before. Did it occur to you that I didn't want company? Or that if I was out, that it was my business and I didn't have to log my whereabouts with you?"

"Sarcasm gets you—"

"Gets my point across," she interrupted. "And another question. Why are you calling Bran Holleran? The account was assigned to me, so I can't think of any reason you'd have for contacting him."

Mia's chin lifted, and her smile, though small, was smug. "We have a friendly personal relationship."

Tatum didn't allow her sister or father to witness how that self-satisfied, arrogant answer affected her. How it punched her in the chest, leaving a hollow ache behind. Leaving jealousy behind. This had ceased to be about business.

This was about her not feeling emotionally safe with either of them.

"Are you removing me from the Greer Motorcycles account, Dad?" she asked, switching her attention back to her father. The calm, flat tone didn't match the cacophony of anger, disappointment and hurt clashing inside her like an out of tune orchestra.

Everything in her stilled as she waited for his answer.

After a long moment, he exhaled. "No, Tatum, you are still on the account. But—"

"No." She rose from her chair and forced her hands to remain at her sides instead of clenching into fists. Or worse, crossing over her chest, telegraphing her vulnerability. "No buts. Yes, I've had a difficult last few months. But my track record at BayStar can hold up against any employee here. If it couldn't, you wouldn't have risked having me handle Greer Motorcycles in the first place, no matter my relation to you. So either you trust that I wouldn't do anything to deliberately harm this investment or you don't."

Not waiting for his reply, and not glancing at her sister, she strode across the office and, after pulling open the door, exited.

But she couldn't leave the guilt and powerlessness so easily.

She couldn't outrun herself.

Twelve

"So are we taking turns popping up on each other?" Tatum stopped at the end of her front walk, meeting the ice-blue gaze of the man sitting on the top step of her home.

"If that's what you want to call it," Bran said, rising, and she tried—damn, she tried—not to soak him in. But she failed. Miserably. She couldn't stop from taking in his tall, wide-shouldered frame clothed in a black pea coat, dark blue sweater and jeans.

A ball of heat coalesced just under her navel and she glanced away from him, focusing on a spot somewhere over his shoulder. Just for a few seconds while she got the need under control. She should've expected that seeing him for the first time after having him inside her would carry more impact.

But God, she'd seriously underestimated just *how* powerful.

She couldn't look at him without seeing that beautiful, rugged face tightened in lust as he came and went rigid above her. Couldn't see him without feeling the phantom brand of his chest to her back and his hand on her thigh, holding it high as he thrust into her from behind. Couldn't see him without feeling his hard, big body surrounding her as they fell asleep.

A shaky breath shuddered out of her and she forced herself to meet his gaze again.

"What would you call it?" she asked, climbing the steps until they stood next to each other.

She didn't wait for his answer but unlocked her front door and entered then held it open for him to follow. Call her paranoid, but after the morning she'd had, privacy on her front stairs had become more of a theory than reality.

Once she'd dumped her bag and purse on the chaise longue, she shrugged out of her coat and hung it on the newel post of the staircase.

"Are you done?" he asked, his smoke-and-midnight voice dancing down her spine.

She halted on her way to the living room and spun around to look at him. The hurt, the anger, the fear from earlier swelled inside her, threatening to take her under. All day, she'd wanted to call him, to hear his voice, to… to have those long, muscled arms around her, cradling her as they'd done the night before. But she couldn't. Couldn't give in to that need, couldn't lean on him.

Last night was last night. In the past, and it had to stay

there. Because she could so easily become dependent on him, and even if he weren't her client, Bran was leaving Boston in a matter of weeks. And who was she kidding? A man scarred by his divorce and a woman left damaged by death and lies didn't make for a healthy relationship.

They should end this now and walk away...

"No," she whispered. "I'm not done."

She stalked over to him, thrust her fingers underneath the bun low at his nape, dragged his head down as she rose on her toes and took his mouth. Not bothering to contain the whimper that clawed free of her, she parted her lips and thrust her tongue into his mouth, taking control of the kiss.

Taking. Taking. Taking.

And he gave. God, did he give.

His hands lightly cupped her hips and he let her have her way with his mouth—nipping, sucking, licking, rubbing. She couldn't get enough of those firm lips with a touch of softness. Drawing back, she grazed his full bottom lip with her teeth, easing any sting with a long, luxurious swipe of her tongue.

Desperation and hunger stole through her, and if she could've crawled up his rangy body, or better, inside him, she would've. But she settled for tugging free his long, dark hair, burrowing her fingers in the strands. Pulling him down again, she reclaimed his mouth, enjoying every scratch of that salt-and-pepper beard over her skin. Not caring that tomorrow might tell the tale if she weren't careful.

She was far past careful.

Ripping a page out of his book, she stepped back from

him and slid her feet free of her heels. Keeping her gaze fixed on his gleaming blue eyes, she reached for the tie at her waist, loosened her dress and unwrapped herself. The front fell open, revealing her purple demi bra and matching thong. Without a word, she shrugged, and the material slipped soundlessly to the floor. Still maintaining their visual throwdown, she slowly bent at the waist, reaching for the silk top of her thigh-high stocking.

"Don't." She paused at the hoarse command, her fingers hooked into each side. A shiver rolled over her at the lust burning in his eyes, tightening the skin over his brutal bone structure so he appeared carved from the hardest, most beautiful stone. "That's mine."

That's mine.

He referred to the action of removing the lingerie— he proved it by striding forward and sinking to his knees in front of her, his hands brushing hers aside.

Yet…

Yet, the command—no, the claim—reverberated inside her chest, and much lower in her sex. Branded her. She'd never believed she would want to belong to someone again, not after the last time had ended up a cruel lie. Mark hadn't been hers; he'd been several somebodies'. And she hadn't been his. How could she be if she was interchangeable?

So she'd given up on that dream, convinced herself she didn't need it.

Until this moment. Until Bran uttered *mine*.

A yearning so wild, so fierce swelled inside her, she had to swallow back a cry. A cry that would've been misplaced in this foyer, where only lust and hunger reigned.

Tunneling her fingers through his thick hair, she scraped her fingernails over his scalp, hoarding the low rumble of pleasure he gave her in return. His hot mouth was high on her thigh just above the lacy top of the stocking. Kissing the skin, he rolled the lingerie down and repeated the caress and the gesture on the other leg.

His palms cradled her hips, and he leaned back on his heels, staring up at her, and maybe she was projecting but it almost looked like reverence in those ice-blue depths. The emotions she'd been fighting all day coasted up her body, swirling, merging, and she blinked against their force. That look called her strong and indomitable and she felt anything but.

"Baby?" he murmured, his calloused palms stroking down her thighs to the back of her knees. With a slight pressure, he bent them and brought her down to the floor, straddling his powerful thighs. Those same hands cupped her face, tilting it down so she had no choice but to meet his gaze. "What's wrong? Talk to me, Tate."

She shook her head. Not now.

Right now she just wanted to burn with him. Drowning in the pleasure only he seemed capable of eliciting from her body.

Circling his wrists, she drew his hands down to her breasts, urging those big palms and long, elegant skillful fingers to cover her. Squeeze her. Make her come. And forget.

Maybe he heard her plea, or maybe the need to touch her surged as hot in him as it did in her. She didn't care. Not here.

As he shoved the bra cups under her breasts and

played with her flesh like she was an instrument he was set on fine-tuning, she kissed him again. Thrust her tongue to engage in another erotic game of hide-and-seek. And below, she rocked against the hard, thick—*God*—long length of his cock. Back and forth. Up and down. She was so wet and was probably making an utter mess of her insubstantial thong and the front of his jeans. It didn't matter. Nothing mattered but him and the pleasure that streamed through her like liquid fire.

"Don't think I don't know you're using me to get off, baby," he murmured against her flesh, flicking a glance at her even as he swept the flat of his tongue over her nipple. Rubbing his thumb around the other tip, he lowered one hand to his jeans and undid them. He slowly reclined on the foyer floor, pulling her with him. Threading his fingers through her hair, he cradled her head and this time, his kiss left her breathless and weak, limbs trembling. "Don't hold back, Tate."

He lowered one hand back to his jeans, jerked the zipper down and pulled his cock free. Hiking his hips up, he shoved the denim down until it gathered just under his ass. Palming his aroused flesh, he stroked a hand up its length, the wide bulbous tip disappearing in his fist before appearing seconds later, glistening with precum. His body arched and strained into the rough caress, and her mouth watered at the thick cock now gleaming with the evidence of desire *she'd* stirred. Desire for *her*. "Fuck it, baby," he urged. "Use it. Use me. That's what I'm here for. For you."

She covered his mouth with her hand. That mouth, that tongue, was temptation, and if he didn't stop talking, his dick wouldn't be the only thing she would beg him for. His raw honeyed urging would propel her right over the edge into release if she wasn't careful.

Lifting, she hovered over his cock…then slid down. And oh God, down. A moan slipped free from her, and the hand not covering his mouth tangled in her own hair. Oh damn. He was… He could… She couldn't…

Oh but dammit, she couldn't stop. The pleasure/burn spurred her on, didn't cause her to halt. She wanted all of it, all of *him*.

"Fuck. Tate." Bran jerked his head to the side, out from under her hand, and he gripped her hips, stopping their steady pulsing. "No condom," he ground out.

She hung her head, her fingers digging into his broad shoulders.

"Pill," she breathed, meeting his bright gaze. "I'm on the pill. And I'm clean. I checked after—*oh God.*"

He thrust hard inside her, stealing the rest of the air from her lungs. Her back arched, her nails denting his skin. Fingers fisted her hair, tugging her head down, and dazed, she stared at him.

"It's just you and me here. No one else." He held her to him, rocking his hips in a tight circle as if trying to screw inside her. Or something. Damn, she couldn't tell anymore. She barely knew who *she* was any longer. "And I'm clean, too. Thank God. Because to go my whole fucking life without feeling this…" He withdrew and plunged inside her again, and she tipped her head back, whimpering. "Yeah, this was worth waiting forty fucking years for."

She'd waited twenty-nine to feel this…free. And she

reveled in it. Threw herself into it with abandon. She rose off his cock, stopped when only the tip stretched her entrance, then dropped back down. And damn, she almost came from that alone.

Almost.

She lost herself in each plunge, each roll, each grind. Beneath her, Bran strained and arched into each stroke, each filthy slide of skin against skin, flesh over flesh. They raced together toward that inevitable, cataclysmic end, even though she ran away from it. Chased it. Dodged it. Chased it. Dodged it.

But when he reached between them and rubbed his thumb over her clit, that's all it took for her to detonate and release into the oblivion of ecstasy. She shook with it, cried out with it.

Gloried in it.

Beneath her, Bran pounded into her, his strokes uneven, fevered, and when he exploded, coming and pouring into her, she sank down onto his sweater-covered chest.

She didn't want to move.

And she didn't have to.

There was a freedom in that, too.

"Okay, you win." Bran leaned against the kitchen wall, arms crossed over his bare chest, while she cooked them omelets. Simple but filling food after two bouts of hot sex. "You won the fucked-up Monday contest."

"Thank you." She performed a half curtsy, almost flashing him from under the hem of his sweater. "I'd like to thank the little people…"

He snorted, his wiry body straightening as he crossed

to her glass-fronted cabinets and opened the one with plates. After liberating two, he walked over and held them out for her, and she slid the eggs onto them. While he carried them to the table in the breakfast nook, she grabbed knives and forks. They sat and dug into the food, and several moments passed with nothing but the scrape of utensils against plates filling the silence.

"This is delicious," he praised. Lifting his wine—because they were classy like that—he pushed the empty plate away from him.

"Thank you." And no, she wasn't blushing.

"I'm not saying I'm surprised…" He arched an eyebrow, the corner of his mouth quirking. "But where did you learn to cook like that?"

"Why wouldn't I know how to cook? Just because we had a chef in our house?"

"Yeah."

"You're right." She grinned. "Nore taught me in college. She refused to watch me waste money on takeout and restaurants after we moved off campus into our own apartment sophomore year. She made me learn simple meals so I could feed myself. Like normal people. Her words, not mine." She laughed, shaking her head.

God, she missed Nore.

"She misses you," he said, and she glanced sharply at him. Did he grant amazing orgasms and read minds? A regular Renaissance man. "Before I met you, I knew one main thing about you, Tatum Haas. You're loved."

She bent her head, slicing into her omelet. Not because she was suddenly so famished—no, to hide the sting of tears. *You're loved.* Sometimes she forgot that.

And sometimes she needed the reminder because she felt so unlovable.

"That's why we're best friends. I love her, too," she murmured.

"I could see that without ever seeing the two of you together. I think that's the only reason she put up with your sister when she came out to Seattle."

Tatum jerked her head, blinking. "What?"

He nodded. "Maybe Nore hasn't said anything, but when Mia flew in for our launch party, they were just cordial. I got the feeling Nore doesn't really care for her."

"No," she murmured, frowning. "She's never said anything."

Although, now that she thought back on it, Nore would beg off from spending time with Mia back in college, claiming Tatum should spend time with her sister. Her frown deepened, and she resisted the urge to grab her cell and call her best friend. Had Mia said something to Nore? Made her feel uncomfortable?

"Knowing Nore, she wouldn't. Of course—" he shrugged "—I could be off. I've only seen them together twice, and both times were in Seattle. For the launch and when she visited Greer for the initial meeting about an investment with BayStar." He set his glass down on the table, propped his crossed arms in front of him and leaned forward, his gaze steady on hers. "Those were the only occasions I've talked to your sister outside of the times here in Boston. With you. There's no relationship between us other than a professional one. Definitely not one that I instigated or encouraged."

A knot that she hadn't even been aware of unfurled

deep inside her. Mia had planted seeds of worry and distrust when she'd intimated earlier that she and Bran were closer than business associates. Given what Tatum had endured with Mark… It had instilled an insecurity inside her that she hated because it wasn't her.

She didn't want it to be her.

"You didn't have to lie to your father about us, though," he added.

Setting her fork down next to her plate, she huffed out a self-deprecating laugh. "One, who I sleep with is none of his or Mia's business. And two, yes, I did."

He cocked his head. "Why?"

"Because I'm a PR problem." This time her laugh abraded her throat. Standing, she grabbed their plates up and then carried them to the sink. "We've talked about why I replaced Mia on your deal. But I wasn't completely honest." She flattened her palms on the counter, staring down at them before lifting her head and meeting his unwavering gaze. "My father replaced Mia with me because, as my sister puts it, I'm a PR problem. The board, our employees, the public—they need to build confidence in me and stop seeing me as 'the tragedy.' So you were my chance to rehabilitate myself and prove I'm able to handle the upcoming open position of COO."

She leaned against the counter. After inhaling a breath, she exhaled it then smiled. It felt brittle on her lips.

"So no, I couldn't tell him that you and I had slept together. Because he wouldn't have seen two consenting adults. He only would've seen me continuing to be a broken, needy PR problem. One so desperate for male validation because of my dead fiancé that I fucked a client. And he would've viewed you as the man taking advantage of his vulnerable daughter. And what we've both worked so hard for wouldn't mean a damn thing. Not to mention, Dad isn't above smearing your name in the business community."

Bran pushed back his chair and rose to his feet. In moments, he stood in front of her, his arms bracketing hers, his chest a breath away from hers, his face lowered until their breaths nearly mingled. To glimpse the anger and frustration there. The simmering lust.

The…

She dipped her gaze to his chin. Here she went, projecting again.

Not being strong on her own but needing a man to want…and love her again. Weak. She'd promised herself she'd never be that weak again. She *owed* that to herself.

"Let's get one thing straight, Tate. I respect your father as a businessman. Neither me or Joaquin would've approached him about investing in Greer if we didn't. But he can't make or break my career. And anyone who would believe you're some vulnerable, fragile creature who can't hold her own in and out of the boardroom is a fucking idiot and not worthy of trying to impress. I don't give a good goddamn about their opinion of me nor do I need their business. I've never hidden behind anyone before—man or woman—and I won't now. So don't use me as the reason for not being honest with your family. And one more thing."

He pinched her chin, tilting her head back. "Not all men lie. Not all men cheat. Not all men will fail and abandon you."

"I know that," she whispered.

"Do you?" He dropped his hand and stepped back. "I have to wonder about that."

Clearing her throat, she ducked her head and rounded him. Because while she did believe that not all men would betray or disappoint her, a tiny, whisper-soft voice insisted that was a lie. At least for her. Insisted she couldn't trust another man because she couldn't trust herself.

She was the problem.

"I'll be right back. I'm going to grab some clothes and return your sweater since it's getting chilly in here."

It was as good an excuse as any. She really needed a moment that wasn't chocolate, oak and sex infused. Not granting him time to object, she dipped out, climbed the stairs to her bedroom and exchanged a black lounge outfit for his sweater. After several minutes, she descended the stairs and reentered the kitchen, a smile back in place.

"Here's your— What're you doing?" she rasped, shock freezing her in the kitchen entranceway.

His sweater fell from her numb fingers as she stared at Bran as he rose from a crouch, holding a small cardboard box, and inside were a black cell phone and a brown leather wallet, among other items. Dimly, she noted the top of the box on the floor along with a watch and thin gold chain. Still, the nausea churning in her belly, the acid racing for the back of her throat claimed most of her attention. Bran glanced at her over his shoulder, but the emotional riot inside her must've been reflected on her face because he dropped the box with the phone and wallet to the table and strode the short distance to her.

"What the hell, Tate? What's wrong?" He cupped her jaw. "I'm sorry about the box. It was on the chair and I didn't notice it until it dropped on the floor. I got most—"

"That's Mark's phone," she breathed, staring at it as if it might lunge out of the container and hiss at her. "Not his regular one. The day I had to leave the movie set? It was because his parents called my mother and father to have them convince me to help clean out his place. I hated it. Every second, I hated being in the space where we'd eaten together, relaxed together, made love." She choked on a bitter laugh. "Or I was making love. But I stayed and his mother insisted on giving me the box of his effects from the hospital. Including that phone. I immediately recognized it's a burner phone. It was so obvious, and there's only one reason for a man in a committed relationship to have a burner."

He lowered his hand from her face and nodded, his eyes narrowed, thoughtful. Glancing down at the phone, he studied it for several moments before returning his regard to her.

"It's not my business, but when I picked it up, the screen illuminated. After ten months, this phone should be dead. You charged it?"

Embarrassment spread through her like a stain, and she bent on the pretense of picking up his sweater when she couldn't meet his gaze.

"Tatum?"

"Yes," she snapped. Then softer, rubbing her forehead, said, "I'm sorry. Yes, I did." Jerking her arm down, she hiked her chin up, and knew she looked defiant, defensive.

But she couldn't help it. That had been her MO for the past months. "I don't know. I've never known," she said.

Circling him, she headed for the wine she'd abandoned on the table. She picked it up and sipped. But she wasn't thirsty; she was stalling.

"You've never known what, Tatum?"

"Who he was with," she blurted. "The police didn't find the woman who called 911—the woman he was having an affair with. And I know it's crazy and self-destructive, but part of me just believes if I knew…if that last part of the mystery was solved, then I could let this anger, this resentment go. I could truly move on. But it's the not knowing…"

She set the glass back on the table and wrapped her arms around herself.

"You can tell yourself that but we both know that's bullshit. Look at me," he ordered, and she obeyed. "You're torturing yourself. Punishing yourself," he said, and though his words were harsh, his soft tone belied them. "What happens if you meet this woman? What will it prove? What will you tell yourself? Everything mean, ugly and hurtful you can think of? You will be mean to yourself, heaping that toxicity on the only innocent person in this whole shitstorm of lies. And one of those lies, Tatum? That you'll let it go. That you'll heal once you know who was lying in that bed with Mark."

He rounded the end and cupped her elbows, giving her a small, gentle shake. Then he pulled her close, ignoring her crossed arms, and brushed a kiss over her forehead.

"You'll heal once you realize the fault lies with people who aren't here to be accountable for it. And you'll start to let go when you accept one unfair, fucked-up thing." He cradled her face, his thumb rubbing over her bottom lip. "Baby, Mark cheating on you with another woman had nothing to do with you. To him, it probably wasn't even personal. What's more, if he were here, he'd most likely swear up and down he loves you. And it might even be true. That sounds crazy to you because *you* were hurt, *you* were betrayed, *you* were about to be his wife. But it's true. That's because he had something missing inside him. Integrity. Honor. Loyalty. Selflessness. The ability to put someone else above himself. So you see, it had nothing to do with you and every fucking thing to do with him."

She blinked. Blinked again, battling the sting in her eyes. Sinking her teeth into the inside of her bottom lip, she tried to contain the tears. His words reached right into her chest, fisted her heart and squeezed until she couldn't breathe.

"No, baby. Don't hold back. Not with me. You're safe here. Right here." His arms enclosed her, his hand sliding into her hair and cradling her head, pressing her face to him. "Let it go without any fear of judgment. Let it go."

As if she only needed those words, the sob ripped free from her. Like a lanced wound, the rage, pain, helplessness, insecurity and fear poured out of her, and she clutched him to her, her haven in this chaotic, scary storm.

She let go.

And he held her.

Just as he promised.

Thirteen

Bran stepped off the elevator on the floor that held Bay-Star's executive offices. As soon as the doors opened, a young Black woman smiled at him.

"Mr. Holleran." She extended her hand. "I'm Tara, Ms. Haas's assistant. If you'll follow me, she's waiting for you in the conference room."

Shaking her hand, he nodded. "Thank you, Tara. It's nice to meet you." He followed her down the hall and dipped his chin again when she stopped in front of a closed door on the left. "Thank you again."

"You're welcome." With a smile, she left him to enter the conference room, and Mia Haas glanced up from papers on the long table, giving him another smile, this one much warmer than her assistant's.

"Bran." She strode toward him, her arms outstretched.

When he halted her progress and aborted what would've undoubtedly been an awkward hug—awkward in that he wanted no part of it—he clasped both of her hands between his. He shook them once and released her.

Her smile dimmed but held firm. He'd admire her for her composure if anger didn't burn a hole in his gut.

"I was surprised to receive your request to see me, Bran. Pleasantly surprised." She swept a hand toward the chairs lining the table like soldiers. "Please, have a seat."

"No, thank you. This won't take long."

She frowned, tilting her head. "I hope everything is okay. Is there a problem with the Greer account?"

"No, everything's perfect there." He studied her, searching for the signs among her loveliness that might reveal the heart—or lack of it—that existed beneath. But nothing. Not one. Damn. Clue. He removed his cell from the pocket of his blazer, located his contacts and scrolled until he found hers. He recited the number. "That's your number, isn't it, Mia?"

Her frown deepened and she leaned a hip against the edge of the table, crossing her arms over her chest. "Yes, that's mine." Flicking a hand toward the cell, she asked, "I'm sorry, but I don't understand. What does my phone number have to do with why you needed to see me?"

Slowly, he shook his head. "I hoped—"

The door to the conference room suddenly opened and Silas stepped inside, his gaze shifting from Bran to Mia, and his dark eyes held a wealth of suspicion. Even though, when he greeted Bran, none of that leaked into his voice.

"Good morning, Mia, Bran." Silas closed the door. "I passed Tara on the way from my office. She said you two had a meeting. Bran—" he slid his hands in his pants pockets "—are you having issues with the deal? Maybe we should get Tatum here—"

"You'll probably want to hold up on that until we air this out." He returned his attention to Mia, holding up his phone again. "Your telephone number. Apparently from the phone you used to call me when I was in Seattle."

"Yes, I already said that was my number. I still don't understand what that—"

"Why was your number in Mark Walker's burner phone? As a matter of fact, you were the last person he called on the night he died."

"What?" Silas barked, striding forward. Bran felt him draw nearer rather than saw him. Because he didn't tear his stare away from Mia. "What number?" Bran didn't have to look back at the phone again to recite it, since the night before, when he'd first glimpsed it on the burner phone's log, the thing was branded into his memory. "That's not Mia's cell number," Silas objected.

"It is." Bran dipped his chin toward the quiet woman whose brown eyes seemed to darken with anger…and maybe some trepidation. "She just confirmed it. Another burner phone, right?"

She didn't reply, but she didn't need to. He had his answer. Had everything he needed to know.

"You were the woman who called 911 that night. You were the one with Mark in that hotel room, and then after making sure the ambulance came for him, you showed up at the hospital as if you hadn't been the woman screwing your sister's man behind her back."

"The hell?" Silas snapped. "That's not true! Mia, say something, dammit. Tell him this isn't true. You would never do that to your sister. I don't know how family treats one another where you're from, Bran, but here we love each other. We're loyal—"

"Dad," Mia quietly said. "Stop."

"Yes. Please stop."

Bran pivoted sharply on the heel of his motorcycle boot. *Shit*. They'd all been so focused on their conversation, none of them had heard the door open or see Tatum enter.

Damn, he wanted to go to her, wrap his arms around her. Shelter her from what was about to come. But he couldn't. He'd tried but he couldn't protect her from the storm that was about to wreck her life. Again.

Tatum moved farther into the room and closed the door behind her. She halted in front of her sister, and Bran tensed, ready to intervene if Mia took one step toward Tatum.

"Go ahead, Mia. Dad's listening, and so am I. Is Bran right? Were you the woman with Mark? Were you with my fiancé behind my back?" she asked, voice even. Too even.

Bran's body rebelled at *my fiancé*. Stupid as hell, but a primal part of him rejected her claiming anyone else. Anyone but him.

Shit.

Clenching his jaw, he shoved the inconvenient and

disquieting thought aside for the moment. Although there was no ignoring it for long.

"Mia," Silas rasped. "Sweetie, no."

Mia's gaze flicked to her father then back to Tatum. Her expression didn't reflect any emotion. Not fear or remorse... Yet, her eyes contradicted the aloofness. They gleamed with a sheen of moisture that Mia blinked against.

"Yes, it was me," Mia admitted, tone cool. "I was with Mark that night. And yes, I had been seeing him behind your back for the last year."

Except for her shoulders and back stiffening, Tatum didn't react. But Silas's rumble of shock and outrage filled the room. He moved toward his daughter, slamming his palms down on the conference table across from her.

"No," he snapped. "No, I won't believe it. I won't accept that you would betray your sister like that. And that you'd lie about it, not just to her and to us and the police, too. No daughter of mine would do that."

"Oh so you remember I'm your daughter when it's convenient for you?" Mia murmured, her lips twisting into a wry smile. "Sorry to disappoint you, Dad, but a daughter of yours did lie and cheat. I don't know how, but you're going to have to find a way to deal with that."

"Is that why you did it?" Tatum asked, speaking for the first time since her sister's heartbreaking announcement. "To get back at Dad for some perceived slight? Or did you do it to hurt me?"

"Both." Her voice lost some of that ice. "You have no idea what it's like growing up in the shadow of the perfect Tatum Haas. That shadow is so long and wide, a person is invisible in it, can never step outside of it. Anything I did you'd already done or had done better. I have never been enough. At home or here." She jabbed a finger on the table. "So yes, I slept with Mark, to take who you believed was yours. To finally be on equal footing with you, even if it was in secret. But that backfired. I fell in love with him. But he wouldn't call off the wedding. In the end, he still wouldn't choose me. And even after his death, you're the poor-is-me fiancée. You're the tragic figure when you weren't the only person to love him. Or the only one he loved."

"You've witnessed firsthand the hell the last few months have been. And you can still stand there and complain because people didn't know you were the side chick? That you're not getting the 'attention' I'm receiving?" Tatum laughed, and Bran nearly winced at the serrated edge of it. "Forget Mark. *You* betrayed *me*. Your sister. Every day for the last ten months, you've made a conscious decision to look me in my face, remain silent through my pain and continue to lie. And somehow you're still making yourself the victim."

"Tatum." Mia's mouth trembled and she sank her teeth into the bottom lip. Glancing away from her sister, she shook her head. "I'm sorry. I've wanted to tell you the truth. It's been hard for me, too—"

"Boo-fucking-hoo." Tatum slashed a hand through the air. "Save it, Mia. Because you haven't changed. God," she chuckled, "there's sibling rivalry, but deep down you must really hate me to do something so dirty, so callous and cold to me. I can never trust you again."

"Tatum…" Silas turned to her, his dark eyes sad. The man seemed to have aged at least ten years in just seconds. Lines creased his cheeks, and he appeared…tired. Ashamed. "Please, take a moment. Don't say anything you might regret later. What Mia has done is terrible, and I still can't believe—" He bit off the rest of the sentence, his head briefly dropping. "But she's still your sister and we're family. We always will be."

Anger roared through Bran and he turned to Silas with a snarl. Once again, he was abandoning Tatum instead of having his daughter's back. The other man might not see it that way, and yes, he was in a difficult situation, but standing up for one daughter didn't mean he loved the other less. It meant he was fucking *parenting*.

"Don't bother, Dad." She held up a hand, palm out. "You're embarrassed over her actions. You're horrified. But this isn't your wrong to forgive, and you won't make me absolve her of it so you and Mom can continue to have the perception of a happy family at dinner. Don't even ask it of me. One day I might forgive you," she said, returning her attention to Mia, "but today is not that day. Especially when I doubt if you're more remorseful over the pain you've caused or just getting caught."

"Tatum, please," Mia whispered. "I am sorry I've hurt you."

"I don't believe you. But worse? I don't believe you wouldn't do it again." Stepping back, she inhaled an audible breath and looked at her father. "Dad, I think you will understand if I take a personal day."

Without waiting for her father's agreement, she spun

around and strode from the room, her shoulders straight, head high. Like a fucking queen. Bran didn't bother addressing Mia or Silas but followed Tatum down the hall to her office. She didn't turn around and look at him when he closed the door.

"Did you intend on telling me what you discovered about Mia and Mark?" she murmured.

"Of course I did," he said, approaching her from behind. "I would've never kept something like that from you."

He wanted to reach out to her, draw her back against his chest. But her stiff posture—and the fact that she wouldn't look at him—didn't invite his touch.

"Last night, you must've looked at the burner phone while I was upstairs. You recognized Mia's number then. Why didn't you tell me last night?" She finally turned around to face him, and shit, the pain in her eyes. He briefly closed his own, but this wasn't about him. And she deserved answers. "Did you think I was too weak to handle the news that my sister had been fucking my fiancé behind my back?" she continued. "Did you think I'd break?"

"Tate, no, nothing could be further from the truth. I just didn't want to inflict anymore hurt on you before I was sure. This morning, I called her, asking to meet to make sure I didn't have it wrong before telling you."

"So everyone in my life has been treating me like a helpless baby who can't fend for herself. Or a china doll that will break at the slightest tap. And you did both."

His jaw clenched, and he inhaled a deep breath. Let it out. *Fuck.*

"You're right," he said. "I shouldn't have tried to shield this from you. It's your life, your decisions and, though this has to hurt almost as bad as Mark's death, you're strong enough to handle it. I messed up, Tatum, and I'm sorry."

"Yes, that's been said a lot this morning." She pinched her forehead then rubbed it. "If you don't mind, I'd rather never hear those words again."

"Tatum." He moved toward her, his hand outstretched, but she backed away from him. "Let me hold you, please."

"No." She shook her head, hands up in front of her. "Don't... Stop. I don't want to be held. I want to be left alone."

A band constricted around his chest and he fought past the tightness to breathe, to not say *fuck that* and storm her. Drag her into his arms and hold her until her body lost that unnatural stiffness.

Until the fear creeping inside him dissipated.

"Okay, I'll give that to you," he slowly said. "I'll just call later—"

"No, don't," she interrupted. "I need space. To think, to..." She briefly closed her eyes, her fists clenching beside her thighs. "I'll contact you when I'm ready."

"Will you, though?" he murmured, the fear swirling, gelling into a hard knot behind his rib cage. "You told me once that you value my honesty. I don't believe in playing games or saying one thing when I mean another. So your turn, Tatum. Be honest."

Her nostrils flared, eyes narrowing on him. Shaking

her head, she warned, "You don't want that. Not right now, Bran."

"I'll be the judge of that."

But she might be right; given the pounding of his pulse and the bracing of his body, he might not be ready for the blow.

"As fucked up as that was—what I just walked away from—it revealed something to me that I've been in denial about. I wear fucking blinders when it comes to people. I am like that defenseless baby because I can't trust myself. Not only did I choose a man who lied to me and cheated on me for at least a year, but I couldn't even see that my sister was the same. I made excuses for them both. I'm dangerous to myself, and I'm so damn tired of being the casualty of my own willful blindness. I can't do it anymore."

"And your solution is to, what? Go scorched earth with every relationship in your life? Baby, life is about risks. It's about taking a leap and hoping the person you love is either with you in the fall or will at least teach you how to land softer next time."

"You're talking to me about risk? Don't be a hypocrite, Bran. When was your last long-term relationship since your divorce?" she jabbed.

"Last night. The night before that. Three weeks before that when I met a woman on a balcony. A woman who challenged me professionally then personally. A beautiful woman who has me believing in second chances."

He stated the truth baldly, laying his heart out there for her. And goddamn, his timing sucked, but she had to know she wasn't defective. She'd *changed* him. Was she perfect? No. But she was his. And he wanted to be claimed by her. He needed to be hers.

"I don't believe you," she whispered, shaking her head. Turning from him, she thrust her fingers through her hair, disheveling the strands. "I don't believe you," she repeated.

To him? To herself? To them both.

"No, you don't *want* to believe me. There's a difference."

"It was a mistake." She whirled back around, and only the desperation in her voice and eyes kept him from snapping at her. Instead, pain and disappointment mushroomed in his chest. Shoving until they filled his lungs, his head. "We shouldn't have become involved in the first place. You know that. I do. And you're leaving for Seattle, anyway. We were never meant to happen or be permanent. Neither one of us wants permanent."

"Anything else you want to throw out, Tatum?" he murmured. "You're too young for me. It's unprofessional. I could lose the investment deal." When she didn't say anything but remained stubbornly quiet, he huffed out a soft, harsh chuckle. "Spoiler alert, Tatum. This deal could go to hell and I wouldn't care. If it came down to the choice of not knowing you, not loving you or funds for a motorcycle? You'd win every time. Business deals come and go, but there's only one you. You're younger than me. Yeah, maybe we shouldn't have become involved. We can't change any of that. And more importantly? I wouldn't. Every. Time," he bit out. "You."

He finally crossed the room and strode straight up to

her, not stopping even though she shuffled backward. Her ass bumped the edge of the desk and still, he kept going, lifting his hands and cupping her face.

"I love you. You don't want that from me. But my love isn't conditional on your acceptance. I can't make you love me, though. I can't erase the fear, the hurt. But I won't stay here imprisoned by it either. Not even for you. When you're ready to truly be free, to not be ruled by the past or allow it to dictate who you are, come find me." He pressed his lips to her forehead then leaned back, smoothing his thumbs over her cheekbones. "Remember, Tatum. Either they write your story or you do."

With that, he released her and walked out of the office.

Because in spite of his big talk, he couldn't bear hearing her say she didn't love him.

Fourteen

The peal of the doorbell echoed throughout Tatum's home. Staring at her security system's image of who stood on the other side of her front door, Tatum longed to ignore the sound.

I can't deal with this.

Not when it hurt her to move, hell, to *breathe*.

Only one day had passed since the confrontation in the conference room with Mia and then in her office with Bran. She didn't possess the emotional bandwidth for more. Yet, she unlocked the door and opened it, meeting Dara Walker's gaze on the other side.

"Dara," she said to Mark's mother. "This is a surprise."

"I called you at the office, but your assistant said you weren't in. Then I tried calling your cell but it went straight to voice mail. I apologize for dropping by unannounced but I needed to speak with you, Tatum. It's important."

God, she wanted to close the door. Instead, she stepped back and allowed her almost mother-in-law to enter. Though she seriously doubted Dara's definition of *important* measured up to hers.

"Tatum." Dara entered the living room and sank down on one of the chairs next to the couch. "Your father contacted Leo and me. He told us about Mark and…Mia." Dara closed her eyes, shaking her head. "I still can't believe it."

Believe that your son had sex with his fiancée's sister or that your son was a liar and cheater?

The question sat on her tongue like a hot lump of coal, but she swallowed it. Lowering to the sofa, she didn't say anything.

Dara sighed. "I can't imagine how you're feeling right now. And I won't presume to. But—" she paused, reaching out and cupping Tatum's knee "—your father also said under the circumstances, you shouldn't be expected to speak at the event we're planning for our foundation. And that he nor your mother would be attending."

What was she saying? Her father had actually stood up for her? He'd placed her feelings above his business and social association with the Walkers? Shock rippled through her, followed by a hesitant, buoyant joy. And relief. She would've never expected that of him or her mother. But…they had. They'd put her first.

"Now, I can understand how receiving the news you have can leave you reeling," Dara said, squeezing

Tatum's knee and reclaiming her attention. "But I'm asking you not to act too hastily. I know you're angry with your sister, as you should be, but this party will benefit students who're going to college. That should be the focus. And you and your family not attending would distract from the purpose. We *need* you to speak and for Silas and Regina to attend."

"No, you mean you need us to show up so people don't speculate about why we're not in attendance. Because if I don't attend, people may believe I'm angry with Mark for not being faithful. They might remember he's not perfect."

Dara frowned, straightening, her hand falling away from Tatum's knee.

"Wait a minute. I understand—"

"Stop saying that," Tatum interrupted, trying her hardest to strap down her temper. "You don't understand. If you did, then you would stop asking me to pretend your son didn't hurt me to my core. Didn't hurt me with someone I loved. Out of all the people in this city, this state, he slept with my sister. If you truly understood, you wouldn't ask me to sacrifice my pride and feelings on the altar of your son's reputation. You wouldn't expect me to grieve like you but grant me the room to mourn in my way, even if you don't agree with it."

Dara blinked, her lips parting, but no words emerged. Her fingers fluttered to the base of her throat, and guilt twinged in Tatum's chest. But she smothered it. No, this needed to be said. It was past time. And more, Dara needed to hear it.

"I loved your son, Dara. I loved him and was getting ready to pledge my heart, fidelity and future to him. And he would've stood up there and mimicked those words knowing he'd been with my sister the night before and probably had every intention of being with her in the future. I get to be mad about that. I get to not want to praise him and ignore his failings. I get to do all of that even if it makes you uncomfortable. Because yes, he was your son and you love him unconditionally and can look past what he did. I can't. I not only have to mourn the man I lost but the man who I believed him to be. And I refuse to live quietly anymore or pretend to be the long-suffering fiancée. You celebrate your son's life. I'm going to move on from your son in death just as I would've done if I'd discovered his betrayal if he were alive."

Dara rose, and Tatum followed suit, preparing herself for a vitriolic diatribe. But it didn't come. Instead, the other woman grasped Tatum's hand in hers.

"I'm sorry my son hurt you. He was wrong, and you did nothing to deserve that kind of pain or disloyalty. And I'm sorry that we haven't been considerate of your feelings. All we saw—" Her voice cracked but she cleared her throat and squeezed Tatum's hand. "Please forgive us, and in your time, please find it in your heart to forgive Mark. Not for me or even his memory, but for yourself. You deserve to be free."

With one last squeeze, Mark's mother turned and left the house, leaving Tatum standing there stunned and, *God*, lighter than she had been in, well…nearly a year.

It hadn't been discovering whom Mark had been with

that had removed the burden from her heart, her soul. No, it'd been finally speaking her truth. It'd been having her own back and finding her own strength.

It was finally…forgiving herself.

Forgiving herself for not seeing Mark's lies.

Forgiving herself for being angry.

Forgiving herself for being silent.

Forgiving herself for loving someone who hadn't loved her the same.

And that was okay. There was nothing wrong with loving. The defect didn't lie with her.

I love you. You don't want that from me. But my love isn't conditional on your acceptance.

She closed her eyes, Bran's words both a balm and an indictment. By grasping so tightly to the past, the bitterness and hurt, she'd almost let a new, fiery, protective love slip through her fingers. She'd hurt Bran—and she couldn't deny it as his eyes didn't lie. The *man* didn't lie—because she'd lashed out, afraid to trust that maybe, out of the worst possible situation, something and someone truly beautiful had come into her life. And she was worth them.

Oh God, she loved Bran Holleran.

And no, the fear didn't magically disappear when she admitted that to herself, but surrounding that kernel of doubt and uncertainty was hope. Hope and love.

Bran had said she was responsible for writing her own story.

Well, she was, staring right now.

Hopefully, he would be there at the happily-ever-after.

Fifteen

"So can you fly back home for a couple of days?"

Bran squinted against the late-morning October sun as he stepped into the revolving entrance of his hotel. These things were death traps waiting to happen. He didn't care what anyone said.

"Yeah," he replied to Joaquin's question as he moved into the hotel lobby. "That's not a problem. I can catch an early plane out tomorrow. Can you send me all the details on the client and what he's looking for?"

"Done," Joaquin said. A pause. "You good?"

Bran drew up short, his jaw clenching for a moment. He'd called his friend the day he'd left BayStar's offices, and Joaquin had listened as Bran relayed everything that had happened since he'd arrived in Boston. Joaquin hadn't torn him a new one about Bran becoming involved with Tatum, hadn't dug into him over not keeping things professional. He'd just stayed on the phone as Bran drank then asked him if he needed to come home. Joaquin offered to take Bran's place in Boston. Because that was the kind of man and friend he was.

But Bran had turned him down. There was no outrunning himself. No matter whether he returned home or stayed here, Tatum would be there with him. There was no escaping her either.

"Yeah, I'm fine," Bran answered.

"All right, then. Once I have your flight information, I'll have it sent over to you."

"Sounds good. I'll see you tomorrow."

He ended the call and tucked the cell in his coat pocket. Maybe going home for a couple of days would be good for him, though. He hadn't even been able to sleep in his own hotel room because the bed, the living room, the dining room—every area reminded him of Tatum. And though the suite had been cleaned several times over, he swore he could still catch her scent. Hear her voice...

"You're leaving?"

He stiffened. Well, damn. His imagination wasn't that fucking vivid. Turning, he locked down the swift surge of joy and lust as he stared down at Tatum. He glanced away from her for a moment because, God, she was beautiful. And it'd been nearly a week since he'd seen her, touched her. But her presence here at the hotel didn't mean shit. He loved her, but yeah, after that last morning in her office, he was wary as hell.

"Yes." He watched, a little confused and a lot interested when she frowned and her fingers twisted together. Her tell. "What're you doing here, Tatum?"

"Looking for you," she said, then tilted her head, frown deepening. "You told me to come find you when I was finally free. And now you're just—" she waved a hand in the direction of the hotel entrance "—leaving?"

"And are you?" he pressed, ignoring her last question. Because damn that. The first part of her statement was the most important. "Are you free?"

Her expression smoothed. Inhaling an audible, low breath, she nodded. "Yes, I am."

"Since when?" He crossed his arms over his chest, challenging her.

He loved her, had prayed to hear those words from her and he wasn't even a praying man. But still… He didn't believe in miracles. And this turnaround—it smacked too much of a miracle. And the thing about them? They tended to be disproven and unbelievable.

"Since I realized all the things you listed that Mark lacked—integrity, honor, loyalty, selflessness, the willingness to be self-sacrificing—you possessed. Every one of them. That man was you. And I was so afraid of being disappointed, hurt and abandoned again that I couldn't see or accept the chance to love again. To *be* loved again. I don't want to exist in the past anymore. I don't want to be handcuffed to the memory of a dead man. Instead, I want to live for the man who I not only deserve but who deserves me."

His heart pounded in his chest, the frantic beat roaring in his ears. She said everything he'd hoped to hear. But a part of him—that part still hurt from her rejection—

was afraid to speak. Afraid that she would rescind those words. Afraid he would believe in them only to have her take them away.

"You should know that I requested my father hand over the Greer Motorcycles account to someone else," she said.

"What?" He stepped forward, scowling. "Hell no, Tatum. I'm not working with someone else. You deserve the credit and the promotion your father promised. I won't let you do that."

"You won't let me?" she repeated, a small smile flirting with the corner of her mouth. "It's done. They will be presenting the deal to BayStar's board next week and I expect it will be pushed through fairly quickly. It's an amazing product. But—" she inhaled a deep breath and then exhaled "—I can't accept that promotion for COO. Because I already have a new job, starting in a few weeks. As of yesterday, I'm now a partner in the Main Event."

The Main Event? Nore's event-planning business? But that would mean...

"You're moving to Seattle?" he rasped, disbelief and hope, so much goddamn hope, mingling and swirling inside him.

"Yes. I'm not running away, though. I've spoken with my family and have made this decision from a place of strength, not vulnerability. I'm making the decision to start over because it's never too late. Because you're in Seattle, my best friend is there. My happiness and peace are there. My future is there."

She reached in her pocket and pulled something free. When she stretched her palm out, the distinctive brooch he remembered from the night they met perched there.

"Nore bought this for me last year. As a wedding gift. See, there's a legend attached to it. The owner will be led to their soulmate. Their path won't be easy, but they'll be destined to find a lasting true love. I'd believed Mark's death destroyed my belief in magic, in love. But you restored it, Bran," she whispered, and he couldn't deny the love that shone in her dark eyes. "You brought the magic of love, trust and belief back into my life. And I want to give all of that back to you. If you'll let me."

He didn't bother answering.

Damn near leaping at her, he swept her into his arms and crushed his mouth to hers. And when her arms closed around his neck and her lips parted for his kiss, joy burst inside him like the brightest sunshine.

"I love you, Tatum," he growled against her lips. "Give me your heart because you have all of mine."

"You already have it." She scattered kisses along his jaw, his chin and finally his mouth. "It's been yours all along," she said then sealed that vow with another kiss.

Did he believe in the legend of that brooch? He didn't know, probably not.

But he believed in her.

He believed in them.

And that was more than enough magic for him.

* * * * *

If you loved Tate's story, don't miss
her best friend Nore's story!
Her Best Kept Secret
by Naima Simone
Available now!

UNDER THE SAME ROOF & KEEPING A LITTLE SECRET

UNDER THE SAME ROOF
Texas Cattleman's Club: Diamonds and Dating Apps
by Niobia Bryant

Investigator Tremaine Knowles was hired to find stolen jewels—not seduce the prime suspect. But Alisha Winters is captivating...and hiding a secret that could change the case *and* the ongoing Winters-Del Rio family feud...

KEEPING A LITTLE SECRET
Texas Cattleman's Club: Diamonds and Dating Apps
by Cynthia St. Aubin

Nothing will derail Preston Del Rio's plan to take over his family's oil empire—except a tryst with Tiffany Winters, daughter of his father's bitter rival. And now there's a baby on the way...

RANCHER UNDER THE MISTLETOE & ONE NIGHT WITH A COWBOY

RANCHER UNDER THE MISTLETOE
Kingsland Ranch • by Joanne Rock

Outcast Clayton Reynolds is back in Montana for Christmas, and all he wants is local veterinarian Hope Alvarez. But she wants no part of the man who ghosted her three years ago, until a heated kiss tempts her to play with fire!

ONE NIGHT WITH A COWBOY
by Tanya Michaels

Workaholic Dr. Mia Zane decides the perfect cure for stress is one wild night with a sexy cowboy. Mia never expected that ranch hand Jace Malone would turn out to be a billionaire...or that she would be expecting his baby!

BREAKING THE BAD BOY'S RULES & THEIR WHITE-HOT CHRISTMAS

BREAKING THE BAD BOY'S RULES
Dynasties: Willowvale • by Reese Ryan

When former rock star drummer Vaughn Reed inherits a run-down ranch, he hires his best friend's sister to fix it up. But annoying little Allie Price is now all grown up—and too dang tempting...

THEIR WHITE-HOT CHRISTMAS
Dynasties: Willowvale • by Jules Bennett

Ruthless businessman Paxton Hart says he always chooses money over love. So life coach Kira Lee vows to show the town's resident Scrooge that Christmas miracles can happen—and their fiery kisses are just the first step!

You can find more information on upcoming Harlequin titles, free excerpts and more at Harlequin.com.

HD2in1CNM1023

Get 3 FREE REWARDS!

We'll send you 2 FREE Books plus a FREE Mystery Gift.

FREE Value Over **$20**

Both the **Harlequin® Desire** and **Harlequin Presents®** series feature compelling novels filled with passion, sensuality and intriguing scandals.

HARLEQUIN
PLUS

Try the best multimedia subscription service for romance readers like you!

Read, Watch and Play.

Experience the easiest way to get the romance content you crave.

Start your **FREE TRIAL** at
<u>www.harlequinplus.com/freetrial</u>.